WITH A LITTLE LUCK

"A professional model in New York," Frank echoed, staring at his daughter in amazement. "I'm so proud of you, sweetheart. Now, we're a little worried about what kind of bad effect this might have on you, but we agree on something else as well. It's usually not what you *do* in life that you regret; it's what you *don't* do. I don't want you to look back one day and wonder what *might* have been."

Frank put his hand over Callie's. "Why don't we all go to New York and take a look at this Whiting place. If everything is on the up-and-up, well, it's just one summer we're talking about. Besides, there are telephones and trains home, you know." He laughed. "It's not like you're going to another planet."

It was a perfect solution, Callie thought. They would go, and if they didn't like the way things looked, she would leave. She smiled happily.

"Thanks, Dad. You're the best."

He pointed a finger at her, teasing. "And don't you forget it."

"It may not work out, of course." He took a sip of his coffee. "But with a little luck. . . ."

For orders other than by individual consumers, Pocket Books grants a discount on the purchase of **10 or more** copies of single titles for special markets or premium use. For further details, please write to the Vice-President of Special Markets, Pocket Books, 1230 Avenue of the Americas, New York, NY 10020.

For information on how individual consumers can place orders, please write to Mail Order Department, Paramount Publishing, 200 Old Tappan Road, Old Tappan, NJ 07675.

KIM ALEXIS

WITH A LITTLE LUCK

KIM ALEXIS AND CYNTHIA KATZ

POCKET **STAR** BOOKS

New York   London   Toronto   Sydney   Tokyo   Singapore

To my Mom and Dad,
who were always there when I needed them
K.A.

To Victoria Skurnick
with love and appreciation
C.K.

———————

An *Original* Publication of POCKET BOOKS

A Pocket Star Book published by
POCKET BOOKS, a division of Simon & Schuster Inc.
1230 Avenue of the Americas, New York, NY 10020

ISBN: 0-671-70757-4

First Pocket Books printing October 1994

10 9 8 7 6 5 4 3 2 1

POCKET STAR BOOKS and colophon are registered trademarks of Simon & Schuster Inc.

Cover photo by Sato Ri/Shooting Star

Printed in the U.S.A.

Acknowledgments

It has been my privilege to work with many talented people over the years. My thanks to all of them for their help, friendship, and support.

Special thanks to the people who provided information and insight for this book, particularly Dottie Franco and Timothy Priano.

I am also grateful to our editor, Jane Chelius, and to Lauren Weiss for their dedication and guidance.

—*Kim Alexis*

For their invaluable help and encouragement, my heartfelt thanks to Meg Ruley, Don Cleary, Carolyn Clarke, Jean Katz, Charles Revson, Jr., Diana Revson, Tom Teicholz, Myra Shapiro, Stacy Higgins, and Mark Steckel.

—*Cynthia Katz*

WITH A LITTLE LUCK

Prologue

*C*allie Stewart smiled brightly at her dancing partner. Her expression revealed nothing of the fatigue she felt and how much her mouth hurt after three straight hours of smiling. Walter Furst maneuvered her around the dance floor in what she supposed was his own particular version of the fox-trot.

Of course, it didn't matter how tired she was; if Walter wanted to dance with her until she dropped, she would be glad to accommodate him. Walter was a group president at Weston Inc., and the one who'd wanted Callie as the exclusive model for their Day and Night Cosmetics line to begin with. It was his signature on her multimillion-dollar contract, and he was the one who could fire her if he felt like it. Callie rarely saw him anymore—they had no day-to-day dealings—but she thought she certainly owed him a dance or two when he asked for it.

The song was ending. Surreptitiously, she glanced over

Walter's shoulder at her watch. It was well after midnight.
Surely she had put in enough time to meet the requirements
of this command performance. She hadn't been too happy
when her contact in Weston's public relations department
informed her only two weeks ago that she was expected at
the Weston Christmas Gala. Nearly a month ago, she'd
accepted a friend's invitation to a birthday party for the
same night, and she felt bad about having to back out. But
she knew better than to complain. This was no ordinary
office Christmas party. It was a black-tie dinner for management and their spouses, but the company also invited key
figures from the makeup and fragrance industry, along with
major distributors and department store buyers. Under-
standably, Weston wanted its famous Day and Night model
there to add a little more glamour to the festivities.

At least she'd been able to come with David, but they'd
barely seen one another all evening; he was constantly off
somewhere with his colleagues, and Callie was kept busy
smiling and chatting with buyers, and dancing with whoever
asked. Arnold Stone, the public relations man Weston
assigned to her, had done a good job, making sure Callie was
introduced to all the right people, whispering names and job
titles in her ear so she would be prepared when the smiling
strangers shook her hand.

By now it was becoming a struggle to keep her eyes open,
but as Walter thanked her for the dance she cheerfully
responded that it was her pleasure and always a delight to
see him. Spotting David in a corner, his head bent in
conversation with someone she didn't recognize, she grace-
fully extricated herself from Walter's grasp and made her
way across the crowded room. David was about to walk off
in another direction just as she reached him, and she put out
a hand, lightly touching his sleeve.

"Sweetheart," she whispered, "do you think we might
go?"

He looked so handsome in his tuxedo. Watching him
purse his lips distractedly, Callie had to resist the urge to
reach up and stroke his face, to lean over and kiss him.

"Not yet," David responded. "There are a few more
people I want to talk to."

"Please, honey. I'm dead on my feet," Callie begged.

He seemed to be thinking about it. "All right. Just let me say good night to Walter and the others. I'll meet you by the coat check."

Callie walked down the long, carpeted hallway toward the building's exit, aware of the eyes on her as she passed other guests. The coat-check girl, who looked to be barely twenty, recognized her immediately, and, without waiting for a claim ticket, slid Callie's midnight blue velvet cape across the counter to her.

"You're so beautiful, Miss Stewart," she breathed, as Callie fished in her evening bag for a dollar to leave in the basket for tips. "I've followed your career, and I have some of your pictures on my wall at home. They inspire me to diet."

"Thank you," Callie answered with a smile. "I appreciate that."

Gently swinging the heavy cape around her and closing the pearl clasp at the neck, she said good night to the girl and turned away. Callie was used to being recognized, but there were still times when she had to stop and wonder at it all. She ran a hand through her long, thick blond hair, freeing it from her collar, feeling it fan out over her shoulders. It was so impossible, too ridiculous to believe. Skinny, unpopular Callie Stewart from Bloomington, Indiana, the girl with so few friends and virtually no dates. Today, she had one of the highest-paying exclusive modeling contracts in the world, with one of the most prestigious cosmetics companies. She had achieved her ultimate goal, the kind of success every model dreams about. Millions of dollars, a limited number of days of work each year, her name practically a household word.

She reached into her pocket and pulled out her long evening gloves, turning her diamond engagement ring sideways on her finger so she could get her left glove on over it. Absentmindedly, she worked the fine leather up over her hand and wrist until she smoothed it out all the way to her elbow. She was thinking about the day she had signed the Weston contract, up in Fredericka Whiting's office at the Whiting Modeling Agency. Whiting was among the top four agencies in New York, but landing one of the most lucrative contracts in the business for one of their girls was a tremendous coup. On that day—unlike so many other occasions—Fredericka and her son, Austin, had been all smiles and kisses for Callie. The office was on the twenty-eighth floor, a panoramic view of Manhattan surrounding them on three sides. Sitting up there on top of the world, signing the actual contract, then posing for the photographer who was recording the moment, Callie had been drunk with it all. The feeling of success, of having made it to the top, had been so heady it was as if she would never be unhappy again, as if she could ward off even time and bad fortune forever. And yet she knew full well it was simply due to whatever twist of fate had given her the face everyone seemed to want at the moment.

She was brought back to the present by the sight of David coming toward her, his mind on other things as he hurriedly retrieved his cashmere coat and put it on. Adjusting a red muffler around his neck, he looked at Callie as if seeing her for the first time that evening. His handsome face broke into a broad grin.

"Hey there," he said, winking at her. "Don't I know you from somewhere?"

He took her arm as they walked to the restaurant's entrance. Two days before, nearly three inches of snow had fallen, but the weather had turned just warm enough tonight to make it a driving rain that was coming down. It must have been raining for a few hours, as the leftover snow had now turned to a watery, gray slush. The parking attendant was nowhere in sight. David looked out at the sheets of water.

"You stay here," he said. "I'll bring the car around."

Callie watched him turn up the collar of his coat and run between the rows of parked cars. At least he seemed to be in a good frame of mind. Maybe they would make love when they got back to the apartment. It had been nearly three weeks since the last time. Callie bit her lip. Lately, his moods had been unpredictable, and she was having a hard time dealing with his brooding, and the biting comments he snapped at her when she annoyed him. He'd been nothing like that when they first started dating. In the beginning, they were wild and passionate together, having fun every minute. She remembered the night he had proposed, how they had stayed up making love until dawn. But it wasn't that way anymore. She supposed that was part of settling in for the long term, preparing to get married; you couldn't expect that kind of passion to last.

The uneasiness she had been fighting off for weeks returned in full force. She knew in her heart that there was no reason for his feelings to have cooled off so much; hers certainly hadn't. The truth was that, except for sporadic moments when the old David reappeared, he wasn't just cooler, he was downright cold and disinterested.

Other things were different about him as well. For one, he had become so secretive. As always, she continued to tell him everything that went on at the Day and Night shoots, and at the occasional television or radio talk shows on which she appeared, guest spots arranged by Weston Inc., ostensibly to talk about her career as a model, but in fact to promote their products. David, on the other hand, told her less and less. Considering that he was director of marketing for Group A, the division Day and Night was part of, he was in a position to help her do a better job of getting along with the people there. True, she had a signed contract, but it was still critical that she remain on everybody's good side, especially if she wanted the contract renewed. At first he'd been constantly looking out for her interests, telling her who was really in control of what, which Day and Night products were up or down in sales, and how people in the company thought she was doing. Now he was closemouthed, unconcerned with helping her, and unwilling to discuss even his own job. And he seemed jumpy and nervous a lot of the time. She worried that something might be seriously wrong with him. Maybe he was in trouble, or hiding some terrible illness from her. Or maybe he was doing something he didn't want her to know about.

She pushed the thoughts out of her mind. He was entitled to prewedding nerves, and that might be all it was. She had to be a little more patient. The wedding was only three months away. She hoped things would straighten themselves out before then.

And if not? she asked herself. She didn't have an answer.

David's navy blue vintage Mercedes pulled up and she saw his arm reach across from inside to unlatch the door on the passenger side. Before she could stop herself she noted unhappily that in the past he would have gotten out to open the door for her, especially in terrible weather like this.

Stepping into the downpour, she tried to get into the car as quickly as possible. Her efforts were in vain; she was soaked in seconds. As she settled into her seat, she looked down at her silk pumps. Ruined. The hem of her evening gown was splattered with dirty water. She shivered as they drove away, feeling cold rainwater trickling down inside her collar, brushing off her wet hair and the soggy shoulders of her cape.

"It'll be great to get home and out of these things," she said, thinking of her warm, thick terrycloth robe on the hook of the bathroom door.

David didn't respond. Callie gave him a glance, but he was concentrating on his driving. She sat back, chastened by his silence. More and more frequently, he didn't pay attention to her, didn't even seem to care whether she was in the room with him. Briefly, she considered saying something about it. But they had a long trip back from Westchester to Manhattan ahead of them, and she didn't want to upset him. Besides, she hated confrontations, and, much as she disliked admitting it, she knew she would do practically anything to avoid them.

The rain was coming down so heavily that it was hard to see more than a few feet ahead, and there were still scattered patches of ice on the ground. They were heading down the long driveway that led to the main road, coming around a curve to an area with more parking spaces. Sneaking another look at David, Callie noticed that he suddenly looked more alert, as if he was watching something of great interest. He had an odd expression on his face. Callie looked out but saw nothing, just the dim forms of a few people hurrying toward their cars to get out of the rain. She was startled to feel the car shoot forward, as if David had accelerated. He *was* going faster, she was sure of it. Much too fast under these conditions.

"Honey, don't you think—" she started carefully, turning to look at him again.

She never got to finish. His jaw clenched, David slammed on the brakes. Callie gasped, seeing a woman right in front of them, looming up as if out of nowhere. Her umbrella, tilted in their direction against the pelting rain, had obscured her vision so that she was unaware of the approaching Mercedes and had stepped right into its path. Only a few feet from the front fender, she must have heard the brakes screeching wildly. Callie watched her raise the umbrella, frozen to the spot, her face illuminated by the car's headlights, her eyes wide with fright.

Callie's heart rose in her throat, but she was flooded with relief as she realized it would be all right, that David was stopping just in time. Then the car struck a patch of ice and skidded forward, only stopping when it hit the woman with a sickening thud. The woman went down, gone from their view in the windshield.

At the same instant, a pair of headlights was reflected in the rearview mirror, momentarily blinding Callie. Another car was coming around the curve, quickly bearing down on them. The grating noise of the other car's brakes reached them, but it was too late.

"No!"

Callie heard David's yell at the moment of impact, as she felt herself being hurled up out of her seat.

Everything was happening so slowly now. There was a deafening crack in her ears, and she was aware of her head breaking through the windshield.

"Unnhhh . . ." The sound quietly escaped from her lips as what seemed like a burning, white bolt of lightning spread through her right side. She was outside in the winter darkness, or part of her was; she couldn't really tell, and for some reason she couldn't see anything. She knew it was cold outside, but strangely, she felt warm all over.

Suddenly she was back home in Bloomington, in her family's backyard. But she was only seven years old, and her father was pushing her on the swing set he'd built. Her little brother, Tommy, was sitting on the ground nearby, sorting through his small but cherished collection of baseball cards. It was hot, unbearably hot. She saw her mother setting up lunch for all four of them on the picnic table. There was a big glass pitcher of pink lemonade, filled with lots of ice, glinting in the sun.

1

*H*arry Sims shifted his weight from one foot to the other and back again, gripping his tennis racquet tightly as he watched Callie Stewart prepare to serve the ball. Even from where he stood on the other side of the court, he could see her determination, the concentrated focus she maintained as she touched her racquet to the ball she held high in front of her, then swiftly brought the racquet behind her and up again, sending the ball whipping across the net. He lunged for the shot and missed. Ruefully, he assumed his position again.

It was a shame, he thought, observing her taking another ball out of the pocket of her tennis skirt. There was hardly anyone around who could give her a run for her money on the court. Not that it was surprising. She was the best tennis player to come through the high school in the ten years he'd been head of the athletics department there. He considered himself a pretty good player, but he had stopped beating her two years back, when she was in tenth grade. Since then, she had won several local competitions and placed second in a statewide tournament.

None of the female players on the school's tennis team could touch her, and most of the boys were reluctant to play her at all, fearing the humiliation of being defeated by a girl, especially one who looked like her—they'd seen the embarrassment on the faces of those seniors who figured they would teach Callie Stewart a lesson. Harry and she played weekly after school, but it was just to keep her warmed up; he knew he no longer presented any challenge to her game.

This time, Harry was able to send the ball back over the net to Callie, and he watched the grace in her movements, the ease with which she extended her reach to get the shot, how textbook-perfect the follow-through was on her swing. He would miss playing with her next year when she went off to college. Although he and Callie didn't usually talk much, they had a quiet, mutual affection for each other based on their shared love of the game. For a time, they pondered together whether Callie should go into tennis professionally. Harry believed she had both the talent and the drive, but it was a big step, and he had put his heart into helping her come to the right decision. In the end she chose college, which meant she couldn't devote herself full-time to a tennis career from a young enough age. But they agreed that she would continue to play at school, and there were other ways she could pursue the sport after that. Harry promised he would always be ready to advise her when the time came. He hated to see the sport lose such a promising young player, but by then he had come genuinely to care for Callie and wanted her to do what was best for her.

She was an exceptional girl, he thought, as he had many times before. He watched her, tall and lanky with long blond hair, her almond-shaped, green eyes narrowed slightly as she followed the ball's progress. The great beauty she was blossoming into was obvious for everyone to see. Everyone except her, it appeared.

As secure and driven to win as Callie was on the court, she

was just as shy and isolated off it. It didn't surprise Harry that many of the girls avoided her and most of the boys were too terrified to approach her; he'd seen plenty of that sort of thing in his years around high school students. But he still felt bad that she didn't have the self-awareness or confidence to see what was going on. He could tell that she thought people just didn't like her. Before practice he would notice her putting so much effort into talking with the other girls, trying to be included in their groups. She genuinely didn't understand that they envied or were afraid of her, a young girl so touched with beauty and ability. But it wasn't his place to interfere or try to explain it to her. His job was to teach her tennis and to see that she made the most of her ability at it, if that was what she wanted.

When Harry sent the ball straight into the net, he shrugged and, with a sheepish grin, called out to her, "Okay, game and second set to you."

"One more set?" Her hopeful question floated across the net to him.

"Sorry, Callie, I've got to get going."

"Right." She nodded as they headed off the court.

Harry smiled and patted her shoulder lightly. "I'm sorry, kiddo. We're having people over for dinner and I promised to get home early enough to pitch in. The holidays are a bear, huh?"

Callie picked up a towel and wiped the perspiration off her long, slender neck. Despite the chilly December air outside, the indoor court was well heated. She and Harry both had a special feeling for this court, a place that enabled them to play all year long. It had been built only three years before, mostly through Harry's tireless efforts to convince the school and the parents that it was well worth the dent in the budget and the extensive fund-raising it had required.

"I'll see you next week, okay?" she said.

"Absolutely." Harry headed toward the boys' locker room. "In the meantime, have a great Christmas."

"Thanks. You too."

Callie gathered up her things and pushed open the door to the girls' locker room. It was quiet inside, just a few students left at this late hour of five-thirty. She headed for her locker and quickly stripped off her clothes and sneakers, grabbed a towel and a bottle of shampoo, and padded in her bare feet to the shower room. Two of the showers, one next to the other, were in use, so she stepped into the adjoining stall.

". . . Christmas party at Janie's. Too bad you couldn't make it." A voice Callie didn't recognize was in the middle of a conversation with whoever was in the second shower. The girl was talking loudly enough for her voice to carry over the running water, making it impossible for Callie to keep from hearing what was said.

"Oh, please, don't tell me about it," came the disgusted reply. "I had a temperature of a hundred, but you would have thought I was dying the way my mother stood over me all night. There was no way I could even have snuck out."

"You gotta hear this," the first voice went on. "I mean, the party itself was great, totally fabulous, everybody was there. But when it was all over and there was no one left, maybe two-thirty in the morning, Mrs. Wynn went down into the basement and found Sue Harwood and Henry Lake on the couch. They were practically *doing it,* with next to nothing on. Even Janie didn't know they were down there."

The two girls screamed with laughter, then continued talking about the incident. Callie wasn't listening anymore. She was thinking about Janie Wynn, who sat next to her in history class. Janie had always been nice to her, and Callie thought they were sort of friends. But Janie certainly hadn't invited her to any Christmas party. She hadn't even mentioned anything about a party. With a small sigh, Callie squeezed some shampoo into the palm of her hand and began lathering her hair. Things would never change. No one would ever really like her, and no man would ever fall in love with her. She would remain a virgin forever and grow old alone.

By the time she let herself in the front door to her house, it was nearly six-thirty. She saw the table set for dinner and smelled the food cooking on the stove, but no one was in sight. Her parents, her brother, Tommy, and she usually ate together at about a quarter to seven, shortly after her father got home from work, and at this hour her mother was always in the kitchen cooking. Her father's sample bag stood by the front door, she saw, so he was already home.

"Hello, anybody around?" Callie called out as she dropped her book bag on the floor and took off her gloves and coat.

No answer. She went into the kitchen and got an apple out of the refrigerator, taking a large, loud bite as she started down the hallway to her room. The door to her parents' room was shut, which was unusual, and she could hear their muffled voices coming from behind it. She paused for a moment, not wanting to eavesdrop but wondering what was going on. *Today seems to be my day for listening in on other people's conversations,* she thought, taking a step closer to the door.

Her father was talking now, but his words were unintelligible. Suddenly, her mother gasped and there was silence. Callie froze, afraid. Then both her parents started talking at once, her mother's words coming rapidly, her father's tone low and soothing. Well, whatever it was, at least they were both physically all right. She hoped nothing bad was going on, but they were entitled to have a secret or two, she supposed, continuing toward her room.

Tommy's door was open, and her younger brother was sprawled across his bed on his stomach, reading a comic book.

"Hey," she called out to him softly.

He didn't look up. "Hiya. When's dinner? Tell Mom I'm starving."

Reaching just inside the doorway, Callie picked up a basketball from where it lay on the floor and threw it hard enough to bounce off the side of his bed. "Nice to see you too, I had a wonderful day, thank you so much for inquiring," she said sarcastically. *What do you expect from a tenth-grade boy?* she asked herself.

The door to her parents' room opened. Alicia Stewart emerged, looking pale. A slender, attractive woman in her midforties, it was from her that both Callie and her brother had inherited their creamy complexions and blond hair. She noticed her daughter standing there, watching her.

"Come to the table, sweetheart." Despite her expression,

her voice gave no indication that she was upset in any way. Without waiting to find out if Callie would follow, she headed to the kitchen.

Curious, Callie remained where she was. In another minute, Frank Stewart came out and caught her eye. He looked tired, his handsome face drawn as he ran a hand through his thick, graying hair.

"Hello, champ," he said, using his nickname for her. "Let's eat."

He turned and went to the dining room table, also apparently uninterested in whether she listened to him. Something definitely was up.

She stuck her head into Tommy's room again. "Dinner. Get out here."

Tommy looked up, his pale blue eyes questioning. "What's the sudden rush?"

But Callie was already hastening to the kitchen, where she got out some ice and a pitcher of water, pouring drinks into four glasses and bringing them out to the table. Tommy sat down at his place across from her, immediately picked up a fork and knife, and began to drum on the table. He seemed not to notice the uncharacteristic silence, their father gazing down at his plate, their mother bustling about, spooning food into serving plates. Callie was now certain that bad news was coming and her stomach tightened up. She prayed that her parents weren't going to announce they were getting divorced. They seemed to love each other so much, but you never knew.

When her mother was seated and everyone had begun eating, her father sighed heavily and looked around at all of them. *Oh no,* Callie thought, holding her breath, *here it comes.*

"I suppose the direct way is best, so I'll just say it," he began. "I got laid off today."

"What?" Callie was shocked, relieved that her parents weren't breaking up, but horrified at the same time. Her father had worked as a salesman for the same stationery supply firm for nearly twenty years—since before she was born. He used to spend a lot of time selling on the road throughout the Midwest, particularly when she and Tommy

14

were small. The traveling had been severely cut back in the past year, which suited everyone in the Stewart family just fine—nobody liked having him away. But maybe, she saw now, that had meant something bad.

"What do you mean? You're fired?" Tommy, pausing in the middle of swallowing his mashed potatoes, his fork still in midair, looked as surprised as Callie was.

Frank gave a small laugh. "No beating around the bush with you two. That's right, Tommy."

"But why? How could they?" Callie looked at her mother. "Three days before *Christmas?*"

Alicia's lips were pursed in a tight line. She looked at Callie and her daughter saw the effort it took for her to smile.

"These things happen, you know," she said, her voice even. "There's not always a good explanation for them. We all realize your father worked long and hard for the firm, but there's no point in going over all that or being bitter. We should look ahead and plan for the future. A good attitude is what's important, staying upbeat."

"Why is it important?" Tommy asked, visibly agitated, his voice growing louder. "Will our *staying upbeat* get Dad his job back?"

"Tommy, that's *enough.*" Mrs. Stewart's tone was sharp.

Mr. Stewart broke in. "All right, everyone. I know we're upset, but we have to face facts. Getting angry isn't going to do any good. When we're done with dinner, your mother and I will go over the budget to see where we can cut back. Right after Christmas, I'll start looking for a new job, and I'm sure something will come up in a few weeks"—he turned his eyes to his daughter—"so don't anybody worry about anything."

Instantly, Callie knew what he was referring to—the tuition money for her to start at the University of Michigan in the fall. Until his reassurance, it hadn't occurred to her that college might be in jeopardy. But if he felt the need to say that, their financial situation must be worse than she had imagined.

She forced herself to smile, showing him she understood, but she wanted to jump up and scream. Getting early admission to Michigan was the most exciting thing that had ever happened to her. They had even given her a partial scholarship, just enough to make her parents feel confident that they could scrape up the rest. The fact that the school was actually willing to give her money to attend had seemed incredible to Callie. And, just as important to her, as much as she hated to leave her family, she couldn't wait to get there and start over. Maybe this time she would do better, make some friends, perhaps even find a boyfriend. If she had to stay in Bloomington, she knew she was doomed to be lonely forever.

The four of them resumed eating, no one saying anything for the moment as each member of the family collected his or her thoughts. *It's rotten of me to be so selfish,* Callie realized. *All I'm thinking of is what I want. What if we lose our house, or even have no food?* She wondered if things could get as bad as that. And there was Tommy. He'd be graduating from high school the year after next, and that meant four more years of college tuition looming on the horizon. Sure, her father might find a new job right away. But he was nearly fifty, and she'd heard plenty of conversations between her parents at the dinner table about how hard it was for other men his age to come up with work once they lost a job.

Callie was too afraid to raise any of the questions racing through her mind. Dinner was over quickly, the others also apparently unwilling to say anything else on the subject. She was glad to escape to her room, where she lay on her bed, staring at the ceiling. Well, she would have to accept whatever came and help her parents any way she could. Her poor father. How terrible this must be for him, getting fired from a place where he believed he was liked and his job secure, having to tell the family and share his humiliation. His suffering was far worse than anything she was going through. If she couldn't go to college, then she couldn't.

Full of resolve, she was determined to be mature about it all, to look on the bright side. But once she was under the covers for the night and the lights were out, that didn't stop the tears from coming.

* * *

"More eggnog, Frank?"

Standing by the dining room table, Alicia was refilling her husband's glass from a large punch bowl of nonalcoholic eggnog she'd made earlier in the day. She ladled out some of the frothy, pale yellow liquid and sprinkled a dash of nutmeg on top before taking the glass back into the living room and placing it on a coaster on top of the piano.

Frank Stewart was seated at the piano bench, indulging in his somewhat rusty playing as he did every Christmas Eve. Callie and Tommy stood behind him, singing along to his halting rendition of "It's Beginning to Look a Lot Like Christmas." Tommy was eating some of their mother's cookies, cut in the shapes of snowflakes and Christmas trees. His voice would fade in and out of the song as he concentrated on licking all the icing off the cookies before biting into them.

The piano hadn't been tuned in a few years, and the off notes combined with Frank's playing to make each tune unique in a way the composers hadn't anticipated. Alicia sat on the couch, sipping her eggnog and laughing at how ridiculous the three of them sounded.

"I suppose I should be grateful," she said with a smile as they paused between songs, "there's no danger you'll be discovered and whisked away from me to become rock stars."

"Don't be so surrrrrre . . ." her husband sang off-key, flipping through the sheet music on the piano to make his next selection.

In the past three days, little had been said about Callie's father losing his job. Life in the household had gone on as usual, but there was a constant heaviness in Callie's chest that she couldn't shake. Not knowing what trouble lay ahead was the worst part of it. Still, if her parents could remain as cheerful as they normally were, she was determined to do so as well. She looked over at the Christmas tree the four of them had had so much fun decorating two weeks before. It was surrounded by lavishly wrapped presents, and she tried not to think that these might be the last her family would exchange for a long time, and that they probably wouldn't have bought them at all if they'd known what lay ahead

She turned her attention back to singing and in a few minutes was able to push everything else out of her mind. When they'd sung all their favorites, and a few particularly corny ones that had Tommy groaning, they sat down for popcorn as their mother told her stories about where the different decorations on the tree came from. It was a tradition: every year Alicia picked three or four of the ornaments and explained how they had come to be in the Stewart Christmas collection. As a little girl, Callie had been fascinated by the tales, which typically depicted long-dead ancestors she'd never heard of, and often revolved around lost children and tearful reunions, or cranky adults who came to learn the true meaning of Christmas.

Not until Callie was eleven years old did she realize that she'd heard more than one story about some of the ornaments, and she came to the startling conclusion that her mother had been making up the tales all along. Outraged by this betrayal at first, she hadn't let on that she knew, but sat stony-faced through the stories for the next few years in protest, fuming because no one even noticed her silence or asked what was bothering her. Eventually she softened, and as she got older she came genuinely to appreciate what a gift her mother's storytelling was. With both children grown, it was now something of a family joke, an unspoken agreement that they would all pretend to believe every word her mother said, and her mother, in turn, acted as if this was to be expected.

When the clock on the living room wall chimed ten, Mrs. Stewart began cleaning up, and Tommy moved to help her. Callie's father asked her if she felt like going for a walk. She nodded. They often went for long walks, sometimes in the evening, sometimes on a Sunday afternoon. Callie really enjoyed the time alone with her father. She realized that they hadn't been on one of their walks in several weeks. The two of them bundled up against the frigid night air and called out goodbyes as they shut the door behind them.

The temperature was in the low twenties, the air crisp and clean. It hadn't snowed recently, so they made their way easily down the dry streets, comfortable in their silence, stopping to admire the Christmas lights strung up on the houses in the neighborhood. Almost every house had some kind of decoration, and many of them were elaborate, ranging from sleighs pulled by reindeer with large, jolly Santas illuminated inside them, to dozens of strings of colored lights hanging from trees and bushes, posts and mailboxes.

"Dad, why am I so unpopular?"

Callie was startled to hear the words come out of her mouth. She had no idea what had prompted her to say such a thing to her father. They'd never even discussed her meager social life, although she supposed he wasn't blind to the fact that she was home on most Saturday nights.

Frank Stewart stopped and turned to his daughter. At six foot three, he was one of the few people who still looked down when he faced her.

"Don't you know, honey?"

Callie was surprised by the question. "Know what?"

Her father gave her a loving smile, touched with sadness. "The girls are jealous of you, and the boys are afraid of you. It's that simple."

"Why?" Callie's voice held all the frustration and hurt she'd felt throughout high school. "Why would they be that way?"

"Because you're so pretty."

Callie was so taken aback by her father's words that she couldn't say anything for a moment. She was okay-looking, she supposed, but she couldn't imagine that anyone thought there was something unusual about the way she looked. Unusual enough, according to what her father was saying, to make them jealous of her.

It was hard for her to get the words out, but she felt she had to. She made herself look her father in the eye. "Do you really think I'm pretty?"

He put his hands in his jacket pockets. "Callie, you're the prettiest girl in all of Bloomington," he answered quietly.

She was stunned. "You're just kidding, right?"

"No. I'm absolutely serious."

Callie thought about how her mother was always telling her how beautiful she was. But Callie had just chalked that up to her being a mother. Her father had never said anything on the subject beyond telling her she looked nice when she got dressed up. But he would never lie or tease her about something like this, she was certain. He must mean it.

"But I don't want to be pretty," she blurted. "I want to be popular."

Frank reached out to stroke his daughter's hair lightly. "Oh, champ," was all he said with a sigh.

They continued to walk, neither of them speaking, Callie no longer seeing what was around them as she tried to make sense of her father's words.

Alone in her room later, she opened her closet door and looked into the full-length mirror there. Way too tall and nearly flat-chested, were her first thoughts. She examined her face, free of makeup as always. Turning this way and that, she scrutinized the prominent cheekbones and straight nose, the full mouth, so like her mother's, and her green eyes beneath long, thick lashes, the same shape and color as her father's. Was she really as pretty as he had said? She couldn't understand what he saw in her. But maybe there was something there. She just wasn't sure.

Callie sat on the floor and drew her long legs up to her chest. Suppose her father was right. If that was the case, there might be a way for her to use her prettiness to help. Maybe she could do some modeling to make money. She'd been planning to work at one of the stores downtown this summer to save whatever money she could for college. But she had heard that models made a lot. She had no idea what a lot might be, but perhaps it was a substantial amount, two or three thousand dollars, even. She already had nine hundred dollars saved up from part-time jobs she'd held over the past couple of years, and she was hoping to add enough this summer to cover money for books and food. No doubt it was just a fantasy, but if she could make enough to do more than that, to help a bit with tuition, possibly it could make the difference in getting to go to college at all for the first semester.

What would that mean, modeling? She hated wearing makeup, and she imagined that models wore tons of it. She'd have to stand around letting strangers take her picture; that could be kind of creepy. How did someone even get into those magazines and TV commercials to begin with?

Moving quickly, she went into the living room and crossed to the small writing table where her mother sat to sort through the mail and pay the bills each month. There was a stack of letters and magazines there. Callie picked up a catalog from a local department store. She flipped through the pages, studying the women whose photographs were inside. Did she look like them? Could she do what they were doing, striking poses, looking glamorous yet relaxed, as if they were having the time of their lives? She had no idea.

She thought for a while, then opened the telephone directory, flipping through the pages until she found the *M*s. Modeling Schools. She stared at the words before her. It was all probably ridiculous and a waste of time. But what the heck. It wasn't like she had anything to lose by making a few phone calls.

2

"This is it."

Alicia Stewart shifted the car into park and referred again to the piece of paper on which she had written down the address. Both she and Callie looked at the squat, gray building, then at each other.

"Well, no one said the neighborhood had to be gorgeous. Just the models," Callie said, smiling at her mother.

They got out of the car and entered through the heavy glass doors. Although she wouldn't have said so, Callie was glad her mother had insisted on accompanying her to the school this first time to check things out.

Looking around, Callie took in the mustard-yellow walls, the black-and-white linoleum. *Kind of broken-down,* she thought. Somehow she'd expected something more fancy, as if she were going into an actual modeling agency. A few yards away was an older woman behind a large metal desk. She smiled brightly at the two women.

"Are you here for the modeling class?" her voice rang out cheerfully.

Callie and her mother approached the desk. "Yes, my daughter is enrolled here," Alicia responded.

A list was consulted, and it was established that Callie owed six hundred dollars, two hundred of it payable right then. Alicia wrote out a check; it had been agreed that Callie would pay her back out of her savings if Alicia decided the school was acceptable. Callie guiltily wondered if she should be giving her savings to her parents instead of spending it on this. She just *had* to do well here. Otherwise, she'd never forgive herself for wasting money the family could have used.

They were directed to room 103. Coming around a corner, Callie saw that the walls of this portion of the hallway were decorated with photographs. Some were magazine covers, other were black and white or color shots of girls' faces. She supposed all the pictures were of Norton Modeling School students or graduates. Every one of them was beautiful. Maybe the school was as good as they had told her they were on the telephone. From the conversation, she'd gotten the impression that they could practically guarantee their graduates would become models. It would take a big chunk of Callie's savings to pay for the classes, but once she had made up her mind to do it, she decided there was no point wondering whether it was the right move. She was going to take a chance. There was always the summer ahead to recoup her money if this turned out to be a failure.

Opening the door to room 103, she saw about ten girls sitting in traditional classroom chairs, wooden seats with a writing surface attached on the right side. A blackboard stood in front of the room and next to it was a long table lined with bottles and jars of makeup and all sorts of black brushes for applying it. There was a stack of folders, probably handouts. The walls here, too, were plastered with pictures of models.

Behind her, Alicia peered in, inspecting.

"Well, it seems to be okay," she whispered to Callie. She shut the door. "I guess I'll leave now, and meet you out front later. You'll be all right?"

Callie nodded. "Thanks, Mom."

Alicia gave her a quick kiss on the cheek and headed back in the direction from which they'd come. Callie was alone in the hall. Steeling herself, she opened the door and entered, slipping into the nearest empty seat.

Nonchalantly she glanced around the room, trying to get a look at the other girls. They were all doing the same thing she was, taking stock of one another. Callie was surprised. Some of the girls were nice-looking, but most of them weren't very pretty, or at least didn't match any of her notions of what a real model might look like. Some were plain or downright homely, with squinty eyes, big noses, acne—she didn't want to be catty about it, but there was just no way she would ever describe some of these girls as attractive, much less as potential models. Maybe she was wrong about what was desirable in a model or what big-time modeling agencies considered attractive. Or maybe these things could all be remedied with tricks of the trade she had yet to learn. She supposed she fell somewhere in the middle of the group. Still, she couldn't help wondering how the school was going to get some of these girls to qualify as faces for their walls.

Several more girls drifted in and found seats. The room was quiet, a few whispers exchanged here and there. Then the door opened once more and in walked a tall, buxom woman, who strode to the front of the room and addressed them all.

"I am Mary Dale. You will call me Miss Dale." Her voice was evenly modulated, yet loud and forceful. "You ladies will come here once a week for the next twenty weeks, and when we're done, you will all walk out of here as someone else. Someone with grace and poise, who knows how to stand, sit, and cross a room like a professional model."

Callie watched her, fascinated. Mary Dale was not beautiful either, but she definitely had a certain presence. She wore a great deal of makeup, and her nearly black hair was sprayed into a stiff bouffant. It was difficult for Callie to guess her age, but she couldn't have been under forty. Her dress was simple, gray with a small, white collar, and she had on big gray button earrings and several gold bangle bracelets that jingled when she moved her arm.

So far I've been wrong in nearly everything I expected, Callie thought, smiling. She had envisioned the teacher as someone petite, with fair skin and a soft voice, maybe even French. Well, so much for her fantasies. This was a get-down-to-business situation, she could see that now. She was learning already: modeling was going to take work. The Norton School claimed they were going to make her a model, and they'd been around for a long time, so she was sure they must know what they were doing.

It was a long two hours. After they went around the room and each girl introduced herself and explained why she was there—which Callie found excruciatingly embarrassing—the teacher took over for the rest of the evening. She explained that in the following twenty weeks they would be instructed in areas such as self-improvement, runway modeling, and makeup. She talked about the illusion of beauty and glamour, how so much of it was subjective and could be learned. How *they* could all learn to project the same kind of beauty that the famous models did. Walking around the room, she paused here and there behind a chair to point to one or another of the girls' flaws, describing—as that girl's face grew red with humiliation—how easily the flaw could be altered or disguised if one knew the right techniques.

There followed a long lecture on the subject of sitting in a chair. Callie had never realized there was so much to say about how to sit down, stand up, and what to do with your hands and feet while you were sitting. Last, Miss Dale discussed photographs. Everyone would have several pictures taken of them that evening and then again at the end of the course so that they could see the difference in themselves—which Miss Dale assured them would be astonishing. Dutifully, Callie took notes on all of it.

Over the next two months, she practiced at home everything she had learned. Tommy thought it was hilarious to see her gliding around the house with a book balanced on her head, working on her walk and perfecting her posture. If he wasn't following right behind, mimicking her fluid motions, he never missed an opportunity to sneak up silently and take a sudden wild swing at the book, knocking it as far as he could across the room, and scaring Callie in the process. He was banned from coming near her altogether when she was practicing her makeup application.

Initially, Callie had gone to a drugstore to buy the makeup she needed, but she'd been overwhelmed by the endless choices and high prices. She wound up borrowing the makeup from her mother's cosmetics bag; Alicia didn't have much, but it was enough for Callie to get by. She'd spread it all out on the rim of the bathroom sink, peer into the mirror, and practice for hours. Her mother would often come in and sit on the edge of the bathtub to observe what she was doing. Alicia didn't say much, but she listened with interest as Callie explained to her what Miss Dale had told them about how to use mascara and shadow or the way to make your nose look thinner, your chin less prominent.

It was in the third month of classes that Callie noticed a stranger sitting in the room one night. He was an older man, his fine white hair shot through with yellow, wearing a stylish European suit and brightly patterned ascot. When Callie looked over at him she saw that he was watching her. In fact, she realized, he was staring at her. When he caught her eye, he smiled. Disconcerted, she looked away, still feeling his gaze upon her. She was relieved when he stood up to leave a few minutes later.

At the end of the evening, Miss Dale told Callie that she was wanted in the office of Jack Norton, the school's owner. Callie's heart sank. They were going to toss her out of school, tell her she didn't have what it took. Six hundred dollars down the drain. She wondered if the man she'd seen sitting in class had anything to do with the decision. Maybe she should have smiled at him. Maybe he was somebody important and had taken a dislike to her; he'd gone right to the head of the school to inform them that she didn't have the personality to be a model.

She entered Jack Norton's office quietly, trying to walk the way she had learned in class, wishing she had worn something nicer than jeans that night. The school's owner was an overweight, unappetizing man in his late thirties.

Callie was nervous as she saw him sitting behind his desk, expressionless, watching her approach. Her heart rose in her throat while she waited for the humiliation to come. Then she noticed that the man who had been in class earlier was sitting in a chair off to one side of the room. So he *did* have something to do with this.

Jack Norton stood up and extended a hand for Callie to shake. Surprised, she took it, trying to concentrate on maintaining her poise. He motioned for her to sit down, and she settled lightly into the chair, crossing her legs at the ankles as she knew she was supposed to do.

"Miss Stewart," he began, gesturing to his left, "this gentleman is Bob Holt. He's a talent scout, meaning he works for modeling agencies, looking for new faces in different parts of the country. He believes you have a great deal of promise."

Startled, Callie looked over at the man. He smiled at her again.

"That's right," he said. "I want to send your photo to a New York agent."

"Me?" Callie leaned forward and pointed to herself, completely forgetting about her posture and proper hand position. "I don't understand."

The man stood up and walked over to the window, looking out at the night, prolonging the drama before turning back to her. "I have little doubt, miss, that you could go to work in New York and become a very successful model."

She sat back, deflated. "No, no, I don't want to go to New York. I just want to do some modeling here so I can save enough money for school in the fall."

Bob Holt laughed. "Miss Stewart, if you came to the Norton School, I have to assume you have some interest in being a model. I'm talking about a *real* model, not prancing around in some runway show for the local store's spring promotion."

Being a runway model for a local fashion show sounded exciting to Callie; it was as much as she would have dared hope to achieve. But nothing could have made her admit that now.

She answered with the simple truth: "Thank you for your interest, Mr. Holt, but I'm serious about college. I really don't want to go to New York."

He regarded her for a moment, frowning. "Won't you consider letting me have a photographer take some photos of you? Just so the people in New York can get a look?"

"Honestly, I don't think you should bother."

She saw the expression of disbelief on Jack Norton's face.

"Any girl would jump at this," he broke in disapprovingly.

Callie's stomach tightened as she realized how displeased they were with her. "Okay," she said, her reluctance obvious. "You can send the pictures they took of me here when class started."

Both men were watching her with furrowed brows. "I'm very sorry, I really am," she went on, faltering. "Please try to understand. This is just so I can make some money for college. It's not a career for me."

Bob Holt nodded and shook her hand. No one said anything else, and Callie left, knowing that she had offended them and, as usual, done the wrong thing. But she was relieved that they had let her go without any further arguing. And, she thought, suddenly feeling lighter on her feet, they hadn't thrown her out of school—just the opposite, they wanted to send her pictures to a New York agent. So she was doing well, and she might actually get some work this summer here in Bloomington. Humming happily, she went to retrieve her coat and headed out to the parking lot. She decided not to mention anything about Bob Holt to her family; they would probably just get nervous about a stranger pursuing her like that.

Only two weeks later, the class had another visitor. Callie watched a thin, sophisticated-looking woman carrying a leather envelope-shaped briefcase enter the room midway through the evening and take the same seat on the side of the room as Bob Holt had occupied earlier. Her dark hair, neatly combed, fell just to her shoulders, framing a delicate face, perfectly made-up. She wore a beige tweed suit, low-heeled beige pumps, and gold jewelry. Callie was struck by the contrast between this woman and her teacher. She couldn't help comparing them, noticing how each thing this stranger wore was just right for her shape and coloring; now that Callie thought about it, everything Miss Dale had on was actually wrong for her.

Callie frowned at this insight, then noticed that the woman was looking right at her. *Maybe I'm getting paranoid,* she thought, *believing everyone's watching me all the time.* But for the next ten minutes or so the woman's gaze wandered from Callie's face only to look down at the small pad on which she was taking notes. The other girls in the class realized what was going on, and a low buzz of whispering started to travel around the room until Miss Dale silenced them with a sharp command. Soon after, the woman left the room without a backward glance.

This time there was no waiting until the end of class for Callie to be summoned to Jack Norton's office. His secretary came into the classroom, said a few words to Miss Dale, then told Callie to follow her. *What now?* she wondered, self-consciously walking to the front of the room, as the other girls started talking among themselves again. When she entered Jack Norton's office, she saw that the woman was already seated there with him.

She stood as Callie entered, crossing the room and extending a manicured hand. Her handshake was cool but firm.

"Hello, Callie." Her voice was soft. "I'm Martha Brady from the Whiting Modeling Agency in New York. We received some photographs of you through Bob Holt, and I've come all this way just to see you in person."

"How do you do, Miss Brady," Callie replied politely, standing up straighter, hoping the woman wasn't about to add that Callie looked nothing like her pictures and the trip had been a waste of time.

Jack Norton stood too, something Callie had never seen him do for any of the other students. He smiled broadly at her. "Miss Brady has something very important to say to you, Callie."

Martha Brady sat down and gestured for Callie to do the

29

same. "We believe you have a certain look many people would find very desirable. With a little improvement, you could be successful as a professional model."

"But—" Callie began.

Martha raised a hand, stopping Callie instantly. "I've heard that you don't want to come to New York; I know the whole story. But I want you to reconsider. You've said you want to model to earn money for college. If you work with our agency, it is entirely possible that you could earn enough in just a summer to pay for your entire first year of college."

Callie inhaled sharply. She had never imagined there could be that much money at stake—her whole freshman year. She thought of her mother, who'd never worked before, now selling in the hosiery section at a local department store, single-handedly supporting the family. Her father hadn't had any luck at all, even after several months of looking. Things were getting difficult for them both, Callie knew, and she was only too aware that they were also concerned about what was going to happen to her in September. If she could earn enough for a year, her parents wouldn't have to give the matter another thought. But was this all for real? It sounded too good to be true.

As if reading her mind, Martha went on, "The Whiting Agency is a very prestigious one, among the top four in the entire industry. You would have no trouble checking that out. This is a genuine offer, I assure you, one that most girls will only get to dream of."

She paused, as if trying to gauge Callie's reaction. "We'll take good care of you, just like we take care of all our girls. Once you join us we set you up in an apartment, tell you everything you need to know, advance you some money, and generally look out for all your interests. It's a big move, coming to a strange place, starting out in a new business, but you would never feel alone. The agency is like a family."

"Do you really think I could earn that much money?" Callie asked. Realizing how crass that sounded, she added, "It's just that going to college is the most important thing to me."

"That's quite all right," Martha answered with a smile. "Yes, I believe you have the potential for it. You'll have to work hard—harder than you can imagine. But the rewards can be great."

Callie was hesitant.

"Callie, please—" Jack Norton was obviously pained that one of his students would even consider throwing away such an opportunity. "Don't be crazy."

"Talk it over with your parents," Martha suggested. She reached into her briefcase and pulled out a small leather case, from which she extracted a business card. "After you've digested the idea for a while, call me collect at the agency and we'll discuss it further."

Callie took the cream-colored card.

"Thank you very much. I'll talk to my mom and dad, and we'll call you."

Martha Brady smiled. "Once in a lifetime, Callie. Just remember that."

At home, Callie told her parents and Tommy the whole story, going back to her encounter with Bob Holt. When she finished, she waited for their response.

"A professional model in New York," Frank echoed, staring at his daughter in amazement. "I'm so proud of you, sweetheart. But I just don't know." He looked at his wife.

"Do you think it's too dangerous, honey?" Callie's mother voiced the concern that was obviously on both their minds. "And will these people take care of Callie? When I think of the stories I've heard about fashion models and the wild lives they lead . . ."

Her husband shifted in his chair. "What do you want to do, Callie?"

She thought for a while. "Well, it's just for the summer, and if I really can make that much money, think about how much easier all our lives would be."

Tommy grinned. "Sounds great to me. I'd do it in a second."

"I don't want to be a baby, but I have to admit, it's kind of scary, too," Callie said in a small voice. "On the other hand, the woman said it was a once-in-a-lifetime thing. I could be a big success."

Her mother stood up. "Let's all sleep on it and talk it over again tomorrow."

Relieved, Callie agreed. She kissed her parents and went to her room and undressed quickly for bed. Excited and frightened at the same time, it was a long time before sleep came.

In the morning, she woke nearly an hour before she had to get up for school. Unable to fall back asleep, she left her room in her bathrobe and found her father sitting at the table, drinking a cup of coffee. Callie poured herself a glass of orange juice and joined him.

"So, what do you think, Dad? What should I do?"

He looked at her with love. "Your mother and I talked it over some more last night, and it's true we're a little worried about what kind of bad effect this might have on you. But we agree about something else as well. It's usually not what you *do* in life that you regret; it's what you *don't* do. I don't want you to look back one day and wonder what *might* have been."

Frank put his hand over Callie's. "Why don't we all go to New York and take a look at this Whiting place. If everything is on the up-and-up, well, it's just one summer we're talking about. Besides, there are always telephones and trains home, you know." He laughed. "It's not like you're going to a different planet."

It was a perfect solution, Callie thought. They would go, and if they didn't like the way things looked, she would leave. She smiled happily.

"Thanks, Dad. You're the best."

He pointed a finger at her, teasing. "And don't you forget it."

"I won't, I promise." Callie laughed.

"It may not work out, of course." He took a sip of his coffee. "But with a little luck, you'll spend a good summer in New York, meet some new people, and have an interesting experience to look back on."

3

*T*ommy, come *on!"* Callie tried, unsuccessfully, to keep the nervousness out of her voice as she yelled for her brother to join them in the driveway. Impatient to get going, but fearful at the same time, she stood in front of their small brown house, squinting into the bright sunshine of the hot June morning and biting her thumbnail. It was just two days after her high school graduation.

Frank finished loading their suitcases and a cooler full of food into the back of the Ford, and after what seemed to Callie an interminable wait, the family was in the car and ready for the drive to New York. Tommy had a week off before starting his summer job as a messenger for a law firm, and Alicia was taking her annual one-week vacation from the store. Frank still hadn't found a job, so he was free for as long as Callie needed him.

Knowing it might be a long time before they would have a family outing like this again, none of them was in a rush to reach their destination too quickly. Taking three days to make the drive, they stopped along the way to picnic from the food in their cooler and to take an hour or so to sunbathe in some inviting spot. At night they checked into inexpensive motels, eating in whatever diner or coffeeshop was nearby. Callie wondered how she would get along without them over the summer, but she realized that she would be going away to school in September anyway, so the time when she would have to say goodbye was simply coming a little bit sooner.

When they finally pulled into New York, all four of them were overwhelmed by the traffic and noise after their peaceful days on the road. Having stopped in a gas station restroom to change from jeans and sneakers into clothes more appropriate for their appointment at the Whiting Modeling Agency, they all now sat rigidly and uncomfortably in their seats.

Frank drove straight to the Whiting Modeling Agency on East Fifty-sixth Street. Unable to find a place to park, he circled around and around the congested city blocks. His nervousness was apparent, his temper flaring when he realized he would have to put the car in a garage for the afternoon; it was a waste of twenty dollars, he muttered; cities were supposed to provide parking for everyone. Finally, he gave up and pulled into a garage two blocks from the agency. Callie and her mother looked at each other, neither having to voice the thought that they were off to a bad start.

The Whiting Modeling Agency was located in a tall white office building off Park Avenue. Alicia consulted a slip of paper with the address in her purse as they got into one of the three elevators. She pressed 6. Suddenly, Callie realized that this was it—they were actually here. She squeezed her mother's hand and received a reassuring smile in return. When the elevator door opened, she took a deep breath.

It was quiet in the reception area. The two leather couches flanking a large glass coffee table were empty, as was the chair behind the reception desk. The four of them walked to the desk, the plush gray carpeting muffling the sound of their

34

footsteps. As they stood there, wondering if they should call out or just wait, an unsmiling, reed-thin young woman in a short black dress emerged from behind a door and took her seat behind the desk.

"Yes, what can I do for you?" she asked in a clipped British accent.

Callie stepped closer to the desk. "I'm Callie Stewart. I have an appointment with Martha Brady. Today. At two o'clock." She glanced at her watch: it was one forty-five. "I guess I'm a little bit early."

She felt foolish, certain she had seemed overanxious. The woman picked up a telephone and, using her knuckle, punched three buttons on her intercom. She had long fingernails painted hot pink. Callie watched them tapping in a bored manner on the desk as the woman waited for a response on the other end of the phone. Without thinking, she hid her own hands with their bitten-down fingernails behind her back.

"A Miss Stewart here for Martha. Yes. Fine."

The young woman gestured for the family to sit down, and they obediently followed her instructions, no one saying a word as they settled uncomfortably on the two couches. Tommy, crossing one leg over the other so his ankle rested on his opposite thigh, began drumming on his pants leg with two forefingers, making rhythmic popping noises under his breath. His mother gave him a disapproving look, and he stopped. Frank Stewart kept running his hand along his tie, unconsciously straightening it over and over. There were some dog-eared copies of *Vogue* on the coffee table, and Callie picked one up. But she couldn't concentrate, and a moment later she tossed the magazine back on the table. The silence stretched on.

It was ten minutes after two when a door opened and another woman came into the reception area. She too was young, thin, and dressed in black, in a way Callie could only describe as New York stylish.

"Callie?" she said, smiling.

"Yes, that's me." Callie jumped up. Hurriedly smoothing the front of her pink V-neck top and white skirt, she sensed she'd made a mistake with her outfit; she should have worn something dressier.

"Come with me." The woman rang for the elevator.

Callie looked at her parents.

"Just you, please," the woman added, sensing what was coming. "If the rest of you wouldn't mind waiting here, we won't be long."

She introduced herself, but Callie didn't quite catch her name, and hesitated to ask her to repeat it as the elevator arrived and Callie followed her inside. They got out on the seventh floor.

Although the furniture was identical, the reception area here was a very different scene from the one a flight below. This room was packed with girls, maybe ten, and a few women who were obviously mothers. The girls were dressed in every sort of outfit from torn jeans to dresses, and ranged in age from what looked to be about fourteen to twenty-plus. Some were heavily made-up, their hair carefully combed, while others appeared as casual as if they'd just come by on the spur of the moment. Several stared straight ahead, as a few chatted and laughed with one another. Each had brought along her book, the big, black portfolio containing photographs of her meant to convince the right people that she was model material—or, better, to actually get work for her.

Callie hadn't brought anything. She knew the agency had the few shots taken of her back at the Norton School, and unlike some of the other students there, she hadn't invested in having other pictures taken by different photographers. Some of the girls at Norton had spent a great deal of money putting their portfolios together, but they said they were certain it would make the difference between success and failure. Callie hoped she hadn't been wrong not to bring other pictures of herself.

Feeling the eyes of every girl in the room upon her, she was ushered past them all and through a door.

"Sorry about that," the woman she was following called over her shoulder as she walked briskly ahead. "You happened to be here during open-call hours. Every week we have a few hours set aside when we'll see anybody who wants to drop by."

"Do you get a lot of models that way?" Callie was surprised to learn that you could just come in off the street and be seen.

"Now and then we get one, yes. It's especially busy in the summer, since school's out and the girls come on vacation with their mothers. And of course the modeling schools keep sending them."

Although they were walking quickly, Callie caught the sights and sounds of men and women in their offices, talking on telephones, looking over pictures and papers, conferring with one another. There were piles of black portfolios in the corners, and every so often they passed stacks of folders and what looked like brochures; Callie had no idea what these things were.

As at the Norton Modeling School, there were photographs on the walls here, but these were of recognizable faces on the covers of well-known magazines. In the past few months, Callie had spent a great deal of time reading the fashion magazines, trying to get some idea of the journey on which she was about to embark. It was a bit overwhelming to see the same faces she'd studied in ads now smiling at her with such warmth from the agency's walls. Other than that, it seemed like any other office, but maybe a bit busier and messier than Callie would have expected. It certainly wasn't glamorous.

Her thoughts were interrupted as the woman opened a door and ushered Callie through. "Right in here. Good luck." Then she turned and hurried off.

A woman sat behind a desk in this room, a manila folder open before her. She smiled at Callie.

"Hello, I'm . . ."

Again, Callie didn't catch the name.

This woman was older than the other one and slightly overweight. Coming around from behind her desk, folder in hand, she pointed to one of the room's white walls.

"Would you stand over there, please." It wasn't a question. "I need to see how tall you are. Remove your shoes."

Callie crossed to where the woman was pointing, seeing as she got closer that there were measurements marked off on the wall. She slipped off her white flats and pressed up against it.

"Five-ten and a half. Good." A notation was made on a page in the folder. "Now just hop on the scale here."

A doctor's scale was off to one side. Callie got on, suddenly wishing she'd thought to diet before coming. The possibility of being overweight aside, she had a lot of muscle weight from all those years of tennis. Maybe they would tell her to leave if she was too heavy. But the woman didn't say anything, just wrote down a figure. She scrutinized Callie's face, then her body, her eyes roaming up and down a few times.

"Have you ever thought of having that mole removed?" She gestured with her index finger toward Callie's face.

Callie's hand flew to her temple. There was a large black mole—a beauty mark was the way she'd always thought of it—next to her left eye.

"Well, I—"

"Doesn't matter. I was just wondering." The woman smiled again. "Okay. Your hair is excellent and a good cut will do wonders. Your skin is pretty good too, although you need a facial desperately to clean up your pores. But you absolutely must lose ten pounds right away, and think about those hips—they're going to give you problems if you don't watch out. There are ways you can disguise them with the right clothes, of course, but that won't help you on a job where you can't control what you wear."

Trying not to show how much her feelings were hurt by the sharp words, Callie nodded. The woman went to her telephone, and Callie listened as she told someone that she was finished here and they could "come for Stewart." Hanging up, she continued to make notes in the folder. Callie stood there nervously, wondering if her presence had been forgotten. The door opened and someone else was there for her, another older woman wearing a severe maroon suit, beckoning for Callie to come along as she took the folder from the first woman. Another trip up in the elevator, this time to the twenty-eighth floor. The lighted directory above the elevator doors indicated that these were the Whiting Agency's executive offices.

The reception area on this floor was altogether different from the other two. It was decorated with oriental rugs, magnificent arrangements of freshly cut flowers in crystal vases, elegant, hard-backed chairs—some kind of antiques, Callie thought—and a large picture window with a breath-taking view of the city. Without a word, the woman walked past the desk where the receptionist sat directing telephone calls on a panel of lighted buttons; the lights were flashing wildly but emitted only a slight hum.

The offices here were different as well. Secretaries worked intently at their desks, some bent over typewriters, others quickly running their fingers across computer keyboards. Several were talking in low tones on the telephone or flipping through papers. They all were well dressed and neatly groomed. Everyone looked busy, but it was very quiet, with all voices hushed. As she passed, Callie uncon-sciously slouched over slightly, feeling out of place and thinking that she looked like a slob.

Finally, the woman stopped outside a door.

"This is Austin Whiting's office. As you undoubtedly know, he is Mrs. Whiting's son and runs the administrative business of the agency."

Callie had never heard of either Austin or Mrs. Whiting, but she nodded. The woman opened the door and Callie broke into a wide smile of relief as she saw her parents and Tommy sitting on a couch at the opposite end of the large office. They all watched as the woman dropped the folder on the large black table with only a telephone on it that obviously served as Austin Whiting's desk.

"Mr. Whiting will be along directly," she said. Then she was gone, and the family was alone once more.

"Been on any magazine covers yet, Cal?" Tommy called out from across the room.

Wanting to hug him for his ridiculous comment, Callie laughed, releasing the tension that was growing inside her.

"Vogue and *Bazaar* both wanted me, but I turned them down," she retorted, joining them. She sat on a wooden armchair, which was very uncomfortable. Her parents

smiled at her. They looked even more nervous than she was, she noticed.

"You okay, honey?" her mother asked.

Callie nodded, glancing at their surroundings. All she could tell from her first impression was that everything in the office had to be awfully expensive. She didn't know why she was so sure of that.

Before she could examine the room any further, the door opened and Austin Whiting entered. Callie saw a man in his midthirties whose noticeably pale complexion contrasted sharply with his slicked-back black hair and dark clothes. He was wearing a navy double-breasted suit, a white shirt, and a brightly patterned tie with a matching handkerchief sticking out of his breast pocket. Beneath his jacket was a vest, a watch chain draped from the pocket. The office was air-conditioned to the point of being almost too cold, but Callie couldn't help thinking it was an oddly heavy outfit for anyone to put on in June.

His smile was warm and welcoming as he approached them. "Mr. and Mrs. Stewart. Callie. So delighted you're all here."

The family members sprang to their feet, as everyone was introduced and proper greetings and handshakes were exchanged all around. Callie found Austin Whiting's hand cold and damp, and his limp touch reminded her of her father's admonition always to give a strong handshake.

Austin urged them all to be reseated, then he pulled up a chair and sat down with them, looking directly at Callie's parents. He inquired about their trip from Indiana and they traded comments about the hot summer weather.

He smiled at Callie. She thought he was kind of creepy-looking.

"I know you must have had your height measured and so on before they brought you up here. Please realize that's just a formality for our records. I trust no one scared you too badly?" He laughed lightly.

"No, no, everyone was very nice," Callie answered politely.

"Good."

Suddenly he jumped up, went to his desk, and rang for his secretary over the intercom as he casually flipped through the folder left there for him.

"I believe we could use something to drink, please, Harriet." He put his hand over the telephone receiver. "Evian sound all right to everybody?" he asked.

They all nodded. He repeated the instruction into the phone and rejoined them.

"I can see where your daughter gets her looks," he said to Frank and Alicia. "You're a most attractive family."

Callie watched her mother blush mildly and smile. "Thank you very much."

Austin went on. "But let's discuss the reason you've traveled all this way. We have high hopes for your daughter, we want you to know that. We wouldn't have invited her here if we didn't believe it would be well worth her time—and ours."

His eyes went back to Callie. "Martha Brady knows what she's talking about when she tells us someone has real potential. That's why she's been with us for years, and why she—and, in turn, we—have been so successful. Seeing you now, I know that as usual she was completely right in her assessment."

He gazed thoughtfully at Frank and Alicia. "This is a very serious step for any young woman, but you must realize this is also our business. We have girls even younger than Callie whose parents trust us to take care of them, to shepherd them through the business and life in the city. We take that responsibility very seriously."

"Exactly what will you do for Callie if she stays here?" Frank asked.

Austin leaned forward in his chair. "First, we put her in an apartment with another girl, someone who can help Callie whenever she needs it. We advance her spending money, so she doesn't have to worry about that. We tell her everything she needs to know, everyplace she should go."

He raised an eyebrow. "Believe me, Mr. Stewart, we're just like parents. We couldn't survive in this business if we let anything happen to our girls. They're treated like fragile

41

jewels. They work hard, I'm not going to deny that. But they build a career for themselves that can be lucrative, gratifying, and fascinating."

Austin sat back. *Lucrative, gratifying, and fascinating.* He'd given this speech so often that by now he could probably do it in his sleep. He resisted the urge to yawn.

The woman who had brought Callie to Austin's office entered with a tray of crystal glasses filled with Evian and lime twists. So she was his secretary, Callie thought; she would have guessed the woman was an executive. It was hard to tell who was what around here.

Everyone picked up a glass. They had barely taken a sip of the cool water before Austin stood up again.

"It's time you all met my mother, Fredericka Whiting. I've just come from her office, so I know she's there and has a few minutes. She'll want to greet you personally."

Another trip down a different hallway, this time with Austin leading the way. They stopped before a set of tall double doors. A secretary, as beautiful as any model in Callie's opinion, sat behind a delicate wooden desk with a vase of irises on it, positioned a few feet in front of the doors. She immediately stood and came around to greet them. Austin exchanged a few quiet words with her, out of earshot of the Stewarts, and, after a quick rap on one of the doors, she disappeared into the office. When she returned, she smiled and asked if she could get them something to drink, perhaps some Evian.

Tommy was staring openly at her beauty, but at the mention of more Evian he snapped back to alertness. "Could I have a Coke?" he asked.

Frank cut him off, speaking with authority. "No thank you, miss, we've just had something. We're fine."

Nodding, she opened one of the doors to reveal the office inside.

Off to the left was an enormous antique brown leather partner's desk with a large matching chair that seemed to dominate the room; expensive-looking leather and gold desk accessories were strewn across the desktop. Other than these two dark pieces, the room was almost entirely beige and white. Thick, off-white carpeting blanketed the floor, while two couches and an armchair, covered in white silk, were grouped in one corner beneath a large abstract painting. Even the painting matched the color scheme, Callie noted; it was white and beige with a little black thrown in. Some type of woven tan fabric covered the walls. Floor-to-ceiling windows on three sides of the corner office revealed a cityscape even more spectacular than the one in the reception area, and dense beige curtains had been pushed open to let the bright sun of the summer day flood the room. The delicate lamps, fresh flowers, and fragile-looking decorative objects placed on end tables added to Callie's impression of having entered someone's living room. *Someone very rich,* she thought to herself. This was the first place she had been that matched—in fact, exceeded—her fantasy of what the modeling world would be like.

She was so intent on studying the room that it took a few moments before Callie realized that standing directly in front of the window on the opposite side of the room, framed by the view, stood Fredericka Whiting herself. Nearly six feet tall, she wore a bottle-green caftan and matching turban. The turban was set high enough on her forehead to reveal a sharp widow's peak of jet-black hair. Heavy gold jewelry dangled from her ears, around her neck, and on both arms, while rings glittered on her fingers. Her dark eyebrows framed large, catlike eyes, made to appear even bigger by green eye shadow and black eyeliner.

Although Fredericka was in her midsixties, most people meeting her for the first time would have guessed her to be ten years younger. That may have been attributable to the porcelain quality of her white skin, sagging ever so slightly around the jawline and neck, but otherwise nearly wrinkle-free and virtually flawless, the high cheekbones still prominent beneath smooth, rouged cheeks. Her lips were painted ruby red, matching her long fingernails. *She must have been incredible-looking when she was young,* Callie thought.

Like a giant butterfly, Fredericka spread her arms wide as if to embrace the family, her caftan fanning out around her. Her smile was broad and gleaming white as she came forward in greeting, the scent of her Joy perfume reaching them before she did. She headed straight for Callie's mother, grasping her hand tightly and bringing it close to her.

"My dear Mrs. Stewart, vot a pleasure. You have come so far and ve are so grateful."

She turned to Callie's father. "You are so kind to take time from vot I know must be your busy schedule."

Callie didn't have a clue where her accent was from, although if she'd had to guess, she would have said Hungary. It just seemed the kind of far-off place such a woman would come from. Too busy staring at this imposing figure to listen to her parents' replies, Callie was unprepared when Fredericka focused her attention on her.

"And this is your daughter." Her eyes traveled up and down Callie as she smiled and nodded in approval. "I have been told about her, I have looked at her pictures, and yes, I see she is for us. A little bit of changes, maybe—" She lightly pinched Callie's cheek. Callie had to keep herself from recoiling at the intimate gesture. "But ve are going to do vell together. Am I right, Austin?"

Her gleaming eyes intent on Callie, she didn't even turn to look at her son, but he smiled at her and the Stewarts followed suit.

"You must be tired from your trip, so I von't keep you," Fredericka went on. She put an arm around Callie, pulling her close. "Vhen my late husband, Mr. Vhiting, and I began this agency in 1969, ve promised that our girls vould be vell taken care of. And they are. You vill be too. They are loyal to us and ve are loyal to them. I vould do anything to help my girls. Ve cannot replace your marvelous family, Callie, but ve vill do our best. That is the reason ve are the top agency, the reason ve are successful for two decades."

Subtly, she steered Callie to the door, her parents and brother following, while Austin stayed where he was. Fredericka looked over at Tommy. "And you, young man, you come see us a little later. Maybe you vould like to be in our men's division." The look of horror on Tommy's face elicited her laugh, a loud, raucous sound. "Ah, but ve are getting ahead of ourselves."

With a grand gesture, Fredericka threw open both doors

to her office. "Now you go to your hotel, relax, enjoy New York. Tomorrow is for doing the business ve have to do, and then a little sightseeing and shopping, yes?"

Before they knew what was happening, the Stewarts were back in the hallway, the large doors shut tightly behind them.

"Wheewww . . ." breathed Tommy in disbelief, reflecting all their thoughts about Fredericka in one long exhalation. "Talk about the Dragon Lady."

The secretary sitting outside couldn't suppress a smile. Callie began to giggle, the stress of the day making her almost giddy. Her father grinned too, shaking his head in wonderment at the scene they had just witnessed, but his wife just pursed her lips.

They checked into the Barbizon Hotel on Lexington Avenue. The Whiting Agency had arranged for everything, a double room for Frank and Alicia, single rooms for Callie and Tommy. Hot and tired, they all showered and changed before gathering in the lobby for dinner in the hotel restaurant. Frank signed for the check as he had been instructed to do; the agency was paying their bills for this trip. Afraid to wander the strange New York streets at night, they retreated to Frank and Alicia's room to watch television until ten o'clock, when Callie and Tommy went back to their rooms to sleep.

In the morning, the four of them were back at the agency. A string of new faces, mostly women again, took them on a tour of the offices. Their guides were friendlier than the people who had assisted Callie the day before, making small talk, trying to answer the Stewarts' questions about the activities taking place around them. Nonetheless, as the family poked their heads into various rooms, they never quite understood what was going on, or what all these people—the majority of them talking rapidly on the telephone—were doing. Martha Brady came by and said hello to Callie, who was glad to introduce her parents to a relatively familiar face after so many strangers.

At one o'clock, Austin Whiting took the four of them to lunch at a French restaurant. Reading her menu, Callie tried to hide her shock at the prices, and she saw out of the corner of her eye that her parents were doing the same. Tommy seemed oblivious to it all, but he followed their lead, declining a salad, appetizer, or anything to drink other than water. As they ate, Austin kept up a nonstop conversation with Callie's parents, drawing them out about their lives at home, what they thought of New York, and, finally, what their fears were for their daughter if she joined the agency. One by one, he addressed all their concerns about how Callie would be taken care of. She could see that both her mother and father were impressed by his sincerity.

As they were finishing the most delicious chocolate dessert Callie had ever tasted, Austin pulled a document from his inside jacket pocket and placed it on the table.

"Everyone at the agency has had a chance to see Callie in person, and we're all in agreement about her potential," he said. "So we've taken the liberty of drawing up a contract."

Frank and Alicia looked startled. Callie's first thought was that she couldn't believe she'd just eaten such a fattening chocolate dessert in front of Austin Whiting after she'd been told to lose ten pounds. She was lucky he hadn't changed his mind about her on the spot.

"It's just a formality really, mostly fill-in-the-blanks, standard stuff. We get Callie modeling jobs, and we give her a paycheck. The agency does all the work—promoting her, booking her, advising her on what work to take and what to pass up, putting her portfolio together, and so on. She doesn't even have to worry about collecting her fees from the clients; that's our headache, and she gets a paycheck whether we get paid or not. It's a good system for the girls, very secure. In return she pays us a twenty-percent commission. Nothing unusual there. Everything is pretty much boilerplate, typical for the industry."

Frank bristled, then broke in. "I suppose it would be permissible for us to look it over before Callie signs it."

Austin took a sip of his espresso. "Naturally. Take it back to the hotel and read it through at your leisure tonight."

He signaled for the check, then said in a reassuring voice, "I completely understand how you feel. Don't worry, Mr. Stewart. You're dealing with the best. We wouldn't get very far in this business if there was anything even the least bit unusual going on."

Austin left them on the sidewalk outside the restaurant after shaking hands all around, waving off their chorus of thank-yous for lunch. Heading back to the office, he breathed a small sigh of boredom and relief that lunch was over. Wooing the parents was the least enjoyable part of his work. Many of them were exactly like the Stewarts, bumpkins from some nowhere place who were certain their precious daughters were being lured to a city of sin and temptation for all sorts of nefarious purposes. He had to placate, soothe, and cajole them—it was all so tedious. They thought the agency would take advantage of their girls, no doubt envisioning leering photographers shooting pornography. And how they worried about men pursuing their little girls, alone and on the loose in big, bad New York City. They even worried about *him* making a pass at their daughters; he could see it in their eyes. *As if I would,* he thought disgustedly.

He stopped at the corner and waited for a traffic light to change. Some days, the whole business made him sick. On others, though, days like this when he had one in the bag, a girl he could see might be a real money-maker, he was content. His mother was in it for the sense of power she got from the whole game; she might pretend that she was a serious businesswoman, but he knew better. She was hooked on the image of herself as the glamorous Fredericka Whiting, a legend in the world of beauty. That was her problem, having to bolster her sad little ego. For him, it was about money, plain and simple, and always had been. Let Fredericka and the rest of them—the girls, their parents, the photographers, everyone who made the wheels go round in the modeling business—let *them* worry about the other stuff. *Just give me the money,* he thought with a half-smile as he picked up his pace.

On their own, the Stewarts spent the rest of the afternoon sightseeing, going to the top of the Empire State Building, walking along Fifth Avenue to Rockefeller Center. That evening, after another large dinner courtesy of the Whiting

Agency, Frank went to his hotel room to read over the contract, while the others stayed in the lobby, talking about everything they had seen. The next day was their last in New York, and they visited Chinatown and Soho, Callie's parents buying a few souvenirs and presents for friends and relatives back in Indiana. Finishing up with a trip to Bloomingdale's, each of them selected one present for him- or herself.

That night, they discussed the contract and what Callie should do. Her parents were a bit thrown by the whole situation, but they were convinced that the agency was a legitimate one, and the contract seemed fair. Alicia added that if Callie saw anything, even the *slightest* thing that looked suspicious or just didn't feel right to her, she was to get on the next plane home. When Callie heard that, she knew the decision had been made. She was staying.

4

"Come in, darling, come in."

Fredericka Whiting didn't look up from the papers she was reading, but she gestured to Callie with a braceleted arm to enter the office. She was wearing a white turban, ruby earrings, and, from what was visible to Callie over the top of the partner's desk where Fredericka sat, a white linen double-breasted jacket that was probably part of a suit. She wore the jacket buttoned up, and instead of a blouse beneath it, a red silk scarf tucked into the neckline, revealing her ample cleavage. Callie wished she could see the rest of the outfit, but Fredericka remained seated at her desk.

Callie had chosen the clothes she was wearing more carefully than on her initial visit to the agency, not wanting to experience again the insecurity of feeling underdressed, especially when she learned her first stop that morning would be an appointment with Fredericka. Before her family had left for Indiana yesterday, she and her mother had selected her outfit for her first day as a real Whiting model. They'd chosen a powder-blue dress with short sleeves and a square neckline, beige low-heeled shoes, and a matching leather pocketbook. Callie had taken special care with her hair, brushing it until it shone, and had put on some pale blue eyeshadow and mascara. She hoped the effect would convince the agency people they hadn't made a mistake in asking her to stay.

Crossing the room, Callie stood uncomfortably before Fredericka's desk. She hesitated, wondering if she should sit or just stand there quietly. Fredericka looked up.

"Darling," she repeated, smiling broadly. Her eyes quickly ran over Callie's outfit, taking in every detail. "Don't you look . . . *sweet.*"

Callie's heart sank. The tone of Fredericka's voice made it clear that the word *sweet* was not a compliment.

"Sit, sit. Ve have things to discuss."

Fredericka watched the young girl uneasily settle herself on a chair. Martha Brady was still a sharp cookie, Fredericka thought with satisfaction, pulling this girl out of that nothing little modeling school. But of course, the great beauties could be found anywhere. Walking down the street, waitressing, working in a shop—you never knew when you'd come upon them, those tall young girls with the magnificent bone structure who'd always thought of themselves as gangly and awkward. This one wasn't a guaranteed winner, but she had definite potential.

Fredericka reached over to extract a folder from a pile of papers at her elbow.

That same folder from the other day, Callie thought. Would it be following her everywhere for the rest of her life? She was suddenly reminded of elementary school, where the teachers always threatened that any breach of behavior would be put on a student's permanent record, whatever that was. She resisted the urge to smile at the memory as she watched Fredericka flipping through the pages, stopping at the photographs taken back at the Norton Modeling School.

"Dreadful, truly dreadful," Fredericka said, holding them up by one corner as if they were too dirty to be touched. "The photographer should be shot. But vhat is impressive is the fact that your look came through, even in such awful vork."

She dropped the photos back into the folder. Leaning forward, her dark eyes boring into Callie's light green ones, her voice took on an intimate quality. "Today is an important day, Callie darling. Today you start as a member of the Vhiting family. Vhich means you are part of a special group: the vorld's most beautiful vimmen. It is an honor and an obligation."

Pausing, she tilted her head. "You have brought the signed contract?"

Hastily Callie dug into her handbag and pulled out the document. "Here it is," she said, placing it gently on the edge of the desk. She wished she weren't so afraid of the woman.

"Good. My secretary vill take it to Legal." Fredericka picked up a gold pen and tapped it lightly on the folder. "I take a personal interest in everything that goes on at the agency and in all my girls. If you have a problem, no matter how small, you must come at once to me or to Austin."

She scrutinized Callie closely, still tapping the pen. "Now, this is vat I think. You lose ten pounds; you have already been told, and there is no question. You also already know you must fix your hair and go to a gym about those hips. Stop biting your nails, get eight hours of sleep each night, drink eight glasses of water each day. This is a serious business, and you must treat it as such. If you vork all day and play all night, you vill pay the price. You vill look bad, and no one vill hire you. Don't be surprised if the suggestion of breast implants is made to you by someone along the vay."

At Callie's shocked expression, Fredericka held up a hand. "I vould never tell my girls to have any surgery they did not vant. Big breasts are vhat the photographers vant right now. I only say it so you'll know vhat to expect.

"Conduct yourself as a Vhiting model should: no scenes or bad language in public, and, most important, good behavior on the set. I promise you, if you act like a prima donna, your career vill be over before it has begun; no one has patience for that kind of nonsense. Always remember,

Callie, time is money and money is tight. Vaste time, or make it hard for the photographer or art director to get the shot he vants, and you are out."

Callie bit her lip. Maybe she should be taking notes on all this. In the back of her mind, an odd realization hit her: Fredericka's English was much better today than it had been when the Stewarts first met her.

"Now, go and enjoy. Vork hard, and ve may make you a very rich girl." Fredericka leaned back in her chair, smiling again. "And congratulations again on joining the family."

She buzzed for her secretary and, almost instantly, one of the doors opened. "Take Callie down to see Grace now, Evelyn," Fredericka commanded, her attention going back to the papers she'd been reading earlier. Sensing she had been dismissed, Callie joined Evelyn, the secretary whose beauty had practically hypnotized Tommy the other day, and followed her out of the room.

"Everything going okay?" Evelyn asked as they waited for the elevator.

"Oh, yes, just great, thanks." Nothing could have induced Callie to admit that she was more frightened now than when she'd begun the day. There was a lot to live up to here, she could see that. She would have to start treating her looks seriously, taking good care of her face and body, things she'd never given a minute's thought to before.

Back on the seventh floor, Callie was escorted to the area where the bookers worked, a room she had seen only briefly during her agency tour. It had been explained to her then that the bookers were the ones who dealt with the clients and scheduled all the models' jobs. Now she was able to get a better look at the room and the people in it.

Three women and two men sat around a big blue table in the center of the room. It was some kind of special table constructed for their job, Callie guessed, because it had a space carved out of the center for a revolving rack with lots of skinny compartments, all of them containing blue and yellow files. Each compartment had a model's name on it. Several of the colorful files were open on the table, and Callie could see they had charts in them with the days of the week written across the top and the hours of the day running down the side. The charts were marked up with penciled entries, some in black, some red.

Each booker had his or her own telephone, and they were all in the process of talking on them as they drank from cans of soda or bottled water. Their clothes were casual, slacks and sneakers. On a low shelf nearby, a radio played softly. Callie looked around the room, seeing a pile of portfolios on a bookshelf along with some paper towels, a bottle of glass cleaner, and a large box of raisins. Stacks of slides in clear plastic casing and oversized envelopes rested precariously in one corner on the floor near two tall file cabinets.

She took a seat in one of the two empty chairs and gazed at the pictures on the walls. Unlike the ones in the hallways, these pictures weren't framed or carefully positioned. They were taped up in rows, obviously used for reference rather than decoration. They must be all the actual Whiting models, she realized, noting that each one had the girl's name clearly printed across the top. Fascinated, she leaned forward in her chair to get a better look.

"Don't worry, you'll be up there soon." A low, gravelly voice made Callie turn around. "Hi, I'm Grace."

The booker sitting closest to Callie was extending her hand. Reaching out to shake it, Callie saw that she was in her late twenties, with shoulder-length brown hair and a pleasant if plain face. She wore blue jeans, a white blouse with the sleeves rolled up, and enormous silver hoop earrings.

"Ready to roll?" Grace gave her an encouraging smile. Callie nodded. "Good. Then take a deep breath."

She rummaged through the papers before her, talking so quickly that Callie had difficulty understanding her. None of the other bookers listened or even looked over at the two of them; they were busy with their own phone conversations or making notations on their charts.

"We've got a list of some of the things you'll need to know. First, where to get your hair cut—and please, don't forget to remind them as soon as you get there that you're with us. We've already scheduled you for tomorrow at ten A.M. Here's the bank we use. You'll probably want to open an account there; most of the girls do, and we can arrange for direct deposit of your paycheck if you want. Here's a gynecologist, an all-night drugstore, and two delis in the neighborhood. Let's see, a facialist, manicurist, and the woman who does a lot of the hair coloring for our girls who need it. That ought to start you off."

She handed the piece of paper to Callie, who glanced at the list of names and phone numbers, but she could hardly make out the handwriting. She would study it later and try to decipher everything.

Grace lit a cigarette, then continued in her rapidfire style. "Normally, we'd pair you up with another girl who was just joining us, but with the crush of new faces around here lately, it worked out that you're going to room with Lanny. She's been with us nearly a year. Her roommate just went back to Wisconsin, so she has an empty bedroom."

"We'll be living together?" Callie asked.

"Don't look so frightened," Grace said gently, giving Callie another slip of paper with an address on it and an envelope. "It's a decent building, on East Fifty-fourth Street. Lanny may actually be a big help to you, since she knows her way around. Don't let her scare you off, though." She lowered her voice conspiratorially. "She's kind of a cold potato, though if you tell anybody I said that, I'll deny it."

"Thanks for the tip," Callie whispered back.

"There's a hundred dollars spending money in the envelope, an advance against future earnings. Your share of the rent will be paid by the agency for now, also an advance that will come out of your paycheck."

Grace picked up one of the blue charts from the table. "Just in case no one told you, you're part of the division known as Taking Off. The more established girls are in the Whiting Women's Division. That's the main division, the biggest one. Then there's the smaller Essential Woman Division, which is the older models. Men's is a separate department, down on six. We'll be scheduling appointments for you, when and if anyone wants to book you, that is."

She brought a chart closer for Callie's inspection. "See, the black pencil is for when they make the appointment; red means it's all confirmed, it's really going to happen."

"Sometimes they change their minds?" Callie asked tentatively.

Grace laughed. "That's one way of putting it. You'll see, nothing is definite till it's definite. There are millions of changes, and we juggle them all on this piece of paper. By the way, if there are ever any problems—a photographer makes you do something dangerous for a shot, the location is moved and nobody told you—you call me right away. We deal with the clients for you. Or let's say you think you'll be in sportswear and they tell you when you get there they need one shot in lingerie. Lingerie is billed at a higher rate. But don't even argue, just call. *Any* problems—you're stranded without money, pregnant, lost—you call and I'll be glad to help you."

"Fredericka said I should also call her or Austin with problems," Callie interjected.

Grace paused, her face expressionless, but didn't reply. Glancing back down at a pad in front of her, she went on as if she hadn't heard. "Now, what name would you like to use?"

"Excuse me?" Callie was startled.

"Your professional name. Some girls use one name only, or you can make up a completely new name."

Puzzled, Callie responded slowly. "Can't I just stick with my own first and last name?"

"Fine by me." Grace made a notation. "It's a nice name, actually. Lots of the girls start out with real doozies."

Callie glanced again at the photographs on the wall. So some of them were fake, she thought, those melodious names printed above the gorgeous faces. Boy, she knew nothing at all.

"One last thing, but most important." Grace stamped out her cigarette in a metal ashtray already brimming over with butts and took a sip from a can of Coke. "After your haircut tomorrow, you're scheduled for test shots. Someone will be there to do hair, makeup, and wardrobe; you don't provide a thing. Just show up looking rested and acting nice. That's really the best advice I can give you, and it'll never change. Looks are one thing in this business, but you'll see that personality is just as critical. If people like you, you'll work. If they don't, you won't." She smiled at Callie. "Simple, right?"

Callie liked Grace's directness. For the first time since she'd come here, she felt that someone was treating her like a real person, telling her the plain truth.

"What are these test shots for?" she asked.

"We use them to start your book, since you don't have any tear sheets—those are real ads or editorial stuff—to show to prospective clients. Modeling isn't about how you look in person really, it's the way you photograph. We need the pictures to convince clients their lives will be utterly meaningless if they don't hire you and *only* you."

Callie nodded. "Thank you, Grace."

"Hey, no problem." She grinned. "And relax, you'll do just fine."

She tossed a checkbook-sized pad to Callie. "Those are your vouchers. Always be sure the client signs one as proof that you were there. You hand them in weekly, and we pay you accordingly."

Grace stretched her arms over her head and rolled her head from one side to the other to get out the kinks. Her telephone rang. "Gotta get that. Call me at the end of the day to confirm you've got the right address for tomorrow. Then you'll call me after the shoot. Right now you should check out of the Barbizon and get settled at Lanny's—she doesn't use any last name." She picked up the telephone receiver as she went on. "The key is with the doorman. Can you handle checking out by yourself and catching a cab with your bags?"

"Sure."

Grace spoke rapidly into the phone. "Grace here. Please hold one minute." She put her hand over the mouthpiece so the caller wouldn't hear what she said to Callie. "No offense. We do have girls fourteen and fifteen who would be too scared to do it themselves. Just asking."

Callie nodded as Grace went back to her caller, simultaneously waving a friendly goodbye. "Freddy, you dog," she yelled into the phone delightedly, her raspy voice ringing out in the room, her visitor forgotten. "Did you really go to Barbados?"

Callie glanced down at the papers in her hand. They

weren't wasting any time. Test shots with a real photographer, already! She wished she could call her parents to tell them, but they wouldn't arrive back home until tomorrow.

A doorman stopped Callie as she entered the building on East Fifty-fourth Street. When she told him her name, he nodded and went into a small cubicle, returning with an envelope containing a key marked 11B. He carried her two suitcases to the waiting elevator, set them down inside, then tipped his hat. She stepped in and pressed the button marked 11, noticing he was still standing there as the door was closing. *Good security,* she thought; it made her feel safe knowing he was watching her until she was safely on her way up. It wasn't until she got out on the eleventh floor that it dawned on her that he was probably just waiting for a tip.

Sighing, she dragged her bags around the hall corner and unlocked the door to apartment 11B. Even though it was the afternoon, the entryway was dark. She flicked on the light switch and looked around. The foyer led into an open dining area, with a spacious living room just beyond. Whoever this Lanny was, she wasn't very neat. In the dining area, the remnants of someone's breakfast remained on the table, a dirty orange-juice glass, cereal bowl, and coffee mug barely finding space amid the junk mail and papers that covered the glass table. Clothes were flung across two of the four chairs.

Walking into the living room, Callie saw more of the same. Magazines, catalogs, videocassettes, loose papers, and what looked like dozens of invitations and flyers littered the floor, scattered around bulging shopping bags propped against the brown couch and armchair. The place didn't look too clean either, she noticed, seeing two dirty champagne glasses sitting in a thin layer of dust on the long, low coffee table.

She stepped over a pair of yellow sandals in the center of the room and went to the window, poking a space in the blinds' narrow slats so she could see out. The buildings of New York waited there, some tall and imposing, blocking parts of the view, some squat beneath her. She didn't know what streets she was gazing at, but just standing there, so high up, made her feel wonderful. She was really here, really doing it.

She walked back to look briefly into the small kitchen—also a mess—and then went to see the bedrooms. One was completely empty other than a stripped double bed and an old chest of drawers. That room was obviously for her, and there was a bathroom nearby in the hall. The other bedroom was much bigger. It contained a king-sized bed with four pillows and rumpled pink-striped sheets, hastily yanked up and smoothed out, a dressing table, and a mirrored closet running the entire length of one wall. Feeling guilty about snooping, Callie resisted the urge to open the closet and peek at Lanny's clothes. But she couldn't stop herself from wandering into the bathroom at the far end of the room.

Wet towels and a silk nightgown tossed on the floor were evidence of that morning's shower. The sink was surrounded by a wide ledge, every available inch covered with bottles and jars, lipsticks and colored pencils. Callie turned on the overhead light. A mirror covered the wall above the sink, while a smaller makeup mirror with lights around it sat on the sinktop.

Fascinated, she studied the items arrayed before her: Lancôme compact, a bloodred Yves Saint Laurent lipstick, makeup base from Chanel, and five or six Dior eye shadows. Callie certainly recognized all the names, but she could never have afforded to buy them. She was surprised to see a pink and lime-green tube—Maybelline mascara—which was what she used at home when she got dressed up, purchased at the local five-and-ten. So she and a high fashion model had that in common. She picked up a black jar with a plain white label on it. The black letters said KIEHL'S VERY UNUSUAL RICH—BUT NOT GREASY AT ALL—HAND CREAM. What on earth was that? There was an open jar marked WILLIAM TUTTLE, with some kind of thick, beige makeup in it. How did these models know which products to buy and how to use them?

A key turned in the front door lock. Whirling around, Callie hurried out of the bathroom and reached the entryway just as the door opened. A girl of nearly six feet stood there, struggling to get her key out of the lock.

"Hi. I'm Callie." She hoped her guilt wasn't written all over her face.

"Damn." With a furious yank, the key came free. The girl looked up, no trace of expression on her face. "Oh, yeah, the new one."

The two of them regarded each other. Lanny's long black hair was swept up in a ponytail on top of her head, casually tied with a purple scarf. She had olive skin and a broad face with a flat nose and wide cheekbones. Her beauty was exotic, a complete contrast to Callie's all-American fair coloring. The tight-fitting, short purple dress she wore revealed bone-thin arms and legs.

"What a morning." Lanny was carrying an oversized black canvas shoulder bag and her portfolio, both of which she dumped on the floor on her way to sinking down into the living room couch. Her tone was disgusted. "Three go-sees, one in the East Fifties, one way over west in the Twenties, the third in SoHo. And all in three hours, no less."

"Go-sees?" Callie echoed hesitantly.

Lanny looked at her with impatience. "Yes, go-sees. Auditions, tryouts, where they size you up and see if they want to hire you for the job. Boy, they don't teach the new ones anything anymore. It's a wonder you can get from one booking to the next."

She kicked off her black pumps and rubbed her feet, and said in a flat, bored voice, "I'm sure you found your bedroom by now. You buy your own groceries, get your own towels and sheets. For now you can borrow a set of mine, but get some soon. I don't cook, so the kitchen is usually free if you're into that."

Lanny got up and walked toward her bedroom, yanking the purple dress up over her head. Underneath she wore only black bikini underpants, and she was so thin that her ribs stuck out. Callie tried to hide her shock at this casual display of nudity, at the same time noticing that Lanny was as flat-chested as a boy.

"I'm going to the gym and then to see my nutritionist."

Callie, still standing in the entryway, watched Lanny close her bedroom door behind her. Grace was right. "Cold potato" was definitely the way to describe her new roommate. She picked up her two suitcases and took them into her room to start unpacking. The closet was narrow, she saw, with only a few hangers inside. Suddenly, Callie realized she was starving. She glanced at her watch: it was already two-thirty. No wonder. She hadn't eaten since seven that morning. It was time to go to one of those delis on Grace's list and get a sandwich. Then she remembered—she had to lose ten pounds right away.

Going into the bathroom, she rinsed out the plastic glass that was in the cup holder and filled it with cold water. Maybe that would stave off the hunger pangs. The water had an odd taste, not what she was used to. She felt a fresh wave of longing for her parents and for her own room in her own house.

But that kind of thinking wasn't going to get her anywhere, she realized. As she finished drinking, she wetted some wadded-up toilet tissue and began wiping off the sink. Instead of spending her money on food, she would find a grocery store and get some cleaning supplies. Somehow, she had to make this place feel like home.

By the time she had scrubbed down the bathroom and the kitchen, and given her bedroom a thorough cleaning before unpacking her clothes and making up the bed, it was eight o'clock, and Callie was exhausted. She went downstairs to the supermarket across the street to get something for dinner. Fearful of eating anything fattening, and uncertain what would be best, she finally settled on a tomato and a head of lettuce, and a plain yogurt for breakfast the next day.

As she was slicing up her meager dinner, Lanny returned, only nodding in greeting before she headed into her room. When she emerged from the bedroom over an hour later, Callie was sitting on the living room couch, flipping through a magazine and trying to ignore the rumbling of her unsatisfied stomach. It had been a long day and she contemplated going to sleep for the night even though it was still early.

"Was that the doorbell?" Lanny called out. "I'm expecting a date."

Callie stared in fascination, her fatigue momentarily forgotten. Her roommate was wearing a sleeveless red dress, even shorter and more form-fitting than the purple one she'd worn that afternoon. Long gold and pearl earrings, the only jewelry she wore, dangled to her bare shoulders, and her hair hung down past her shoulders in a thick, straight curtain. She had on the sheerest red stockings and red high-heeled pumps, and was stuffing a lipstick and brush into a small beaded evening bag of the same bright shade. Her eyes were made up with gold eye shadow, and fire-engine-red lipstick made her mouth look wet.

Lanny was so chic, Callie thought. She could never be that way in a million years. Where could her roommate be going in that dress? She wondered if this was the way models lived, going out on dates in the middle of the week, actually looking in real life as if they had just stepped out of a magazine. Callie tried to imagine herself in an outfit like Lanny's but it was such a farfetched idea that she had to smile.

"Well?" Lanny asked, annoyed.

"What?" Callie couldn't remember what Lanny was asking about. "Oh, the doorbell. No, no, it hasn't rung."

Lanny crossed over to where she had left her canvas shoulder bag that afternoon and bent over, rummaging inside it to take out a few more items for her purse. The dress rode all the way up her thighs, revealing the white lacy garters holding up her stockings. A garter belt. Callie had never known anyone who actually wore them—maybe older women did, but not the sexy kind like Lanny's.

The two were silent as Lanny continued with her preparations to leave. Callie wanted to fill the quiet and somehow make Lanny like her.

"I'm already scheduled to do some test shots tomorrow," she said, glad to have thought of some news she could share. "It's my first real job and there'll be hair and makeup people and everything."

Lanny turned to look at her, and her bored tone made it clear that she felt compelled to explain the obvious. "That's good. But don't think they're anybody important. They're just starting out, the same as you. They're nobodies, like whoever the photographer is who's shooting."

"What do you mean?" Callie sat up straighter on the couch.

"It's part of the system," Lanny answered, taking out her lipstick again and reapplying it. "They all need shots to put in their books so they can get work. Nobody's getting paid. You get pictures for your book, the photographer gets pictures for his book, the makeup guy gets pictures for his book. Get it? It's not like it's a real job. It's the pictures that count. You can't get work without pictures, but you can't get pictures without work. This is the way everybody has to get started."

"Oh, I see." Callie was deflated.

The doorbell rang. Lanny grabbed a red chiffon stole from a shelf in the hall closet and draped it loosely around her shoulders. Then she opened the door and was gone. Callie hadn't been able to see the man standing in the hall, but she envisioned a gorgeous male model in a tuxedo.

Well, she reassured herself, the people on the set might be starting out, but there was nothing so terrible about that. It was still a professional job, and Callie was going to do the best she could.

She stood up. Early or not, she was going to bed. She wanted to be well rested when she got to the set the next day. And she was sick of trying to pretend she wasn't hungry. Sleep would take her mind off it. *What I wouldn't give for a cheeseburger and fries,* she thought ruefully, heading into her bedroom.

The lobby was small and dirty, and Callie hesitated, checking the address on her slip of paper. She was definitely in the right place. There it was on the directory: John Vine, second floor. She rang for the elevator, looking around nervously, hoping no one was about to spring out from behind some corner and mug her.

Finding the photographer's studio had been something of an ordeal. Having asked the receptionist at the hair salon how to get to the address Grace had given her, Callie had been directed to a nearby subway. She must have taken the wrong train, though, because when she got out and asked a man walking by which way it was to Grand Street, he laughed and told her she was way uptown. In the end, growing panicked and afraid she'd be late, she'd swallowed her pride and stopped at a telephone booth to call Grace. Grace had been patient and reassuring, slowly going over the directions until Callie was sure she understood.

She took several deep breaths. It was okay, she was here now, just half an hour late, not good, but not the worst thing that ever happened. And she had a new haircut that should make her look more acceptable, more like a real model. That had been an experience all by itself. The salon on East Sixty-third had been so busy and noisy, full of beautiful women and employees rushing around. Callie had stood unnoticed by the front desk until she finally forced herself to tell someone she had an appointment. She remembered to tell them that Whiting had sent her, and she saw that the information was passed along from the receptionist to the girl who shampooed Callie's hair to Salvatore, the man who cut it.

Upon learning that she was a Whiting model, Salvatore had introduced himself immediately and told Callie that he cut the hair of all the best models in New York. He then commenced to rave about her beauty, holding her chin between his thumb and forefinger, turning her face left and right, making kissing noises into the air.

"Veddy gorgeous," he said in his heavily accented English. He inspected her hair, announcing that Callie could keep her own color and it would be left long, but shaped and layered. The haircut itself took only a few minutes, but even Callie could see that it made a significant difference. She normally wore her hair parted in the middle, but Salvatore had cut wispy bangs and moved her part to the left side. He snipped off two inches from the back and sides, shaping it into a soft curve. When she got up from the chair, she took a last glance in the mirror. It was hard to say exactly why or how, but the girl who looked back was more sophisticated and prettier than the one who had initially sat down.

"Bella," Salvatore had pronounced, delighted with his

handiwork, brushing the air near Callie's cheek with his lips. "You tell everyone Salvatore cut your hair."

The elevator opened with a grating squeak. Callie got in, ignoring the smell of urine. Photographers just starting out must not be able to afford nice offices, she supposed. She only had to go up one floor, but the ride seemed to take an eternity. The door opened directly into the studio, a large room with virtually no furniture in it other than a wooden chair on casters and a table with a black telephone on it. Grime covered the two windows on the opposite wall. At the far end of the room Callie saw a long sheet of heavy white paper suspended from the ceiling. It was too long, so the bottom curved onto the floor and extended about four feet into the room. Two lightstands had been positioned on it, along with a camera on a tripod, ready to shoot. Nothing too fancy for a set, she thought, but that was obviously where she would pose.

"There you are!" an angry voice rang out. Callie tried to guess where it was coming from. "What the hell kept you?"

A man in his twenties with wavy dark hair stepped out from behind the white backdrop. "You girls—how do you expect to get anything done if you're this late?"

Callie was mortified. "I'm—I'm so sorry," she stammered. "I got lost on the subway and—"

"Yeah, yeah, I don't want to hear about it." He moved one of the lightstands a bit to the left. "Just get ready."

She hurried over to where he stood and saw that behind the white sheet was a small recessed area equipped with a stool and counter. A young man sat on the stool, setting out makeup on the counter before him. Seeing Callie, he jumped up and smiled.

"I'm Leon. I'll be doing your hair and makeup."

Callie extended a hand. "Very nice to meet you, Leon."

They shook. Seemingly from nowhere, a young woman appeared beside them. She looked no older than Callie. Her eyes were heavily outlined in black and she wore an orange jumpsuit. She smiled, although her tone was businesslike.

"I'm Anne, the stylist. Take off your clothes so we can get changed."

"Everything?" Callie asked.

Anne nodded. "Except your panties. If you're wearing a bra, we'll see if it interferes."

Anne and Leon stood there expectantly. Were they both going to watch her remove her clothes? Apparently. Callie kicked off her shoes, then reached under her dress to pull off her panty hose, stalling for time. Leon came over and started running a brush through her hair as Anne moved her shoes off to one side, then came around behind Callie and started opening the buttons that ran down the back of her dress. She slid the garment off Callie's shoulders and Callie stepped out of it, resisting the impulse to cross her arms over her white bra. But Leon, she saw, was engrossed in picking out eye shadows, and Anne was busy smoothing the front of a flowered sundress. Neither of them were the least bit interested in observing Callie in her underwear.

"Put this on."

Obediently, Callie held up her arms as Anne slipped the sundress over her head. The stylist eyed her critically, frowning. "No, that's all wrong. Take it off."

Callie obeyed as Anne turned to consider several other garments hanging on a metal rack, finally selecting a peach-colored dress with cut-out shoulders. "A little sixties looking," she said, "and I think just right for you. Slip off your bra straps and try it on for me."

Callie got into the dress and Anne smiled. "Good."

"So that's the color you want her in?" Leon asked.

Anne nodded.

"How do you see the hair?" Leon took Callie's chin in his hand and was turning her face right and left, running his hand through her hair, fluffing it up, smoothing it down again.

Anne considered the question. "The dress is funky but kind of retro chic, so something new and interesting."

"Okay, take a seat here," he said to Callie. "Let's get started."

Anne helped Callie out of the dress, giving her a thin towel to wrap around herself. Tucking the ends tightly, Callie hopped up onto the tall stool. Leon sprayed a white cloud of styling mousse into one palm, then rubbed it onto both hands and applied it quickly through her hair. Callie sat patiently while he used a blow dryer on it, then pinned it up, pushing her bangs off to the side and clipping them separately. Then he turned his attention to the makeup on the counter.

She looked at herself in the mirror. After using mousse and spending that time drying it, why had he just stuck it on top of her head? Wasn't it ruined? She hoped this wasn't the hair style he had in mind—it looked dreadful.

"Leon," she asked timidly, "is this how my hair will be?"

He looked at her, startled by the question. "Of course not, honey. But your hair was clean, so I had to put something on it to give it some resistance—sort of make it dirty, so it'll hold the style. Clean hair is too slippery to work with for what I want."

"Oh." Embarrassed, Callie resolved not to ask any more questions.

She watched Leon's eyes traveling from the dress to the makeup before him as he selected the appropriate colors. There were so many things there, jars and shadows and pencils. Silently, she followed his movements as he picked up and discarded different colors, carefully selecting what he would use.

Anne ripped open a package of panty hose and brought them over with a pair of white pumps, gesturing for Callie to put them on. Leon held up a bottle of foundation next to Callie's face, then another, apparently debating which was better for her skin tone. His decision made, he grabbed a white triangular wedge of sponge and began hurriedly applying the thick face makeup in short, quick strokes. Trying to keep her face steady for him, Callie wriggled into the panty hose and slipped on the pumps. After clipping white daisy-shaped earrings onto Callie's ears, Anne left her alone while she ran a small steamer along the front of the dress, smoothing out a few wrinkles.

"It's getting late. Move it back there." The angry voice of the man Callie had first seen when she entered boomed back to the three of them. Leon looked panicked, his hands traveling more quickly across Callie's face. The voice must belong to John Vine, the photographer. Callie wanted to groan. She'd already made a great impression on him.

"We're moving as fast as we can. Do you want a good shot or not?" Anne retorted.

Callie admired her nerve; she would never have dared to answer back that way. She wished she could see what Leon was doing, but he was in front of her, blocking the mirror on the wall. As he applied the eye shadow, she saw his hands shaking slightly. So he was just as anxious as she was. She smiled to reassure him.

"Good, keep smiling," he instructed her, reaching for a lipstick brush and jabbing it into a pot of pale peach lipstick. The smile frozen on her face, Callie had an irresistible urge to scratch her nose. When she could stand it no longer, she reached up, but Leon pushed her hand away.

"Now close," he instructed her.

She stopped smiling, and he stuck the brush into the corners of her mouth, making sure the lipstick was evenly applied. It was a strange sensation.

Anne was standing behind her. "Almost done?"

Leon got out of the way just long enough for Anne to slip the peach dress over Callie's head and zip it up the back. Leon moved around behind Callie to brush out her hair. In the mirror she saw him teasing it, spraying and combing it until the sides stayed back off her face, then curling it out into a flip. He fussed with her bangs, spraying and poking at them with the thin end of a comb until they achieved the wispy effect he wanted.

The stylist fussed with the dress for a moment, as Leon came back around and went over Callie's lips again with sheer lip gloss. Then they both stood back, appraising their handiwork, and Callie got a quick glimpse of herself in the mirror. The dress was practically as short and tight as Lanny's purple one the day before. Her face looked—what was the word—*contoured* somehow, as if it had more planes and shapes in it. Her green eyes appeared a deeper shade than normal, and much larger, staring out from beneath the bangs Salvatore had given her only two hours before. She barely recognized herself.

Leon followed her as she walked around to the front of the white paper, still spraying her hair, then dabbing powder on her face. "You look great," he whispered encouragingly.

"Thanks," she whispered back, wishing she could hug him for that.

John Vine was standing behind his camera making adjustments, then hurrying over to move the lightstands a little bit in one direction or the other. He looked up to see Callie come toward him.

"What would you like me to do?" she asked, keeping her voice cheerful.

"Stand on the seamless, please," he said, pointing.

That must be what the white paper was called. She should have known that, she thought, moving to find a place in the center of it as he scrutinized her. Her heart was pounding so loudly that she was afraid they could all hear it. She hoped the photographer wouldn't comment on her being too fat.

He came over to her, holding a small black box near her face.

"What's that?" Callie asked pleasantly.

He was annoyed by her question. "Light meter," he said brusquely.

She admonished herself; she'd sworn not to ask anything else today. Frowning, John Vine spoke more loudly, his comments addressed to Anne. "Okay, I want the hair fuller, and change the earrings. The white ones are no good."

Leon and Anne rushed to do his bidding, as Callie breathed deeply, trying to keep calm. *You can do this,* she told herself.

For the rest of the day, Vine barked instructions at Callie and she did her best to follow them. She turned, she jumped, she shook her hair, she frowned, she laughed, she pouted sexily—or what she hoped was sexily. Her cheeks were killing her from so much grimacing, as she held her expression for what seemed hours on end. Between rolls of film, the photographer had Anne change Callie's outfit three times, and Leon stepped in each time to freshen up her makeup and redo her hair, putting it up in a ponytail and finally a French twist. Callie was surprised to note that far more time was spent fixing her hair and makeup and dressing her than on the actual taking of photographs.

Callie smiled sweetly at every break in the action, but inside she was frightened and upset by the commanding tone in the photographer's voice. She kept reminding herself that if Lanny was right, he was just starting out too, so maybe he was as nervous as she was. It didn't help much, though. No matter how nervous she was, she would never speak as roughly to anyone as John Vine was speaking to her.

When he announced they were finished, Callie was so relieved that she could have kissed him. Anne helped her out of the last outfit, and Leon brushed out the French twist so that her hair was loose again, although still sticky from all the hairspray he'd used. Callie didn't want to take off the makeup just yet; it would be fun to go out wearing it, she decided. Back in her own clothes, she said goodbye to the two of them and that she hoped she'd see them again soon. The three shook hands all around. John Vine was nowhere in sight when she came out front to leave. She called out to him, but there was no reply.

Back on the street again, Callie was exhausted but jubilant. It was over and she had survived. That practically called for a celebration, she thought excitedly. Hurrying up the block, she didn't know what to do with herself. Then she remembered that she was supposed to call Grace at the agency. Digging around in her purse for change, she hurried to the corner and found a telephone booth, dialing the number she had already memorized.

"Grace?" she said breathlessly when the booker answered her line. "It's Callie Stewart. I did it! We had the shoot!"

She could barely hear the reply over the noise of the traffic on the street behind her.

"Oh, honey, that's great," Grace said warmly. "Everything went all right?"

"Oh, yes, everybody was terrific." The entire experience was already taking on a rosy glow in Callie's mind.

"How was John Vine? We want to know if he's going to amount to anything."

"He was wonderful." Callie was sincere, generously reflecting what a difficult job his was, having to produce just the right picture.

"Good. We should have the proofs in a couple of days. Now take the rest of the day for yourself. You earned it."

"Thanks, Grace." Callie felt almost drunk as she hung up the phone. The thick foundation Leon had used on her face was heavy in the summer heat. But it didn't bother her. There was a definite bounce in her step as she walked uptown, too happy to contemplate getting into the subway. It was a nice day anyway, she thought, and the exercise wouldn't hurt in shedding those extra pounds; she'd walk from Grand Street up to Fifty-fourth.

The admiring gazes of the men she passed on the street didn't escape Callie. No one back in Bloomington had ever stared like that as she walked down the street. Or maybe they had and she'd just never noticed.

It was after seven when she got back to her apartment. She couldn't resist calling her parents, even though she knew she shouldn't be splurging on long-distance telephone calls. Her father answered, clearly thrilled to hear Callie's voice. She told him about the shoot, leaving out the less pleasant parts and dwelling on how fascinating it had been, how nice Leon and Anne were to her.

"You're on your way, baby," Frank told her proudly. "We knew you could do it."

"Thanks, Daddy." Callie was filled with an overwhelming longing to see her family, but she didn't want her father to be aware of the loneliness that washed over her as she continued to talk to him. He would only feel bad if he knew. She remained upbeat, telling him how sensational Grace was, how helpful the agency was being.

"So they'll get the proofs in a couple of days," she went on with her story, feeling very important to be tossing around the industry jargon. "I'll let you know how it turns out."

"Do that, champ. We'll be waiting." His voice was filled with love. "You take care of yourself."

"I will, Daddy. I love you."

"We all love you, too, honey."

Sadly, Callie hung up the phone. She wandered around the apartment, reluctant to wash her face and erase the last traces of her triumphant day. There was no one else to call, no one else with whom she could discuss all the exciting things that were happening to her. She wished Lanny would come home. Eventually, she got out of her clothes and headed for the shower.

When Grace called her two days later to say the proofs had come in, Callie practically flew over to the agency. She had spent the preceding day alone, looking at health clubs. Although she was horrified to learn what the membership fees were, she finally resigned herself to paying the price, and selected a club that had tennis courts along with its exercise equipment. But the only people she had spoken to were the club's employees, and she'd passed the two nights prior to that by herself in the apartment; she hadn't even seen her roommate since their last encounter before Lanny's date. By now, she was desperate to talk to a friendly face, and couldn't wait to see Grace.

The receptionist on the seventh floor at Whiting directed Callie to go in. Heading toward Grace's office, she passed an open kitchen area, where two models stood talking and giggling with a dark-haired man. When he turned so Callie could see his face, she saw that he was more than attractive; he was, she thought, what the girls back home would have called gor-gee-us. Catching her eye as she passed by, he gave her a broad smile, and winked. Callie looked away, her face flushing beet red. A woman she had never seen before was standing in the hallway, flipping through a stack of papers; she must have witnessed the scene because she whispered something as Callie passed.

"Excuse me?" Callie wasn't sure the woman had been talking to her.

"Some of the photographers can be very dangerous, especially for the new girls," the woman whispered again with a smile, raising an eyebrow knowingly.

"Oh. Thank you," Callie whispered back. She really would have to be careful.

When Callie stuck her head in the bookers' room, Grace was on the telephone, but waved her in immediately and tossed her a thick gray envelope. Inside were nearly two dozen glossy pages, each revealing several rows of small black and white pictures of Callie. Sitting down as she flipped through them, Callie was amazed to see how many pictures had been taken that day. *There must be hundreds here,* she thought. Going back to the beginning, she reviewed them again, more slowly this time.

It was incredible. She looked like a model. Her face showed every imaginable expression, and, there was no question about it, she looked beautiful. And the clothes— moving as she jumped in the air, skirts billowing as she spun around—she really looked like one of the girls she saw in magazines.

"What do you think?" Grace's low voice interrupted her reverie.

Callie looked up, her face shining. "They're great." Then, abashed at her lack of humility, her face fell. "I shouldn't say that. Maybe they're not so great, huh?"

Grace laughed. "Don't worry. We're all fairly pleased with them. We can definitely use them to get you some work, though I wouldn't count on being on any magazine covers for the time being. But it's a start."

Callie nodded.

"Okay," Grace said, lighting a cigarette and getting down to business. "We'll pick a bunch of shots, blow them up, and put them in a portfolio for you. You'll start with one portfolio, but as there's more demand to see your book, we'll make you more. The agency deducts five hundred dollars for the cost of each book and developing. Of course, you pay the messenger fees to send the book around town—and that fee goes on for as long as you're with us."

Grace paused to make sure Callie was taking all this in.

"When you have more pictures, stuff from jobs," Grace went on, "we'll put one of these on our head sheet, which is the big fold-out page with all the girls' faces on it. Photographers put them on the wall—it's like a poster to refer to the girls. And we'll make up a composite for you. You know, they're about six by eight inches, and they have a few different shots to show how versatile you are, along with your sizes—height, measurements, shoe size, eyes, hair color, and so on."

Callie nodded again.

"Here's another hundred dollars spending money." Grace handed her a white envelope. "And, let's see, what did I do with that?" Bending over, she rummaged through a stack of envelopes on the floor next to her. "Ah, got it."

She handed Callie a bound, black leather book. "Courtesy of the Whiting Agency." She smiled. "This is your appointment book. Live with it, breathe with it, sleep with it. Write down all your go-sees and appointments and everything else in the world. There's a pocket in front for your vouchers. It'll be your lifeline."

Delighted, Callie thanked her, taking the book and running one hand over its soft front cover.

Grace picked up the phone. "I gotta make an important call, so I'm throwing you out now. But stay in close touch. I'm working on a job for you, and I should know tomorrow."

Callie waved as Grace punched the buttons on her telephone. It occurred to her that no one ever seemed to say goodbye around here. They were all off onto the next thing before the conversation was even over, so gestures had to suffice. She walked back down the hall. The kitchen area where she'd seen the models with that photographer was empty now.

So, she thought, *it's actually going to happen.* She would model and save up enough money for school and go on to do everything she'd wanted. And it was turning out to be so easy.

5

Callie stood at the corner of Eighth Avenue and Twenty-third Street, waiting for the light to change and trying to ignore the blaring horns and fumes spewing from the rush-hour traffic that crawled past her. Exhaust smoke mingled with the humidity of the July day, making the late afternoon air heavy and wet beneath the hazy summer sun. A young man in a dirty white T-shirt caught Callie's eye from inside his beat-up van. He leaned out the open window, banging loudly on the outside of his car door as he whistled long and low.

"Hey, baby," he called out, "you're just my type. And I bet I'm *your* type too."

Callie looked away, angry and embarrassed. The light turned green and she crossed, weaving in and out of the cars trapped in the intersection. Her hair, damp with perspiration, was sticking to her neck. In what was now her daily routine, she'd spent half an hour that morning coaxing it with a round brush and a blow dryer, attempting to make it look the same as when she'd initially had it cut. Listlessly, she brushed her bangs away with her hand; they were glued to her forehead, greasy with makeup. The foundation on her face seemed to weigh a thousand pounds, and she could practically feel the mascara forming raccoon circles beneath her eyes every time she blinked. Her mouth was caked with lipstick and gloss.

Please let this day be over soon, she silently begged no one in particular. Her black canvas bag slipped down off her shoulder and she shifted her portfolio to her other hand as she stopped for a moment to hoist the bag up again. It hadn't taken long to discover she needed one of those big bags she'd seen Lanny carrying that first day. It was the model's job, she'd learned, to show up prepared for anything.

She remembered how fascinated she'd been when Lanny dumped her bag's contents on the dining room table one morning, rummaging through it for something. Callie had quickly taken in its contents: a bulging makeup bag, a black brush and comb, hot rollers, the same Whiting leather appointment book Callie had, Tampax, bikini underpants, two pairs of panty hose, a bra, a body stocking, a pair of black pumps. Lanny also had a couple of Polaroid shots of herself in different outfits, obviously snapped on various sets. The next day, Callie had rushed out and bought a satchel as similar to Lanny's as she could find, then stocked it with most of the same items. Another investment of money. Callie didn't even want to think how much the agency had advanced her by now; she'd be paying it off forever.

She sighed, making her way down the block in the stifling heat. The bag must weigh fifteen pounds at least, she guessed, sarcastically noting to herself that she might as well leave it home from now on, because it certainly didn't look like she was in any danger of being asked to use anything in it on a go-see, much less on a job.

Two solid weeks and no one had hired her for anything at all. The shoot Grace had been so hopeful about the day

Callie had gone in to look at her first proofs had never materialized, and it was beginning to look to Callie as if no job ever would. Every afternoon she dutifully wrote in her appointment book the times and addresses for all the go-sees Grace arranged for her, and every morning she set out for them promptly, carefully dressed and hoping she had been successful in emulating the expert makeup job she saw Lanny perform on her own face. Sitting on the steaming subway, plotting the day's course with the aid of her new bus and subway map, she gave herself pep talks, reminders of how important it was to remain upbeat and friendly. At night, she would practically collapse on her bed at home, exhausted and down, her feet hurting, her head throbbing. Busy with her appointments, she'd seen nothing of New York's sights since her parents had dropped her off the preceding month.

As July progressed, she found the city heat unbearable, adding to her depression and constantly growing loneliness. She wondered how long Whiting would keep her on if she didn't make any money for them. Like a lot of the other new girls, she had taken to hanging out at Whiting in her free time, listening to the gossip and chatter, getting advice from the photographers and models who came through. Maybe she shouldn't be doing that; the Whiting people might get annoyed at seeing her around so much, a constant reminder of the financial drain she was becoming for them.

She had thought it was going to be so easy. People would jump to hire her, she had been sure after seeing those first test shots. *What a laugh,* she said to herself now. Day in and day out she marched through a series of advertising agencies and photographers' studios, only to be told she was all wrong, her eyes were too close together, her shape wasn't right, she needed to have her breasts enlarged and the mole near her eye removed—they hadn't been kidding at Whiting, she saw, when they warned her about those last two items.

Even Grace had admitted to her that they were slightly surprised by the lack of response to Callie. Men and women whose jobs and functions she never discovered examined her with contempt, some eyeing her and then turning away with indifference, apparently annoyed at the intrusion in their busy day, others flipping through her book, then silently shoving it back across the table to her without even making eye contact.

To add to her confusion, sometimes a photographer or one of the people at the ad agencies broke into a broad smile when she came toward them, and raved about her pictures; she was the perfect face for them, they would say, exactly the look they wanted. There was always a lot of talk about her *look,* she had noticed. If her look wasn't passé or a waste of time for this or that client, then it was classic, or that of a winner. Callie had been so excited the first couple of times she'd heard the encouraging phrases. She couldn't understand why none of those kind words had led to a job so far.

She knew the goal was to be hired for ads, which paid the most. But first, Grace had told her, she was hunting for editorial work, the fashion or accessory spreads in magazines. They only paid around a hundred fifty dollars a day; even after you'd worked repeatedly with a publication for as long as a year, you could expect to get the fee up to only about two hundred fifty. That was far less than ads paid, but the advertising people scoured the editorial pages for new faces to promote their products. Callie needed to get her face in places like *Elle, Cosmopolitan,* and *Glamour;* even better would be *Vogue* or *Bazaar.*

She located the building. It was small, with an intercom outside, only one of its three black buttons labeled. She pressed that button, next to the word *studio,* and waited.

Finally, she got an irritated response. "Yes?"

"It's Callie Stewart. From Whiting."

The buzzer sounded and she hastily yanked open the door, not wanting to miss the moment and have to ring up again.

The lobby was similar to the one where she had gone for her first shots—dark and dank. Since that day, Callie had learned that lots of photographers had studios in run-down or what she considered creepy buildings that she would ordinarily stay away from. These places apparently were often the ones that offered spaces large enough for a full studio, so the prestige of the photographer really couldn't be judged by his address. She climbed a flight of stairs to the second floor, hearing rock music blaring from behind the studio's large, heavy door. She rang the bell. A girl with close-cropped hair and wearing yellow pants opened it, smiling at Callie but quickly walking off without saying anything.

The room was full of people, although everyone was milling around, apparently on a break. Callie saw a cluster of models, all wearing forest-green turtlenecks and leggings, standing over in one corner, talking and laughing loudly as they sipped from bottles of water and juice, some of them moving in time to the music's driving beat. Normally, she would have stood there until someone approached her, so fearful was she of interrupting or antagonizing a potential employer. Today, she was too hot and irritable to worry about that.

"I'm supposed to see Jacques Duval," she said to a man standing near her, raising her voice to make herself heard. "Which one is he?"

The man pointed. "Over by the picture box."

Callie followed the man's finger and saw the photographer, a tall, graying man with a mustache, scrutinizing slides set up on some kind of small lighted board. She walked over to him, having practically to yell her name until he heard her above the music, and indicating to him that she had brought her book.

"Okay, let's do this fast," he said in a loud voice, reaching out to take it.

He flipped through, the same few images she had grown so used to seeing whizzing past yet again. Now that she'd had a chance to glimpse other models' books in the course of her time at the agency, she knew hers was sadly lacking. *Really pathetic, trying to get work with these,* she said to herself, standing there quietly, barely maintaining her smile. She'd never get anywhere without actual tear sheets, samples of real jobs paid for by real clients. The photographer glanced at her again.

"I don't have anything for you, but I'll keep you in mind."

He took one of her composite cards from the pouch in the back cover and returned the book without interest.

"Thank you very much," Callie responded, not bothering to find out whether he could hear her this time. Another wasted trip. She could have screamed. But at least she was free to go home now.

Downstairs, she headed for a phone booth to check in with Grace, who usually had a few words of good cheer to keep Callie's spirits up. Today, the booker's normally low-pitched voice rose when she learned it was Callie on the other end of the phone.

"You got one!" she cried. "Your first booking has been confirmed."

"You're kidding," Callie exclaimed, her exhaustion instantly lifting. As usual, she battled the street noise to make herself heard on the line. "What is it?"

"Dodd's catalog. You're booked for a full day. Twelve hundred fifty dollars. You're at the low end of the pay scale, of course, but Dodd's is a great place to start. They like to mix well-known faces with some new ones, and you're one of the new ones this go-round. It's a good sign. Since money is so tight these days even the catalogs demand super-looking girls."

"I can't believe it," Callie practically squeaked. "How did it happen?"

"Someone at their ad agency saw your book and liked it. That's all it takes. Congratulations, and be there at ten A.M. sharp. There'll be other girls there, but you'll start a little later because there are so many of you. Expect to stay a little later at the end of the day." Grace gave her the photographer's address.

"Thank you, thank you." It was as if the entire rotten day had never happened. Callie made a mental note to pick up some yogurt for dinner so she could go home, take a shower, and get to bed early. Tomorrow was going to be a big day.

The photographer's studio was the largest one Callie had seen so far. She stood in the doorway hesitantly, feeling her customary uncertainty about what she should do, whom she should speak to. The soft strains of classical music were being piped in through the stereo system, and she noticed a group of people clustered around a table laden with juices, coffee, croissants, and platters of fresh fruit. It wasn't hard to distinguish who the models were, but she had no idea who everyone else might be. Taking a few tentative steps forward, she noticed the dressing area behind a half-drawn curtain. It was bigger and better equipped than those she had seen in other studios: large, lighted mirrors lined the walls, reflecting a long, low counter, and there were three comfortable-looking barber chairs and several racks of clothing.

A woman—in her thirties, Callie guessed—was standing in front of one of the racks, apparently counting the dresses hung there. She was dressed elegantly in neatly pressed navy blue pants and a creamy beige silk shirt. A pair of scissors hung from a navy grosgrain ribbon around her neck. Turning to the counter, she opened a large green fishing tackle box, sifting through compartments of pins, threads, and buttons.

Callie saw an extensive array of makeup and brushes set up on paper towels along the countertop, a sight she was now used to seeing in the studios. She recalled how impressed she had been at her test shots back at John Vine's, when she'd seen the makeup artist's display of products; now she realized that Leon hadn't had the better products, and in fact his selections were minimal compared to what most makeup artists had. Briefly, she wondered what had become of him.

Near the makeup area were rows of shelves containing shoes, handbags, hats, and other accessories she couldn't quite make out from where she stood. A manicurist was at work on the hands of a model, the two women's heads practically touching across a tiny table as they chatted intimately. Next to them, an elderly woman stood ironing, hard at work.

A young man in blue jeans and a black T-shirt came over to Callie.

"You are . . . ?" he inquired politely.

"Callie Stewart."

"Great. Come this way." He smiled and Callie was reassured. Maybe the people on this shoot would be nice. They might even like her, she thought hopefully. Was he the photographer, Bill Meyer? Someone from Dodd's? She didn't dare ask.

He led her to the table of food. "Help yourself to some breakfast, then you can start getting ready. I'm Bill's assistant. He'll be here in a few minutes, so you have some time before we start."

Callie smiled, grateful for the information, and reached for a glass of orange juice. It was delicious, fresh squeezed. She hadn't had fresh-squeezed juice since last summer at home. Suddenly she remembered how many calories were in it and, frowning, put it back down on the table. She'd lost only four pounds so far, and she was determined to shed ten, as Fredericka had instructed. The other people were starting to drift toward the makeup area, so she figured it was just as well there was no time to eat.

She followed the group, putting her bag down in a corner. Everyone seemed to know everyone else. They were talking about their agencies, about who was working what job, about some couple who had broken up. She sat down in one of the barber chairs, trying to be inconspicuous. A model with short, dark hair came rushing in, her clattering high heels making a racket on the wooden floor as she ran across to the dressing area and dumped an oversized pocketbook and two shopping bags on the floor. She and another of the models spotted each other and broke into broad grins.

"Hey, I didn't know you were going to be here." The one who had come in late gushed delightedly as they hugged and exchanged quick pecks on both cheeks.

"Where've you been hiding?" asked the other.

"Shooting in Germany. It was great. Malina Ivor and I did two weeks there. If she wasn't a wreck! She's on the edge of being history—everybody knows about her coke problem. So she bought a pair to give a little lift to her career."

"A little *lift?*" the other one said. They both laughed.

Callie wondered who and what they were talking about. Bought a pair of what?

"And damned if it didn't work," the model went on. "She was a complete bitch, always late, too, but they kept her the full two weeks. I met a guy there and it was total heaven."

As the two continued their animated conversation, Callie turned her attention to the model who had been having the manicure. Barefoot, wearing only a white cotton robe, she was walking in Callie's direction, blowing on her wet nails. Spotting Callie, she stopped and gazed intently at her for a few moments, first staring at her face, then running her eyes up and down Callie's body. She didn't look pleased.

"Hello," she said briefly. "Who are you with?"

Callie smiled. "Whiting."

Something flashed in the girl's eyes. "I see. Well, my name is Vida. I'm with Whiting as well. Nice to meet you."

"Nice to meet you too, Vida. I'm Callie." She held out her hand. Vida wriggled her fingers, indicating that her nails were still wet, then nodded and moved away.

What on earth was wrong with her? Callie wondered. Was there something about Callie that bothered her? Maybe she disliked Callie's face and didn't want to be seen in the same catalog with her. That seemed pretty silly, though, since they both had long blond hair and fair skin. In fact, Callie thought, she had the same sort of eyes Callie herself had, although Vida's were blue. Vida slipped off her robe and stood there naked except for her white lace panties. Callie's weeks of go-sees on busy sets had helped her get used to the models' casual attitude about nakedness, and she was able to force herself to take an objective look at Vida's body. Their bodies were pretty similar, too: not too much on top, a little bigger in the hips, but slim and muscular. *We could be sisters,* Callie said to herself.

Her thoughts were interrupted.

"I'm Ron Passo. Hair and makeup."

Casually brushing back sandy-colored hair off his tan face, his blue eyes crinkling in a friendly way, Ron wore tight jeans and a red shirt. Callie would have guessed him to be a model himself, somewhere in his midthirties, but apparently he wasn't using his good looks in front of the camera. She introduced herself as he came to stand behind her chair, sipping from a steaming cup of coffee.

"You're new, right?" he asked pleasantly, putting down his cup to gather Callie's blond hair in one hand as he picked up a black brush. With swift strokes he began drawing the brush through her thick hair.

"That's right." She sat still, wanting to make his job easier.

They were both silent as he let her hair fall loose again, then he examined it, pushing it this way and that, studying her reflection in the mirror. He picked up a tube of styling gel, squirted some into his hands, then ran them through her hair. Next he turned on a small blow dryer and moved it rapidly back and forth around her head. When he turned it off, he spoke again as if there hadn't been a pause in the conversation. "With Whiting?"

Callie nodded, relieved that she knew from her experience with Leon that he was just preparing her hair for styling, and she didn't have to ask about it.

"Well, keep your eyes open around here. There's a lot to learn." Walking around, he kneeled and brought his face close to hers, casually examining her features. He smelled pleasantly of a light aftershave. "Actually, Bill's a pussycat, a breeze to work with. You know, you have incredible eyes. And I know just what to do with them."

He was so close she could almost have kissed him just by puckering her lips. Still kneeling in front of her, he reached around to tie her hair back with an elastic, and gave her a quick wink. There was a small flutter in Callie's stomach. *You're being an idiot,* she said to herself as he pinned her bangs off her forehead. *He's not interested in me, he's only doing his job.*

"Anything you need or want to know, just ask me," he said. He ran his fingers over her cheeks. "Are you dry?"

"Dry?"

Before she could say anything more, he had a bottle of moisturizer open and was applying it all over her face. Then he took a small triangle of white sponge. She watched him dip the sponge in a glass of water and squeeze it out, then pour a thick, tan makeup base onto it.

Maybe he could help her with some of the jargon being thrown around here. "Actually, I do have a question." She hesitated. "It might not make any sense to you. What does it mean when someone's 'bought a pair'?"

"I beg your pardon?" He stopped in the middle of applying the makeup to her forehead. "Run that by me again."

"Someone said a girl named Malina Ivor bought a pair. What does that mean?"

Ron laughed loudly, and Callie felt her face turning red. "I'm sorry," he said. "I shouldn't laugh. It means she had breast implants. Surgery to make her boobs bigger."

"Ohhh."

"And thanks for the news." He picked up a large, fluffy makeup brush and dipped it into a jar of loose face powder, patting the excess powder off on the back of his hand. "Malina's got a bad coke problem. Maybe it helped."

How on earth does everyone know so much about everybody else? Callie wondered as Ron powdered her face. That was what Fredericka had mentioned that day in her office— buying a pair. Well, Callie wasn't about to have models laughing about her personal business on other sets. If there'd been any chance of her considering such a thing—which there wasn't—just the thought of it now was enough to make it certain she never would.

Ron scrutinized her as he rubbed a thinner brush into a pot of taupe eye shadow, tapping off the excess onto the paper towel on the counter. Callie was intrigued to see that he had about a dozen open pots of shadow glued onto a palette, like an artist's paints, ready for use. That way, she guessed, he didn't have to fuss with opening and closing each one. He put a piece of tissue under her eye.

"Close your eye so the lashes are on top of the tissue, please. We don't want the shadow falling on the base."

Callie did as she was told.

"Malina is a holdover from the bad old days," Ron went on. "The days of drinking, drugs, and disco."

Callie's eyes opened wide in question.

"Don't move," he reprimanded her, reaching for a different brush and dipping it into another color. "In the sixties and seventies, modeling was a big deal, and all that stuff came together—good times, free love, the drug thing. It peaked in about eighty-two, I'd say. Now it's all business. Everybody's working out, counting their money, acting professional. I guess it's all for the best." He turned to pick up a different brush and sighed. "It was an awful lot of fun, though."

"That's all over?"

"Basically. The young, new girls hang out at night, I suppose. Wherever there's a lot of money, there's always a party in life. But now it's mostly work from nine to five, then dinner out instead of dancing till four A.M."

The first shot was getting under way. Callie observed from her seat as Ron continued to work on her face, carefully applying shadow on the outer corner of her eye, then painstakingly putting on black eyeliner.

Vida and another girl were posing together, both wearing silk shirtwaist dresses. Callie noted that they were barefoot, so she assumed the picture wouldn't include their feet. The stylist, the photographer, and two other people conferred behind the camera tripod. One of the photographer's assistants came forward with a light meter, holding the small black box close to their faces, then moving it up and down their bodies; it made Callie think of a security guard in an airport checking passengers with a metal detector. She heard a clicking sound, and the models closed their eyes as the lights flashed on and off repeatedly. More conferring, and a few alterations were made in the lighting. The light meter was brought back. The group behind the camera talked again. The models' accessories were changed and the stylist turned up the cuffs on Vida's dress. Then, finally, the camera started clicking.

The strain of sitting so still while Ron ministered to her eyes was causing Callie to blink repeatedly.

"Not much longer," he reassured her, holding yet another brush close to her face. "Look up."

She raised her head to look at the ceiling.

"No," he smiled, "just with your eyes. Keep your face facing forward."

She sat quietly as he put more loose powder underneath her eyes, but the powder got into her eyes and caused them to tear. *Oh no,* she thought, *now I've ruined the makeup!*

"A little smear here." Ron picked up a Q-Tip. "Open your mouth, please."

She did, and he quickly rolled the Q-Tip around on her tongue to moisten it, causing her to screw up her nose at the cottony taste. Gently he dabbed the swab under her eye, repairing the damage. After a few minutes more of going over her eye shadow, he picked up a small silver instrument. Callie had no idea what it was.

"Would you like to do it or would you like me to?" he asked.

"Why don't you go ahead," Callie answered.

He gripped it and positioned the instrument over her eyelashes. She realized then it was an eyelash curler.

"Is it okay?" he asked.

"Fine."

The curler gave her eyelid a painful pinch. "Youch!" she yelped, her eyes watering.

Ron looked apologetic. "Sorry."

While he got busy blotting her again with Q-Tips and tissues, she craned her neck to keep watching as the shoot continued. Fascinated, she saw the two models moving only slightly every so often, altering the tilt of their heads, the positions of their arms or hands, shifting their body weight, turning a little more to the right or left. Sometimes the photographer told them how to change their stance; the rest of the time they kept it up on their own, asking him if this was okay, was that what he wanted.

"Suck your cheeks in." Ron had finished putting on her mascara and was holding up a fat brush to apply blush to Callie's cheeks. She saw that he had an assortment of powder blushes glued onto a second palette. He used several shades on her cheeks. When he was finished, he sharpened a lip pencil, dulling it a little on his hand before outlining her lips. Then he picked up a plastic vitamin server, the small compartments labeled with the days of the week. As he popped open one of the containers, Callie saw it held lipstick, which he carefully dabbed onto her mouth with a brush. He blotted her lips with more tissue. She noted that he had accumulated a large pile of dirty Q-Tips and balled-up tissues, and his hands were covered with different colored lines and markings. Everything that had started out so spotlessly clean was now a streaked mess.

The stylist, hurriedly mentioning that her name was Susan, approached Callie and told her to get ready to be next. Ron yanked the elastic out of her hair to start combing it out. He pinned one side of it behind her ear, and with wide, circular motions sprayed it into place. Callie coughed from the hairspray as he combed out her bangs. Inspecting her face, he picked up something and leaned forward, putting one finger lightly on the outer edge of her right eye. As his other hand came toward her, she saw it was holding a straight pin. She tensed in the chair.

"Don't worry," he said soothingly. "I just have to fix your lashes. They got a little clumped."

Callie gritted her teeth and held very still as he used the pin to delicately separate each eyelash, amazed that he didn't touch her eye at all. He powdered her face again. When he was finished, she was glad to escape to the clothing racks, where Susan assisted her in getting into a pink button-down-collar blouse and navy skirt, with navy tights and low-heeled shoes. Callie was comfortable in the clothes; it was an outfit she might have worn at home. She was glad that on her first shoot she hadn't been asked to put on anything too revealing or strange.

Ron came over to brush and spray her hair once more. "Go get 'em, tiger," he whispered to Callie as the stylist slipped two gold chains around her neck and clipped on some tiny earrings.

"Next shot," the photographer called out.

Callie caught her breath and looked at Susan, who nodded. She walked onto the set, passing Vida and the other model as they headed off. Vida gave her a cold stare. Something was definitely bothering her, but now wasn't the time to find out what it was. Callie moved to the blue seamless where they had stood, careful not to trip over the thick black cables and wires running along the floor and the tripod stands supporting the lights. Some of the lights were up high, while a few were on short tripods close to the ground. She could feel the heat they generated, although they were actually facing away, open umbrellas positioned behind them to bounce the light back onto her. The umbrellas' handles—actually silver bars—were pointed directly at her face.

It was so bright on the set that she was having difficulty seeing out into the studio as she listened for the photographer's instructions. All she knew about him was that he was older and graying, and when she had told Lanny about the booking, Lanny had informed her that Bill Meyer was an important photographer and did a lot of work for *Vogue* and *Bazaar*.

Callie waited quietly, ignoring the muffled conversations being held around her, for what seemed an eternity. The same assistant who'd come forward with the light meter before approached her. He held the box up to get a reading on her face, so close it was practically touching her. She smelled tobacco on his fingers. Click. The lights flashed, startling her. He moved the meter around, clicking it continuously, and she closed her eyes. Apparently, the little box was hooked up to the lights, because his clicking turned them off and on.

She waited, feeling hot and constricted beneath the makeup, the hairspray, and the clothes. She had a powerful urge to rub her eyes and twitch her face. Two assistants came back onto the set and made adjustments. The light meter came back. There were more discussions. How long would this take? Ron came up to her, a leather pouch around his waist holding hairspray, a hairbrush, powder, and an assortment of makeups and brushes.

"Hang in there. It'll be fine," he said, smiling as he touched up her lips and powdered her nose and forehead yet again.

When at last Bill Meyer called out to her, his voice was gentle. "Okay. Look at me like you're greeting your best friend."

Callie smiled brightly.

"No," the voice remained patient, "we need more energy. Give me more . . . more enthusiasm."

She drew her shoulders up and grinned as widely as she

could. Surely he would tell her she looked like a demented maniac.

"Good, that's good." As surprised as she was, his approval was music to Callie's ears.

He took a lot of pictures, but it was hard for Callie to keep track; maybe it just seemed like a lot. When he told her he was finished, she nodded, said thank you, and walked off the seamless as the next model walked on. She wanted to yell with joy. She had done it, her first professional picture at a real job.

The rest of the day passed quickly. Callie had three other shots taken of her after that, and before each one, Ron altered her hair and makeup. He laughed and joked with her as he pinned her hair up in a bun for one picture, set it in hot rollers and brushed it out to be wild and full for another. Susan gave her a pair of wire-rimmed glasses to wear with a fleece running suit, and long pearls and a satin evening bag for a beaded evening blouse and black skirt. The skirt was too big for Callie, so Susan applied a small clamp in back to keep it up and make it appear to fit more snugly. Everyone fussed over the smallest details of the clothes, her makeup, and the way the light fell on her jewelry. She posed with another model for one shot, and did her best not to look like the amateur she knew she was, imitating the girl's fluid movements. Callie's eyes were open wide as she tried to learn from it all.

When the day was over, she was happily exhausted. Hers was the last shot, and as she posed, she heard the other models getting ready to leave, putting their hair up in ponytails, tissuing off eye makeup and lipstick, exchanging goodbyes and hurrying out. By the time she was finished, they were gone. She dressed slowly, fatigue spreading through her entire body. Susan was packing up her tackle box, straightening the pins and sewing materials, hairclips and buttons spread out in the various compartments.

"Oh, brother." Ron was still there, the makeup that had been strewn along the counter now packed up in his tan canvas bag. He looked on the floor under the barber chairs.

"Something wrong?" Callie asked as she emerged from behind a rack, buttoning her blouse. The others might get dressed and undressed in front of the immediate world, but she still couldn't bring herself to, not if there was any other choice.

His expression was resigned. "Someone took my Mason Pearson. They always do if I don't keep an eagle eye on it. I must have lost twenty of those brushes on the sets."

"Are they expensive?" Callie stepped into her flats. That black hairbrush was the same kind Lanny had, the same one she'd noticed a lot of models using.

"Expensive enough." Ron regarded her. "And you should have one yourself if you don't already."

She made a mental note to buy one.

He took a step toward her, smiling shyly. "Listen, would you consider going to a party with me next Friday night? It's at a club and it should be fun. A bunch of friends are giving it."

Callie was taken aback. *Don't blow it,* she told herself. *Act nonchalant.* "Friday? That would be fine."

"Good." He flashed her a bright smile. "I'll pick you up at ten."

"Ten at night?" As soon as the words were out, she could have kicked herself. She'd seen Lanny go out at ten, eleven, even midnight. People in New York went on dates at incredibly late hours.

He only nodded and fished out two business cards from his back pocket. "Here, you keep one in case you need to call, and write your address and number on the other for me."

Callie dug around in her bag for a pen, hoping he wouldn't change his mind if she kept him waiting. When they were finished trading addresses, he waved and was gone. She stood there for a moment, watching the photographer and a few others whose names she'd never learned labeling small yellow rolls of film and cleaning up around the studio. Susan was finishing up, and Callie walked over to her and thanked her for all her help that day. The stylist looked mildly surprised at the comment, but only said a quick you're-welcome.

It had been quite a day. Callie was suddenly so tired that

she could barely walk. She had promised herself she would go to the health club and work out after the shoot. Besides, one of the trainers there was trying to line up a tennis partner for her, and she was curious to learn if he'd had any success. But there was no way she could make herself go. In fact, she'd treat herself to a taxi back to the apartment. Then she would call home and tell her parents about her big day. This was a special occasion, after all, in more ways than one. Her first job plus a date with a great guy. She might leave out that part about the date when she spoke to her mother and father, she decided, slinging her bag over her shoulder. Things were definitely starting to look up.

"Pull over right here."

Ron extracted a ten-dollar bill from his wallet to pay the cabdriver as Callie peered out the window, wondering where the club was; the area was just a bunch of darkened warehouses. She smoothed down the front of her dress, a blue and white print with short sleeves. Having changed clothes three times before Ron picked her up, she still was uncertain that she'd made the right choice. And he'd looked so incredible when she opened the door, casual and just right in his tight jeans and cowboy boots, a collarless white shirt open at the neck.

The cab drove away and they were left on the deserted street. There was no sign indicating a club or restaurant anywhere around. Ron, obviously knowing exactly where he was going, turned and opened an unmarked door, then proceeded down a narrow, dark flight of stairs. Callie hurried after him. Strains of faint music grew louder as they descended, and she was amazed to realize the club was underground somewhere, hidden from view. She'd heard about places like this in New York, but it was hard to believe she was actually going to see one.

The heavyset bouncer at the front door nodded at Ron and let them pass through to the club inside. Callie was surprised that the man hadn't asked for any proof of her age. Her eyes slowly adjusted to the relative darkness, the only light in the room a diffuse red glow. It was packed, she realized—there had to be more than two hundred people crowded around the bar and on the small dance floor. The air was thick with cigarette smoke. People were talking, laughing, shouting at one another.

"I'll get some drinks. What'll you have?" Ron yelled to her.

"White wine, thanks." Callie rarely drank, sometimes taking a glass of wine on her birthday or special holidays, but she wasn't about to admit that to Ron. And it seemed as if no one here was going to question whether she was old enough to be served alcohol. She watched Ron disappear into the crowd, trying not to panic as she stood there alone. A tall, thin man stepped on her toes protruding from her white sandal, and she winced with pain. He didn't even notice her.

She looked around. A lot of the women had on skin-tight pants or miniskirts with form-fitting tops, many with sequins or in shimmering gold or silver. The men wore their hair in long ponytails, crewcuts, or slicked back, and their eyes were hidden behind sunglasses even in this dim light. Everyone was so . . . *New York,* she thought. She glanced down at her dress. *I look like I just got off the bus from the farm,* she told herself unhappily. She'd never pull off dressing like these people did; she couldn't even learn how to do it, much less have the nerve.

Ron returned with two glasses in his hands and another man in tow. As he gave Callie her drink, he shouted introductions, but Callie couldn't make out the name over the din and didn't see any point in making him go through it again. The two men put their heads together, talking shop, no doubt, she thought, standing there patiently.

Ron didn't make Callie wait too long. After another minute, he tossed back the contents of his glass in one gulp, then grabbed her hand and pulled her onto the dance floor. As she would have guessed, he was a great dancer, and she did her best to imitate his smooth moves. When they stopped for another drink, she found that the second glass of wine helped her loosen up a bit when they got back out on the floor. Little by little, she began to enjoy herself, not

WITH A LITTLE LUCK

worrying anymore about whether she appeared silly or wasn't dressed right. It was fascinating, all of it. The people, the energy, the whole forbidden flavor to the place, even though nothing illicit was going on that she could see. She was sorry when Ron told her they had to go at one o'clock. The evening had been much too short.

He dropped her off at her apartment with a soft kiss on the cheek and asked her to have dinner with him on Sunday night. Thrilled that he would want to see her again, Callie immediately accepted. She was so wound up from her first big night out in New York that she didn't fall asleep until nearly two o'clock. The next day she woke up after eleven, something she couldn't remember ever happening.

On Sunday, Ron took her to a restaurant downtown where they ate with two other couples. He hadn't mentioned anything about the arrangement to Callie, but she was happy to meet them. It would be nice to make some new friends after spending so much time alone. They all had what seemed such glamorous jobs: one of the men said he was an independent film producer, another told Callie he was a buyer for a department store, and both women said they worked in the art department of an ad agency, which was how they'd originally met. All of them were dressed in black.

Dinner was pleasant, although Callie was well aware of what an outsider she was as she listened to them discussing people and places she had never heard of. As they ate dessert—Callie going off her diet for a piece of cheesecake, her favorite—Ron put his arm around her. When she said something he found funny, he tweaked her nose gently and kissed her on the cheek. It made her feel wonderful and secure, sitting there basking in his affection. When the meal was over, Ron took her straight home and dropped her at the door with another gentle kiss and a promise to call soon. Although she was a little disappointed, she also thought gratefully what a pleasure it was to date such a gentleman. She'd been so afraid she would have to fend off sexual advances on the first or second date, and she knew that would probably wind up just driving him away; the fact that he spared her that was a welcome relief. Maybe they could really build something substantial together.

"Hi, Lucy, how are you today?" Callie greeted the receptionist on the seventh floor, enjoying the fact that she now knew the girl's name and could chat with her as she breezed past into the Whiting offices, no longer a civilian. As one of the other models had told her, "civilians" was what they called the girls who were just starting out and hadn't hooked up with an agency yet. Knowing those sorts of inside tidbits made Callie feel more as if she belonged.

She didn't have an appointment or any real reason to be there, but since she was in between go-sees, she had come by as she often did to pick up the latest news and advice. Not that she had as much time to do it anymore; Grace was trying to make the most of Callie's Dodd catalog booking, using it to persuade potential clients to see Callie. On just one day last week, Callie had gone on fourteen go-sees. That had to be an all-time record, she thought, and one she didn't hope to repeat. That was another day that she was too exhausted to get to the health club for a workout; it was hard to stick with it at the end of these long, hot days, but Callie was usually able to force herself to go at least twice a week and always felt better afterward.

But all her walking, taxiing, and subway riding was paying off somewhat, as she did get two more jobs, both for catalogs. They hadn't been as easy as the Dodd's job. The photographers were less patient, one of them actually yelling at her in frustration when he couldn't get the expression he wanted. She tried her hardest, but it wasn't easy to be instantly sad, happy, sexy, or pensive on command. Still, it was encouraging overall. She hoped it wouldn't be too much longer until she could get copies of the new pictures to put in her book.

Walking toward Grace's office, she stopped to get a cup of tea at the kitchen, then paused at an open door to a small conference room. Three models were sitting around a table, dozens of pictures spread out before them. They were working on their books, she saw, slipping photographs in and out of the plastic sheets inside the big black portfolios.

A model's book, Callie now knew, was an ongoing project, never completed, always in need of updating or improvement. One of the models was scrutinizing her composite. While a book always had to be retrieved, a potential client could keep the composite card as a reminder of what the girl looked like and what her measurements were. No model was ever satisfied with her composite.

She entered the room with a friendly greeting. As three heads looked up to see who had come in, Callie realized that Vida was among them, the only one she knew by name. Vida gave her a frosty smile as the other two called out their hellos. Callie took a seat as far from Vida as she could get, sipping quietly at her tea, listening.

They were discussing a model whose name Callie didn't recognize, talking about how she had started believing her own press and thinking her success was a given, taking it easy, not putting out the effort on the set; after she'd thrown a few tantrums on top of that, her bookings had dropped way off. The three of them shook their heads at her foolishness, then quickly moved on to the topic of their boyfriends. One of the girls complained that hers was completely unreliable and she never knew when he was going to call, much less if he would actually show up for a date.

Callie's thoughts immediately turned to Ron. She hadn't heard from him in nearly ten days, since their dinner date. She wondered what was wrong, but she would never have telephoned him; that just wasn't her way, to be aggressive enough to call a boy. A couple of times she had almost brought the subject up to Lanny, wishing her roommate were the kind of person with whom she could talk about such things. But Lanny, on the few occasions when Callie actually saw her in the apartment, was so cold and disinterested in Callie that she couldn't bring herself to mention it. Lanny probably didn't know much about this kind of problem anyway; she went out with a steady stream of different guys.

Should Callie say something to these girls? Judging from their banter, they certainly seemed to know their way around men. Maybe they could give her a little advice. And perhaps sharing a confidence or two was a good way to get Vida to warm up to her a little. That in itself was worth a try. She waited until there was a lull in the conversation.

"I've been having some boyfriend trouble of my own," she offered hesitantly.

Three pairs of eyes regarded her expectantly. She cleared her throat. "Well . . . I've been seeing someone and he hasn't called in a while. I'm not sure if I should call him or just wait."

"Tell all." A redheaded model leaned forward.

"There's not much to tell," Callie said, relaxing a bit. "We went out twice, and things were great. Then, nothing."

"Who is it?" The other model, a brunette Callie realized she had seen once in the waiting room at a go-see, held a picture of herself up at arm's length, eyeing it critically. "Someone in the business we would know?"

"Maybe you know him. He does hair and makeup. Ron Passo."

Callie watched as looks were exchanged among the three of them. She couldn't imagine what that meant. It was Vida who finally spoke, her eyes filled with amusement at being the one to tell Callie the news.

"Ronnie Passo is gay, but he tries to prove he's not by going out with all the new girls. Or the girls who don't know about him." Her tone indicated that although she might be new, Vida herself was clearly not one of the girls who didn't know; she was far too savvy to be caught up in that kind of nonsense.

Callie leaned back in her chair, startled. This Vida was really mean.

"It's true," the brunette chimed in. "He doesn't want to face the fact, and he doesn't want people to think he's gay. So he dates lots of the girls, the ones who don't know about him, and makes sure he gets seen around town with them. But he's—"

She was interrupted as Fredericka and Austin Whiting came into the room. Austin was wearing a white suit, in sharp contrast to the short black dress and turban his mother had on. The other three girls were instantly all smiles and warm hellos, but Callie was too stunned by what she had just learned to say anything.

"Hello, my lambs," Fredericka greeted them. "I'm glad to see you're fixing your books, but I'd rather hear you are out showing them to people who are falling madly in love with your faces." She smiled widely to show she was only kidding, her large teeth breaking through the bright red slash of her mouth.

Her comment was greeted with laughter and chatter. She walked over to stand behind Vida and picked up a few of her tear sheets. "This one," Fredericka declared, putting a black-and-white ad down on the open plastic pages of Vida's book, "but definitely not this other one." She tossed a color ad aside. "It makes you look like a horse."

Vida nodded brightly. "Thank you."

"Come and see me in my office in a half-hour. I vant to talk to you." Fredericka glanced over at Callie. "You have taken off a few pounds, Callie. That's good. But you're not done. At least five more, please, and don't take so long about it." She put a hand on Vida's shoulder, her long red fingernails vibrant against the white of Vida's shirt. "When Vida joined us four months ago, she had to take off a bit too, but she did it in only a few veeks."

Callie was spared having to answer, as Austin looked at his gold watch and said, "We'd better go now, Fredericka."

She didn't acknowledge her son's words but nonetheless moved toward the door to leave. "Goodbye, darlings, and get a good night's sleep tonight. You all look haggard. Not one of you says the vord *healthy,* the vay you should. All vork and all play . . ." she trailed off, the warning unspoken. "Vitality, life, happiness—that's vhat they vant to see."

There was a nodding of heads, everyone indicating that they understood and agreed.

"And, you, Mia," Fredericka said to the redhead, "see a doctor if you're going to insist on making yourself throw up every time you eat. In the long run, that just makes you sick, you should all know that by now. And then you can't vork at all. Foolish, very foolish."

Then the two of them were gone.

"More words of wisdom from our very own Cruella DeVille," Mia said spitefully. Callie stared at her, amazed that the girl didn't seem the least bit humiliated at having such a private matter spoken about in front of other people. Callie would have crawled into a corner with shame. And how did Fredericka even know about Mia's eating problem?

"I thought Austin was looking particularly androgynous today," added the brunette. "Is the betting pool still open? I want to put another ten dollars on *no* sexuality. There's no way he could be with either a woman *or* a man. Impossible —they're all beneath him. But never literally." There was general laughter. "And Cruella was quite divine, all in black like a mortician." She turned to Vida. "What does she want with you?"

Vida shrugged. "Maybe it has something to do with Lyle. I just got a booking with them confirmed, three days shooting in Nassau."

Callie struggled to hide her shock. Grace had told her that *she* was the top contender for that job with Lyle Sportswear. Just yesterday, Grace had said it was practically a lock. It would have been Callie's first big ad. She regarded Vida. Yes, they looked very similar—Callie hadn't been mistaken about that when she'd first seen Vida at the Dodd's shoot. It dawned on her that this might not be an insignificant thing. Maybe it meant they'd be competing for the same jobs, for people who wanted their kind of look but would choose only one of them. Vida must have understood that right away, as soon as she'd seen Callie on the Dodd's set. No wonder she'd been so cold to her.

Callie drew her hand across her eyes, suddenly tired from her own stupidity. First, Ron. The signs had been so obvious, she realized, the short dates, the quick good-night kisses, no desire to be alone with her for even five minutes. Now this. She recalled the sight of Vida's head bent in so close to the manicurist, the two of them whispering. Vida knew how to find out what was going on; she would never permit herself to be as ignorant as Callie was.

Callie stood and said a quiet goodbye. Vida didn't even look up from what she was doing, while the other two gave her cursory waves, engrossed again in their books and in a discussion about the benefits of using egg versus clay masks on their faces. Callie decided to talk to Grace to find out what was going on. If Vida was doing so well, the agency might decide they didn't need a lookalike and fire Callie.

Panic welled inside her. She'd been working so hard and she wanted so much to succeed. Besides, she'd devoted the better part of the summer and had hardly a cent to show for it. Most of what she'd earned from her few jobs went to paying back money the agency had advanced to her. They were still taking care of her expenses, but the whole point had been to go home with savings at the end of the summer, not just break even. She hurried down the hall, hearing Grace's voice talking on the telephone even before she got to the booking room.

Callie greeted the other bookers by name and made small talk with them as she waited for Grace to hang up. They inquired about her parents, her younger brother. Whiting really was like a family, Callie thought. They'd gotten to know her and seemed genuinely to care about her.

"Just the person I wanted to see." Grace was off the phone, grinning. She jumped up.

"Grace, I—" Callie's shoulders slumped.

The booker interrupted, reaching for her lit cigarette in the ashtray. "You look rotten. But that's beside the point now. You lost Lyle to Vida Moore." She inhaled deeply on her cigarette. "Sorry about that. Now here's the great news: you're going to Europe. Two weeks in Paris, magazine work all lined up for you and two other girls. You should come back with some great editorial pages for your book."

Callie stared. "Are you serious?"

"I didn't want to say anything until I was sure it was going to pan out. You leave August eleventh." Grace sat back down in her chair and put her legs up on the table. "See, there are lots more fashion magazines in Europe, and they're more open to using unknowns. So, a lot of the new girls go over there to get some decent pictures. It'll be a great experience. The photographers are very creative, they do terrific stuff. Those editorial pictures should get you editorial work here, which will get you the ads."

Paris. Callie couldn't believe it. She'd never been out of

the United States, much less to the most glamorous city in the world, a place she'd always wanted to visit. Her spirits soared.

"I'll see if my busy schedule will permit me to go," she said teasingly.

Grace arched an eyebrow. "You do that."

Callie threw her arms around Grace, laughing.

6

Callie forced herself to take another sip of espresso. She didn't like coffee, and this was so strong and bitter that she could barely swallow it. But she needed the caffeine to jolt her awake, and this powerful brew was the only thing available. She glanced at her watch. Six-thirty in the morning, and the Paris heat wave was obviously going to continue for at least another day; the humidity was already setting in, making the cramped trailer stifling. Longingly, she pictured her bed back in New York with its two fluffy pillows and cool white sheets.

For at least the twentieth time in two days she told herself she was an ingrate. She should be thrilled to be in Paris, appreciative of the incredible opportunity Whiting had given her. She'd so looked forward to the trip and had packed for it with great anticipation. She'd been so excited when she got her passport. Now she could just pick up and travel anywhere in the world; it felt so grown-up. She reached out for another croissant. *Empty calories,* she silently lectured herself half-heartedly, but she was too depressed to care.

She bit into the buttery flakiness as she watched the makeup artist bend over one of the models, scrambling to work his magic in the tiny quarters. He was talking to her in broken English, complaining about how little money he had made for a job he'd done the preceding week. So, it was the same around the world, Callie mused wryly; she had noticed in her trips to the agency and on go-sees that complaining about money was a popular pastime in the industry. The other model sat in a corner writing a letter as she listened to a tape on her Walkman, her head bobbing up and down to the beat only she could hear.

Everything had gone wrong from the beginning. As soon as she'd arrived at Kennedy Airport, Callie had sensed that, as usual, she would be completely out of place. She'd been wearing a dress, sheer stockings, and high heels, and had carefully fixed her hair and makeup, thinking it was only proper to get dressed up to fly to Europe. She got to the gate an hour and a half early, and sat there alone, trying to pick out two women who might be the models accompanying her, wondering if she'd misunderstood the instructions, if this was the right flight.

When the other two models from Whiting showed up together ten minutes before boarding, Callie saw that they were both in jeans, old shirts, and cowboy boots. They wore sunglasses and no makeup at all. One had her hair in a ponytail, the other tucked under a hat. As she introduced herself, finding out their names were Linda and Nan, Callie hoped they couldn't tell how ridiculous she felt, like a little girl all fixed up to go to a birthday party.

That had only been the start, she recalled, pouring herself half a cup more of the vile coffee. She was seated on a padded bench at a table built into the trailer, a small version of a restaurant booth. Breakfast food, bottled water, and a pot of espresso were set out in front of her. The makeup artist was chain-smoking unfiltered French cigarettes, and its powerful odor at this early hour made her stomach heave. Everyone in France seemed to smoke. Sighing, she reached for a jelly-filled pastry to distract her and help her get down the rest of her coffee.

Her thoughts returned to the disappointing moments when she had reached France. It had been such a thrill when the plane landed. She was actually here, in *Paris*. But the taxi ride from the airport was so long, in a noisy Mercedes speeding along at a terrifying pace, and everything was so flat and dreary. Was this Paris? Nothing around but farmhouses, then the congested neighborhoods cropping up out of nowhere, laundry flapping in the breeze outside the windows of ugly, dull yellow buildings. The driver had the window open, and she was dismayed to find his powerful body odor carried by the breeze directly into the backseat, where she sat with Linda and Nan, mingling with an unpleasant smell from outside—she supposed it was some sort of fuel. They went through a few tunnels, then suddenly they were in the city. The cab darted in and out of traffic, coming to a sharp stop outside the hotel. Feeling disoriented, Callie got out.

Although she wasn't expecting anything fancy, she had nonetheless been taken aback at how dreary the hotel was into which Whiting had booked the three of them. Or maybe it was the French magazine that had chosen it. Callie wasn't sure. After taking an elevator no bigger than a telephone booth up to the second floor, she found that her room was, like the rest of the hotel, small and dark. It depressed her to be there. Even though the room was sweltering, without air conditioning or fan, it was still unpleasant to discover that there was no hot water. The icy trickle that came out of the rusty showerhead wasn't any relief from the heat when Callie got up at 5:00 A.M. to get ready for the day ahead. There wasn't even a television set for some distraction.

It was all made worse, she knew, by the fact that she didn't understand a word anybody said to her. Fortunately, Linda spoke fluent French and had handled the cab from the airport, because Callie wouldn't have had any idea how to get one or pay for it. She was still struggling to figure out how much a franc was worth, mentally converting the money back and forth into dollars. The agency had given her some

French money so that she would be prepared as soon as she got there, but it hadn't been much help. People spoke so quickly, impatient with her ignorance, and she couldn't tell how much she was supposed to pay or what it represented in American money; she just gave people what they asked for. When it got too complicated, she let them take the amount from of a handful of bills and change she held out before them.

Although she'd been determined to make the most of her visit, the first morning there Callie found that she was exhausted from the trip and too frightened to venture out by herself. Instead, she had stayed in her hotel room most of the day, trying to nap so she wouldn't be jet-lagged when they had to shoot the next day. She'd been unable to sleep that night, though, and she felt like a zombie the following morning. Someone had knocked on her door at 5:00 A.M., barking something in French, and she guessed that must have been her order to wake up. The three models were shepherded into a trailer on the narrow street outside the hotel and driven to another tiny block paved with cobblestones.

Grace had explained these logistics in advance, noting that this was an unusual arrangement; typically, she would have had to get herself to the location. The trailer remained parked on the block there all day, while a stream of people came in and out, getting the three of them ready in fur coats and boots. Callie had ventured from the cramped van into the street a few times, but they kept calling her back to change for yet another shot, so she had seen virtually nothing and had no idea where in the city they were. Three other models, all French, dressed in another trailer nearby, and the six of them posed in various combinations, sitting on the curb, their fur coats dragging in the gutter, slouching on car hoods, arms around one another, leaning against the old, crumbling walls of the small buildings on the street.

Nan told her that Paris had been experiencing a heat wave for over a week, and Callie was sure the temperature had to be at least ninety-five degrees. Perspiring inside the different fur coats she was assigned to wear, she mopped her face and neck with a damp, scratchy paper towel, careful not to get the coats wet; she didn't know what they were, but they seemed awfully expensive, long-haired and lush—maybe lynx or sable; she'd heard that those cost a lot. It made her nervous, worrying about getting food or dirt on them, but none of the other models appeared concerned.

When Grace first told her about the assignment back at Whiting, Callie had assumed that the two girls going with her would also be new at modeling. But that wasn't the case. Both Linda and Nan had worked in Europe several times and were veterans of the business. Linda even had a boyfriend in Paris, and disappeared in a flash as soon as they'd checked into the hotel, and every free minute she had after that. Nan was around more, and acted friendlier, but Callie had refused her invitation for dinner the preceding evening, too exhausted after a second twelve-hour day to do anything but go back to her hotel room.

She'd been so down that she'd put in an overseas telephone call to Bloomington. It was great to hear her parents' and Tommy's voices, and she made sure to remain upbeat, full of excitement and good news. But when she hung up, tears of loneliness and fatigue stung her eyes as she turned out the light. What was the point of this? she wondered. She wasn't even getting paid a lot—around ninety dollars a day—and much of that would be taxed. She was just wasting her time. It was such a roller coaster, every day up and down, thinking she was about to get somewhere, certain she was going to fail.

Well, today was a new day. Even though she was still tired this morning, she was finally beginning to feel a little bit more like herself. The jet lag must be passing, she decided. She would ask Nan if the dinner invitation was still good for this evening. No matter how tired she was, she should make the most of the few hours she had at night to experience Paris.

"Hi, everyone. I'm Kate."

Callie looked over at the trailer's tiny doorway. A young woman had poked her head in. She had chin-length brown hair and wide-set brown eyes peeking out from under thick bangs. Dressed in lace-up sandals, a miniskirt and tank top, big sunglasses perched on her head, she had the stylish look of the other French girls Callie had seen, but her accent made it clear she was American.

No one else seemed to hear or to notice her. Callie smiled in greeting as Kate hopped lightly up the trailer's two steps and came in. She was carrying a small metal box.

"I'm the stylist." She returned Callie's smile, putting the box down on the floor and popping a small pastry into her mouth.

"Callie Stewart." Callie gave a little wave. "But there was a French stylist here for the past two days. What happened to her?"

"Flaked out." Kate opened the box she had brought. It was full of the usual endless supplies of small odds and ends that might be needed on a shoot, Callie saw, the staples of a stylist's job. "Just quit last night, said she had to go someplace. The French—I love 'em." Despite her sarcasm, her good-natured smile indicated that she really *did* love them.

"I don't remember seeing you on my plane over. Which flight did you take?" There had been a few people sitting behind Callie who turned out to be involved with the shoot, but she'd learned that it wasn't required for everyone to be on the same plane or sit together unless they wanted to. She recalled how seeing Linda and Nan head for seats next to each other in the smoking section had added to her sense of isolation on the trip.

"I've been here for two years," Kate responded. "But I'm going back at the end of next week. It's time to go home to New York, pick up my work there."

Imagine living in Paris for two years, Callie marveled to herself. It was so exotic.

"Are you married?" As soon as she spoke, Callie wondered what possessed her to ask such a personal question of this stranger.

Kate laughed merrily. "Me? I'm the original spinster. A hopeless case. I'll never get married—not that I don't want to. But, hey . . ." She shrugged and moved over to examine the hooded cashmere jackets scheduled for the day's shots.

There was something about Kate that Callie liked, an open friendliness that seemed genuine. And throughout the rest of the day her first impression didn't change, as Kate chatted with her, interested to learn about Callie, then talking about how much she liked living in Paris but how ready she was nonetheless to go home.

Callie had found most stylists to be preoccupied with the details of their jobs, and less inclined to talk and gossip than were many of the other people on the set. Like Kate, though, they usually wore the most interesting outfits or were the best-dressed ones around. Still, they had so many things to attend to—dressing the models, satisfying the photographer and the client, having to make an article of clothing or accessory materialize according to somebody's whim, watching the model on the set to make sure her clothes didn't wrinkle or bulge, always pinning and fixing with their rolls of doubled-edged tape—it was no wonder they didn't have the time to get as friendly as the makeup people or the various assistants that roamed the sets.

Kate was relaxed and talkative, though. With the other models caught up in their own activities, Callie was delighted to have someone to pass the time with, and the day went by much more quickly than the previous two. Once Kate discovered that Callie was new to the business, she passed on whatever helpful hints or information she could as they went along. She explained that it was really the fashion magazines that dictated the current look for the models; if the editorial spreads in magazines used voluptuous girls or girls with full lips, short hair or aquiline noses, the influence spread to the advertising side. Catalogs were about a year behind the magazines in featuring the new looks, she noted, and of course summer clothes were shot in winter, winter clothes in summer. Intrigued, Callie listened with rapt attention.

When the photographer declared it was a wrap for the day, Callie asked Nan if they might get together that evening and if it was all right to invite Kate along. Nan agreed, telling Callie she was meeting a group of people for dinner, but the more the merrier.

After a nap and a shower back in her hotel room, Callie was feeling a lot better as she dressed for the evening. Zipping up her white skirt, she paused. She'd been watching the French women, not only the models on the shoot with her but the ones that passed by in the street. It was true what they always said in the magazines: the French had a sense of style that was unmistakable. Maybe it was time for something a little more daring for herself.

A small mirror hung above the bureau, and Callie hopped up onto the narrow bed, bending this way and that, trying to see her entire reflection. She reached under her blouse and rolled up her skirt's waistband a few times, hiking it several inches above her knee. The blouse hung over the waistband's folds, so they weren't noticeable. Stepping back down onto the floor, she opened the top button of her blouse, and, instead of flats, put on high heels. The effect startled her, but she liked it. She considered her eye makeup. Now that she thought about it, she rarely saw any of the models wearing blue eye shadow like hers when they were out on their own time. And none of the makeup people she'd observed at work ever used it. She walked into the bathroom and tissued hers off, reapplying instead a little pale beige shadow on her lids and adding more mascara to make her lashes fuller. *There,* she said to herself. *Better.*

Nan had told her they would meet at the hotel front desk at ten-thirty. Having been up since sunrise, ten-thirty seemed awfully late for dinner. But during these past few days she had found that this was the way things were always done in Europe. Nan and Kate were both waiting there when she emerged from the elevator. They managed to get a taxi, Nan directing the driver to a small bistro on the Left Bank. Following the other two women in, Callie decided the restaurant was exactly what she would have pictured for a French nightspot, right down to the red-and-white-checked tablecloths. Every table was taken, and people milled about in the narrow passages between them, waiters pushing through in annoyance, large silver trays poised high above their heads.

The three of them made their way over to the far end of the room, where six other people were seated. As usual, Callie had no idea who anyone was or what was going on, but she'd learned by now to sit back and just watch instead of worrying about it. The air was thick with cigarette smoke, and as she settled herself into a chair, a Frenchman passed by and leaned down to whisper something in her ear, his lips brushing her neck, before moving on. She barely heard him—and she wouldn't have understood what he'd said anyway—but she was completely flustered. She hoped no one had noticed.

Someone put a glass of wine in front of her and she picked it up, grateful to have something to do. Taking a sip, she realized she was seated next to a dark-haired man who was watching her with mild amusement in his large, dark eyes.

"This is your first time in France?" He spoke gently, his French accent barely discernible.

She nodded. "You can tell."

He shrugged, reassuring her. "No, no. Just a guess." He extended a hand. "Jean Trignon. I'm the fashion director at—"

Callie recognized the long word that was the name of the magazine she was working for, although she still had no idea how to spell it or what it meant in English. She really ought to find out.

"I'm modeling for them," she said, feeling uncomfortable. Jean Trignon was extremely attractive.

He smiled. "Yes, I know."

Callie bit her lip. Of course he would know. Why was she always the fool? Her eyes straight ahead, she watched his tapered fingers reach for the wine bottle, and he added some wine to Callie's glass before refilling his. Desperately looking around for help, she saw Kate engrossed in conversation with another man, Nan at the other end of the table talking to a woman whose hair was practically fuchsia.

"Have you eaten in this restaurant before?"

Callie forced herself to look directly at him. "No. I've only been here a few days."

"Would you permit me to order for you? There are a few specialties on the menu I think you might enjoy."

"That would be lovely." Callie relaxed, sitting back in her chair. There was no reason to be so nervous, she told herself. He was a nice man, only a few years older than she was, in fact, and she was out on her first big night in Paris. Now she was going to experience real French food, not the sandwiches and sweets from snack bars she'd been subsisting on ever since she'd arrived.

The waiter came by, harried and impatient. Jean spoke to him in rapidfire French and gestured for more wine all around. Then he turned his attention back to Callie, giving her a slow, warm smile.

"You're the fashion director?" she asked, wanting to deflect the conversation away from revealing any more of how little she knew about Paris. "You seem young for such an important position."

He tilted his head slightly. "Maybe so. I'm twenty-five. But we are open-minded about things like age in France. If you have the creativity, that's what is important."

She nodded, sipping her wine.

"You like modeling for us?"

She hesitated. "It's been an unusual experience."

"I see." He laughed. "You mean it's boring and hot and hard work."

Surprised, she laughed along with him. "Oh, you've been out on the modeling locations."

"Many times."

"So you meet a lot of American models." Callie wasn't sure what had prompted her to say that; it was nasty. She broke off a piece of bread from the loaf in the basket nearby and brought it to her lips. The aroma was delicious.

"Yes, I do," he answered as the waiter set a plate before him. "But not many of them are as nice as you appear to be. They can be hard—like Nan over there."

"Nan?" Callie looked over at the model, who was smoking a cigarette, sharing a laugh with a man to her left. Her view was blocked as the waiter next bent down to put a plate in front of her. She looked at it: some kind of steak in a sauce. Full of butter and cream, she decided. It looked and smelled delicious. She could hardly wait to taste it.

"Nan's all right, but she's been many places and seen too many things," Jean went on. "You are not, well, jaded as she is."

Callie was confused. To her, her innocence seemed a burden, yet this man apparently liked it. He put his hand lightly over hers.

"And she's not nearly as beautiful as you are." His eyes crinkled with a smile. "Now please tell me what you think of your dinner."

Posing on the Pont Neuf the next morning, Callie had a chance to get a bit more of a view of the city. Wearing skin-tight tops, bicycle pants, and vibrant green sneakers, she and Linda sat on the ground, two bicycles carelessly tossed down beside them, as if they had suddenly abandoned their ride to enjoy resting in the sun. Passersby stopped to watch, but Callie was certain she was far more interested in them than they could ever be in her. She was studying the way they dressed, trying to discern what made them so sophisticated-looking. Even the children were chic, she thought, with their long pleated dresses and ribbons as sleek finishing touches to their outfits. And it all seemed so casual, so unstudied. But Callie was beginning to get the idea that this wasn't the case; it took work to achieve that look.

"Look over your shoulder, you, *gauche*," the photographer barked.

Callie wasn't sure whom he was talking to. *Gauche* wasn't a complimentary word, but perhaps it meant something else in French. She glanced at Linda, who signaled with her eyes that he had indeed been referring to Callie. Four days and he still didn't know her name, she thought, turning her head obediently. He really wasn't a very pleasant man; he'd been high-handed and irritable with her at every turn. She had somehow assumed that French photographers would be patient, caring, great artists dedicated to their work.

"No, no," he cried in annoyance. "Purse your lips. *Comme ça.*" He made a face, screwing up his mouth as if blowing a kiss in extreme boredom. *"Gauche, gauche."* Frustrated, he searched for the English word. "Left!"

She quickly turned her head the other way. There at the far end of the bridge stood Jean Trignon. Callie's stomach jumped with surprise and excitement. He was making notes on a pad, his eyes hidden behind black sunglasses. When he looked up, he saw Callie's face turned in his direction. He smiled. She had to restrain herself from reaching up to smooth her hair, wanting to be perfect for him, wishing she could stop the ridiculous pouting she had been instructed to do.

Last night had been so wonderful. They had talked all through dinner, and afterward, when the crowd was breaking up, he had invited her to go someplace else for a late drink, just the two of them. He took her to a dark bar, full of Parisians, where he ordered cognac, which Callie had never tasted. They sat and talked until three in the morning, sharing the stories of their childhoods; Jean had been brought up in the city of Angers, she learned, coming to Paris when he was eighteen. They talked about what they wanted in the future. Callie was pleasantly surprised to learn that Jean loved children and eventually wanted to have three or four. She was completely comfortable with him and found it a great relief to talk freely to someone about what was important to her; it had been a while since anyone other than Grace at the agency had taken an interest in what she was thinking, she realized.

Aside from feeling comfortable with Jean, Callie was very attracted to him. Remembering Ron, she was a bit wary, but there was something in the way Jean looked into her eyes that told her this definitely wasn't a similar situation. Jean was attracted to her as well, it was obvious. When he dropped her off at her hotel at three-thirty in the morning, he'd given her an impassioned kiss, and she hadn't resisted. She had left him feeling as light as air.

Now here he was, watching her, his long dark hair combed back off his forehead, his beige linen pants and jacket wrinkled but cool-looking on this hot day. As the magazine's fashion director he hardly needed an excuse to come to the shoot, she supposed. She hoped she wasn't jumping to conclusions, assuming that he was here to see her, but she hadn't seen him around in the past three days. When the photographer called out that it was time for a lunch break, she stood up and Jean immediately approached.

"*Bonjour,* Callie," he said, lightly touching her hair. "May I steal you away for an hour if I can get the okay from our photographer?"

She broke into a wide smile. "Just let me change. I'll be right back."

It took her some effort to keep from running instead of walking back to the trailer. Once inside, she tore off her clothes and hurried into her jeans and blouse, leaving the last few buttons open and tying the cotton fabric into a knot just above her navel.

"What's the rush?" Kate asked, folding some clothes as she watched Callie scramble to brush her hair.

"Lunch with Jean Trignon," Callie answered breathlessly.

Kate batted her eyelashes. "Ah, he is truly divine." She turned and fished through her strongbox. "Here, wear these." She held up a pair of large, gold hoop earrings.

"Thanks." Gratefully, Callie put them on. Kate was digging around in a pile of shoes in one corner, then triumphantly held up a pair of sandals with heels. "Great," Callie agreed, abandoning her black flats and slipping into the sandals. She still had a lot to learn, but at least she felt she looked like an adult today.

With so little time for lunch, Callie and Jean stopped at a nearby bistro for onion soup and a bottle of wine. That night, he took her to dinner at the most incredible restaurant she had ever seen, full of elegant couples in evening wear seated at tables glittering with crystal and sterling. They shared a bottle of champagne and gave each other tastes of all their food, from the mussels and châteaubriand to the crème caramel and chocolate cake.

Later, they went to a club to dance. Callie was the only American, she saw, and not a word of English was heard in the din of laughing conversation and clinking glasses. Afterward, they took a long walk. Callie got her first glimpse of the Eiffel Tower, brilliantly lit against the Paris skyline. Taxiing over to the Seine, they strolled along the water's banks until four-thirty, when Jean took her home. Their good-night kiss in front of the hotel lasted much longer than the one the preceding night, and Jean finally released her reluctantly and told her he would see her the next day.

For the next week, Jean and Callie were never apart when she was off the set. Their third night together, he invited her to his apartment for hors d'oeuvres before dinner. Jean lived in a large one-bedroom with high ceilings and intricate moldings. Callie wandered around the living room, examining the antiques, the fashion layouts spread across his desk, the art on the walls.

Sitting on his couch, sipping champagne and listening to jazz, she felt as if she were in a movie, an old black-and-white French film about a daring American girl who takes Paris by storm. It was silly and fantastic. They held hands as they drank and kissed, and she was disappointed when Jean announced they'd better leave for the restaurant. For the first time, she knew she was ready to make love. But the thought frightened her as well. Was Jean the right one? Would she be sorry later? She was grateful that he didn't push the matter in the next few days, and she stopped worrying about it.

By the second week of her visit, Callie was feeling at home in Paris. She jumped out of bed each morning to get to the trailer, no longer bored, but humming and excited to be working. No matter how late she and Jean had stayed out the night before, she never felt tired. If he could get away from the office and the shooting schedule permitted, they had lunch together. Otherwise, he met her after she was finished for the day. Twice he took her out with his friends, after which they both agreed that they would rather be alone.

They roamed the city arm in arm, Callie knowing that this was a state of enchantment too good to last. She saw all the sights of Paris, both the tourist attractions and the side streets with their out-of-the-way shops and cafes that were part of a Parisian's daily life. Poking around the shops, she splurged on presents for her family: a soft leather wallet and belt for her father, a silk scarf from Yves Saint Laurent and a bottle of Joy perfume for her mother, a cashmere sweater and a framed pencil sketch of Notre Dame for Tommy.

As a present to herself, she selected a black leather miniskirt, which Jean applauded admiringly when she stepped out of the dressing room to show him. In a moment of sheer daring, she asked him to take her to the best hairdresser in Paris. He made an appointment for her at a salon the next day, where, at her request, she emerged with short hair, the kind of pixie cut, she told him with a laugh, that she'd had as a little girl. Her bangs were almost as long as the rest of her hair now, just barely reaching the tops of her ears. The new haircut made her feel reckless and free, especially when Jean told her he was crazy about it.

The next day, which Callie had off, she asked Jean to help her pick out some new clothes; after all, he was the fashion director of a leading magazine, so if anyone could tell her what looked right for her, he could. He was delighted to spend the afternoon taking her to both the better shops and the bargain haunts, where she acquired virtually an entire new wardrobe. Their last stop was at the makeup section of a large department store, where he assisted Callie in selecting new colors in foundation and eye shadow that would best set off her skin and green eyes. It frightened Callie to spend so much money on herself, but she was sure she was doing the right thing. The time had come for her to grow up. And Jean made it all so much fun.

It was toward the end of her second week that she found herself back at Jean's apartment, their kisses growing more passionate, her feelings for him more urgent. Lovingly, he stroked her hair, her breasts, her back. She unbuttoned his shirt, hungrily taking in his scent and the smoothness of his bare chest. It was time, she knew; she was ready. Jean was a good, kind man. It felt right to do this with him. But somehow she had to tell him about herself first.

"Jean." Her voice was tentative, so quiet he barely heard her. "Jean, wait."

He looked at her. "Yes, my sweet."

"I'm . . . You should know something." This was agonizing. He would laugh at her, she was sure. "I've—never done this before."

"What do you mean?" He nuzzled her cheek softly.

Callie forced herself to say it again. "This is my first time."

He pulled back, regarding her in amazement. *"Tu es une vierge?* You're telling me you are a virgin?"

Callie hung her head. "I'm sorry."

Jean gathered her in his arms. "You have nothing to be

sorry about," he whispered. "Thank you for giving me such an honor. I'll do my best to live up to it."

He led her into the bedroom. Slowly, kissing her and touching her gently, he undressed first her, then himself. He lay beside her on the bed for a long while, holding her close, letting her get used to the feel of his naked body alongside hers. When they made love, she was ready, amazed at his tenderness, at how right it seemed. For so long she had wondered what sex would be like, half-curious, half-afraid. With Jean, it was perfectly natural, as if it was simply meant to happen. Afterward, she fell asleep contentedly, their arms and legs entwined. And in the morning, she woke to his smile and the coffee and baguette he brought to her in bed.

They made love every night of the few she had left in Paris. She knew that when the trip was over he would go back to his work and she would return to New York; there was no point in pretending it would be otherwise. That didn't keep her from crying at the airport as Jean held her and kissed her goodbye.

"Callie," he told her, stroking her hair as she wept, "it's been a perfect two weeks. You are a glorious girl, and you'll come back, you'll see. There will be more work here and we'll be together again."

"Thank you for everything," she whispered, barely getting the words out through her tears. "Thank you for all you've done for me, and for making me feel so beautiful. I'll miss you so much."

He smiled at her. "The truth is one day you'll be a big star and you will forget all about me. I am certain of that."

Callie looked at him doubtfully. A voice on the loudspeaker announced the boarding of her flight. Out of the corner of her eye she saw Linda and Nan moving toward the gate. Kate was rushing to catch up to them, toting two overflowing leopard-skin-print bags; she had arranged to go back to New York on the same flight, seated beside Callie.

Her eyes full of sadness, Callie pulled back and wiped the tears from her cheeks as she gave Jean a small smile. Then she bent down for her carry-on bag and turned to go. She didn't dare look back, afraid she would break down.

Jean watched her walk away. He would miss her, the special quality she had, so giving and sweet, yet totally real in her emotions. His eyes followed her, a tall figure in tight blue jeans, new cowboy boots, and a blue workshirt. Dangling earrings, revealed by her short haircut, swayed as she moved. There was no question, she wasn't the same girl he had met that night at the restaurant. She was far more sophisticated—her clothes, her walk, the way she held herself. He hoped she wouldn't lose her quality of innocence altogether, but he supposed it was unavoidable.

"*Bonne chance*, Callie," he murmured wistfully. He pulled out his sunglasses and put them on as he headed in the opposite direction.

When Callie woke the following morning, she stretched lazily, relishing being back in her own comfortable bed. Then Jean's face flashed in her mind, and sorrow flooded her. Their time together had been such magic. After several minutes, she forced herself to push away the image of him; it wouldn't do any good to give in to the pain of being separated from him. She got out of bed quickly, determined to keep busy. Instead of calling in to the agency, she decided she would go over in person.

It was strange to be back in New York, the noise and bustle so different from the easygoing atmosphere in Paris. She strolled along, the breeze gently lifting the skirt of her new dress, Jean's face still in her mind. Approaching Whiting's building, the familiar sight brought her back from Paris with a jolt, distracting her from the lingering sadness. As she pulled open the door, a man whistled at her from across the street, and she smiled. It was a magnificent day and she was happy to be alive, to be young and lucky enough to be a model. She sailed past the receptionist on seven with a huge smile and warm hello, heading toward Grace's office.

She came quickly around the corner and into the bookers' room. Startled, she froze in her tracks. Fredericka sat on the edge of the table, wearing a red silk suit and turban, as the six bookers all listened in rapt attention to what she was saying. The telephones, normally ringing off their hooks, flashed silently; the calls must have been forwarded elsewhere. Fredericka stopped in midsentence when she saw Callie enter.

"Oh, I'm so sorry," Callie stammered. "I'll come back another time."

Fredericka's eye roved up and down, taking in Callie's appearance. "No, no, dear, stop a minute. You've just returned from Europe." It wasn't a question.

Callie nodded, amazed again at the way Fredericka kept track of everyone's comings and goings at the agency. "Yes. It went very well, I think."

"Your hair." Fredericka made a disapproving, clucking sound. "I like it, but this is a big mistake, cutting it vithout discussing it vith us." Her voice was sharp. "You *never* change your look on a vhim—vhich is vhat I suppose it was."

Callie saw Grace giving her a sympathetic look. She felt very small. "I'm sorry. I . . ."

"In fact, there is some good news for you, and I hope this von't be a problem. Not only do you have a catalog booking for tomorrow, but you are set for your first editorial spread on Friday. Sportswear for *Mademoiselle.* Grace has done an excellent job in getting you these bookings. But, of course, they are based on your pictures with the long hair."

She turned to Grace. "The catalog shouldn't be too much trouble. But if Callie's short hair bothers *Mademoiselle,* offer them Vida. I don't vant them getting upset because they get something they didn't expect."

Anger flashed in Callie's eyes. If the magazine had picked her, then it was *her* job, not Vida's. Vida might be ambitious, but Callie could play that game too. She didn't know what Fredericka was up to, pitting them against each other; this was the second time, she realized, and she didn't like it. Suddenly, Callie knew that she was not going to fail at this, no matter what.

"It will be all right, Fredericka," she said coolly. "I'll make sure it's all right."

Fredericka raised her eyebrows but her tone was even. "Good, Callie. Now, if you vill excuse us."

Callie nodded and left, all eyes in the room watching her

retreating back. When she was gone, Fredericka smiled and nodded in satisfaction.

"Europe never fails," she said, shifting her weight to look once more at the men and women quietly gathered around the table. "They get some polish and learn how to dress. Like magic—it vould take us months to teach them as much."

She rapped her knuckles on the table in satisfaction. "You can learn a lot about the business right here if you pay attention. This Callie vas determined to leave after the summer. But I know she vill not. I knew it vhen she kept trying after several bad weeks vhen no one vanted to hire her. The rejection either drives them away or makes them more determined. Normally, I vould never send a girl to Europe in August if I think they might leave, but I follow my instincts. And they tell me this girl *must* vin. So now she looks like a model and she vill get vork. And she vill stay because always a bigger success vill be right in front of her, and she must pursue it. It's her nature."

Fredericka sipped from a tall glass of iced tea. "You must have the talent, yes. But the desire to follow through makes for success. Now, vhere vas I?"

Back on the street, Callie hailed a cab and went directly to the health club. The more she thought about her encounter with Fredericka, the more angry she became. She was *not* going to fail at this. Hurrying into the gym, she went to her locker and got into her sweatshirt and cut-off shorts, noting that, as usual, she was the scruffiest-looking of the women there; so many of them had matching leotards and tights, even headbands and little belts around their waists. That wasn't her style.

She was glad to see that the Stairmaster was available, and she hopped on. *Good,* she thought, willing herself to put her all into it, *I got here and I'm doing it.* The effort, she'd discovered, wasn't in the working out but in persuading herself to go to the gym in the first place. Not all the models exercised, she'd learned. A lot of them didn't seem to need to; they just stayed thin, and that was enough.

Over in the far corner she spotted Lisa Parks, one of the other models at Whiting. *Imagine,* she thought, pleased, *I recognize someone here.* Observing her, Callie was surprised to see that Lisa was walking slowly on the treadmill, her expression bored, barely exerting herself. Just before she'd left for Europe, Callie had read a magazine article in which Lisa was interviewed about her routine at the gym. She'd described it as being extensive and grueling, talking about the joy of her difficult cardiovascular workout, her love of running. Callie smiled, redoubling her efforts.

Back at her apartment, Callie poured a tall glass of water, not even minding for once that she had to pass up soda or juice to save the calories. She sipped it as she gazed out the window. When she was finished, she went to the telephone.

"Hello?" Alicia Stewart's voice was always a little bit anxious when she answered the phone, as if she expected bad news.

"Hi, Mom, it's me."

Her mother's tone became more anxious. "Callie, darling, how are you? Is everything okay?"

Callie smiled. "Of course. Is Dad home? Could you ask him to pick up the other extension?"

"Hold on." Relieved, Mrs. Stewart called out to her husband and there was a pause until he picked up the second telephone.

"Champ, is that you?" His deep voice revealed his pleasure at the unexpected call.

"Hi, Dad. You both on?"

"We're here. What's up?"

"I've been giving it some thought," Callie began. This was going to be harder than she'd expected. "Things are going very well for me, but I can't accomplish what I set out to in the few weeks left. I'm booked for *Mademoiselle*. That's the big break I've been waiting for, a real editorial spread. It will give me exposure and . . ." She trailed off.

"Yes, honey, go on," her mother said encouragingly.

She might as well just blurt it out. "I don't want to start school yet. I want to stay longer—just a semester, I figure, until I make some real money. I'm almost there, really."

There was silence on the other end.

"Mom, Dad, are you there?"

Her father's voice was solemn. "We're here. We're just a

little surprised. Are you sure about this? It was only supposed to be for the summer."

"I know," Callie said rapidly, "but the summer wasn't enough. They'll hold my place at school for a semester, I'm sure of it. I really want to do this, Dad. It's silly to come so far and then walk away just as I'm about to have some success."

"Frank?" her mother questioned from her extension. "Will she lose her place in college?"

"I doubt that," he answered, "but this isn't what we all had in mind."

"Please, I know what I'm doing," Callie interjected.

She heard her father take a deep breath. "Well, you've always known what you wanted, and there's no reason this should be any different. We trust you, honey, and if you say this is best for you, we're behind you a hundred percent."

"That's right. Your father and I always support your decisions, you know that," Alicia added.

Relief surged through Callie. "Thank you both. You're the best. And I won't let you down. I'll make you proud of me, I swear it."

When they'd finished their conversation and Callie had hung up, she fell back onto the couch, amazed at the step she had just taken. Now she really had to do it, had to make it work, and she had only a few months to succeed.

7

"What time is the big blowout tonight?" Kate asked, piling her plate high with pasta and shrimp. She picked up a basket of hot herb bread and gestured toward Callie with it, offering her a piece.

"Ten-thirty, eleven, somewhere in there," Callie responded, shaking her head no to the bread and instead reaching for the serving spoon in the large glass bowl of strawberries.

A man in a gray suit came up next to them, plate in hand, ready for a second serving. Obviously the client, Callie decided. It had taken a long time, but after ten months in modeling, Callie had learned the system and caught on to the rules that made it work. Whatever the person's job, if he or she was connected to the ad agency or the company whose product was being advertised, they were referred to as *the client*, in contrast to the various technicians and assistants and whoever else might be roaming around on the sets.

"How are you doing there?" Callie flashed him a warm smile.

"Okay," he replied, eyeing the elaborate spread of food before them. He turned to her. "You looked good this morning. The shot should work out well."

"Thank you, I appreciate that." Callie leaned in toward him, her voice intimate. "Don't pass up the brownies. They're the best."

"Got it," he said. "Christopher always puts out a nice lunch, doesn't he?"

"Absolutely."

Callie gave a little wave and walked off to catch up with Kate, who had already taken a seat at the table along with the six other people working on the shoot. The talk there was quiet but animated, about a well-known model who had jumped from one modeling agency to another; despite making noise about taking legal action, it looked as though the first agency would let it slide, even though the move violated her contract. They kept their voices down because several men and women, all of whose business clothes indicated that they were probably from the ad agency or Day and Night itself, sat on two low couches off to one side, talking softly among themselves. No one wanted to be heard gossiping by the clients. As they talked, everyone hungrily consumed the meal a caterer had just finished assembling.

From what she had observed in her months on various sets, it was Callie's theory that the smartest photographers always served a really good, catered lunch. That way, the client could come, watch for a while, and throw in a few comments as they were enjoying the lunch break. Depending on their particular jobs at their companies, some of these clients were used to being around sets, but for others it was still something exciting, a change in their routine. Serving gourmet or special food made the shoots that much more fun for them and, as far as she could see, was just smart business.

There were so many small things that made for smart business, and they could add up to the difference between success and failure. Callie understood that now. Although she was still in the dark when she walked into a studio about who served what function—and might never find out in the course of the day who some of the people were—she understood that it was typically the advertising people who controlled the hiring for a job, not the actual company that was footing the bill and whose product was being advertised. Once things got rolling, the ad agency's art director was the one who appeared to have the most headaches, as he or she was responsible for the success of the shoot.

When it came to dealing with the ad agency people, some models were talkative and friendly, while others were disinterested in doing anything but putting in their day's work and leaving. It was up to each girl, Callie had determined, to decide how she wanted to handle it; no one dictated putting out the extra energy to make conversation, but she was certain it was the sensible thing to do.

At the shoot, the photographer was the one who had to answer to the client, and she had observed how differently they behaved, depending on their style. Some were friendly, chatting with the people who employed them; others made sure they looked busy and important every second, if not actually taking pictures, then examining slides on their lightboxes or consulting with assistants; still others remained cold and aloof, or nervous and impatient—whatever their personalities dictated—and appeared oblivious to everyone around them. Regardless of whether the client was present on the set, in the studio the photographer was the boss over everyone laboring to achieve the right shot. Some were egotistical and concerned only with themselves—like many powerful, creative people, she supposed—although others were a delight to work with. It amazed her how different each studio could be, one atmosphere strained and formal, another raucous and fun.

Callie had learned. Slowly, but she had learned. It wasn't enough to have the right look. Yes, it was important, and a girl had to have the necessary look to get hired, but that wasn't necessarily what got a model hired a second time. It was exactly as Grace had told her all those months back. Assuming you had the look, if you could make the set a more pleasant place and acted professionally, or, better, made the experience of working with you a fun one for everybody involved—if they *liked* you, plain and simple—you worked. If you were difficult, showed up late, or acted sullen or uncooperative, no one would hire you again. Some of the big-name girls, the really famous models, could get away with almost anything. But outside of those few, she had seen the principle hold over and over. The same was true for the hair and makeup people, maybe even more so for them; the ones everybody liked were constantly booked, while the ones who were considered downers or short on personality dropped out of sight.

Callie went to the refrigerator, looking for something to drink. Bottled water rested next to film bricks, the shrink-wrapped rows of film found in every photographer's studio. She took a bottle of water out and squeezed next to Kate on the bench lining the long table, setting down her plate and retying the sash of the robe they'd provided for her.

"How do you think it's going?" she whispered to Kate.

Kate nodded, chewing. "Good," she whispered back. "My guess is they'll want one really sexy shot this afternoon. Give it all you've got."

Callie smiled, signaling that she understood. She had been thrilled to discover that Kate was the stylist on this shoot when she'd shown up this morning. Despite their having become close friends since meeting in Paris the previous summer, they didn't often have an opportunity to work together. Even though fast friendships might be struck on a set or on location, you never knew when you would see someone again whom you had met at a booking, and Callie wasn't famous or powerful enough to request Kate as her stylist. Other models, she knew, could demand that certain people be hired to work with them on a job, but they were in a different league.

She and Kate spent plenty of time together socially, but when they ran into each other at work, that was an added bonus. It was great for Callie, who loved having someone around she could count on to tell her the truth about what was going on and how she was handling the shoot. And who would, of course, make Callie look her best, rather than trying to make a statement about her own styling talents at Callie's expense.

That was especially important today, as this was a major job for Callie. She had never before worked for Weston, the company that owned Day and Night Cosmetics. These cosmetics ads were both prestigious and lucrative. She thought Grace had mentioned that she would get eighteen hundred dollars for today plus an added bonus for usage of the ad. That meant, Grace explained, more money for the right to use the ad for a certain period of time—in this case, six months—in magazines or anyplace else they wanted, along with displays such as countertop cards in department stores.

"You mean I'm getting paid for them to shoot the ad, and then paid again for them to *use* it?" Callie had asked in amazement.

"I guess you could put it that way," Grace had laughed.

Christopher, the photographer, passed by, a glass in his hand. "Hello, birthday girl," he said to Callie, lightly putting a hand on her shoulder. "Congratulations."

She grinned. "Thank you, you're so sweet to remember." Callie was certain that someone, probably his secretary, had just told him it was her birthday, but that was beside the point; it *was* nice of him to say something about it. A chorus of happy-birthdays rose from those at the table who hadn't known it was her birthday, and she acknowledged them all, then took some of their good-natured kidding, responding by throwing a few well-aimed strawberries at some of the guys across the table. They all laughed as someone brought a scone with a candle in it over to Callie, who screwed up her face to show she was making an important wish, then huffed and puffed, as if struggling to blow out the tiny flame. The candle went out, and, amid applause, everyone headed back to work.

While Callie was having her makeup touched up, Kate selected a tangerine-colored evening gown, sleek and low-cut, for her to wear next. After helping her into it, she spent a long time considering the collection of necklaces arrayed in front of her before settling on a strand of crystals. Callie recognized it from Kate's own jewelry box.

"These'll be good with the lipstick," she told Callie as she slipped the necklace over her head. "Not distracting, but a bit glittery in the light, complementary."

Callie tried to nod, but the makeup artist grabbed her chin, holding her head steady. "Don't move," he said, starting to outline her mouth with lipstick pencil.

She sat very still. The lipstick was why they were here, and she wanted the shot to be so good that the ad agency couldn't resist using it. Day and Night was one of Weston's most successful lines, a combination of products that claimed to take a woman through every situation. A few basic products, like the foundation and undereye concealer, could be used for either day or night wear; then the wearer worked with others—actually, the majority of the products, such as the eye shadows and lipsticks—to make herself perfect for everything from office work to an evening at the opera.

This shoot was for a lipstick from the Night products, a color close to that of the dress Kate had chosen. Callie was pleased with the result when she stood and glanced in the mirror: with her fair coloring and blond hair, now grown out past her ears, the lipstick was a good shade for her.

Although one person often did both hair and makeup, this shoot had two people for these functions. Zeke, the man doing hair today, approached Callie for a final comb-out. By this stage, Callie could tell practically from the first brushstroke whether a hairdresser knew what he was doing, whether he was confident or tentative. Some could fuss over her forever, putting in her hair what seemed like a pound of goo, and she still wound up looking just as she had when she started out; others could transform her hair with what seemed a few quick flicks of the brush. Zeke was good—she knew that from having worked with him before—even if he was pretty obnoxious most of the time, full of his own superiority.

"Hey, Zeke," Callie said warmly. "How's your adorable little dog?" She knew he loved his tiny black poodle more than anything else on earth.

Zeke's face softened. "She's super. A real terror, but I adore her."

Satisfied, Callie smiled widely and was rewarded with a smile back from Zeke.

"Let's do it, people," a voice called out.

The makeup artist hurriedly colored her eyebrows and shaped them with a toothbrush before letting Callie go. Her skin and eyes were sore from so many people touching them, and she was relieved to get out of the chair and hurry onto the beige seamless. Callie was the only model working on this job, and they had been at it since eight that morning, although this was just the third shot. The two they had done before lunch featured more toned-down clothes for evening. Later on, she supposed, the Day and Night marketing people would decide if they wanted an ad featuring Callie in a long silk dress or a camisole and black suit, the outfits she'd worn for the other shots, or in the evening gown she had on now.

Two of the assistants on the set had just finished centering a blue velvet couch. They kept tossing plump needlepoint pillows onto it, seeking just the right casual effect. Someone else was in the process of hammering a framed picture above the couch, sinking nails into a tall piece of plywood propped up behind the seamless. Callie concentrated on Christopher, clearing her mind and preparing herself to do whatever he requested. Someone placed a champagne glass in her hand. Another hand appeared before her, pouring ginger ale into her glass to simulate champagne. The music, silenced during lunch, came on again. It was a reggae record, loud and pulsing.

As usual, there was extensive discussion about the lighting between the photographer and his assistant, several changes were made, Polaroid pictures were snapped and examined, and the light meter was repeatedly brought near her face, her hair, and her dress. More powder and lipstick for her face, more repairs to her hair. Then, abruptly, she was alone on the set.

"Sit down, Callie. We're going for sexy," Christopher called to her. "I want a big, open mouth, laughing, inviting. The most energy you can give." He was fussing over his camera, continuing to talk as she settled in on the couch. "You're a woman who's been around, seen it all, and is still incredibly excited by everything life has to offer. You *love* life."

Kate had hit the nail on the head, Callie thought. The big, sexy shot. She took a deep breath. These were the hardest for her. Suddenly, someone tripped over a tripod supporting one of the lights. There was a startled silence, then exclamations of annoyance from different people as the stand had to be repositioned and the light meter brought back, everything held up while the lighting was set up again. Callie sat patiently, not wanting to add to the growing tension on the set. She noticed Zeke off in a corner doing the hair of a woman from the ad agency, laughing with her and offering her styling advice. He was well aware, Callie supposed, that it couldn't hurt him to get friendly with those people.

Finally, everything was ready.

"Here we go. Throw your head back and laugh," Christopher instructed.

Callie complied. She didn't hear the camera clicking.

"Again."

Do it right, she instructed herself sternly. She let her mind drift away, forgetting where she was, gazing into the glass of make-believe champagne. She thought of Paris, how carefree and happy she'd been with Jean all those months ago. Those memories were tinged with longing but always made her feel wonderful. Of course, she hadn't felt wonderful when, after arriving home from her trip to Paris, her period had been six weeks late. She and Jean had used protection, but the scary possibility that she was pregnant sent her scurrying to the gynecologist Grace recommended. She wasn't pregnant. The doctor had blamed the delay on jet lag and the too-strict diet Callie had adopted upon her return from France; Callie had sat through a long, disapproving lecture from the doctor about starving herself. She'd made an effort to eat more low-fat, healthful foods since then, but it was so hard to keep the weight off. Would she ever be free of the hassle of worrying about it?

There was silence on the set. She took a deep breath and held it. Then, suddenly, she tossed her head back and let out a loud laugh.

"Good!" The camera clicked furiously. "Tilt your head, part your lips."

Callie listened to Christopher's commands, attempting to block out everything but the sound of his voice and the beat of the music. He talked and shot continuously, and they worked in tandem, she responding to each word. Then there was a pause as he waited for his assistant to change the film.

A voice she didn't recognize said, "Could she lick her lips, make them wetter?"

"Maybe we could try one with a little longing in her smile." That was someone else she didn't know. Both of these people had to be the client, but she couldn't see past the lights to make out who in particular was talking.

"Did you hear that, Callie?" Christopher asked.

She understood that he was cuing her to follow their instructions.

"Yeah, gotcha." Callie licked her lips and altered her expression.

They went at it for more than two hours, the lipstick reapplied and her hair and makeup repaired every few minutes. Christopher had a test roll of film sent out to be developed right away so he could see what he was getting. Beauty shots were difficult and required attention to the most minute details. Callie felt fatigue setting in, but she refused to let it show.

"One more roll and we're set," the photographer called out.

She resisted the urge to smile. Callie had learned that "one more roll" was jokingly referred to as the biggest lie in the business, a photographer's trick to keep exhausted models going a little longer, promising them it was almost over. Some of the more experienced models had told her that the way to get the photographer to live up to the lie was to stop moving, to stop giving him anything new that might encourage him to keep shooting. Otherwise, that "one more roll" turned into two or three or more. But Callie couldn't be that way. She wanted them to get the best picture possible. And, though she'd had a lot of jobs so far, this was the most important one. As far as she was concerned, Christopher could shoot all night if he wanted.

In fact, he shot just two more rolls, then called it a wrap. Gratefully, Callie walked off the set and sank down into a chair, kicking off her shoes while Kate took off her jewelry and unzipped the dress. The makeup artist offered her some makeup remover, which she took appreciatively since it was a courtesy on his part—he wasn't required to bring that along. As everyone finished up around her, she and Kate solidified their plans to meet later that night at The Salon, the club where a crowd of friends were getting together to celebrate Callie's birthday.

It was a bit chilly outside, and Callie pulled her trench coat tightly around her as she headed for the subway, thinking how glad she was that she'd bought the coat, a rumpled, drab olive green that tried to look like silk, so *out* it was chic, and a true find at the army-navy store for twelve dollars. Heading down the subway stops, she paused, realizing she had completely forgotten about her meeting with the real estate agent. They had an appointment at five-thirty, when Callie was supposed to see another apartment.

For a moment she contemplated just continuing on her way, anxious to get out of her clothes and relax, but she forced herself to turn around and head for the phone booth on the corner. She would be late, but she could still make it. Besides, she'd had to cancel several other appointments with the agent when she was held up on jobs. Not only was it rude, but she was never going to find an apartment if this kept up.

While she was at a phone, she decided, she might as well check in with the agency.

"Grace?" she said when she reached the booker. "Hi, it's Callie. What's up?"

"Hey there," Grace replied. "Sorry, but Alistair's canceled next Tuesday's booking and it looks like Loops is backing out of the Virginia shoot. But Teriano is talking about two days in North Carolina. Call me in the morning, okay? Gotta run."

Unsettled, Callie headed back to the subway. Two canceled bookings at once. It was so hard to know if that meant anything. Maybe it was a coincidence; bookings got canceled all the time. Or was something wrong with her, with the way she looked? Her anxiety grew.

Half an hour later, struggling to put her worries aside, Callie hurried into the lobby of a highrise apartment building on East Sixty-fourth Street near Third Avenue. It was a good location, she noted approvingly, close enough to Whiting but a few crucial blocks removed from the bustle of midtown shopping.

The prospect of buying an apartment outright for herself had seemed too daunting and permanent, but she was more than ready to rent one. The time had definitely come to be on her own, living alone. Lanny's coolness and disinterest in Callie hadn't changed in all these months, but it had proven to be an advantage over time, since their relationship was always on an even keel—no arguments, no dramas, no problems. Now, though, she wanted more space, privacy, and a sense of reward for having done well in her work.

The agent, a woman in her late fifties who had shown Callie six other apartments in the past few weeks, was waiting on a bench in the lobby and greeted her with a broad smile. They went up in the elevator to the eighteenth floor, and she led the way to the last door at the end of the hall.

"You're going to like this one, I'm sure of it," she said, inserting a key in the lock. "It's a killer place, a steal."

As soon as they had stepped inside, Callie knew this was going to be her new apartment. Passing through the foyer into the spacious living room, she saw light flooding every corner, the effect bright and welcoming. She hurried into the bedroom. Enormous, with a huge closet and tall windows revealing a panoramic view.

"How much is it?"

The agent consulted her notes. "Twenty-five hundred a month. Divine, isn't it?"

Twenty-five hundred dollars a month to rent an apartment! An image of her parents flashed through Callie's mind as she walked slowly into the kitchen, taking in the long white counters and high cabinets, the spanking-new appliances, the space for a breakfast nook. Her mother's kitchen, even if the appliances were ancient, was twice the size. Her parents would never be able to grasp the idea of spending so much money for rent. Well, she wouldn't tell them the real amount anyway, although even cutting it in half would elicit shock from them.

She gazed out the small kitchen window. It seemed that lately she told her parents fewer and fewer things about what was going on in her life. They just wouldn't be able to understand. The late hours and parties, dating lots of different men—her social life would have frightened and worried them needlessly. And although it was perfectly harmless and under control, she knew that if her parents were aware of how much she and her friends drank when they went out, they would be horrified and start preaching at her. It was better to let them think she was still going to sleep at nine o'clock every night, keeping to herself and a few close girlfriends, shying away from the lures and temptations of New York.

They were already upset about her having put off college for the entire year instead of only one semester, as she had promised at the end of last summer. They hadn't been as agreeable about this second delay in her schooling when she had called them in early December and sprung her decision on them; that news, coming on top of her telling them that she'd be too busy with work to come home for the holidays, had elicited angry words from her father and a lot of pained silence from her mother. If she wanted to be completely honest with herself, the prospect of leaving modeling to go to college at all was growing dimmer and dimmer in her mind. The truth about the rest of her life now would only lead to further arguments and trouble, and she had no desire to hurt them.

Besides, she told herself irritably, unsettled by her thoughts, what she did was her business, and her work was practically supporting them all. Her father had finally found another job, just a few months before, but it was at a far lower salary than his previous one, and the family would have been struggling had it not been for Callie's contributions. They wouldn't accept much from her, although she would have been happy to give them more. She had already decided to pick up the cost of Tommy's college tuition when the time came. Her father would probably refuse at first, but she was sure that reason, in the form of her mother, would eventually prevail. They wouldn't tell Tommy, though. She could imagine his negative reaction to having his big sister support him through school.

Money made things so complicated with the people you loved, Callie reflected with a sigh. She had been enjoying the fruits of her hard work, and she wished her family could do the same. She couldn't imagine when she'd be able to break it to them that she had bought a BMW. That would floor her parents. But, hell, she was entitled. When the bookings had started coming in for her, she had taken them all, working five and six days a week, grueling hours every day, willing to do anything as she fattened her portfolio and watched her bank account expand.

At first she'd been afraid to spend any of the money she made, just letting the thousands of dollars accumulate in a simple savings account. But being around the best of everything—from clothes and food to cars and furniture—learning from the people in the business what was in good taste, what was too much or trying too hard, she had wanted to be part of it all, to enjoy some of the finer things for herself. And she could now.

She turned back to the agent. "If the lease looks okay to you, I'm ready to sign."

The woman's face lit up. With the commission from this rental, she could redecorate her living room.

Back on the street, Callie strode briskly downtown. It would be another two weeks before she could move, but she'd better start making some arrangements. Crossing on Fifty-seventh Street, she was so deep in thought that she almost missed the cover staring out at her from the newsstand as she passed.

She stopped, startled. Her face was smiling out from the cover of *You* magazine. She had posed for the picture three months earlier, ecstatic to be booked for her first possible cover shot, but there had been no way of knowing whether they would actually use it. And now here it was.

She scrambled to find her wallet and bought two copies. It was a good picture, it really was, she thought. Her hair looked great, her expression looked natural, and the feeling of it was very nice. She remembered when it was taken, how amazed she had been to find out that the photographer on the job was Jacques Duval, the man who had shown such complete disinterest in her book on that unbearably hot summer day. You never knew what was going to happen. It turned out he had been the one to suggest her as a cover possibility. Of course, by then he would have seen her pictures around in other publications, but still, she could recall so well how dull his eyes had been when he met her in person that afternoon, how she'd felt that her trip to his studio had been a waste of time.

She walked along, staring down at the image of herself. It was unbelievable. There she was, on the cover of one of the top fashion magazines in the country. No wonder they paid so little for these shots—what was it she had made, a hundred fifty dollars? It didn't matter; it would have been worth paying *them* for the thrill of this. This was even more exciting than when they had moved her from Whiting's Taking Off division to the Women Division, the sign that she had truly arrived as a model and was part of the established group of successful girls.

Engrossed in studying the cover, she didn't even remember getting upstairs to her apartment, but once inside she headed straight to the telephone and called home. Her mother had not only seen it, she informed Callie in a voice bursting with pride, but the picture was already out being professionally framed for a place of honor above the fireplace. They talked and giggled about it for nearly half an hour. Callie's mother wished her a happy birthday, wanting to know if Callie had received the present they had sent her, a long, red and white flannel nightgown. Smiling, Callie told her she had gotten it yesterday and that it fit perfectly. The truth was that Callie would never wear it, but she wasn't about to tell her mother that she now slept either in nothing or in silk nightgowns or teddies. When she got off the phone, Callie was determined to find a way to spend more time with her family and get them to enjoy her success more, as she did.

It was only when she started toward her bedroom that she noticed the enormous basket of irises on the dining room table. The card propped on the table next to them had her name on it. Lanny must have brought the basket inside, she figured, opening the small envelope and pulling out the card. *Happy birthday, Callie darling. Our love and congratulations from Fredericka and Austin Whiting and the entire Whiting Agency staff.*

How beautiful the flowers were, she thought happily, carrying them into her room. And how terrific that the agency had remembered her birthday. They were obviously pleased with her if they went to the trouble of remembering and including such a friendly card from Fredericka and Austin. She set them on her windowsill with a sigh of pleasure. It was good to be nineteen, truly on her way as an adult.

"The guy in the iridescent suit sent this over," the waiter yelled, with a jerk of his head to the left to indicate who had requested he deliver the drink.

Callie paused in her dancing just long enough to take the glass from him. "What?" she yelled back, trying to hear over the din of music and noise in The Salon.

"Over there," he repeated, with the same motion.

Callie gave up trying to understand and nodded her thanks as she took a sip. Everyone knew that stingers were her drink, and this must have been the tenth one sent over by one or another of her guests so far tonight. She turned back to her dancing partner.

"Here, Jake." She handed him the drink and he took it, both of them still moving to the music.

Jake was a model with Whiting's Men's Division, and he and Callie had become casual friends. Although some of the other male models were far worse, he was still a bit too vain for her taste. Besides, she thought, he lacked something, and didn't have quite as much—what was the word?—*character* as some of them did. Male models weren't all empty-headed boys, as a lot of people perceived them. Far from it: some of them had other jobs or wanted to use the money from modeling as a springboard to serious business ventures. Those guys read *The Wall Street Journal*, invested their money shrewdly, and treated modeling only as a means to a secure financial end. A number of them wanted to go into acting. Some, she knew, felt modeling was a joke but would never admit it. They did earn less than the women models overall, and their careers moved more slowly, many of them starting out doing catalog work in Europe for a while. But their careers lasted longer than the women's—as long as fifteen or twenty years.

When the song ended, Callie kissed Jake on the cheek and turned to go. She and Jake had worked together twice, and it was fun having him on the set; whatever his flaws might be, he kept everyone laughing and made sure the mood stayed light. She thought about how different he was from Les Hardwick, the model she'd worked with the week before. Les was so full of himself, and so touchy about every little comment, as if whatever anyone said was somehow a veiled criticism of him. The ad was for an expensive line of Italian shoes, and Callie had been instructed to wrap her arms around Les's neck as if he were her great love, stare into his eyes, and bend one leg out behind her. She hated the smug expression on Les's face, as if he *knew* she was secretly thrilled to be so close to him; she hated the sickeningly sweet smell of his cologne, the feeling of his hands on her back. She'd never been so relieved as when the photographer announced they had the shot and she was free to go. If only all these guys could be like Henry Keel, a model she'd met on a shoot for *Cosmopolitan*. Henry was smart, funny, a perfect gentleman, and a pleasure to work with.

Jake gave her a friendly slap on the behind as she darted off, and she glanced back at him, wagging a finger in mock threat, then smoothing down the back of her dress. It was an ice-blue minidress with spaghetti straps, so short she didn't dare sit down. But she'd been so elated when she tried it on, seeing that having lost an extra five pounds brought her hips down enough that she could wear something so tight. It had been impossible to find shoes to match, and she'd wound up having white silk pumps dyed to match. In the skimpy dress and high heels, and with her hair swept up, she felt free and cool despite the heat generated by so many people packed into the club. She looked just the way she wanted to look—dressy yet relaxed, unadorned except for small diamond post earrings and her new Cartier dress watch, her birthday present to herself.

She spied April standing near the bar and moved in her direction; it was the first time she'd seen her friend all evening.

"Callie, I love you, honey!" One of the male bookers who worked at Whiting appeared before her, hand in hand with his boyfriend. "Happy birthday!"

Callie kissed his cheek. "Karl, you're the best. I love you too and I'll wait for you forever."

Karl and his lover guffawed as Callie moved on. Stopping to exchange more quick kisses of greeting and a few words with different guests as she made her way, her face glowed with the excitement of being the center of so much attention.

It took a full twenty minutes before she was able to get close to the bar. The distasteful thought suddenly flashed through her mind that she was unable to be direct with most people now, as if she could no longer turn off the personality, the carefree facade she had struggled to perfect. She shook her head slightly as if trying physically to rid herself of the idea, and slipped in between two men to reach April.

"Hey, birthday baby!" April greeted Callie with a hug, her thick, waist-length brown hair immediately getting tangled up between them.

April's hair was her trademark, making her instantly recognizable when she had started modeling two years before. She sometimes considered cutting it, unsure whether keeping the same look for so long was benefiting her or losing her jobs, despite the fact that she worked constantly. But she wanted to go further, to work with hot new photographers, in television and eventually film, and had become fixated on the idea that her hair would be a decisive factor in her success. Callie voted for a new, shorter hairdo, but April couldn't bring herself to make the decision.

Callie had initially met April at the agency one afternoon, both of them there between bookings. They had struck up a conversation, but it probably wouldn't have led anywhere were it not for the fact that they found themselves working on the same job four days later. Just three weeks after that, they were surprised to find themselves booked together again, and from there the relationship had developed from surface pleasantries to a real friendship. Callie had introduced April to Kate, and they too got along well, so the three of them had dinner together or took in a movie when they were all free—which was rare.

"Having a good time?" Callie asked as she gestured to the bartender to freshen April's drink. "Are you with anybody?"

"Yeah, I brought Louie, but I lost him about twenty minutes ago. He's around somewhere." Louie was April's on-again, off-again boyfriend, also a model, but they had been together for over a year and spent most of their time fighting and then, according to April, passionately making up, which was the best part of their relationship.

"As the guest of honor, do you have an official escort?" she asked Callie.

"No, I wanted to be unencumbered, free as a bird," Callie answered airily with a laugh.

"Where's that guy, whosie?" April asked with a frown. "The one from the dinner party last week that you liked."

Callie waved her hand dismissively. "Didn't work out. He was dating two other models and just wanted to add me to his roster. A jerk."

April shook her head. "We've got to find you somebody decent."

"He's out there. I'm not worried," Callie replied, grabbing a handful of mixed nuts from the bowl on the bar and tossing a few into her mouth. She'd have to work out for an extra hour at the gym tomorrow to make up for all this eating and drinking.

"By the way," she went on, "this guy called yesterday and said Mitch Astin would like me to—get this—join him on his yacht next weekend."

"*Mitch Astin?* Oooooo . . ." April sighed appreciatively. Astin was one of the year's hottest singers and as handsome as any movie star. In fact, rumor had it that his good looks were going to take him from a career in singing to one in films. "Are you going?"

Callie held up a hand to the bartender, pointing to herself, and he nodded to indicate he would bring her another drink. "Of course not. I told the guy if Mitch Astin wanted to ask me out, he could call me himself."

April made a face. "I would have been there as fast as that guy could have given me directions. You're crazy."

"Maybe so." Callie saw some people she knew on the dance floor waving their arms to get her attention. She waved back.

"Now, girls, what's going on here?" Kate said with mock severity as she approached. "You're talking about something important, I can tell, and you're leaving me out of it. Unless you're talking about me, that is, in which case I don't want to know."

April gave Kate a look that reflected her disgust at what she had just learned. "Callie turned down a weekend on Mitch Astin's yacht."

"That's our Callie." Kate put her arm around her. "No brains. Now listen, it's too busy and noisy here to celebrate your birthday properly. What do you say I take you to lunch on Saturday. Or maybe tea at the Plaza. We can wear white gloves and big hats with fake fruit glued onto them." She regarded April. "You come too, please. My treat."

Callie smiled. "Thanks, Kate. That sounds terrific."

"I'd love to," April said. "I have plans on Saturday, but I'll change them."

There was a commotion on the far end of the dance floor. The three of them looked over. Someone was bringing out a huge chocolate cake ablaze with candles. Wasn't it wonderful, Callie thought, having friends who cared about her that way. She gave Kate a little hug. Nineteen was going to be a great year for her, she just knew it.

8

Callie was one of the first passengers off the plane when it landed in Indianapolis. Her carryon bag slung over her shoulder, she tightened the sash on her black cashmere coat as she hastened out to the baggage area where she knew she would find her family. She'd told them there was no reason for them to make the trip to the airport, that she would be glad to hire a car to drive her home. It was over forty miles to Bloomington, and she didn't want them to make the long drive back and forth. But her father had insisted. He always left plenty of time to catch or meet planes, trains, and the like, so Callie guessed he had hurried her mother and brother to the airport, and they'd all probably been waiting around for at least forty-five minutes.

She spotted them immediately, her parents anxiously scanning the incoming passengers' faces, Tommy standing slightly apart from them, his head buried in a book as he shifted his weight from one foot to the other. For an instant,

Callie paused. Suddenly it dawned on her that more than a year and a half had passed since she had last seen her parents. It had never occurred to her that they might look different from the day they had dropped her off in New York the summer before last. But they did look different—a lot different. Older, smaller, as if they had somehow shrunk. Her father's usually thick, lustrous gray hair appeared thinner on top, and her mother's face looked pinched. She felt a stab of sadness.

Tommy, she saw, was even taller, easily six feet by now, and, in contrast to their parents, he looked better than before. His blond hair brushed his shoulders and his face had filled out a bit; she would no longer be able to tease him about his long, skinny chin by whinnying like a horse, something she used to do that drove him crazy. In fact, her little brother had become extremely attractive. He could probably get modeling work if he wanted it.

Fredericka had seen his potential that day when they all came to New York, Callie recalled, thinking back to the remark about Tommy's joining Whiting's Men's Division that had so horrified him. At the time, Callie had assumed that Fredericka was just kidding to put the family at ease, but she had come to learn that the head of the Whiting Agency had absolutely no sense of humor and never joked about anything, especially when it came to the business. You had to hand it to Fredericka, she really knew how to spot the talent. But Tommy was off to college in the fall, and Callie was certain he wouldn't even consider taking a stab at modeling.

Alicia saw Callie first, her eyes lighting up. She tugged at her husband's sleeve and they both rushed forward to greet her, Tommy bringing up the rear. Callie dropped her bag to the ground as she and her parents exchanged long hugs. Tommy gave her a quick, awkward kiss, careful to avoid any possibility of coming into contact with her lip gloss.

"Oh, sweetie," her mother said, her eyes filling with tears of happiness, "we're so glad you could come home for Christmas. It was awfully sad without you last year. And look at you—you're so gorgeous and grown-up."

"How's my favorite girl?" Frank asked, taking her hands

in his and standing back to appraise her. "You're too skinny, Cal."

Callie laughed and turned to Tommy. "Hey, baby brother, what's doing?" she said brightly.

She watched him taking in her coat, the Hermès scarf draped around her collar, her Italian leather boots. She had been careful to dress conservatively for the trip home, but her clothes were of good quality; that was all she bought now. Her brother would have no idea where these things came from or how much they really cost, but he knew they were expensive, she could see that much in his eyes.

He tilted his head and regarded her. "Why are you wearing all that makeup?"

"Tommy." Callie hadn't heard her mother's familiar tone of reprimand for so long, and she smiled at the sound.

"Okay, everybody." Frank bent down to pick up Callie's carryon bag. "We have a lot of eggnog drinking to do at home. Our schedule is tight."

"Right you are, Dad." Callie's voice echoed his joviality as she moved toward the luggage carousel, peering to see if her two suitcases had come down the ramp yet.

On the drive home, Callie kept up a steady stream of conversation, entertaining her parents with tales of New York and modeling, careful to leave out anything that might shock or worry them—which meant diluting the stories down to their bare bones. But they seemed not to notice and continued pumping her with questions. Tommy said nothing.

When they reached Bloomington, Callie glanced out the window every few blocks, continuing to talk but taking in the sights of the streets, which were covered with grimy snow left over from several days prior. When they finally approached their neighborhood, she saw how run-down it was. Like her parents themselves, the houses and yards looked so much smaller than she remembered. Everything seemed gray and dirty, in desperate need of a coat of paint.

It was a shock to her when they pulled in the driveway to their house. Was it possible that the house had always been this tiny? Whenever she thought of it now, it was as a middle-class home, and a very comfortable one; clearly, though, it was located in a lower-middle-class area and was an extremely modest house, actually ugly, she couldn't help thinking. Ashamed of her disloyalty, she began talking faster, filling the air with her chatter and laughter.

Stepping inside, her new impressions were confirmed. Everything was run-down here, too. The walls needed painting, the furniture was old and worn, and the rooms were small and dingy. How had the four of them managed to live together here? She could barely breathe. Her apartment in New York was so open and airy with its white couches and expanses of polished parquet floors. Here, the dark wood furniture was oppressive, the atmosphere made even heavier by the old pictures and keepsakes that seemed to clutter up every wall.

Passing the living room on the way to her bedroom, she stopped in her tracks. There was the framed picture of her hanging over the fireplace, the cover of *You* that Callie had spotted walking down the street on her nineteenth birthday eight months before. Since then she had gotten at least ten more cover tries and four of them had been used on magazine covers. But her mother insisted that this was the best because it was the first.

Callie hadn't seen the picture in a long time, and with a critical eye she walked over to examine it more closely. The lighting was flat. What could Jacques Duval have been thinking? And there was a small bump in her hair. Why hadn't anyone seen that and smoothed it out? The necklace was all wrong for the blouse. She would never let that happen now, but back then she hadn't been savvy enough to know what accessories would have been better. Even the makeup job was no better than passable. She grimaced, wishing the picture weren't hanging in the most prominent place in the room, where all eyes would be instantly drawn to it.

It was a long night for Callie. Her mother had obviously gone to a lot of trouble in preparing dinner, but the fried chicken was limp and soggy, and the peas and mashed potatoes with gravy were bland. She must have served that same dinner to the family a thousand times before, and Callie had always loved it, but none of the food tasted the way she remembered it. Besides, she never ate like this anymore, preferring to stick to low-fat foods, splurging on things that weren't good for her only when she was in a decent restaurant where it was worth going off her diet.

She pushed the food around on her plate, distracting her parents from the fact that she wasn't eating with tales of her days at work. They wanted to know more about her friends Kate and April, whom Callie always mentioned when she talked to them on the phone. Callie knew her parents imagined that they were like three sorority sisters, sitting around the house doing their nails and talking about boys, and she did nothing to correct that image. She was glad when she was able to jump up and clear the dinner plates. Dessert turned out to be Jell-O with whipped cream. She ate quickly, barely tasting it, then went in to help her mother wash up.

After dinner, her father insisted on playing the piano and singing carols, despite the fact that Christmas Eve was two nights away. Callie was bored but tried to be a good sport about it. At ten-thirty her parents went off to bed and Tommy retreated to his room. Callie, wide awake, had nothing to do. She wandered around the house, not eager to go back into her old room, which had been no less of a shock than the rest of the house when she initially went in to drop off her bags. The ruffles around the bed, the ornate brass handles on the old white chest of drawers, the fading pink carpet—it didn't seem possible that she had lived here. None of it was remotely to her taste anymore. The truth was, she thought guiltily, she wouldn't be caught dead in a room like this now. She drifted into the kitchen and opened the refrigerator, leaning against the door as she absentmindedly ate a chicken leg left over from dinner.

It was after two in the morning before Callie went to bed, and she didn't get up until ten the next day. Her father had gone to work and Tommy was off somewhere. Her mother had taken the day off, so they were alone in the house. While Alicia went down to the basement to put a load of laundry in the washing machine, Callie made herself a pot of strong coffee and sat at the dining room table with it, reflecting that she would be missing the annual Whiting Christmas party that night. Whiting threw an incredible party every year. She'd had so much fun at the last one and met a man she'd wound up dating for three months. That wasn't the only party she was missing. She envisioned the stack of invitations back in her apartment. Christmas was a great time to be in New York.

The telephone rang. Reluctantly she dragged herself out of the chair and went to answer it.

"Is this Callie Stewart?"

Callie didn't recognize the voice. "Speaking."

"This is Suzie Peters from the *Bloomington Mirror*. We heard you would be in town this week, and we'd like to send a reporter and photographer to your house to do a story."

"What kind of story?" Callie asked, taking another sip from her mug. Thank goodness for coffee, she thought, or she'd never make it through the mornings.

"Bloomington is your hometown and now you're a famous model. What could be a better story than that for us?" the woman answered.

"Oh." Callie wasn't sure what to say to that. It made sense, though, she supposed, that they might want to do an article on her, the local-girl-makes-good angle.

"Would tomorrow morning at eleven be convenient?"

"I guess so."

"Great," Suzie Peters said. "We'll see you then."

No sooner had Callie hung up the telephone than it rang again. The caller sounded a bit breathless.

"Callie? Callie Stewart?"

"Yes."

There was a little squeal. "Oh, it's you. This is Marnie Franks. You know, from high school. Remember me?"

Marnie Franks, the most popular girl in their class, cheerleader and steady girlfriend of Jim Meehan, the star of the swim team. She had never so much as looked in Callie's direction.

"Hello, Marnie. How are you? What have you been up to?" Callie asked in a friendly tone.

"Oh, nothing as exciting as you, but keeping busy. Jim and I are married now, and we have a little boy. I'm pregnant with our second right now. Can you believe it?"

Her voice was oddly loud. "Anyway, it's hard for us to get out much these days—you can never find a sitter when you need one, you know—but we would just *love* it if you would stop by for a little visit. We'd invite the whole gang over for an afternoon, watch some football on the tube. Or maybe have dinner here. Whatever you want."

The whole gang? Callie couldn't imagine whom Marnie was talking about. She must mean her own gang of friends from high school. Callie had certainly never been part of any group of friends, much less all those popular girls Marnie had hung around with.

"That's very nice of you, Marnie. It's a little bit hectic here, but I'll try my best to make it. Can I get back to you?" She knew she wouldn't call Marnie back, but she couldn't bring herself to say no to the invitation.

"Sure, Callie. Great to talk to you again. Welcome home."

Callie hung up the phone. *Great to talk to you again.* Unbelievable. They'd never exchanged more than two words in the past, and here Marnie was acting like they were best friends.

The rest of the morning brought more of the same. Two other local newspapers called about doing articles on Callie. Half a dozen of the girls and boys with whom she had gone to high school called, all wanting to see her. Most of them were married and had children or were starting their families. The two boys who were single asked for dates. She remembered them both, good-looking athletes who never seemed to notice she was alive before. Everyone was either shy and reserved, as if afraid of her, or falsely intimate the way Marnie had been. She did want to see some of the kids from school, but it was all very peculiar and uncomfortable. At around noon, Janie Wynn called and asked if Callie would like to go shopping with her and two other girls from their old class. Callie had always liked Janie and agreed to get together the day after Christmas.

It took forever for Christmas Eve to roll around, and by the time it did Callie was beside herself with boredom and sorry she had planned the trip for an entire week. She loved her parents but she couldn't take much more sitting around the house with nothing to do. Back in New York, her days and nights were filled with parties, restaurants, flirting, and laughter; at work, she was accustomed to strange hours, four-letter words, gossip, the models' nudity, and quick friendships formed in the lulls of waiting. The pace was just so much faster. Here, everything was so prim and correct, and so *slow*.

On Christmas Eve, Callie again endured another round of caroling, keeping the smile on her face while wondering why her father continued to pretend he could actually play the piano. She helped her mother serve the eggnog and cookies, the same cookies she'd been putting out every year on Christmas Eve since Callie could remember. They weren't really very good, she thought, biting off the head of a pink snowman. When Alicia offered to tell her stories about the tree decorations and how they got into the Stewart collection, Callie begged off, saying she was tired. She thought she saw the hurt in her mother's eyes, but she just couldn't sit through another session of those stories. She was too old for that—they all were.

She was only glad she had brought so many gifts for the three of them, so that they would know how much she loved them. For starters, she had engraved stationery from Tiffany's and antique pens for both her parents, a new leather briefcase for her father, a silk blouse for her mother, and a CD player for Tommy. Pleased, she glanced over at the tree, noting with satisfaction that there must have been twenty presents from her under it. At least she'd done that part right, she thought. And her parents had seemed to genuinely enjoy the fuss of being photographed and interviewed by the different reporters who had come to the house over the past few days. It was torture for Callie, telling the same stories over and over to these smalltime reporters, answering such silly questions. And they all wanted her to pose for pictures. But she was pleased that she could give her parents the excitement of being local celebrities.

When it came time to meet Janie Wynn and the other two girls for her shopping date, Callie put on a black jumpsuit and kept her makeup to a minimum. She didn't want to seem out of place or too *New York* to them, which was the way she knew they would regard her. They were to meet at a coffeeshop downtown. There were Janie and Tina Hart and Lisa Montgomery, all smiling anxiously as they watched Callie enter and walk over to join them in their booth. All three were married, Callie learned, and Lisa was four months pregnant. She asked them about their lives, but they avoided discussing themselves, telling her that they weren't interesting, just going to work every day. They only wanted to hear what it was like to be a model, how it felt to live in New York, and if Callie knew any famous people.

After several cups of coffee, Callie persuaded them that they should get going if they were going to shop, and the four of them headed out.

"We thought we'd go to Brack's and then on to Samson, if that's okay with you," Janie told Callie as they walked along.

Callie nodded. Of course, she realized, they would all be on tight budgets, buying their clothes in the discount shops, as Callie used to do. It dawned on her that she could now afford anything in any of Bloomington's better stores. Not that she would want anything from the Bloomington stores. She was used to designer clothes and the kinds of shoes and accessories one could find only in the international shops of New York. Although she tried her best to get into the spirit of the day, oohing and aahing over their selections, she knew they understood the truth as well, that she wouldn't be caught dead in these kinds of clothes anymore.

And they had little else in common. Even in her simple black jumpsuit, Callie somehow looked completely different from the three of them in their stretch pants and sweaters, their short boots, and their blouses with small collars. She walked faster, talked more quickly, and had to censor what she said, afraid of seeming cynical or snobby. Sensing their envy, she tried to make light of their differences, but it was awkward and she was relieved when the day was over and she could retreat to her parents' house.

It seemed an eternity before the week finally came to an end. Packing her bags, Callie reflected unhappily that this visit hadn't rekindled her closeness with her family as she had expected it would. On the contrary. And Tommy had barely said a word to her all week. She'd noticed how he had quietly been observing her through narrowed eyes, disapproval clearly evident in his expression. More significant, she was horrified to discover that her parents actually embarrassed her. They were just two hicks, really. She'd never known that before. They'd spent the entire week telling her how wonderful she was, how proud they were of her. It seemed they were just as taken in by the image of her as a high-fashion model as everyone else around here. The thought made her cringe.

She zipped her suitcase and glanced at her watch. It would be such a relief to get back to New York. Only another half-hour before they left for the airport. When she got home, she would send her parents something nice to say thank you for the visit. She was well aware that they'd gone to a lot of trouble on her behalf that week, and she didn't want them to think she didn't appreciate it. In the meantime, she would go in to say goodbye to Tommy, who wasn't going to the airport with them. She headed to his room.

"Hey, it's me," she called out, knocking on his closed door. "Can I come in?"

She barely heard his answer, a mumbled "sure." Opening the door, she saw he was sitting on his bed, lacing up his sneakers. Probably going to play basketball in the school gym, she thought.

"I'm leaving soon, baby brother," she said brightly. "Just wanted to say *adieu.*"

He turned to her with an expression of disgust. "Don't call me *baby brother.* And what's with that *adieu* crap?"

Callie bristled slightly. "I didn't mean anything by it. Just being friendly. If you want to know the truth, you haven't been too nice to me this week, but I'm trying to overlook it."

"Don't do me any favors." He bent his head down, focusing on his sneakers again.

"What's that supposed to mean?" she asked, her voice rising.

Tommy stood up, reaching for his jacket on the bed. "Look, Callie, everyone's been fussing over you and telling you how *faaabulous* you are." He sarcastically drew out the word. "Well, I don't have to do it too. If you want my opinion, you've become a real asshole."

Stunned, Callie said nothing.

"So go back to your little model buddies and fancy photographers in New York, where everybody knows how important you are and you can be all phony—and everybody thinks it's adorable when you play your little games."

Callie found her voice, her eyes flashing. "You've got a lot of nerve, Tommy. I'm not playing little games, as you call them. Modeling is *work*. And, you know something, it's hard work. It might seem like a joke to you, but it's a serious business."

Her brother let out a snort of disbelief. "Oh, yeah, very serious. Real hard. Practically brain surgery."

Callie exploded in anger. "It may not seem like brain surgery to you, but whose hard work do you think is going to pay for your college tuition next year?"

As soon as the words were out, she regretted them. She had sworn to herself never to let Tommy know she was going to pay for his education, and here she'd already blurted it out before he'd even graduated high school. Seeing his stricken expression, she wanted to kick herself, or run over and hug him, tell him she was sorry.

He recovered his composure quickly. "Keep your damn money, Callie. You need it for your clothes and cars. I don't need it. And you know what?"—his voice rose to a yell—*"I don't want it."*

So that was going to be his attitude. Callie's face reddened with anger as her feelings flip-flopped from regret back to indignation. "If that's the thanks I get for trying to help you, fine, just forget it," she yelled back.

She turned and left the room, slamming the door hard behind her. A few seconds later she heard Tommy leave the house, but she made no move to go after him. She didn't mention the scene to her parents, and she struggled to hide her impatience when they dropped her off to catch her flight, delaying her with a shower of hugs and advice. Once the plane took off, she leaned back in her seat, overwhelmed by it all—Tommy, her parents, the whole visit. Confused and ashamed, she began to cry. Had she changed or had they? What was so wrong with being a successful model, learning to improve herself, and enjoying some of the better things life had to offer?

It was a miserable flight back to New York. But when she saw the city skyline coming into view as the plane descended for its landing, she started feeling better. If her family couldn't understand the things that had happened to her, then that was just how it would have to be. This was her new life and she loved it. And no one was going to ruin it for her.

9

It was seven o'clock. Kate and April wouldn't be there
for another fifteen minutes—assuming they were on time,
of course, which was unlikely, as April was famous for
being late. Callie, dressed and ready to go, picked up the
large envelope Whiting had sent over the day before. Having glanced inside when it first arrived, she knew it contained fan mail, but this was the first opportunity she'd
had to go through the contents. Fan mail. She couldn't
believe it. It was hard to imagine that people who had
seen her pictures had gone to the trouble of finding out
who she was, then actually taken the time to write to
her.

Dear Callie,
   *You are the most beautiful model ever. I want to be
just like you when I grow up. I'm thirteen and not much
happens in the town where I live. But I know if I come to*

where you are, things will be different. Maybe you could show me how to be a model too. I love you.
Crystal Toomey

Callie was touched. She wondered how she should answer. This young girl was sitting at home in—she glanced at the return address on the envelope—someplace in Texas that Callie had never heard of, thinking about Callie and dreaming of a future for herself. She opened the next letter.

Dear Callie,
I'm writing a paper for my eleventh-grade social studies class and I'm asking famous people to tell me what they think is the most important issue in current events today. Could you send me an answer? I'd also like an autographed picture of you. Thanks.
Your friend,
Sunny

Amazing. The time and caring behind these letters. She would have to give her answer to this one some special consideration, so that Sunny, whoever she was, would be happy with the response and have something useful to put in her paper for class. As far as an autographed picture went, she supposed she would use one of her composites. She wondered what the standard was, what the really famous models sent out.

The house phone buzzed, interrupting her thoughts. It was the doorman calling to tell her that her friends were downstairs. Not bad—only a half-hour late. Callie slipped all the letters back into the envelope and left it on the couch, grabbing a black leather blazer as she left. The past week had been unusually warm for early March, and she figured the blazer should be enough, particularly since Kate and April had somehow maneuvered for a limousine to drive them directly to all their stops that evening.

The doorman tipped his hat, holding the building's glass door open for Callie as she dashed out into the street. A chauffeur was standing by the curb, one hand on the open car door. Kate and April were ensconced in the backseat.

She hopped inside and kissed both of them lightly on the cheeks.

Callie had seen April just the night before. They'd gone out for dinner together and stayed out until two in the morning, having afterdinner drinks at the bar, flirting with the men there, talking shop. Callie had worked during the day, so April had come by the studio to pick her up. It was Callie's fifth ad for Day and Night. The cosmetics line did a great deal of advertising, constantly promoting the products through magazines, billboards, point-of-purchase displays, and every other form of media. Callie was pleased that they had booked her for so much print work, but she couldn't help hoping they would consider her for one of their television spots. That was really big time, and she felt she was ready.

Last week, she had gone so far as to request a brief meeting with Austin Whiting, telling him that she wanted to work in television and asking how the agency might help her break into commercials. Austin had merely told her that they would look into it and given her a patronizing pat on the arm as he ushered her out of his office. For the moment, though, print work kept her busy enough, with bookings nearly every day.

Having April come by yesterday's shoot had been great, perking Callie up at the end of the long day. How unlike the last time she had worked for Day and Night. She frowned, thinking back. Not that the company had anything to do with it being such a rotten experience. Their ad agency had booked Callie and Vida to pose together for what would eventually become a life-size cutout to go near the makeup counters. One of them was to represent the Day line, wearing the foundation and rouge and some light eye makeup, and dressed in a simple suit as if for work. The other represented Night, and the makeup and gown she wore stood for glamour, a night out on the town.

Both of them wanted to do the Night shot, but Vida had finessed Callie out of it. Somehow, Vida appeared almost immediately in the evening gown—just trying it on to see who fit into it best, "for the good of the shot," she said. She pointed out how terrific the dress looked on her, suggesting that Callie might have "just a touch" of trouble with it in the hips. The photographer obviously didn't care who took which part and waved his hand to indicate that the arrangement was fine, they should just hurry and get ready so he could start shooting, the Night girl first, please, since that would be a more difficult picture.

For the rest of the day Vida had upstaged Callie at every turn, delaying the start of shooting with requests to change her hair, consuming the photographer's attention, coming up with new ideas, wanting to try different things. None of this was Vida's typical style, Callie knew, which was to play all the political angles but to get finished with the shots as quickly as possible. Vida was just stalling, using up the day so there would be far less time for Callie's shot. Sure enough, when they finally got to her it was nearly four o'clock, and Callie was so frustrated that she was practically in tears.

This was supposed to be a fun night, though, and there was no reason to be thinking about Vida. Callie turned her attention back to the two women beside her.

"Are you recovered yet from last night?" she asked April.

"Sure I'm recovered. Hey, I'm perfect. Don't I look perfect?" April responded playfully to Callie's inquiry, twisting in her seat to show off a skimpy black blouse and striped pants. "I did have a killer headache this morning. But it's long gone, and I can't wait to see this movie. It's supposed to be great."

Kate looked outrageous as usual in a fuchsia dress, matching shoes, chunky black jewelry, and a black hat. On anyone else the outfit would have been awful, but Kate made it seem ultrafashionable and stylish.

"Thanks for taking us as your dates," Kate teased. It was April who had been invited to the premiere, and managed to arrange to take two guests along instead of one, as specified on the invitation.

April tossed her long hair back over her shoulders and out of the way. "What I'm really looking forward to is the party afterward. Everybody in the whole world will be there."

"Including Louie?" Callie asked archly. April and Louie were in one of their fighting phases again, which was why

April had chosen to bring her friends to the premiere instead of her boyfriend.

April replied airily, "If there's justice, Louie is rotting in hell this evening. If there's none, I suppose we may see him there."

Kate laughed loudly. "Well, I happen to know that a certain someone, an assistant photographer who shall remain nameless—namely Hal Arden—is going to be at the party," she confided. "And yours truly plans to move in on him, carefully, casually, but steadily."

"Like a spider moving in on a fly," Callie said with a grin.

They were all laughing as the sleek black car pulled up in front of the office building where the screening was held. The chauffeur opened the door for them and they rushed out, yelling their thanks as they went, telling him they would be back in two hours. Upstairs, the guests had already finished the complimentary cocktails and hors d'oeuvres and were settling down in the screening room. Scrambling to find seats, Callie and her friends grabbed the last three together in the back row, calling out greetings to the few people they recognized. They pretended not to notice all the heads turning to see who these three girls were; it was just something that happened, especially when models went out in groups. Callie and April were used to it.

As the houselights dimmed, Callie saw the door just behind them open one more time to admit a man. He was alone, and he slipped into a seat at the end of the row where Callie and her friends were, three chairs away. Tall and blond, dressed in a suit, the bright light that emanated from the screen lit up his face to reveal a startlingly handsome profile.

Callie felt a slight flutter in her stomach. He was incredible-looking. She had no idea who he was. Wanting to focus on the movie, she found she kept turning to glance at him. She really should pay attention, she told herself, especially since the movie was about something so close to home, a wildly successful model-turned-actress and her slide into oblivion. Finally she gave up all effort to watch the movie and just stared at him, wondering how she could manage to meet him. When the houselights came back up, she felt absurdly foolish, amazed she had wasted her time daydreaming and staring at this stranger, and had practically no idea what had happened in the film. The man didn't wait to read the credits, she noticed, but got up and slipped out of the room as unobtrusively as he had come. She could only hope he might turn up at the party.

The three of them went to the ladies' room to freshen up before leaving, Kate and April talking about how much they had liked the movie, despite the inaccuracies about the modeling business in it. Half-listening to their conversation, Callie brushed out her hair and reapplied some pale lipstick. She straightened out her short black skirt and smoothed down her taupe silk top, not completely displeased with her reflection, but wishing she had worn something a little more eye-catching in case she ran into the man from the screening later.

The party was at Manny's, the hot downtown spot of the moment. It was mobbed by the time Callie and her friends arrived. They got drinks and made their way through the narrow bar area, stopping to hug and kiss people they knew, exchanging exclamations of delight when they saw someone they hadn't seen in a while, gossiping with those they ran into more often. It was quite a scene, Callie thought, taking in the noisy crowd and the smattering of famous faces from the modeling and acting worlds.

Without wanting it to look like she had any destination, she worked her way through the crush of bodies, trying to get a glimpse into the back room where a late supper would be served; unless she checked out the whole restaurant, she wouldn't know if her mystery man was here. Kate and April fell away at different points. Callie caught a glimpse of April and Louie standing together, April shaking her head in annoyance as Louie talked animatedly, pointing his finger for emphasis. A few feet away, Kate was engrossed in conversation with a guy in a leather jacket; Callie hoped it was Hal Arden, the one Kate had mentioned.

She covered the length of the bar area and peered into the back room. He wasn't there. About to give up, she turned around and saw him just entering the party. Slowly retracing her steps, trying not to appear obvious, she watched him greet several people. He was even better-looking than she had thought, with piercing blue eyes and an aquiline nose. He must have gone directly from work to the screening, she decided, noting his well-tailored, conservative gray suit and paisley silk tie.

Here was her opportunity. He had stopped to talk to Michael Leeds, an art director Callie knew. She hastened over, slowing down just as she approached to make the meeting seem more casual.

"Michael, hi!" she called out, as if just noticing him for the first time.

He turned, his face brightening at the sight of her. "Callie, love, how nice to see you. Come here and give me a hug."

She obliged. When they separated, Michael turned to the man he'd been talking with.

"Callie Stewart, let me introduce David Long. David's director of marketing for Weston. David, Callie is with Whiting."

David Long extended a hand. "I'm glad to meet you."

Callie gave him a firm handshake. "Nice to meet you too. Actually, I've done some modeling for Weston. For the Day and Night line. I just did my fifth print ad for you the other day."

He frowned. "I'm very embarrassed, then. I should recognize you. Day and Night is in my group of product lines, and I usually know all our models."

"Don't give it a second thought," Callie replied with a laugh. It was hardly surprising that he didn't associate Callie in person with the heavily made-up and coiffed girl in the ads; many people had difficulty making the connection, because many models looked completely different in real life from the way they photographed.

"No." He shook his head. "It's not right. And I'll have to make it up to you."

He was flirting with her. Callie gave him her biggest smile, wanting to sigh with relief that he thought she was attractive.

"Let's see what we can come up with," she tossed back with an innocent look.

Michael, standing next to her, laughed at their obviousness, and she gave him a gentle, joking punch on the shoulder. Taking his cue, he drifted off into the crowd, leaving Callie and David alone.

"Were you at the screening?" he asked.

She nodded, hoping he wouldn't ask her anything about the film.

He reached out to take an hors d'oeuvre from a passing waiter's tray. "What did you think of the movie?"

She glanced away for a second, knowing that averting her eyes only made it look more like she was lying but unable to stop herself. "I liked it a lot. It was a bit sad to watch." *At least I hope it was,* she added silently, assuming that if the model in the movie fell from stardom it couldn't have had too upbeat an ending. She remembered Kate and April talking in the ladies' room. "And some of it wasn't all that accurate."

"Good performance by that actress, though. She's going to be a big star herself, maybe in another picture or two."

Relieved, she gently touched his forearm, eager to change the subject.

"Have you eaten anything tonight? I'm starving, and they're starting to serve dinner in back."

David held out his arm for her and said in an exaggeratedly formal tone, "Shall we dine, then?"

"I really don't understand why this happened." It was hard for Callie to speak so directly, but she forced herself, even though her tone was gentle and gave little indication of how angry she was. "Couldn't you have told me earlier what I should be doing?"

She closed her eyes in annoyance and resignation as she listened to the answer. A bunch of nonsense. This guy had to be the worst accountant in the world. Having gotten his name from her old roommate, Lanny, she had employed him the preceding year to do her taxes, but she hadn't made that much money between July and December, so it was all pretty straightforward back then. She hadn't given it a thought, assuming he had done what was right.

But from this past January to December was another financial story altogether, and he hadn't given her a word of advice. Today was the first time she was hearing her total income for the year—over two hundred thousand dollars—and not one dollar of it had been invested or put to any practical use. She had dutifully reported to the accountant everything she had earned, figuring he would let her know when and how she should do something with it. But he had told her nothing, beyond the delightful news today that she was going to pay a walloping amount of taxes and that she had earned nothing more on all of it than the interest of a savings account.

It's my own fault, she berated herself angrily. *I should have been more involved.* But even as she thought it, she knew she didn't want any part of these things. She would just have to find someone better for next year. And a lawyer, too. At the agency, she often heard models talking about their investments, and some of them were involved in complicated business dealings. Even if she wasn't the kind who loved discussing the ins and outs of her finances, she had better get on the stick and do something with her money. She didn't want to be one of those models who frittered away their earnings.

Ending the conversation, she dejectedly flopped down on the couch. *I'm not going to be as stupid next year,* she vowed. And with that, she got up to prepare for her booking, which was for a very upscale catalog, with two lingerie shots. Nothing tacky, she knew, or she wouldn't have taken the job no matter how good the money was. Lingerie ads paid five hundred dollars an hour, with a minimum of two hours; the clock started ticking on the lingerie segment of the shoot from the second a model walked onto the set until the second she walked off, the time billed in fifteen-minute increments. Grace had extracted assurances from the client that Callie would be posing in a one-piece teddy, or tap pants and a camisole—no bras and panties or garter-belt stuff, even if it was a respectable catalog and the photographs were considered fairly artsy by people in the business.

Callie went into her bedroom and began to get dressed. Tonight she had a late dinner date with a man she'd met at a party the week before, and she estimated she would have enough time for a quick nap after her booking before she had to get ready for the evening. *Good,* she thought. She was overtired, working long days and staying out late practically every night. It wasn't a smart policy, she was well aware of that, and very unlike her normally. But recently she had begun to feel as if she was missing something, as if life would pass her by if she didn't get out and grab every second of it.

Maybe it was because she couldn't find a decent boyfriend. She'd certainly tried, but nothing ever worked out. There were plenty of men around who were eager to date a model, but no one gave her the sense of security, of belonging, that she'd experienced with Jean in Paris. She smiled at the memory of him, faded but still able to elicit a warm feeling. She remembered how she'd cried over him in the months after leaving him, wondering if the happiness had been worth the pain. They'd written to each other for a while, but there hadn't been another opportunity for Callie to go to Europe, and eventually the letters and calls stopped.

Since then, she had watched other women moving in with their boyfriends, marrying, or getting involved in long-term relationships. But nothing had ever worked out that way for her. It wasn't that anything bad happened—just that no one really special came along.

After that night of the movie premiere, she'd had high hopes—irrationally high, she saw—for David Long. There was something about him that made her feel comfortable and protected. His air of self-assurance and success was matched by a sharp intelligence and wit. He was everything she wanted, and she had tried hard to make him like her. But at the end of the evening he had given her a good-night kiss on the cheek and left, without even asking for her telephone number. That had been more than two weeks ago.

Two weeks ago. With a start, Callie realized it was nearly the end of March. That meant she had missed her mother's birthday, on March fourteenth. She sighed deeply. Birthdays were considered a big deal in her family. Yet, neither of her parents had called to remind her or even to berate her for not sending a present or phoning her mother this year. In fact, it had to be at least five or six weeks since she'd last spoken to them. Maybe longer. There was so little left to say to them, it seemed. And she and Tommy still weren't speaking, though by unspoken agreement they both hid that fact from their parents. As she slipped into a pair of white jeans, she guiltily told herself she would call as soon as she got home from her booking; there was no time left now. As it was, she would be late if she didn't get out of there in the next five minutes.

The doorbell rang. Buttoning up a white shirt, she ran to answer it. A messenger stood in the hall, envelope in hand. Callie signed for it and closed the door. Her name and address were written in caligraphy on the front; there was no return address. She tore open the heavy ecru envelope, revealing a card of thick stock inside with black script engraving on it. Probably a wedding invitation. As she read, a broad smile spread across her face.

Mr. David W. Long
requests the pleasure of
Miss Callie Stewart's exquisitely charming company
for an evening of dinner and dancing
The Rainbow Room
Saturday at Eight o'Clock
Can you make it?

The maître d' escorted them to their table. Callie was pleased to see many of the other patrons casting glances in her direction as she and David passed their tables. She had made a good choice in wearing the strapless, bronze-colored gown. She'd wanted to look just right tonight, and it had taken her hours to decide on the dress, set off with small pearl earrings and a simple double-stranded pearl bracelet, her hair pinned up in a French twist. The admiring look in David's eyes when he picked her up had been reassuring. Now she felt even better as eyes followed them through the crowd.

David was even more handsome than she remembered, tall and lean in his tuxedo. His warm smile and the way he held her hand as they went down the elevator to her lobby had her practically floating into the waiting limousine. The maître d' pulled out a chair for Callie and she perched on the edge of it, watching everything going on around her, thrilled to be in such a beautiful restaurant high above New York with this exciting man.

Champagne arrived. Their glasses were filled, then the bottle was placed in a silver bucket on a stand beside their table.

"To a wonderful night," David toasted, lifting his glass to her.

"It's already wonderful," Callie answered softly, returning the toast.

They took their time over dinner, enjoying the food, talking quietly. David told Callie that he was the eldest of four children, had grown up in Seattle, come east to college at Dartmouth, then settled in New York. His parents and siblings still lived in Seattle, within a few miles of one another.

"How did you get into the cosmetics business?" Callie asked, taking another bite of her chicken.

"I started with a computer company, then I moved from job to job in that field before getting to a small cosmetics firm, and finally to Weston."

"Wasn't that a big change from computers?"

David shook his head. "Marketing is marketing. I've been lucky in that I've been able to apply the business principles I believe in at Weston, and they've worked. So I've been promoted a lot, and pretty quickly."

"You must be very good at what you do," Callie said sincerely.

David smiled. "I like to think so. Now I'm in charge of marketing for Group A. The group includes several product lines along with Day and Night, some of them more expensive, some less. Thanks to Joseph Mann, I've got a great deal of autonomy in my job."

"Joseph Mann?"

"Weston's CEO. He's my personal role model, a real self-made guy. I admire Mann for his combination of brains, directness, and vision."

With that, David wanted to hear all about Callie for the rest of the evening. Refilling her champagne glass, he began asking questions, learning about her family, and how much had changed in her life since she'd come to New York. She found herself telling him how lonely she'd been as a teenager, and how awful her visit home had been over Christmas, one kind of isolation from her peers having been traded for another. He listened with obvious sympathy, and agreed with her that changes and breaks with the past were unavoidable as some people grew and went on to become successful while the rest stayed behind.

It seemed as if they had just sat down when the band began to play and David asked her to dance before they ordered dessert. He escorted her onto the dance floor and took her in his arms. Callie felt the strength in his hands, the easy but firm way he held her close. She leaned her cheek gently in to touch his and closed her eyes happily, relishing the moment. They moved together effortlessly, David expertly gliding her around the floor. Callie inhaled his light aftershave, and the delicious smell of him underneath that scent.

As the music ended, she pulled back to look at him, their eyes meeting for a moment. Then, slowly, he brought his mouth to hers. They remained there without moving, the softness of her lips pressed against the giving firmness of his, the intensity of feeling growing between them. The music started up again, and they reluctantly pulled apart, David putting one hand gently on Callie's cheek. Nothing had to be said.

They walked off the dance floor and gathered their things, David quickly taking care of the bill. The limousine took them directly to David's home on Sutton Place. Callie barely had a chance to look around the large apartment before David took her in his arms again, his kiss gentle at first, then more urgent. He ran his hands up her bare arms, caressing her shoulders, her cheeks. With one deft move, he loosened her hair, stroking it, whispering her name. She sighed with pleasure.

Her hands went inside his jacket, to slip it off, and he shrugged it from his shoulders with her help, then pulled her to him again. She heard the sound of her dress's zipper being opened in one long, slow motion. They sank down on the oriental carpet together, helping each other out of their clothes, their kisses probing and hot. Callie saw the desire in his eyes, and she reveled in knowing how much he wanted her. Their lovemaking was hurried, their hunger demanding. When it was over she lay in his arms, their clothes in disarray on the floor beside them. She was shocked at herself, at her response to him, but she loved what they had just shared.

David reached over and grabbed the edge of the carpet, pulling it over to form a cover for the two of them. He took a deep, satisfied breath. This girl had a lot of potential, he could tell. Of course, when they were initially introduced, he had recognized her as one of the models they used for Day and Night—what kind of director of marketing would he be if he hadn't?—but he didn't have to tell her that.

It had all worked out smoothly. This girl would make a perfect replacement for Sabrina. *She'd* been a mistake, that was for sure. Sabrina had been doing well as a model, but then her career suddenly went flat and she'd driven David crazy with her complaining. Six months of her had been more than enough. But this one had some class, and she was far more beautiful. Callie was the perfect woman with whom to walk into a room—he'd seen that tonight, the way everybody stared at her. She was just what he wanted, just the kind of woman he should be with. Young, giving, incredible to look at, and obviously ready to fall in love with him.

He leaned over to give her a kiss on the forehead, and she smiled up at him contentedly.

In the weeks that followed, several people at the agency and at her shoots commented on the way Callie practically glowed. It wasn't hard to figure out that she was in love, and her co-workers teased her mercilessly. She didn't care, laughing at their comments, happy to join in on the fun at her own expense. Kate and April were amazed at the change in her. Although she had always been fun-loving and easy to be with, they said, now she was positively ebullient. That David Long was definitely a good influence on her.

Callie couldn't have agreed more. It was as if she had finally found the man she had been waiting for, searching for all these months. He was so solidly grounded and made her feel so safe. At just twenty-eight, she raved to her friends, he was incredibly accomplished professionally and knew exactly where he was going in life. And Callie was certain after only a few weeks that, wherever he might be going, she wanted to be there too.

His executive status at Weston was impressive, but it also meant that he worked long hours, and she tried not to show her disappointment when he called to break a date or, worse, told her he would be too busy to see her for the next week, possibly longer. When they were together, Callie knew he cared for her, and she lost herself in their lovemaking, happier than she had ever been. In their free time they went everywhere in New York, to all the tourist sights she had missed or learned to avoid as being too hokey—with David, they were fun. They would go shopping, walking, scouring art galleries and museums, exploring new restaurants and neighborhoods she'd never seen before. Her favorite times were the Sunday mornings they spent in bed, eating bagels and reading the *New York Times,* the phone turned off as they made love off and on all day and into the night.

She tried not to think about how elusive he was at other times, not even calling during those periods when he said he would be too busy with work to see her. Sometimes she would call him after a week or ten days had passed, and he always sounded happy to hear from her, ready to see her within the next day or two. Each time, she secretly wondered what would have happened if she hadn't called him. How long would it have been before he called her?

During those periods she became increasingly anxious and fearful that he would just disappear or suddenly break the news that he had a new girlfriend. When he wasn't around she couldn't think of anything but him, and she hurried home at night in case he should call. Kate had warned her about becoming hooked on him, setting herself up for a fall, but Callie wasn't interested. David Long was the man she wanted, and she was determined to have him.

David was also helping her professionally, beginning to give her some advice about her career. He could teach her things, starting with the fact that she was making a lot of money for Whiting now and should stop acting as if she worked for them. It was the other way around. Callie had never thought of it like that before, always assuming they could fire her at any moment. But of course what David said was true, she was worth a lot to them now, and she could say no to jobs she didn't want.

He also told her to demand that Whiting lower their commission when her contract came up for renewal. There wasn't anything wrong with Whiting's taking 20 percent of her earnings, but other models paid less, as much as 10 percent less, depending on how powerful they were and how much they brought in to the agency's coffers. Callie would never have known about any of this, or had the nerve to do anything about it, without David's urging. It took her a few weeks to work up the courage, but she went to Austin and told him she wanted the agency's fee lowered. She was stunned when Austin told her they would review the contract in Legal and work something out. It was so easy. If only she had found David earlier, she thought. He could handle things like this; he knew what to do. Other models had husbands and boyfriends who went to bat for them or advised them. Now, she did too.

Everything was changing so quickly, it seemed, and Callie began to see it more clearly on a morning in mid-May. The day had started off with an obscene phone call from a so-called fan, a heavy breather who kept whispering her name into the phone. *What a delightful way to wake up,* she said to herself as she hurried into the shower, resolving to get a new, unlisted number. An hour later she had received another call, this one from the agency telling her that an actor, a hot star who was in a new hit movie, wanted to know if Callie would go to a party with him. Callie declined. It was the third such call she had received in the past two months, famous men she didn't even know calling to ask for dates. Several of the models, she knew, had met their boyfriends that way, rock stars and actors having spotted them in magazines and called up the agency to track them down. These girls were heroines of the day when they came into the agency giving out free tickets to their boyfriends' rock concerts or movie premieres. But that wasn't Callie's style. Besides, she had David now.

She filled the kettle with water for tea and set it on the stove, wishing David had come over last night. He'd called at six-thirty to break their date, telling her he was up against a deadline, apologizing, and promising he would try to make it over later that night if he could manage it. He had never shown up.

Her glance fell on a pile of fan mail on the kitchen table, still to be answered. There were more and more letters coming in, she realized. And yesterday she'd been recognized on the street twice. Two teenage girls walking on Third Avenue had squealed and poked each other when she turned a corner and came face to face with them; Callie had heard her name whispered as she passed. Later in the day, a woman in her twenties had stared at Callie as they both stood in line at the drugstore, her expression making it clear that she knew who Callie was. This sort of thing was occurring a lot more frequently now.

Something was definitely happening, Callie reflected. Her book was overflowing with ads, editorial spreads from the best magazines, and cover shots. She now had regular meetings with an accountant and a lawyer, who suggested investments that were too complex for her to understand, but who bandied about numbers that startled her; it was hard for her to imagine that she could afford these investments, despite their assurances that she could. She just kept busy working, taking all the bookings that came her way as long as they weren't anything she considered immodest or dangerous, such as shots posed on high ledges. People obviously liked her, since she got a lot of jobs from the same clients over and over. Day and Night, for one, had hired her over a dozen times now. And it had been a treat doing that swimsuit editorial in the Caribbean two months ago, as close to a vacation as she was likely to get for some time.

Beyond that, she didn't see much of what was happening around her. Or *to* her, apparently, she thought. She turned her eye to a pile of magazines on the far end of the table. All of them contained shots of her, and she hadn't even had a chance to look at them. Things were changing, there was no question about it.

10

Callie rummaged around in her red canvas bag until she located the small Thermos of martinis. Pulling it out, she leaned over to refresh the half-empty drink David had put down in the sand next to his beach chair.

"Want something to eat with your drink, sweetheart?" she asked.

"No. I'm just going to sit here like a log and enjoy the sunset," he answered, stretching his legs out in front of him.

Callie refilled her glass and put the Thermos back into the bag. Then she too leaned back in her chair, and they sat silently watching the red ball of sun dropping in the sky. It was quiet now, most of the swimmers and sunbathers having left, retreating for showers and naps before their Saturday night began. Callie loved the beach here, and this was her favorite time of day, when the area was nearly deserted and so peaceful.

"I suppose we should be getting back," she murmured

halfheartedly, adjusting her wide-brimmed straw hat. "Tate will be wondering what became of us."

David's eyes were closing in contentment. "Not yet. And Tate has a houseful of other people to play with. We're not on his mind at all, I promise you."

That was probably true, Callie thought. David's friend Tate Winters always surrounded himself with people. Whenever they met up with him in New York he had an entourage of at least four, often more. At his summer house in Southampton there were rarely fewer than eight guests on any given weekend. David and Callie had already come out twice this summer. Callie felt a bit guilty for continually accepting his hospitality without being able to reciprocate in some equivalent way, but David had reassured her that this was the way his friend wanted it. Tate, he insisted, would have been miserable without swarms of friends, acquaintances, and general hangers-on noisily filling the well-appointed rooms in the rambling Winters family house that overlooked the water. That was simply what Tate did, he said, have people over to dinner or for the weekend or as guests in his Aspen ski house.

Callie could now understand that, having met more and more people like Tate in the past year or so, young men and women with inherited wealth who had never worked, and who spent their days—well, *socializing* was the only word she could think of to describe it. Always fun and ready for a party, Tate was completely aimless, seemingly not the type of person her hardworking, disciplined David would befriend. Yet he had a great charm and ease about him. Callie had observed him at dinner parties, able to draw out even the most shy or dull companion, always adding a special spark to the evening. That was a skill unto itself, she knew. Besides, she saw how much David enjoyed the few breaks they took here at the house, how much he liked meeting the wild assortment of guests who showed up. Often they were powerful or influential people from the business world, David had told her, and he made valuable contacts over the lobsters and fresh corn on Saturday night or eggs Benedict at Sunday brunch.

Brushing sand off her legs, Callie got up from her chair and kneeled down on the blanket next to David. His eyes were still closed. She gazed lovingly at his tanned face, framed by blond hair bleached even lighter by the summer sun. David, it turned out, was an excellent tennis player, and they tried to play together whenever they could find the time. Too busy to practice as often as she would have liked, Callie's game had slipped, and, while she occasionally let David win, once in a while he beat her fair and square in spite of her best efforts.

Grains of sand clung to his forehead. She gently brushed them off, leaning in to kiss him lightly on the mouth.

"Mmmm," he responded in satisfaction.

She started to pull back, but he surprised her by quickly reaching out and grabbing her by both shoulders, his eyes open now.

"Where do you think you're going, my pretty?" he cackled in his best falsetto imitation of a witch.

Callie laughed as he wrapped his arms around her. He brought her to him for a deep, long kiss. Later, when they got up to leave, the sun had fully set, leaving blazing streaks of color to paint the sky.

David's mood was less sanguine the following evening as they sat in traffic, barely crawling along the Long Island Expressway on the way back to Manhattan.

"Damn, we should have left earlier," he muttered in irritation.

Callie bit her lip. She couldn't stand it when David got annoyed or angry, even if it had nothing to do with her. In the five months they'd been dating, he was usually even-tempered, but when he had a difficult day at work or the considerable pressures of his job got to him, he angered easily and turned a sharp tongue on her.

Exasperated, he finally pulled out of the right lane and began to drive along the shoulder of the road.

"David, honey, please don't do this," Callie pleaded. "You'll get a ticket. And it's dangerous."

She saw his face harden in anger.

"Don't tell me it's dangerous. I'm a great driver," he

snapped. "And we've got to get back. I've got projections to go over before tomorrow, and I'll be up all night."

Callie recoiled from the sting of his words. "I'm sorry," she said quietly.

She shouldn't have said anything; it was obvious that she would only start an argument. Besides, he *was* a great driver. The old Mercedes was his pride and joy, and he loved to drive it at high speeds, zipping along the highway, the radio blasting. It was his way of letting off steam, she knew.

They rode in silence for a few minutes. David swung the car back into the right-hand lane, cursing under his breath. She cast around in her mind for something to say that would distract him.

"Oh, I completely forgot to tell you," she began lightly. "I've got another booking for Day and Night tomorrow. That makes— I've lost count by now."

"Which product?" David asked with only mild interest.

"A mascara, from the Day line. Come on, 'fess up. You're the one who's secretly been arranging for me to get all this work from them."

David glanced at her in annoyance. "Callie, you know better than that. We've already talked about how it would compromise me completely to start pushing my girlfriend as a model for the company. That hasn't changed. You can't imagine I would be so unprofessional." He paused. They had stopped moving again, and he pressed the heel of his hand on the car horn in frustration. Callie restrained herself from pointing out that honking would do no good.

"I know, but there've been so many bookings, I thought . . ."

"The ad agency makes the selection and we give final approval," he said. "I've seen you come up as a choice a number of times, but I've never even hinted that they should use you."

"Oh." Chastised, Callie looked straight ahead. She had naturally assumed that David had something to do with the accelerated rate of bookings she'd been getting from Weston in the past few months. But she could see that of course he was right, it would be inappropriate for him to suggest using

Callie in their ads. Although she was a little taken aback that he hadn't done anything to help her, she also realized it was far more of a compliment to her: David was indirectly telling her she'd gotten all that work strictly on her own merit. Knowing that made her feel good. She turned to gaze out the window on her side, hiding the smile she couldn't suppress.

Lying in bed, snug under the white down comforter, Callie watched the snow fall outside her window. Thanksgiving was just a couple of days away, and she was taking today off. Tomorrow she had a booking for another Day and Night ad, and then she and David were off to spend the holiday weekend with friends of his in Vermont.

She stretched lazily. She had noticed how the bookings from Day and Night had dropped off slightly after the summer before picking up again in early October. At first she'd been afraid she had done something wrong, or that the ad people were annoyed that she was dating David and didn't want to use her for that reason. When they started asking for her again, she wondered if they had been trying out other models, then deciding in the end that they liked her after all. It was so hard to tell, considering how much shooting they did. For all she knew, they could have dozens of girls they liked to use, and she was just one among many. But she was delighted to note that, for whatever reason, she was back in their good graces. They had even chosen her as the face for an entire print campaign for an eye cream from the Night Skincare line.

With things going so well between her and David, she took extra care to be especially friendly yet professional on the Day and Night sets. She would never want to do anything that would embarrass David if it should get back to him. He had changed her life so much, making everything easier, letting her know in so many little ways that he would take care of her.

It was a vast relief to have someone to lean on, knowing he had an eye on her interests. He continued to push her to stand up for herself at the agency and not do anything she didn't want to do. The security of his love made her bolder, and she found herself able to turn down the more distasteful jobs that she would never have dared decline before. Together, she thought with satisfaction, they were building some kind of foundation. Ever since the summer she had been entertaining fantasies of marriage; she was afraid to say anything about it, but she hoped that the idea had planted itself somewhere in the back of David's mind and would eventually work its way forward.

She threw off the covers and headed to the bathroom for a shower. Just as she placed a foot under the inviting stream of water, the telephone rang. Callie wrapped a towel around herself for warmth and hurried back to the bedroom to answer it, her one wet foot leaving tracks across the wooden floor.

"Hi, it's me."

Callie recognized Grace's low voice immediately.

"Hey there. How are you, and what's up?" she asked.

"Nothing really." There was a slight pause. "But I had an idea and I wanted you to think about it over the holiday. It's just a germ of a twinkle of a spark, really."

Callie laughed. "Sounds like something very definite."

"I was going over your bookings, and the Day and Night people are obviously very hot for you. They hire a lot of girls, but you've been getting work consistently from them, and they're for good ads now, the big national stuff, not just regional promotions and the like. The public has seen you connected with Day and Night a lot." Callie heard Grace taking a puff from her cigarette. "Anyway," Grace went on, "it occurred to me that there might, *might,* mind you, be the possibility of an exclusive contract here. If they like you as much as they seem to, maybe they would consider it."

"Grace, you're kidding."

"Why would I be kidding?"

Callie was speechless. An exclusive contract meant a model was so desirable that a company was willing to pay big dollars to keep her from working for anyone else. The model could make a huge amount of money, and become famous as the face of that particular company, especially if it was a nationally known, prestigious cosmetics company. She would have a limited number of work days per year, which was far easier than the unpredictable day-to-day grind of regular modeling, and would give her plenty of free time. An exclusive contract with a firm as big as Weston was pretty much the greatest success a model could hope to achieve.

"Sleep on it over the weekend," Grace said. "Think about whether you would want us to pursue this. Not that I'm saying it's actually a possibility, but we'd have to know it's what you want before we even broached the subject."

Callie grinned. "There's nothing to think about. I'm not crazy. Of course I'd want it. What would you say to the Weston people?"

Grace considered the question. "Just something along the lines that they seem to like you, you like them, and maybe there's an interesting possibility for exclusivity here. You know, we'd try to convince them that this is like a couple dating, and the company has to make a commitment to the relationship."

"Well, I'm all for it."

"Okay, just sounding you out. I'll take the idea to Austin and Fredericka. These are very sensitive discussions, and they usually fall apart at the drop of a hat. So remember, not a word to anyone that we even speculated about this."

"Even to David?" Callie asked wistfully.

"Especially David." Grace sounded alarmed. "For now."

"I understand. And thank you, Grace. You're terrific."

"At the very least," Grace replied playfully. "Gotta run. I don't have time to fool around with the likes of you."

Hanging up, Callie stood where she was. What an incredible idea, having an exclusive contract. It would never happen, the whole thing was only a fantasy. The Weston people would just laugh at the Whitings. Still, she wished she could tell David that Grace had even suggested it. It would be horrible to keep a secret from him. But Grace was right, this wasn't the time to blather on about such a thing before the agency had a chance to broach the idea with the right people. There would be plenty of time later to talk about it—and, unfortunately, to laugh about it, since it was so unlikely. But it was a tantalizing thought and incredibly flattering. Humming, she walked back to the bathroom and showered.

Unlikely as it seemed to Callie, the Weston people didn't laugh at Grace's idea. Throughout December and January, they talked about the possibility. Grace told Callie that it was all in the preliminary stages, no mention of money yet, everything barely creeping along. But at least they were talking.

In late January, Callie was surprised to get a call from Austin himself, who brusquely instructed her to be at the Weston offices the next day at 9:00 A.M. sharp to meet Walter Furst, president of Group A, Day and Night's division. By this point, Austin's abruptness was to be expected, Callie having learned long ago that the charm he'd exhibited when she and her family first met him was only brought out on occasions like those, where it would be most advantageous to the agency. Typically, she found he was disdainful of the models and had as little to do with them as possible, preferring to spend his time negotiating deals and contracts, handling the running of the business. She politely thanked him and told him she would be there on time.

As thrilled as she was, Callie hadn't anticipated how anxious she would be about the interview. She turned to David in a panic, who by now knew all about the contract negotiations. He couldn't help her land the contract by influencing his people, he told her, but he would be on the sidelines rooting and advising her in any way he could. When he heard about the meeting, he quickly gave her the lowdown on Walter Furst: an older, conservative man who demanded a certain decorum from the people who worked around him. They determined that she should be upbeat but reserved. With David's help, Callie picked out an elegant Chanel suit for the meeting, its shorter skirt and sleek lines an updated version of the traditional.

On the morning of the meeting, dressed and applying a quick spray of cologne, her nails freshly manicured, her hair swept up in a chignon, Callie took a deep breath and tried to stay calm. She went downstairs to meet the limousine Weston had sent for her, checking and rechecking her makeup in her compact's mirror, and fussing with her skirt and blouse, certain she was going to make a fool of herself. This was more nerve-racking, she decided, than the first day she had come to Whiting over two years before. Then, she'd had no idea what was at stake. Now she knew all too well.

The limousine dropped her off at Weston headquarters on West Fifty-seventh Street. Callie took the elevator to the fortieth floor and the receptionist immediately summoned Walter Furst's secretary, who ushered her inside, their footsteps in the hall silenced by the thick beige carpeting. The offices were quiet and luxurious, she saw, bespeaking the money and success behind Weston's considerable clout in the cosmetics industry. Framed photographs of the company's products were arranged on the walls as carefully as if they had been paintings in a museum.

The secretary poked her head into an office, then held the door open for Callie to enter. Walter Furst was coming around from behind his desk, balding and portly, a friendly smile on his face. They shook hands and sat down in the two French Provincial chairs by the window. Callie glanced around the room. It was as understated as David had said Walter himself was, decorated in browns and beiges, nothing jarring to the eye.

"So, I hear you're going to do something special for Day and Night," Walter said. "Work some magic for us, eh?"

"I'd like to," Callie replied. She was suddenly reminded of the evening she'd been summoned to Jack Norton's office to meet Bob Holt, the talent scout who had discovered her. Was it another lifetime ago? How hard she'd tried to sit still and hold her hands properly. She had the urge to revert to those lessons again. She crossed her legs at the ankles, but forced herself to settle back a bit in the chair, wanting to appear less rigid. The secretary entered and set down on the coffee table a tray with bone white china cups and saucers and a sterling coffeepot. Callie declined the coffee, afraid she might spill it on herself in her nervousness.

Walter rested his hand on the chair's arm, his forefinger tapping distractedly. "This is a big decision," he said.

"True. But I'll bet you'd like to get the damn thing made and over with as much as I would," Callie blurted.

There was silence for a moment. Callie froze. She couldn't believe she had said such a thing. But Walter Furst broke out into a loud laugh.

"You're an honest one, aren't you?" he said, his eyes twinkling with amusement. "I like that."

They continued to talk. Callie soon discovered he came from Indianapolis. With that, they launched into reminiscences of Indiana and everything they loved or hated about their shared home state. The time passed easily, and she was amazed at how relaxed she felt by the time he looked at his watch, signaling, she thought, that the meeting was over. Quickly, she rose.

"I appreciate all the time you've given me, Mr. Furst," she said.

"Walter, please," he corrected her. "And I don't want you to leave yet. I'd like you to come meet Joseph Mann, Weston's president and CEO. He'll have the final say. He's seen your pictures, naturally, but he should get acquainted with you in person. He's expecting us."

"Of course. I'd be delighted, Walter." Callie spoke warmly, though her heart rose in her throat at the idea of having to pass muster with a second top executive that morning.

Walter walked Callie to Mann's office, and Callie comforted herself as they went with the thought that David was at work on the floor below. Joseph Mann's office was twice as large as Walter's, decorated with antiques but a minimum of bric-a-brac and personal items. The desk, couch, and coffee table were all of the finest quality, and virtually clear of clutter.

Clutter, Callie saw, would not become the man who greeted her there. Well over six feet, with silvery hair and a chiseled face, Joseph Mann looked polished and important. Callie registered his expensive suit, his pants and jacket perfectly tailored, the white shirt beneath undoubtedly custom-made. He was definitely from Central Casting, she thought, repressing the urge to laugh, the perfect company chairman.

"Miss Stewart." He came to the door to greet her, taking her right hand in both of his. His voice was low and well modulated, and his brown eyes gazed into hers as if there were no one and nothing else on earth. She felt the power of his presence.

"It's a great pleasure to meet you, Mr. Mann," she said.

Kim Alexis & Cynthia Katz

He led her to the beige tweed couch and they sat down. Walter positioned himself in a chair nearby.

"You know, we've never had an exclusive face connected to a Weston product line before," he told her, sitting forward. "This would be a big step for us. It would be something of a grand experiment, and we would put our every resource behind making it a success."

There was great intensity in his words. No wonder David was always talking about him, about how inspiring he was, what a role model he made, Callie thought. Instinctively, she knew this was a man who could get people to push themselves to perform for him, to exceed even their own expectations of themselves with his encouragement.

"It would be a big step for both of us," she replied, "but I believe it would be a good one. I've done a lot of work for Day and Night, as you know, and I'd like to think I understand the kind of face and image you want to represent the line. I would do my best to be that image for you."

He gazed at her in silence. Callie tried not to show her discomfort at his scrutiny. Then a smile crossed his handsome face.

From that day on, the discussions between Weston and Whiting moved forward at a slow but steady pace. Grace told Callie that things had progressed far enough for her to get a lawyer. Having no idea whom to use, she asked the Legal Department to recommend someone, and they sent her to Rick Fields, the absolute best for things like this, they told her. After spending two hours in Rick's office discussing the details of what had to be negotiated, Callie felt comfortable with him, relieved that he would be handling what was obviously a very complex deal. She couldn't believe all the areas that would be covered in the contract, everything from prohibiting Callie's use of obscenity in public, to maintenance of her weight and appearance, to what would happen if she became pregnant.

Now, as Grace put it, the dance began in earnest. She advised Callie on what jobs to accept while the negotiations were in progress, telling her to refuse ads for competing cosmetics firms or products such as deodorants or sanitary napkins, anything that might even slightly turn off Weston to her image. Callie was bewildered by the intrigue of it, but Grace insisted everything had to be handled just right.

When Callie was booked to model for a top fashion magazine, Grace held discussions with them about the types of cosmetics that would be used on the shoot. Callie must appear only in Weston products, she told them, or the photos would have to be held for at least six months. These kinds of talks with other clients were very sensitive, the booker confided in Callie, since the agency didn't want the news of the negotiations getting around the industry, but the restrictions had to be imposed.

Callie quickly got to see for herself how delicate the process was. Day and Night was still hiring her for work, but they often seemed to be testing her now, keeping her in front of the camera for long hours at a stretch, dressing her on location so that she was either overheated or freezing all day long, finishing her makeup job and then insisting it be completely redone, having her pose in difficult conditions. In May, Callie and David took their first vacation together, but their long-planned week of isolated rest and relaxation on St. John's was interrupted when Day and Night called her back for a shoot right in the middle of their trip. Grace agreed with Callie that the company was indeed testing her, finding out if she had the disposition they wanted for their Day and Night girl. With so much money at stake, they couldn't afford to make a mistake. Callie remained good-natured at all times, refusing to let even a hint of displeasure cross her face.

As spring turned into summer, Callie came to believe that the whole thing would never happen. It had taken too long, she thought, dragging on for well over six months. She hadn't even heard from her lawyer in weeks. She had a hard time fighting off the disappointment. But what difference did the contract make? she asked herself, annoyed for having believed it would actually come to pass. She was earning plenty of money and would just continue doing what she had been doing.

Then, on a Friday afternoon in mid-July, Rick Fields telephoned her at home to announce that the deal was done.

The contract was waiting for her signature, and the big event was scheduled to take place in Fredericka's office the following Monday. As the Day and Night girl, he told Callie, she would be earning four million dollars, paid out in escalating amounts every six months over the course of three years, working twenty days a year for Weston and no one else. The deal called for a mix of print and television work, plus personal appearances at up to twenty public functions that Weston deemed appropriate. They were paying for her exclusivity and her commitment to them as a spokesperson. After three years, they would have the option to renew the contract.

After the signing of the deal, he went on, the Weston publicity machine would crank into high gear, and her name and face would be everywhere they could get exposure for them, starting with the announcement of the contract, and then as Day and Night's image. She would be the look of today; she would set the trends.

Callie was so shocked by the amount of money involved and the realization that it had actually happened, she barely managed to mumble a thank-you to her lawyer before she hung up the telephone. She sat down cross-legged on the floor, not knowing what to do with herself. For a long time she remained there, motionless. Then she thought of David, and leaped up to grab the phone, almost too excited to dial his number. *Wait until he hears the news!* she thought. *Can life be any sweeter?*

"Honey, I got it! *I got it!*" she burst out the second he picked up the phone.

"What?" he asked distractedly. Realizing what she was talking about, he laughed. "Oh, baby, you mean the contract? It's great, isn't it? I found out two days ago, but I didn't want to spoil the surprise."

"You *knew?* And you didn't tell me?" Callie yelled in indignation. "How could you keep a secret like that?"

"It wouldn't have been as much fun for you," he replied. "Congratulations. We'll celebrate later."

"David," she half-whispered, suddenly serious, "it's *so* much money." At the same time, she wondered how it compared with what the other top models with exclusive deals were getting. The financial terms of exclusive contracts were well-guarded secrets, and though she'd heard of amounts going as high as six million dollars, she had no idea if that was accurate.

"If you don't want all that money, tell them to forget about it," David teased.

"Not on your life." She wished he were there so she could throw her arms around him, kiss him, make love with him. "Hurry over, okay?"

"See you around eight-thirty."

"I love you," she said, already planning their evening.

It was a jubilant Callie who floated into Fredericka's office on Monday morning. She discovered a room full of people waiting for her: Fredericka, Austin, Rick Fields, and two men who she assumed represented Weston, along with a photographer apparently hired to record the moment.

"Darling, oh, *darling,*" Fredericka gushed when she turned around and saw Callie in the doorway. For this special occasion, the head of the agency wore a lemon-yellow turban and a linen suit of the same color. She hurried forward to embrace Callie. "Vhat a happy day for all of us, no?"

Callie had long ago noticed that Fredericka's grasp of English lessened when she was around people from whom she wanted something or hoped to impress. In the course of everyday business, her grammar and sentence structure were perfect, and it was only the pronunciation of *ws* that still seemed to elude her. But today Callie was in far too good a mood to reflect on Fredericka's affectations. Besides, it felt wonderful to be in Fredericka's good graces. No matter what the other models said about her, they all desperately wanted her approval. Callie responded to the hug she received with one of her own.

Austin came forward as well, offering kisses on both her cheeks. "Great job, Callie. We're proud of you," he said warmly.

Rick Fields also had a kiss on the cheek for her, as he led her to Fredericka's desk, where five copies of the contract sat waiting for her signature. It was thick, Callie thought, picking up the top copy and flipping to see that the last page was numbered 25. She wished there were an opportunity to read it through and study it a bit, but that would take hours and they were all obviously expecting her to sign it right then and there. Taking the pen Rick handed her, she turned to the last page and signed her name with a grand flourish, smiling for the benefit of the group. The photographer snapped away as everyone applauded. *It's done,* she thought, *it's really done.*

Champagne corks popped and glasses were passed as Callie signed the other four copies. The photographer made her pretend she was still signing as he continued to take pictures. Then everyone posed together, talking noisily and happily, shaking Callie's hand and kissing her again. Callie herself took Polaroid pictures of the group for her own photo album.

Her excitement grew as what had just happened began to sink in. This was the peak, the absolute top. Fredericka and Austin were virtually fawning over her, their most valuable model—and one of the most highly paid models in the business. As she drank her champagne and continued smiling for the photographer, she glanced out at the panoramic view of New York. She had conquered it all—the city, the agency, the entire modeling business. This was the success every other model dreamed of. And she had done it.

From Fredericka's office, Callie was ushered down to the agency's lower floors, where everyone wanted to congratulate her, shake her hand, or kiss her. It was slow progress to get to the bookers' room, but Callie made her way there, thanking all the well-wishers as she went. When she stuck her head in and Grace spotted her, the two of them grinned at each other and hugged tightly.

"Thank you, Grace," Callie whispered, hoping her friend could hear her above the din of people laughing and talking. "I know you made this happen."

"Wasn't nothing, kiddo," Grace whispered back, giving her another affectionate squeeze as the other bookers crowded around for their chance to hug and congratulate Callie. "Any old time."

The rest of the day passed as if it were a dream. Callie was dazed and happy, surrounded by people who shared her excitement. Fredericka took Grace and Callie out for drinks to mark the event. At three o'clock, Callie went home to call her parents with the good news and then met Kate and April for another celebratory drink. She left enough time to bathe and change leisurely before dinner with David. He had promised her something special that night, so she took extra care getting dressed. When she was finished, she gazed at her reflection with satisfaction. The pale blue evening gown was form-fitting but elegant, and she loved the way the elbow-length white gloves looked.

David was right on time, wearing a tuxedo and carrying two dozen yellow roses for her. The limousine drove them first to a restaurant they both loved in SoHo for drinks, then on to dinner at Lutece. Callie ate everything she wanted, not giving a second thought to the calories or the fact that she would be hung over from so much champagne. This was the night to celebrate.

"I'm so proud of you, Callie," David told her, reaching across the table to take her hand as their dessert plates were cleared away. "I knew you were a winner from the first minute I met you, and you've done even greater things than anyone could have hoped for."

"Thank you, sweetheart." Callie's heart was filled with love for him. "But you helped me so much. I never would have done all this if it hadn't been for you."

The waiter set down two brandy snifters. David picked his up and swirled the dark fluid.

"A toast to you," he said, holding the glass up slightly.

Callie picked up her drink.

"Thank you for filling my days and nights with more happiness than I deserve." He spoke tenderly.

Callie gazed at him, thrilled by his words. She watched as he brought his glass to his lips and took a sip, then she followed suit. She was surprised to see that there was something in the bottom of her drink, clinking against the side of her glass.

"What's this?" she asked.

Delicately, she reached into the snifter and picked out the

object: a three-carat emerald-cut diamond ring set in platinum with two baguettes. She looked at David, stunned.

"Will you continue bringing me happiness forever?" he asked softly.

Tears of joy filled Callie's eyes. Truly, she thought, her life was absolutely perfect.

11

Callie finished combing out her wet hair and slipped into a pair of jeans and a clean sweatshirt. She knew she could dispense with drying her hair, putting on moisturizer, even tweezing her eyebrows; it would all be taken care of for her at the shoot. Yawning, she sat on the edge of the bed and put on a pair of sneakers. It had been hard to drag herself out of bed; 7:00 A.M. was earlier than her usual pickup time. The limousine would be waiting downstairs, and it was nice to know she didn't have to rush, or worry about getting to the studio on time by cab. David, of course, was long gone; he always left for the office early.

If I hadn't moved in with him, Callie thought as she stood up, *I'd never see him at all.* She'd been hesitant about the move, protesting that they should be married first, but David had convinced her that she was being silly, that they would be married soon anyway and this was a better arrangement for both of them. And it *had* been exciting, seeing her clothes hung up in the closet next to his, settling in with him. It had been the right decision.

She'd looked at the script for the commercial the night before, and she grabbed it from the hall table as she went out the door. Settling back into the limousine's comfortable seat, she idly flipped through the pages again, then sat back and looked out the window. This would be her second television spot for Day and Night, but she was still a bit nervous about it. As opposed to print shoots, the sessions for TV spots were somehow much more . . . serious, she reflected. There were more people running around, and the decisions seemed bigger. No doubt because there was so much more money at stake.

Grace had told her who the director would be, but Callie hadn't recognized the name. The limousine was turning on Thirty-fourth Street to go over to Tenth Avenue. She took a few deep breaths. *It'll be fine,* she told herself.

The soundstage, a cavernous space with vast white walls, was dusty, cold, and drafty. It was crammed with film and video equipment, wires and thick cables running everywhere. Half a dozen men were busy setting up, attending to lighting, moving cameras, ripping off large pieces of silver duct tape from thick rolls to secure wires and platforms. A still-photographer's set tended to be peaceful in comparison, often with music piped in, but there was no music here and the atmosphere was one of controlled confusion.

Callie put her bag down by the makeup station, recognizing Reed Timothy in the process of setting up.

"Hey there, Reed," she greeted him. He'd done her makeup on another Day and Night shoot.

"Madame Callie." He smiled. "How's tricks? You know Jules? He's doing hair."

Jules smiled hello. "I'm glad to meet you. I've got some good ideas for you today."

"Glad to know you too, Jules. But right now I'm starving and I'm off to the food. Can I get you guys anything?"

They both shook their heads. Callie went to the long table set up with an assortment of juices, fruit, and muffins, helping herself to a few slices of cantaloupe and honeydew.

Slowly, watching what was going on around her, she wandered back to Reed and Jules and settled in a chair. Reed was assessing the large lighted mirror on the wall, removing several of the bulbs on the perimeter, then changing his mind and putting them back.

A woman wearing black pants and a brightly striped shirt came over, a clipboard in one hand, a stopwatch on a long black string around her neck. "Hello, Callie. I'm Alice, the producer for this spot. Do you have everything you need? We'll be ready to go in half an hour."

"Thanks, Alice. I think I'm fine." Callie finished her fruit and put the plate aside as Jules began to prepare her hair.

"Holler if there's anything I can do," Alice said as she walked off.

Callie spotted Arnold Stone, her publicity contact from Weston, over in a corner talking with someone. He caught her eye and waved. She liked Arnold, and he was a big help in making her feel comfortable in all the new situations that kept coming up. Public appearances as a corporate spokesperson were still scary for her, so she appreciated his coaching and encouragement. She also noted Stan Hollings getting himself a cup of coffee. He was Day and Night's art director, an older man with a dry sense of humor; as usual, he was wearing a beautifully tailored suit, looking distinguished and poised. He walked over to talk with some other men, probably from Weston's advertising agency, she thought.

Jules tied her hair back as Reed conferred with the lighting director, asking what was being planned and how heavy a base he should use on Callie. Satisfied, Reed took over and began the long process of her makeup. Callie sat, comfortable now with the situation, her confidence returning. She knew some of the people here, and Day and Night was *her* company, the one she represented. It was still important that she be nice and avoid criticizing anyone directly, but she wasn't the outsider here or some disposable face booked for a half-day. She belonged.

Callie saw the director, a slight man with a dark beard, conferring with his crew members. He was busy, but after a few minutes he broke away from the group and came over to her. Reed stopped what he was doing and stepped back, out of the way.

"Callie, I'm Michael Antaro and I'll be directing the spot." The man picked up a folding chair and sat down in it facing Callie. "Thanks for coming. Can we get you anything?"

"I'm fine; thank you for asking."

"Okay then. We're doing a few scenes here today. Tomorrow we'll all troop uptown for the location scene. Everything will be shot in thirty-five millimeter. You know all that? You're ready with your lines?"

Callie nodded. "Yes, thanks."

"Oh, you're so polite," he teased her. "I love the polite ones. They give you such a sense of *power.*"

They both laughed. Michael stood and put the chair back where he had gotten it. "See you in a few minutes."

The noise level was increasing. Reed was hurrying, as Jules stood by, observing. Another woman, young and dressed all in black, was pressing clothes over in a corner. Callie recognized her; Nancy Louis had been the stylist on a shoot for *Elle* that Callie had done. Jules went over to ask her something and the two stood there talking, Nancy shaking her head in disapproval of whatever Jules was saying. Callie turned her attention back to Reed as he gave a sigh of exasperation at being interrupted yet again, this time by a young man holding a copy of the script.

He extended a hand for Callie to shake. "Judd Rogers, the copywriter. You all set?"

"Judd, hi." Callie gave him a big grin. "The spot should be terrific." She hesitated, then gathered up her courage. "Do you think it would be possible for me to say, 'It makes life so easy' instead of, 'It makes *my* life so easy'? Something about those two words when I have to say them out loud—*makes my, makes my* . . . I don't know."

"Makes my . . ." He thought for a few seconds. "I don't have a problem with losing that word. Let me run it by Michael."

Callie smiled as she watched him head for the director.

There was a time when she would never have dared to ask for a change in anything. She felt proud of herself now, speaking up that way.

Her train of thought was interrupted when Nancy Louis came over, clothes slung over her arm, her face tense. "Good morning, Callie. I'm Nancy Louis."

"I remember you, Nancy, don't be silly," Callie said. *"Elle."*

"Right." Nancy clearly didn't care whether Callie remembered her; her mind was on other things. "There was a problem with the shoes for the Day segment, so we'll have to make do with a size six pump, okay?"

Callie nodded. Shoes or clothes were often the wrong size, and were either pinned or stitched to appear as if they fit the models properly. Shoes that were too big were one thing, but standing for hours in a pair two sizes too small wasn't a pleasant prospect. The clothes and accessories were Nancy's responsibility. Callie could have made a fuss, but she had no desire to get Nancy in trouble. "Not a thrill, but we'll deal with it," she said.

A woman in her early twenties approached Callie tentatively. "Excuse me, but you need to sign this." She held out a clipboard. Callie saw that it held a release form. She frowned, thinking that this sort of thing should have been covered in her contract.

"I doubt I'm supposed to sign that. Call Whiting and talk to them about it, okay?"

The girl nodded and disappeared. Callie didn't see her again.

When Callie finally walked out into the center of the soundstage, she was instructed to stand in a specially constructed doorway frame with ornately carved moldings and an elaborate paint job of faux marblizing on the plywood walls surrounding it. She adjusted the cuffs of the silk blouse she wore under a beige suit, trying to get a bit more comfortable. Nancy immediately appeared at her side, helping her, smoothing down the blouse, wanting to be sure Callie didn't do anything to mess up the outfit. Jules and Reed were standing off to one side, their arms crossed, casting a critical eye on Callie as they discussed the work they'd done on her. Michael and the lighting director circled her, conferring, pointing.

When shooting got under way nearly an hour later, Michael spent a few minutes going over what he wanted Callie to do: stand behind the wall and, at his cue, stick her face around the corner of the doorway so the camera could see her, then pause and say her line.

"Do it the way it was written originally, okay, Callie?" he said sweetly but firmly, his tone letting her know that he wasn't going to argue with her about it.

She conceded at once.

The lights were intense and hot. Unlike the strobes that went off and on with the camera's clicking on a still-photographer's set, these lights stayed on continuously. Over and over, Callie popped into the doorway, paused for a beat, then said her line. "It makes my life so easy," she repeated brightly, sweetly, lovingly. No one told her whether she was doing a good job; Michael just continued to direct her to try something new. "Try it like you're surprised to see us. . . . Now come at it like you've just discovered the greatest thing in the world. . . . Show us what a good time you're having." She couldn't see out past the lights, but she could hear constant whispering. Was everyone talking about her?

It was a relief when Michael declared that they had the shot and were breaking for lunch. But she only had time to grab a sandwich and take it back with her into the chair to be made up for the afternoon's shooting. Lunch for the crew was an hour, and she had to be ready to roll as soon as they got back. It was a long afternoon. When she climbed back into the limousine at five o'clock, she decided to head straight for a hot bath, then climb into bed early with a yogurt and a good book. David wouldn't be getting home until ten that night, she knew, and she doubted that she would even see him; she'd probably be fast asleep long before then.

The next day seemed even longer. She was made up in a trailer parked on East Sixty-fifth Street and stood around in a full-skirted evening gown while the shot was set up, unable to sit down for fear of wrinkling the dress. She had to emerge from the intricately designed entranceway of an old, elegant brownstone, say her line, then walk down the block, where a male model in a tuxedo would run up to her and put an arm around her shoulder.

"It makes me everything I ever dreamed of," she said again and again as she came out through the entrance. The noise of traffic, a passing helicopter, a dog barking—every time Callie felt she had done it just right, something ruined the sound. When it was blessedly quiet and the moment was perfect, she flubbed the line, or didn't move as fluidly as she knew she had to. A small crowd gathered, but Callie tried to block them out, knowing that to make eye contact with someone was to encourage them to come up and talk with her, despite the barricades around the area.

At the end of the day, she couldn't believe how tired she was. She would sleep late the next morning, she promised herself. But the telephone awakened her the following morning at eight-thirty.

"Hello," Callie answered groggily.

"Good morning, Callie. This is Arnold Stone at Weston."

She struggled to wake up. "Hi, Arnold. Everything go okay yesterday? I thought it went pretty well."

"Great, great. Just wanted to let you know we booked you on *The Paul Shelby Morning Show,* but they want you there tomorrow. Everything's happening at once, eh? The car will come for you at seven-fifteen, and you'll be on around nine-thirty."

Callie sat up, fully awake now. *"Paul Shelby* is live, isn't it?"

"Yup," Arnold said. "If you like, we can coach you a little, give you some idea of what they'll be asking and how you might answer."

"That would help," Callie said gratefully.

"You want to come down here about three today?" Arnold asked.

"Right."

When the limousine picked her up the following morning to go to the show, Callie knew she was as prepared as she could expect to be. She told herself that it would be a fun experience and to make the most of it. But as she heard the driver say into his car phone, "We're four blocks away," it was all she could do to control her anxiety. When the driver opened the door for her, she saw a small crowd of people standing around. "Who is it?" they whispered to one another, pens and papers poised for autographs. None of them recognized her as she walked by. A security guard checked her name off on a list, and a young woman was waiting in the lobby to escort her backstage.

She was pleased to see Reed waiting to do her makeup. Arnold had told her that Day and Night would have their own makeup person, instead of using the show's staff artist.

"Long time no see. Good morning," he said, as she sat down in front of him. He put some tissues around her neck to protect her dress from the makeup. "Nice outfit. Good for your skin tone."

"Thanks." Day and Night had messengered the designer dress to her the day before. Thank goodness she'd been spared the agony of having to pick something from her closet, she thought.

The room was busy, guests being made up, people filing in and out. Someone shoved a form at her with blanks for her social security number, her agency, the address to send the two-hundred-fifty-dollar fee for her appearance. She filled it in, not sure whether she should, and signed.

When Callie was ready, a production assistant brought her to the green room, where she sat with two men and a woman watching the show get under way on a large television set. Snacking on the doughnuts, bagels and cream cheese, and coffee set out there, the men were talking to one another, but no one spoke to her. She poured herself a glass of sparkling water, relieved to see Arnold Stone come in. He complimented her on the makeup job and sat down beside her to give her a few last-minute tips.

At nine-fifteen, a woman who identified herself as the associate producer came to get Callie. She brought her out near the set; Callie could see the show in progress, Paul Shelby wrapping up an interview with an author about his latest book.

"What's it like to be a supermodel? When we come back,

one of the biggest will be with us," she heard him say. "Stay tuned to meet Callie Stewart."

The woman with Callie handed her a wire attached to a small leather pouch shaped like a thin pack of cigarettes. "Remember," she said, helping Callie hide the pouch in her panty hose, "once you're miked with this, everyone in the control room can hear you. So watch what you say, unless you want your words overheard by all those guys. And consider whether you really *have* to use the ladies' room. The mike picks up everything."

As soon as she said that, Callie was seized with the urge to go to the bathroom. But she stood there, waiting, her fear growing. During the commercial break, the cameramen were joking with one another, as Paul Shelby sat off to one side, going over some papers. She saw the stage manager, an older man wearing a headset, pacing about and appearing to be talking to himself. "I'll tell him," he said into the air, apparently communicating with the control room. He raised his voice. "One minute out, people."

After what seemed like a year to Callie, everyone resumed their places.

"Okay," the stage manager said, "going in five, four, three . . ." Silently, he used his fingers to count off two and one, then pointed directly at Paul Shelby to indicate that they were back on the air.

The show's host sat up straighter and his face instantly became animated. "What would it be like to be a supermodel, one of the world's most beautiful women? Why don't we find out? Everybody, let's welcome Callie Stewart."

Callie smiled broadly and stepped out into the bright lights as the audience applauded. Paul Shelby stood up, and for a moment she panicked, not sure if she was to take one of the two seats on the set or just stand there with him. He took her hand and guided her to a chair.

"You are indeed lovely, Callie," Paul gushed, leaning forward.

"Well, thank you, Paul. But you're not so bad yourself." She smiled at him innocently.

He guffawed insincerely, then turned to gaze directly into

the camera. "Callie's now the exclusive face for Day and Night cosmetics. This is the big time, folks." He looked back at her. "Tell us. Where did you come from? How does it feel to be *the* face of today?"

This was the hard part. Somehow, she was supposed to work in references to Day and Night products, particularly their new mascara and a perfume called Sunlight.

"I don't know about being the face of today, Paul. I do work with Day and Night a lot, which has been a wonderful experience for me. I travel with them, too—just last month we were in Mexico shooting an ad for their new waterproof mascara. And I have to tell you, with all that sun and water, the mascara really worked. They've got a new perfume out too, which I'm wearing. It's called Sunlight." She put out her wrist. "What do you think?"

He took an exaggerated sniff of her wrist. "Very nice. But on you, I suppose anything would smell good."

He went on, the questions continuing in the same vein: what was it like to be a supermodel, how did she get there, what did her future hold? Callie tried to be succinct and direct. She knew her slot was to run four minutes, and she was surprised when he thanked her for coming and broke for a commercial; it had gone by so fast, she would have sworn she was on for less than a minute.

Her segment over, Paul Shelby walked away without a word. Callie headed offstage, and someone removed the mike. Abruptly, she was standing there alone, uncertain what to do, watching the next guest, a girl of about sixteen, talk with the associate producer. She wondered if she'd done a good job, if Day and Night would be pleased with her. She didn't see Arnold anywhere, and there wasn't anything else for her to do there. The limousine would be waiting outside to take her anyplace she wanted to go. She might as well go back to David's apartment.

As soon as she arrived, she called David at the office. He'd said he would be sure to watch her on a television set there. But he was in a meeting, so she could only leave a message. She dialed Grace next; the two of them had talked the day before about Callie's getting booked on the show, and Grace had promised Callie a full critique on her performance.

"Hi, hon," Grace cheerfully responded to her greeting above the usual background noise of the bookers' room. "How're you doing?"

"Did you see me on *Paul Shelby* today? What'd you think?" Callie couldn't wait to hear Grace's comments; they would doubtless be useful for the next time she had to be on TV.

There was a momentary silence. *"Damn.* Oh, I'm sorry, I completely forgot. I planned to watch but I overslept—well, the excuse doesn't matter, I'm just sorry. Do you have a tape of it?"

Callie kept the disappointment out of her voice. "Sure."

"Great, bring it next time you're in."

Callie didn't point out that she had no reason to come by the Whiting Agency, that in fact she hadn't been there in close to three months. Before the Weston contract, she would typically call in three or four times a day to find out how her appointments and go-sees were shaping up, or stop by in person to check her schedule or just shoot the breeze, finding out what the various models and clients were up to. There was no need for any of that now that she worked only for Weston, her schedule set well in advance. She supposed she could go in anyway but it would be obvious that she was just hanging around with no real purpose. She was Callie Stewart, the agency's top model; she would look pathetic, collaring the other girls, hoping they could take time to chitchat.

"Tell me what else is new," she said to Grace.

"The usual mayhem and madness." Grace's next words were spoken with affection. "Hey, now, admit it, you've got to be wondering if clients have been asking for you."

That was exactly what Callie was wondering but she would have died before admitting it. Being out of touch with the daily goings-on in the industry, she sometimes felt as if everyone had forgotten her.

Suddenly the level of noise in the bookers' room increased. Grace put her hand over the receiver but Callie heard her muffled voice telling someone she'd be with them in a second.

"Hannah Kroft just walked in." Grace was back on the

line. "She got back from L.A. yesterday—an editorial spread for *Glamour*—and she brought us all these tacky Hollywood souvenirs."

Hannah was seventeen, a promising new face whom Grace had taken under her wing, just as she had done for Callie—it seemed like centuries before. There was a loud hoot of laughter. Callie envisioned the scene, everyone opening their gifts, the jokes flying, Hannah bright-eyed with the thrill of so much attention.

"You wouldn't believe what she brought Jo-Jo." Grace chuckled. She'd obviously forgotten that she had been about to tell whether any clients were still trying to book her.

"Sounds like Hannah's doing well," Callie said, realizing she was stalling, trying to keep Grace on the line.

"Yeah, she is." Grace was distracted. "Listen, hon, call anytime. And take care. Okay?"

"Okay. Thanks."

Callie hung up with a sigh. She looked around, uncertain what to do next, restless, still charged up. Her eyes fell on the two shoeboxes stuffed with fan mail on the floor next to her desk. Now seemed like as good a time as any to tackle them. As she crossed the room, she thought again how pleased she was that she had bought the antique desk; it had been expensive but a real bargain for what it was. She sat down and lifted one of the boxes onto her lap, taking a satisfied glance around the living room of David's apartment. *No,* our *apartment,* she corrected herself. It was still hard for her to think of the place as anything but David's, even with all the changes she'd made. A lot of work had gone into redecorating it, but with the help of an interior designer she'd done a pretty good job. The apartment had been nicely furnished before, but it had had a heavier, more masculine feel. When David had given her the go-ahead to redo the living room and bedroom, she'd gotten down to the task right away.

All that time to decorate, what a luxury that had been. This week had been incredibly busy, but for a while before that, Day and Night hadn't used her for anything. Released from the everyday grind of her business, spared from having to run around town on lots of different jobs, she'd been able to spend hours poring over choices in fabric showrooms, antique stores, and furniture auctions. It was heaven, and now she had the results to enjoy permanently. Imagine, she thought with a smile, making so much money yet still having so much time to herself. She'd even gotten back to her tennis, playing three days a week at the club, sometimes with April, usually with one of the two men she'd gotten friendly with there during her workout sessions, both of whom were strong players. Her game had quickly come back. She couldn't believe she had let it slide for so long, barely playing at all for months on end. She would make sure that didn't happen again.

The plants needed watering, she noted, her gaze traveling around the room once more. And something wasn't quite right with the arrangement of paintings on the far wall; they looked off-balance somehow. She'd have to call her decorator about that later. Pouring herself a glass of water from the crystal pitcher by her elbow, she wondered for a split second why plants and picture arrangements suddenly seemed important to her. Didn't she have anything else to occupy her mind? Frowning, she quickly pushed away the thought.

She made a mental note to talk to a real estate agent about going to see some country houses. The other night David had said they should buy one, that it was a good time to check out what was available, maybe an old farmhouse in Connecticut. That would be tomorrow's project, she decided. Right now the fan mail was waiting. She concentrated on the box in her lap, picking up the top envelope as she opened the desk's narrow drawer and reached inside for her sterling silver letter opener.

Callie spent most of the next three weeks researching possibilities for a country house. She didn't tell David anything about what she was doing, wanting to surprise him by having done all the legwork first and simply taking him on a tour of the best five or six choices. He'd been in such a bad mood lately, maybe this would cheer him up. Nearly every day she drove around with real estate agents, running in and out of the huge houses, trying to imagine herself and

David in each one, barbecuing for friends out back, breakfasting in the sun-drenched kitchens, making love in front of the fireplaces. It was great fun. Having carefully narrowed the choices, she was delighted with her final list. Any one of them would be a happy haven away from the city for the two of them—and, in the future, for their children as well.

On Thursday morning she roused herself from sleep to catch David before he left for the office. He was standing at the kitchen counter, sipping a cup of coffee as he looked through a file.

As she entered the room, he glanced at her briefly, then went back to his papers. "What are you doing up? It's only six-fifteen."

Knotting the sash in her silk robe, she was unable to suppress a grin. "I want to put in a special request, and I know I'd better give you lots of notice. Would you keep all day Saturday open for me?"

"Saturday?" His eyes returned to her face and he frowned. "I don't think so—no, I can't."

The grin faded from Callie's face. "Are you sure? This is for something great."

"I'll be working on Saturday, then I've got a game of golf with Van Samuels." Having finished his coffee, he set down the cup, picked up his folder, and turned to leave.

"Oh . . ." Callie hadn't wanted to tell David what she was up to, hoping to keep him guessing as she drove him up to Connecticut. But she could see that wasn't going to work. "I've picked out some houses for us over the past few weeks, wonderful places in the country. I want you to come look at them."

David stopped and turned back to her. His tone was flat. "You've been looking at houses?"

"Yes, just seeing what was around." Callie faltered. It was clear from his expression that he wasn't pleased by her research efforts. "Isn't that what we wanted, a country place?"

"Where did you get that idea?"

"But you said—"

David interrupted sharply. "You know how much business I do over the weekends, and if I'm not at the office, there are dinners, things like that. That socializing goes with my job. I could never be away every weekend, not at this stage of my career. And I wouldn't want to be anyway. Besides, a country house is a pain in the neck."

"I see." Callie bit her lip, her dreams of long walks in the woods disintegrating.

"Our next step should be to buy a decent brownstone and renovate it." He spoke with irritation. "I hope you didn't waste too much time on this. I can't imagine why you thought we were going to buy something out of the city."

She followed him out as he grabbed his briefcase, which was propped against the wall in the foyer.

"Honestly, Callie, sometimes you can be so . . ."

Not bothering to finish, he shut the door behind him. She stood there smarting from the sting of his unfinished thought. Then, remembering something, she pulled open the door, relieved to see he was still there waiting for the elevator.

"David, you won't forget that we're supposed to meet at Tiffany at three-thirty? The silver patterns."

The elevator opened. "Right," he replied brusquely, stepping inside without looking at her. "Earth-shakingly important, silver patterns."

Slowly, Callie closed the door. Whatever was bothering him lately, she certainly hadn't made matters any better between them. But he got angry with her so easily these days. She searched her mind, wondering if she had done anything to provoke his ongoing bad temper. Well, if she had, she couldn't imagine what it was. It was probably pressure at work getting to him.

The telephone rang.

"Hi, it's April. Sorry if I woke you, but I'm on my way out. Are we still on for lunch today?"

No point in burdening April with her boring little problems. "Absolutely," Callie said cheerfully. "How does twelve-thirty sound?"

It had been nearly four weeks since Callie had last seen

April, and she was unprepared for the sight of her friend, her trademark long hair now shorn and slicked back against her head, with bangs across her forehead.

"My God," Callie burst out, rushing to the table where April was waiting for her. "What made you finally do it?"

"You like it?" April turned her head left, then right, so that Callie could view her from different angles. "I just realized it was about time. No big deal."

They both laughed at April's pretense that the decision had been an easy one.

"Fantastic!" Callie couldn't get over the change. "You look about twelve years old, and it really brings out your cheekbones."

April smiled. "I wish I'd had the nerve to do it before. It saves me an hour in the bathroom every morning."

"What did Fredericka say? How did you persuade her to let you?" Callie asked, opening a menu.

"She was the one who persuaded me, actually. Old Fredericka knows when the time is right for change. In her inimitable warm fashion, she informed me that my look was dead and that short hair would get me new jobs."

Callie reached for a breadstick. "And has it?"

"Like crazy," April said happily. "It's like I started a new career. I'm working every day I want to."

"That's great."

Callie sat back, a smile on her face. She was genuinely glad for April, but at the same moment a pang shot through her. April was busy, in the thick of things, sought after. In comparison, Callie was bored and lonely, cut off from all the action. *I'm an ingrate,* she silently reprimanded herself. *Here I have everything and I'm selfishly griping that it's not enough.*

April interrupted her thoughts. "Even Austin had a kind word for me, believe it or not. He said the hunt is on for someone for the new Joie de Vivre perfume campaign, and this haircut is going to put me in the running. Plus, Prescott Glen wants me for a series of five ads, all eveningwear."

Callie smiled, but she couldn't stop the unhappy feeling that washed over her. Who besides Weston would ever want her again? Who would even remember her by the time the Weston contract was over?

A horrible thought suddenly occurred to her. She had reached the pinnacle in her business. She was at the top. There was no place left to go but down.

She did her best to hide her feelings from April as they ate their lunch, talking about the agency, what different people were doing, how April was seriously considering breaking up with Louie. Callie was startled to see that it was almost three o'clock when she glanced at her watch. She had to hurry to meet David at Tiffany. It had taken such effort to get him to take twenty minutes out of his afternoon, she didn't dare keep him waiting.

April and Callie exchanged hugs on the street and Callie hurried over to Fifth Avenue, then up to Fifty-seventh Street. Here and there, passersby recognized her and nudged one another or openly stared. She smiled at them. Approaching the store, she saw David standing in front, tapping his foot impatiently. He turned, frowning as he saw her rush up the block. She waved.

"This was a mistake," he said almost before she was close enough to hear him. "I must have been nuts to say I'd come out in the middle of the afternoon."

"It'll only take a minute," she said soothingly, leading him toward the big revolving doors. "If we don't register soon, we'll never do it."

Callie had narrowed the choices for sterling flatware down to two, one with plain, straight lines, the other with a more intricate pattern. She pointed them out to David. He immediately chose the simpler one.

"The other is awful. Too fussy," he said firmly.

"Maybe," Callie ventured uncertainly, "but it's a little more traditional."

David's tone was sharp. "You asked me to pick and I did. If you were planning to ignore what I said, why did you drag me here?"

Callie kept her voice low, but she couldn't stop herself from saying, "Honey, this is so unlike you. Please—I *know* something's bothering you. Tell me what it is. Talk to me."

He looked at her coldly. "I've got to get to a meeting. See you at home later."

Callie watched his retreating back. This had gone no better than their conversation that morning. She knew he wasn't likely to be as interested in things like flatware and dishes as she was, but she couldn't very well make these selections without even consulting him, could she? Well, she was here, so she thought she might as well take a look at some other things. She headed to the crystal department.

As she picked up a large vase, her attention was distracted by a conversation between another shopper and a sales-woman.

"No, that's ugly," the woman shopper was complaining in a loud voice. "Don't you have anything else?"

The saleswoman said mildly, "I've shown you what we have, madam."

"What about that?" The woman pointed.

"It's well outside the price range you gave me."

"You're a big help," the woman said sarcastically. "I ask you to find me a gift and I'm walking out of here empty-handed."

Callie watched them. The customer looked to be in her late forties, darkly tanned, her hair bleached almost white-blond. Her face was overly made-up, her mouth set in a dissatisfied line beneath bright crimson lipstick. The clothes and jewelry she wore were expensive but loud. *Probably has nothing else to do but shop,* Callie thought.

Uncomfortable, she turned away, suddenly losing interest in the task at hand. She got onto the elevator. What would happen to her as she got older, after Whiting had no further use for her? Would she try to hold on to her looks, having nothing to do all day but get manicures and facials, roam the stores, spend money, feel useless?

A sense of panic welled up in Callie. What *would* she do? She had no skills besides modeling, no goals other than the one she had already accomplished. The elevator door opened and she got out, her chest feeling constricted, her palms wet with perspiration. She imagined herself in two years, Weston cutting her loose, everyone in the industry laughing at the idea of booking used-up Callie Stewart. By that time she'd be twenty-three. Could she really start college at that age, after all she'd been through? That was a picture: the ex-supermodel sitting around a classroom with a bunch of seventeen-year-olds, all of them staring as she flubbed an answer.

Her breath was coming in short gasps. What was happening to her? Rushing to the nearest exit, she made her way out onto Fifth Avenue, her hand to her chest, trying not to panic. A few people glanced at her curiously, then looked away.

I'll be okay, she reassured herself over and over, leaning against the building for support, her breath finally slowing down. *I made the best career move anyone could ask for. And there's David, wonderful David. We'll have children, create a family. We'll share our lives together. David will help me figure out what to do later.*

Feeling calmer, she took a long, somewhat shaky deep breath, then exhaled slowly. She'd had good luck up until now. There was no reason to think it wouldn't hold. Everything would be just fine.

12

Will there be anything else, Mr. Long?"

David shook his head, and his secretary left the office. He glanced at his watch: ten after three. The days when he had these meetings were always interminable, an eternity until four-thirty finally arrived. He picked up a computer printout of the latest sales figures, then tossed it back down. It was no use—he couldn't concentrate. He might as well leave now.

Emerging into the crisp November afternoon, he stalled for time by walking west on Fifty-seventh Street for a few blocks, then decided he had waited long enough and hopped into a taxi. He got out at Riverside Drive and Ninety-second Street, heading toward the Hudson River. It was twenty-five past four but Lawrence Richards was already there.

This was David's third meeting with Richards, a corporate vice president at Miracle Corporation, one of Weston's major competitors. Richards was a good-looking man with an affable manner, but David was well aware that he was considered a real shark in the industry. He'd been the one who put out feelers to David when they'd run into each other at industry events and a few charity benefits. He was very subtle, carefully circling the idea, then slowly, cautiously moving forward until he and David understood each other and eventually came to terms of agreement.

They walked along the water's edge. Keeping his voice low, David tersely listed the dozen new colors to be added to several of Weston's product lines, then explained the concepts behind two face creams and a lipstick in the works, as well as the latest on marketing plans for Caring for Him, Weston's line of skin-care products for men.

Richards asked a question here and there, making notes on a small pad. None of what David told him was a surprise; the products he mentioned were nothing earth-shattering, and once they were on the shelves anyone could copy them. It was the secrecy about their development that was important, the key weapon in the battle of the marketplace. By knowing Weston's moves in advance, Miracle could formulate a plan of attack.

"That's it for the moment," David finished.

"Thank you very much." Richards smiled politely, as if David had simply suggested a good restaurant or complimented him on his tie. "The payment will be made to the Maryland account by Monday afternoon." He shook David's hand. "Give my regards to your lovely girlfriend," he added.

The two men parted without another word, walking in opposite directions. Searching out a taxi to take him back to the office, David breathed a sigh of relief. He was always nervous until these meetings were over. But again it had gone smoothly; no one at Weston had any idea what he was up to. This was his third meeting with Richards in as many months, and those three payments already added up to a tidy little nest egg, just waiting and earning interest for him in that Maryland bank.

For a moment he allowed himself to contemplate what would happen if he got caught selling Weston's secrets. He shuddered. It wasn't that he had any moral compunctions about what he was doing. In his opinion, the cosmetics business was nonsense anyway, and the damage he was doing to Weston's sales in the short term were justified by his personal goals right now. Weston would recover as soon as he stopped leaking the information; they were the industry leader and could weather a brief storm. But if he should be found out, his career would be over. He might even wind up in jail. Unthinkable. He just couldn't permit that to happen.

Spying an empty cab, he hailed it. He was on his way up at Weston, no doubt about it. If his excellent performance continued, he could go all the way. But for now he needed more money than his job paid. It was critical if he was going to maintain the right lifestyle. He couldn't *become* more successful unless he already *looked* successful.

Nothing was going to get in the way of his success. He wasn't going to be some poor loser like his father, struggling along working two waiter's jobs, blind tired when he finally got home at the end of his second shift, disgusted, angry, always needing those few drinks before he could face going back to it the next day. David never told anybody what his father had really been like, and he was glad the old man was dead so he couldn't show up to embarrass David in the life he'd so painstakingly constructed for himself in New York. David wouldn't settle for anything less than living at the top, and he planned to get there while he was still young enough to enjoy it.

These days, he was immensely satisfied to note, it looked like his plan was going to stay right on schedule. Aside from the visible job and the money, there was Callie. She was perfect for the image he wanted to project, and he congratulated himself on the way he'd spotted her as a winner right off. Of course, he'd been as impressed as everyone else when she'd landed such a monster contract with Weston; and in truth he'd had nothing to do with it, she'd managed it all by herself. But he couldn't be more pleased with the way it had worked out. He was the object of everybody's envy, his famous girlfriend looking at him adoringly, their picture in the papers and magazines at openings and restaurants.

The cab pulled up in front of his office building. He

handed the driver a ten-dollar bill, still thinking about Callie. A frown crossed his face. As perfect as she was in some ways, lately she'd been a real pain in the neck. For one thing, she'd taken to questioning him about his moods, trying to find out what was bothering him. Of course, he would never tell her about the situation with Miracle, that was completely out of the question. Maybe he *had* been a little jumpy since this whole business had swung into high gear, but that was just too bad. But on top of that, she'd started worrying about her future, asking him what he thought she should do when her contract ran out, how he saw their life together down the road. If she was going to turn into a clinging, whiny nag, he would have to cut her loose. Maybe it wasn't smart to marry a woman who was *too* successful.

Overall, though, life was proceeding smoothly, he reflected, hurrying through the building's vast marble lobby. He'd had good luck so far. There was no reason to think it wouldn't hold.

The next day, David was sorting through a pile of phone messages when Barbara Hutchinson stuck her head in the door.

"Hi. Got a minute?" she asked pleasantly.

He gestured toward a chair. "For you, anytime."

Barbara worked in his group, but she was a vice president in the finance area. They had a very surface relationship, nothing more than the typical interaction in the course of their business dealings and pleasantries exchanged in the halls. They did run into each other frequently in the elevators, as they seemed to arrive at exactly the same time nearly every morning. David knew little about her other than having observed that she was very ambitious, aligning herself with the right people, asking the right questions, making sure she was included in the important meetings whenever possible.

"Just a funny thing . . ." she said, taking a seat and crossing her legs. David noted silently that her legs were long and slender. She wasn't bad-looking, he thought. Her body was still good for thirty or so, and she had nice lips, but he could have done without the short haircut.

"Can I have Adele get you some coffee?" David asked.

She shook her head. "No, I only wanted to tell you about a weird coincidence. You know, usually I'm here pretty late, but I happened to leave early yesterday because my little girl Julia was sick. I went home to be with her at around four-thirty. We live over at Ninety-first and Riverside."

At the mention of her address David felt his stomach tense, but he willed his face to remain impassive.

"I hope she's all right," he said in a concerned tone.

"Oh, she's fine," Barbara answered with a smile, her pride in her daughter apparent even in those few words. "A fever, but it passed. Anyway, as I'm coming up the block, I think I see someone who looks just like you across the street by the river. At first I figured it was my imagination. What would you be doing way over there during the workday?"

She paused, tilting her head as she regarded him. "But I came closer and sure enough, it was you talking to Larry Richards. Isn't that crazy, that we should both be there at that time on a weekday afternoon?"

David felt a surge of anger and fear in equal parts. Of course Barbara would recognize Lawrence Richards too; he was a well-known figure in their industry. She suspected that David was up to something, and she was playing with him. He wanted to throttle her but he was also afraid. If she put it together . . . well, he wasn't even going to contemplate that. He would never let things get that far.

Barbara laughed. "You dog, Miracle's trying to woo you away, aren't they? Hey, if they give you a great deal, promise you'll take me along?"

Despite her teasing, she was watching him expectantly, waiting for an answer as to why he had been with an arch rival in such an odd location. No matter how senior David might be, job offers and negotiations rarely took place on out-of-the-way street corners. She knew that as well as he did. He thought fast.

"Look, Barbara," he began, lowering his voice conspiratorially, "don't repeat this, but I happen to be old friends with Larry, and he had a problem. It's too personal to go into. But he asked for my help, said he wanted to talk in private, and asked if I would meet him. So I did. It's as simple as that."

Barbara gazed into his eyes for a moment. He could see that she didn't buy his story.

"Well, that's what I said, a weird coincidence." She rose to go. "Next time you're in the neighborhood, please come up and have a drink with my husband and me."

As soon as she had left, David cursed aloud. Would Barbara Hutchinson let it drop, or would she try to find out what he'd been up to? It would be unbearable, waiting to find out, seeing her in the office, not knowing if she was shrewd enough to realize that she might be onto something politically valuable for her, or if she'd just let it go. But then he set his mouth determinedly. He'd dealt with enemies and colleagues hoping to sabotage him before, and no one had gotten the upper hand on him yet. He wasn't going to permit this Hutchinson babe to be the first.

As Thanksgiving came and went, David began to relax about Barbara Hutchinson, reassured that she'd forgotten about seeing him with Lawrence Richards. But the scare had made him more determined to take precautions to safeguard his career. Late one night he went out to a telephone booth and called Richards at home, informing him that the price for his services was going up and the location of their meetings would have to be changed to a spot of David's choice.

Not wanting to remind Barbara of what she'd seen, David made sure to avoid her for a few weeks, arriving ten minutes earlier than his usual 7:30 A.M., even missing a meeting he knew she'd be attending the week after she'd come to his office to question him. But eventually he decided he'd hidden from her long enough. Either she was going to make a move or she wasn't, and by now it appeared that the whole thing had blown over.

When several more weeks elapsed, he wasn't even concerned when he heard her calling his name moments after he left the office building on a rainy Friday night the week before Christmas. He was opening his long black umbrella as he walked, and turned to see her hastening toward him.

Barbara normally dressed in conservative dresses and suits appropriate for a woman in management, but whenever it rained or snowed, she wore a bright red plaid plastic raincoat with red rubber boots and carried an emerald-green umbrella. Whenever David encountered her in the elevator on such days, he always had the same thought—that she looked like an overgrown child. Once he'd almost asked her why she dressed so outlandishly for the rain, but he'd immediately thought better of it, not wanting to get into anything personal with her, and not really caring anyway.

She was prying open the green umbrella as she caught up to where he stood waiting for her.

"I tried to get you on the phone, but you were in a meeting nearly all day," she said amiably but loudly enough to be heard over the noise of the heavy traffic on Fifty-seventh Street. "Those meetings can be grueling."

He smiled noncommittally. Surely she hadn't stopped him in the rain to sympathize about his workload.

"I'm glad I caught you," she went on, her voice even and pleasant, "because we need to talk. You see, David, I know why you were talking to Larry Richards that day near my house. I *know*."

David gripped his umbrella handle tightly but remained calm. He smiled. "Of course you know, because I told you. And I asked you to keep it a secret, remember?"

She laughed humorlessly. "Don't patronize me. It took a while, but I've got proof that you've been selling out Weston."

David froze. At that moment, one of the vice presidents from Sales walked by and waved. They both smiled at him. David didn't want to keep standing there where other Weston people might overhear them.

"Let's walk a bit," he said.

Barbara shrugged. "If you like."

They turned and moved away from the building. *Maybe she's guessing,* he reassured himself, *just bluffing.*

"Barbara, whatever you're talking about can't be right," he said casually. "Someone's feeding you something, probably to get back at me. You know how that works."

"Oh, I don't think so," she said coolly. "Three meetings, three deposits to a special bank account in Maryland . . ."

David's stomach heaved.

"That's ridiculous," he protested, as if hurt by her lack of trust.

Barbara grew annoyed. "Let's stop this, shall we? You and I both know that you're involved in cutting the knees out from under Weston for your personal profit. I imagine the powers that be in this company would frown upon that."

He stared at her. All he could think was how stupid she looked in that idiotic outfit. *This woman has the power to destroy me in the palm of her hand,* he said to himself, *and I'm fixated on her red rubber boots.* This whole thing wasn't happening, it couldn't be. *What am I going to do?*

"It's a lie," he said angrily. "How could you accuse me of that?"

She drew herself up, matching his anger. "Don't waste my time denying it. If that's how it's going to be, I'm leaving."

She turned away from him. David panicked.

"Barbara, wait," he cried out.

She looked back expectantly.

He lowered his voice. "There's a lot of money involved. Enough for both of us."

She burst out laughing. "You're offering to 'cut me in,' as they say?"

He cursed silently. That was the worst thing he could have done. If only he'd kept his calm. He *knew* better, knew he should have denied it to the bitter end. Barbara still had an amused expression on her face. He wanted to strangle her.

His words were low and angry. "Don't think I'm just going to stand around and let you ruin me. Let me warn you right now: you'd better not mess with me. You'll be very sorry."

She wasn't intimidated. "Don't you threaten me. And let me warn *you.* You're going to have some interesting explaining to do at the executive meeting in January." Her distaste for him was evident by the expression on her face. He was

startled to realize that she disliked him that much—
probably had all along. "You always put on such a polished
performance at those meetings. Let's see how you handle
this one."

Then she spun around and walked off, the rain coming
down harder now, furiously bouncing off her bright little
green umbrella.

13

"Callie, you've been at it for hours. *Let's go!*"

David paced irritably in the living room, adjusting his shirt cuffs beneath his tuxedo jacket. The last thing he was in the mood for tonight was the Weston Christmas party. And Callie was, as usual, nearly an hour late in getting dressed.

"Okay, I'm coming," she called, emerging from the bedroom.

He looked up, stopping where he was. Even after living with her, after growing used to seeing her every day, her beauty could still overwhelm him at times. Impossibly lovely in a pale blue dress, her gleaming hair fanning out across her bare shoulders, the smile she gave him was outright stunning.

"How do I look?" she asked, turning around for him.

Normally he never told her she was beautiful or made a fuss over her looks. As he'd said to her, everyone she encountered all day talked about her face and body, so he wasn't about to do it too. But tonight was an exception.

"You look like an angel," he answered truthfully. "You must be the most beautiful woman in New York tonight."

Callie seemed slightly stunned by his comment. Then she smiled again, almost shyly.

"Thank you," she replied quietly. "And you are unquestionably the most handsome man in New York."

For a moment, David was able to forget everything that had been bothering him—the tension of worrying about what Barbara Hutchinson might do, how he would save his skin at Weston, the way Callie had been nagging at him, demanding so much closeness. Staring at her, he was happy to think that he would go out tonight with this gorgeous woman beside him, this woman who loved him totally and completely. Suddenly he was certain that he would find a way out of his problems.

His feeling of euphoria was short-lived. Once they got to the party, Callie was whisked off to play her part as the company's famous model, and David was left to contemplate how all the people in the room would cut him off as soon as they got wind of what he'd been up to. And he was smart enough not to delude himself about getting any support from Larry Richards. The people at Miracle would also dissociate themselves from David. They wouldn't want to be connected to someone known for selling secrets. He'd be hung out to dry alone.

But it wouldn't do to show any tension or fear tonight. This was the time for damage control, however late it might be. Of course he would deny everything Barbara said at the meeting in January, although he was chilled by the thought of what kind of proof she had. For now all he could do was cement his relationships with his Weston colleagues in the hope that it would help him rally support later. Maybe he would somehow get lucky at the meeting, maybe they wouldn't believe Barbara, or maybe she would change her mind and keep her mouth shut.

Feeling the tension in his clenched jaw, David worked the room. While Callie talked and danced with a steady stream of men, David joked with other Weston executives, innocently charmed their wives, and traded light shoptalk. Staring into the smiling faces, knowing these were the same people who wouldn't deign to look at him once the word got out, he was desperately turning over options in his mind. Then suddenly he saw Barbara across the room, standing next to a tall, dark-haired man who was probably her husband. David's eyes narrowed with hatred and he quickly looked away. Spotting Walter Furst and his wife, he headed in their direction, a pounding headache coming on.

Around midnight, in the middle of a conversation with one of Weston's distributors, he felt Callie's hand on his sleeve.

"Sweetheart," she whispered, "do you think we might go?"

He turned to her, thinking he should probably put in another hour or so trying to shore up support.

"Not yet. There are a few more people I want to talk to."

"Please, honey. I'm dead on my feet," Callie begged.

But then he realized that most of the important people had left. Besides, making polite chitchat tonight wasn't going to help. The solution was out there somewhere, he just had to find it. His head was throbbing.

"All right. Just let me say good night to Walter and the others. I'll meet you by the coat check."

Ten minutes later, David retrieved his cashmere coat from the coat check girl and headed toward the exit, adjusting his red muffler, still wondering what he was going to do. He saw Callie just a few feet away, watching him. There was no point in getting her started again, asking him concerned questions, trying to soothe him when she knew nothing of his problems. He forced himself to smile broadly.

"Hey there," he said, winking at her. "Don't I know you from somewhere?"

They reached the entrance and he saw the driving rain outside. The snow that had fallen two days before had turned into a partially frozen, slushy mess. The parking attendant wasn't around, but David was too edgy to stand there until he returned. He told Callie to wait while he brought the car around himself. Turning up his coat collar, he hurried through the parking lot to his blue Mercedes.

By the time they were both settled in the car, David felt panic threatening to overtake him. Callie was talking about something or other; he wasn't paying attention. He told himself to keep cool, but seeing the entire executive staff assembled in one place that night had made it painfully clear that at best they would toss him out, end his career. At worst . . . He didn't even know what that might be. If it turned out there was a real possibility that he would be prosecuted, he would definitely leave the country. He wasn't going to go through that.

It was raining so hard that he had to abandon his train of thought to concentrate on the road, driving around a curve that led to another area of parked cars. Startled, David abruptly sat up straighter. There was the bright green umbrella, the lower part of the red plaid raincoat showing beneath it, the red rubber boots. Barbara Hutchinson was about to cross the road right in front of them, alone, heading toward her car.

It came to him suddenly. This was the perfect opportunity. He would scare the wits out of her, drive right up to her, then screech to a halt. He'd stick his head out the window to ask if she was okay, making sure she saw that it was him behind the wheel. She wouldn't be able to accuse him of deliberately trying to hurt her, but she'd have to go home a little bit frightened, unsure what lengths he might go to keep her from revealing what she knew. He could plant the seeds of uncertainty in her mind, get her wondering if it was worth it to expose him, just in case he might actually be a little unbalanced. It was a great idea. And being so comfortable with his car, he knew he could get within inches of her and still stop on a dime.

He lowered his foot on the gas and the car shot forward. Callie turned toward him. "Honey, don't you think—"

Concentrating intently, David drove right up to Barbara, then slammed on the brakes. Triumphant, he saw her raise the umbrella at the screeching sound of the tires; the look of terror on her face. But the car hit a patch of ice and he felt it skid forward, knocking her down. Shocked, he then heard a noise behind them and saw in the rear view mirror that another car was careening around the curve, headed straight for them.

"No!" he yelled.

It was too late. The other car rammed into his and he heard the deafening impact of metal on metal as he was violently lifted out of his seat, then yanked sharply back by his seatbelt. Callie hadn't put on her seatbelt, and she went right through the windshield with a terrifying force, the glass shattering loudly. Her blood splattered everywhere, and he instinctively put up his arm to cover himself.

Then he was alone. He could hear the muffled sounds of the other car's doors opening and closing, people calling out to him, fear and panic in their voices. Callie lay draped across the hood of the car, blood all over her beautiful face, not moving at all. He watched as the rain soaked her clothes and plastered her hair across her bloodied features, smearing the blood, turning it pale and runny. The sound of rain pelting the roof of the car seemed to grow louder and louder until it became almost deafening.

He cursed, smacking the steering wheel over and over again with his hand. Why was all this happening to him?

14

*T*here were flowers, so many flowers. Fuzzy, hard to make out. What were they called? Too difficult to remember. All those colors.

Now everything was white. Callie couldn't move. Her mouth was so dry. She was gazing up at a long, blank expanse of white. Slowly her mind began to work, telling her that she was alive, that she was *someplace*.

The Weston party and the rain. The woman in front of their car, then the headlights in her eyes, the noise of the crash. This was a hospital, and she was looking at a ceiling. She tentatively turned her head, the motion bringing on a sickening stab in her chest and awakening pain throughout her body. She hurt everywhere. Her head, her limbs, everything inside—it was terrifying, the sensations overpowering her, making her desperate to escape them. She shut her eyes and moaned.

* * *

"Callie?" Alicia Stewart leaped up from the chair, dropping her knitting, and rushed to her daughter's bedside. "Honey, are you awake?"

With enormous effort, Callie tried to open her eyes again. Something was wrong. Her right eye was bandaged, she could feel the pressure of it, the eye forced closed. That entire side of her face hurt. And her right leg was stiff, in some kind of awkward position; she strained, but she couldn't move it. She saw flowers. Those must have been the ones she'd seen before, dozens of arrangements lining the broad windowsill. Her mother's anxious face moved into view.

"Baby, can you hear me?"

Callie tried to answer but couldn't get any words to come out. *Mom, oh, Mom, you're here.* She wanted to sob with gratitude. The most she could manage was a soft, guttural sound. She shut her eye, crying silently, her shoulders shaking. The movement made her insides hurt so badly that she didn't think she could stand it. Taking a labored breath, she drifted back to sleep.

Alicia and Frank Stewart were standing there talking to each other, their backs to Callie, the next time she woke up. The sight of them overwhelmed her. She wanted to crawl into their arms and hide there forever.

"Thank you . . . coming," she managed to get out.

They turned around at the sound of her voice. Alicia leaned forward to stroke her hair.

"Shhh, honey, don't tire yourself," she soothed. "As if anything on earth would have kept us from being with you."

Frank took his daughter's hand in his and bent to kiss her cheek, pain for Callie's suffering evident in his eyes. "How's my champ doing?"

Callie felt tears forming again, burning sobs welling up in her chest. She loved them both so much.

"I'm sorry," she whispered. "I've been . . . such a terrible daughter."

Frank was taken aback. "Callie, you're the best daughter any parents could ever dream of."

Alicia hastened to add, "And you always have been." She

smiled. "You've given us nothing but joy from the minute you were born."

They didn't understand. Callie lay still. She had betrayed them by choosing a life alien to all the things they believed in. Then she had deceived them by pretending her life was different from what it really was. They didn't realize that she had left them far behind, not only literally but in every way. The terrible truth was that she had come to look down on them. That was the worst betrayal of all.

"Do you hurt, champ?" her father was asking, still clutching her hand.

"What happened, Dad?" Callie managed.

Her parents exchanged glances.

"You were in a car accident," her father began. Her nod told him she remembered that much.

"David . . . is he all right?" she asked weakly.

"They said he was fine, just a few bruises. But you got banged up pretty good." He didn't seem to want to say anything more.

Relieved that David was unhurt, Callie shifted her gaze to her mother and asked, with more urgency in her whisper, "What *happened?*"

Alicia spoke softly. "It was a serious accident, honey. But don't worry, you're okay."

Her mother was lying, Callie could hear it in her voice. Was she permanently crippled or disfigured? Her modeling! What would happen at Weston if she'd been cut or bruised? She was almost too afraid to go on, but she forced herself. "My face?"

Alicia looked to her husband for support.

"You'll be fine, honey," Frank soothed Callie. "You've got a few cuts, and they did some work on your eye. But everything will be fine, we're sure of it."

His voice told her he was lying as well. So, it was even worse than she had feared.

"Callie, do you know what month it is?"

She sighed, tired of answering the doctor's questions. What year was it, who was the president, on and on. "December."

"Good." The doctor was satisfied as he finished examining the cast on her right leg that ran from her foot all the way to her groin. "Now, is there anything you want to talk about?"

Callie looked at him, standing by the side of her bed. She knew only his name and the fact that he had taken care of her when they'd brought her to the hospital two days before. According to him, she'd been asleep most of the time since then, with the exception of her conversations with her parents. Alone with him now, she hoped he would tell her the truth about the extent of her injuries.

"Dr. Grant, what's wrong with me?"

The doctor put his hands in the pockets of his white coat. In his fifties, with snow-white hair, he had so far spoken in a detached, professional manner as he examined her, probing, poking, checking on what was healing and what needed attention. At her question, though, his face softened and he looked at her with a caring expression.

"I wasn't sure if you wanted to know. Not everyone does."

"Tell me."

"You've got a number of broken bones. Your leg, your collarbone, four ribs. Bad contusions and lacerations as well. There was a fair amount of internal bleeding, but I think we've got it checked now."

Callie took this in.

"It's a bad break in the leg," he went on. "You've fractured your tibia and fibula. You're going to need physical therapy, I won't lie to you. Because of some of your other injuries, you won't be able to manage crutches yet. Unfortunately, that means a wheelchair for a while." He paused. "You know, you're very lucky to be alive."

"My eye?"

The doctor straightened up. "The ophthalmologist who operated on it will be in to see you later. He should be the one to explain it." Seeing the fear on her face, he hurried to add, "He took some glass out of it when they first brought you in. I don't want to tell you anything that's not right, so we'll let him go over that."

Callie knew there was no point in pressing him further. "Thank you, Dr. Grant."

"Now get some rest." He glanced around the room at the flowers and gifts stacked everywhere, the piles of cards and telegrams on the night table. "We've had a devil of a time keeping photographers and all sorts of people out of here. Now that you're a little better, it'll be up to you who you want to see. But hold the number of visitors down to an absolute minimum. And keep the visits short; no more than a few minutes."

The doctor left. *Visitors,* Callie thought. Of course, people would be coming by. They would see her. The doctor had said photographers were trying to get in, hoping to get a shot of the famous model—disfigured, grotesque. She closed her left eye and lay there, frightened. David could help her, he could make it all right. She wanted him desperately. Where was he? Why wasn't he there with her?

Alicia stuck her head in the door.

"Honey, your friend April is here. Do you feel up to it?"

"Mom," Callie asked as evenly as she could, "where's David?"

Her mother's expression showed nothing. "I don't know."

"He came while I was asleep, right?"

"There was a Pete and an Elliot, but no one named David came by." Alicia kept her tone neutral, hoping she wasn't revealing her own crushing hurt at the way her daughter's fiancé was behaving. She'd never met the man, but if she ever did, she'd have to restrain herself from smacking him. He'd put her daughter in this hospital bed and hadn't even had the decency to call or show up; he'd just sent flowers and a couple of fancy nightgowns, as if that would make up for it. "I'm sure he's been calling the switchboard, checking up. He sent those magnificent roses along with some beautiful satin gowns. He'll probably come today."

Callie was stunned. Two days, and he hadn't come by even once.

Alicia wanted to get her daughter's mind off him. "Should I send April in?"

April, yes, it'll be good to see her. She nodded.

Full of energy, her friend burst into the room, her arms overflowing with presents for Callie.

"What is the meaning of this unconscionable slacking off, this silly pretense for missing work," she began, obviously planning to make light of the situation to cheer up Callie. But she stopped short as she saw Callie lying there, her face bruised and swollen, half-covered in bandages, her leg in a cast with only her toes protruding, her arms all black and blue. April tried to hide the shock in her eyes, but she wasn't fast enough; Callie saw it. So, her worst nightmares were true, Callie realized. She was a hideous sight, mangled and deformed.

"Oh, honey, are you okay?" April quickly dumped her packages onto a chair and went to the bed.

Callie nodded and struggled to give her friend a smile. "Never better."

"What on earth happened? Everyone at the agency is talking about you, asking me how you are. We've all been so worried. But the hospital wouldn't let me up here until now, and David hasn't returned my phone messages."

Callie winced. She'd always dreaded being the subject of everyone's gossip in the business, and now they had ample material about her to chew over. And David had ignored even April. How was that possible?

"April, all I know is that we were driving in the rain and we nearly hit a woman. Then another car hit us. That's all I remember."

"Yeah, I read that in the paper," April said sympathetically.

Callie was surprised. "In the *paper?*"

"Of course," April replied, surprised in turn that Callie didn't know. "It's been in the headlines for two days. All the papers are reporting it. They've run pictures of you, some of you and David together. And a picture of that poor woman."

"The one we almost hit?" Callie was instantly alert. "Is she all right? She must have been so frightened. I hope she wasn't hurt."

April looked at her strangely. "You haven't seen or heard anything about this, have you?"

Callie didn't like the expression on her friend's face. "What's wrong, April?"

"Well . . ." She was reluctant to say more.

Straining, Callie raised herself on one arm, ignoring the pain that shot through her. "Tell me," she demanded.

"The woman worked for Weston. Her name was Barbara Hutchinson."

Callie's fear rose. "Go on."

"The papers said she had a heart condition—had for a long time," April said gently. "She wasn't hurt by the car, but it knocked her down, and she had a heart attack. She died on the way to the hospital."

Callie fell back against the pillows. "Oh, no. Oh, please, no."

"I'm sorry to be the one to tell you." April stared at her lap, not knowing what to say next. "Is there anything I can do for you?"

"Who was she?" Callie whispered. "I mean, how old was she? Was she married? Did she have children?"

April said softly, "She was about thirty-two, I think they said in the paper. Married, with a six-year-old daughter."

Callie turned her face away. "I don't mean to be rude, but I need to be by myself for a while. Would you mind?"

Sadly, April patted her hand. "I'll come back tomorrow. Rest."

Left alone, Callie released the tears she'd been holding back. A young woman with a husband and child was dead, and for no reason at all. She and David had ruined a family, killed the mother, left the father and little one alone forever. Guilt washed over her. *It was an accident, an* accident, she said to herself over and over. But it didn't do any good.

It's our fault, she thought, *David's and mine. We're responsible for this.* She replayed the evening in her mind, recalling those minutes when she got her cape, when David brought the car for her, how they'd come bearing down too quickly upon that poor woman. *If only I'd told David to slow down sooner,* she thought, clenching her fists. *If only we'd gotten into the car a few minutes earlier or later.* She went over all the details again, straining, as if she could alter what had happened by changing the facts in her mind.

She *had* to talk to David. With a great deal of effort, she reached for the telephone and dialed his office. The woman who answered told Callie that he was out for a few hours. Where was Adele, David's regular secretary? Callie asked. At home sick with a bad flu, the woman answered; she was just a temp. Callie asked that David call her as soon as he returned. When she didn't hear from him after two hours, she tried again, and was put off once more. She called back twice before giving up.

Callie felt nauseated. David didn't want to see her, he was revolted by the thought of her face, injured and disfigured. When the nurse brought in her pain medication, Callie was grateful to take it, relaxing enough to fall asleep and push David from her mind. She just couldn't stand to think about it.

When she woke up, another doctor was standing next to her bed. He looked to be in his midthirties and wore wire-rimmed glasses.

"Who are you?" she asked groggily.

"Dr. Leigh, the ophthalmologist," he said mildly. "I treated your eye injury when they brought you in."

Callie was silent. She didn't want to hear what this doctor had to say.

"We removed the pieces of glass that were embedded in the eye, but there'll be scarring on your cornea, and I suspect we're looking at a corneal transplant down the road." He reached over, making some minor adjustments to her bandage.

"A transplant," Callie whispered, frightened.

"It also appears that you've developed a cataract," the doctor went on.

"Don't you get those when you're older?" Callie asked.

"A cataract can also develop after a trauma to the eye. We'd want to remove that and implant a lens." At the look of fright on Callie's face, he hastened to reassure her. "I'm very optimistic about it."

Callie's voice was small. "Do you mean I might be blind in that eye?"

He looked at her squarely. "Let's take it one step at a time. Right now, you'll probably be able to make out light and shadow. We'll go from there. First, you need to get your body back in shape. Then we'll consider your options."

When he left, Callie lay silently, her hand lightly probing the bandage over her face, struggling not to let the panic she felt claim her.

Later, she asked her parents to bring her the newspapers from the past few days so that she could read about the accident. Unhappily, they complied with her wishes. She pored over the harrowing words. Apparently, both David and the man driving the car that had crashed into his had been questioned by police, but it was established that neither of them had been drinking and they were cleared of any wrongdoing. The episode was deemed a simple accident, due to treacherous road conditions.

She stared at the pictures of herself, shots from old ads, a couple from her more recent Day and Night work, different photos used by different newspapers. They all ran the same photograph of Barbara Hutchinson, a blurred shot of her with her husband, a tall, dark-haired man, and a sweet-looking child with long brown hair. Callie studied the woman closely, the fine features, the short haircut. A nice woman, she decided, a close family. Her own pictures showed a woman representing the height of glamour, her hair flying, her face heavily made-up. How ludicrous they appeared to Callie next to the one, somehow sad picture of the small family, now shattered. And there were pictures of David, one of her and him rushing into The Four Seasons for a private party being held by an actor back in September. She remembered that night so well, how handsome David had looked, how proud she'd been to be with him, how happy she'd been.

Remorse hung over Callie, weighing her down, emotionally deadening her. Her parents and Kate—the only other people she permitted in the rest of that day—did their best to cheer her up, reassuring her that she and David weren't responsible. But she didn't hear them. The nightmares she was having every time she dozed off told her otherwise. Again and again she saw Barbara Hutchinson through the car window and was blinded by a bright light. She woke up drenched in sweat, tears streaming down her face even before she was fully awake.

Callie asked her parents to find out when Barbara Hutchinson's funeral would be. When they learned that it was scheduled for the following afternoon, Callie had them send an enormous arrangement of flowers in her name. Then she called Kate, begging her to go to the service in her stead. At first Kate refused, telling Callie it would only upset her more. But Callie was insistent; she wanted to know about the woman, know about her family. The urgency in her voice persuaded Kate to relent.

Callie continued to try to reach David, but he was never at home, and his temporary secretary always insisted that he was out or in meetings. Overwhelmed with feelings she couldn't begin to sort out, Callie refused to think about it. When a messenger appeared with a package from David containing two best-selling novels and an enormous box of Godiva chocolates, Callie silently gave it all to her mother, who put it away in the closet without a word.

Kate came straight to the hospital after the funeral. Callie was propped up against two pillows, waiting anxiously.

"Tell me all about it," she demanded as soon as Kate entered the room.

"Callie, please, don't upset yourself so much," Kate said soothingly.

Callie's mouth was set determinedly. "Was her husband there?"

"Yes."

"Describe him."

Kate spoke with great reluctance. "He's nice-looking, early thirties, but of course he was very upset. He was keeping it under control, I suppose for the sake of his little girl. He spent most of the time holding her, comforting her."

"The little girl. Julia." Callie knew her name from the news reports. "What was she like?"

Kate shook her head, obviously unhappy at contributing to Callie's misery.

"Go on, Kate."

"She was a pretty little thing, but she was crying, clinging to her dad." Kate paused. "That's all, Callie. It was a lovely service. A lot of people were there."

"The little girl was crying," Callie echoed, staring down at her hands.

"You've got to stop torturing yourself this way," Kate burst out. "It's terrible, we all agree. But it's not your fault. You weren't even driving the car."

Callie looked at Kate helplessly, tears sliding down the side of her face that was free of bandages. Kate put her arms around her friend, her heart breaking for Callie's anguish.

"Of course it's my fault," Callie whispered into Kate's shoulder. "Of course it is."

15

Alex Hutchinson unlocked the apartment door and went in. He yanked off his overcoat, stuffing the plaid muffler he'd been wearing into one of the sleeves before hanging it up. The apartment was silent; it would be another hour before Julia got home from school. His footsteps quiet on the oriental rugs lining the long hall, he walked into the bedroom.

The chairman of Columbia's English Department had told him to take a few weeks off, that they would find someone to teach his classes. But after the horror of the past few days and the funeral, he thought he would lose his mind if he didn't get out of the house. He'd spent so many hours in the living room, the book-lined walls closing in on him while relatives and friends dropped by, bringing food, attempting to distract him and cheer up Julia, asking what they could do.

What they could do. *Here's what you can do,* he'd wanted

to shout, *explain to me why Barbara's dead*. But he simply smiled and thanked them for their concern. Only thirty-two years old, and she was gone in an instant, her entire life, their ten years of marriage wiped out just like that. Now he had to start over, alone. And he had a little girl to raise with no mother.

He'd thought it would help to get out, go to his office at the university and do a little paperwork. But he couldn't focus on anything, and he left after an hour, walking back to the apartment on Ninety-first Street, welcoming the painful sting of the frigid winter day on his face and ungloved hands. Before Julia got home, he decided, was as good a time as any to go through some of Barbara's things, start the gruesome process of getting rid of them.

Sunlight sliced through the blinds in the large bedroom. A pair of Barbara's shoes rested in the corner where she'd left them the night she died, hurrying to change clothes for the Weston Christmas party, late from the office as usual. A half-drunk glass of water and an open novel lying facedown were on the nighttable next to her side of the bed. Alex had continued to sleep in the room after she died but he'd never noticed these objects there until now.

He had no idea where to start. Crossing to the tall wooden chest of drawers they shared, he picked up Barbara's cloth-upholstered jewelry box and sat down on the bed.

Barbara was always so neat, he thought, opening the box to reveal earrings, rings, and pins in orderly rows. There were the dangling gold earrings he'd given her when they'd gotten engaged, the day they both graduated from Kenyon College in Ohio. The small diamond stud earrings he'd bought her when she got her M.B.A. degree from New York University. A marcasite pin that had belonged to her mother, one of Barbara's favorite pieces. He lifted up the tray to see necklaces and bracelets underneath, immediately recognizing the long strand of pearls she'd treated herself to when she learned she'd gotten the job with Weston. He recalled how he'd hit the roof when he heard how much they cost, but she had only smiled and walked off, unperturbed; later he'd apologized, telling her she was entitled to a reward after all her hard work getting to this point in her career.

He poked through the other pieces. There was so much,

all the accessories she used to finish off her professional look when she headed out every day to her job, or to complete a stunning outfit for a Saturday night out. Dozens of images of her collided in his mind. Barbara in college, her hair long and flowing, in a turtleneck and jeans; the day Julia was born, his wife's tear-stained face red and worn with the exhaustion of sixteen hours of labor, but blissful also, as the doctor handed the screaming infant to her for the first time; Barbara unpacking cartons the day they moved to New York, perspiration dripping down her face in the ninety-eight-degree heat. He could see her so clearly, seated at the ballet, emerging from the ocean at Fire Island, weeping at her mother's funeral four years before.

He closed the lid. It should all go to Julia anyway. After a moment's thought, he reached inside again and took out the gold earrings and the marcasite pin. Those he would present to Julia that night, the earrings as reminders of her parents' love for each other, the pin a link with her mother and grandmother. The rest he would put away for her until she was older.

His eyes fell on a large plastic bag in the corner. He couldn't remember exactly how it had gotten there, but he knew what it contained: Barbara's purse and the clothes she was wearing the night of the accident. Her friend Allison had dealt with all that, selecting the outfit Barbara had been buried in, asking Alex to approve her choice of one of Barbara's black dresses. He'd barely been able to look at the clothes, mumbling that he was sure whatever she picked was fine, was what Barbara would have wanted. He should probably retrieve her purse, he thought, deal with the credit cards, her checkbook, whatever else might be in it. But he couldn't, not yet.

With a start, he realized that he knew exactly how much money would be in her wallet, that it contained a ten-dollar bill and a twenty-dollar bill. He'd given her the twenty at the Weston party. At around nine o'clock, he'd called home from the party to check in with the babysitter. To his vast annoyance he discovered that the sitter, a woman they'd never used before, had misunderstood them and could only stay with Julia until ten o'clock that night. Alex knew it was important to Barbara that her presence at the party be visible to the higher-ups at Weston, so he had volunteered to call a car service to take him from Westchester back to Manhattan; Barbara could drive the car home herself whenever she was ready to leave. He thought he was doing her a favor, leaving her with the car, letting her conduct her business. As he was going, he asked her if she had enough money with her, since she'd be alone. She looked in her bag.

I only have a ten, she'd said. *I didn't get a chance to go to the bank today.*

Take another twenty, just in case, he'd replied, giving her the bill from his wallet and kissing her on the cheek. *See you later.*

Why had that misunderstanding with the babysitter happened? And why was it so damned important that Barbara stay there, when she could have come home with him then and that would have been the end of it? He could have prevented all of it, *should* have prevented it. Barbara should still be alive.

The noise of a key in the front door startled him. Hurriedly, he got up and replaced the jewelry box on the dresser, not wanting Julia to catch him sitting there with it. She was so attuned to his pain, she would see instantly that he'd been sitting there brooding. He didn't want to do that to her. Her own sorrow was tragedy enough. But it was her awareness of *his* sorrow, the way she attempted to comfort *him* during the days, that tore Alex's heart.

He saw Julia standing in the foyer as her regular daily sitter, Esther, locked the door behind them. She had dropped her bookbag on the floor and was slowly removing her woolen mittens, intent on her task.

"Hello, baby," he said, coming to greet his daughter.

She looked up at him. The strain of the past few days showed on her face, just as it must have been showing on his, he thought. Like him, she had wanted to get out that morning, had insisted on going to school. And just like him, he realized at once, it hadn't helped.

Her eyes, usually so clear and bright, were dull, swollen from crying, and had dark circles under them; since Barbara's death, Julia had been unable to sleep at night, sitting up in Alex's arms and sobbing for hours. Worn out, she would sleep until eleven or twelve the next day. Her smile had always come so easily, but he saw the effort it took for her to produce it now, and her normally rosy complexion was pale. Alex noticed that her long brown hair was sloppily tied back; he realized she must have fixed it herself that morning. Was she old enough to brush her own hair? Had Barbara still been doing that for her? He'd always spent as much time as he could with Julia, but there were still so many things he didn't know about his daughter, all the little things he'd never dealt with before.

"Hi, Daddy," she answered quietly.

He knelt, enveloping her in a hug. He felt her arms go around his neck tightly, her head coming to rest on his shoulder. She didn't say anything else, just stood there, her breathing soft in his ear. Tears stung his eyes.

"Tough day at school, eh?" he asked gently.

She only nodded, her face burrowing farther into his shoulder.

Dear Lord, he thought, stroking her head, *what's going to become of my little girl?*

He stood up, taking both her hands.

"You know, I've got a yearning for a nice cup of hot chocolate, with lots of little marshmallows floating on top." He smiled at her. "Care to join me, champ?"

16

Holding the remote control in one hand, Callie idly changed channels without really seeing what was on the large TV set anchored on a platform high on the opposite wall. She was too depressed to watch anything, too distracted to think about anything. She hit the Off button and turned her head toward the window.

David hadn't shown up in four days. His gifts kept coming—nightgowns, robes, flowers, books, and gourmet treats, all arriving by messenger—but not even a call from him. After that day when she'd tried unsuccessfully to reach him by phone, she'd stopped calling; if he wanted to see her, he certainly knew where she was. But it seemed that he didn't even want to talk to her, much less see her.

He was revolted by the idea of her being disfigured, she just knew it. Her beauty had been part of what he loved, and without that, he didn't love the rest of her enough to care. The feeling had been gnawing away at her as soon as she discovered he hadn't been by her side from the beginning, as she would have expected him to be. She thought she had a right to expect that of him, the man she was going to marry. If their positions had been reversed, and he'd been the one in the hospital, nothing could have kept her away from him.

But she was Callie Stewart, the model—she had to remember that. That's what people expected her to be, and apparently what David expected her to be. Now she was ugly, deformed, disgusting. And he didn't want to be around her anymore. There was no other explanation. She felt cold inside with the terrible knowledge of it.

Callie shut her eyes, wishing she could doze off. The truth was that, once she'd had some success in modeling and accepted that she was considered beautiful, she'd become dependent on her looks. She'd grown more and more fearful that her beauty was the only thing people loved about her. Now it seemed that she was justified in her fear. Had David completely stopped loving her? She didn't know what she would do without him, how she could stand it if he left her.

"Hey, how about a smile from my honey?"

Callie froze at the sound of the voice. Slowly she turned her head to see David standing in the doorway, flowers in one hand, unbuttoning his overcoat. There was a broad grin on his face.

"Oh, David," she whispered. After the tension and pain of the past few days, she felt tears of relief coming to her eyes. "Where have you been?"

He slipped off his coat and hung it in the room's narrow closet. "I'm sorry, Cal, I really am. I *wanted* to come, but you know how I am about hospitals."

She stared at him. No, she *didn't* know how he was about hospitals; the subject had never come up between them. After all this time, his excuse for leaving her alone was that he didn't like hospitals?

"You know I'm practically phobic about them. Always have been." He spoke with false brightness as he unwrapped the roses he'd brought, shoved them into a plastic pitcher, and went into the bathroom to add water. He turned on the faucet and continued talking to her, calling out over the noise of the running water. "But you got all my presents, right? I hope you liked them. I thought you'd look really nice in that blue gown, the one from Saks."

Callie didn't answer. Four days without a call or a visit, and he couldn't be bothered to come up with a plausible excuse. Since he'd arrived, he hadn't kissed her hello, had barely even looked at her. Now he was rambling on with all this ridiculously phony cheerfulness.

He emerged from the bathroom, holding the pitcher out in front of him so none of the water would spill on his suit, one hand covering his silk tie to protect it. He set down the vase, admiring the flowers. "Not bad. It wasn't easy, getting out in the middle of the day and making time to get flowers too." He turned to her. "See what I go through for you?"

Callie raised her chin slightly, afraid to let him see her but at the same time angrily determined that he get a good look at her, at her bandages, at the fading bruises. She watched him for a reaction, but his face was expressionless.

His eyes, she thought fearfully, *his eyes are totally blank. He doesn't feel disgust at the sight of me. But there's no sympathy either, no sorrow, no hurt for me. He doesn't feel anything at all.*

"They taking good care of you around here?" David asked, pacing around the room.

"Yes," Callie answered quietly.

"You gave us quite a scare, but you're going to be fine, just fine."

She nodded.

"Food here's terrific, too, I'm sure." His smile was forced.

Why was he talking to her like that, like a total stranger, mouthing clichés? She wanted to scream at him, to pound him with her fists. *Stop it, stop it,* she cried silently.

"David, please, we need to discuss the accident. This Barbara Hutchinson—"

She was shocked to see a momentary flash of anger in his eyes, disappearing as fast as it came. Before she could go on, they were interrupted by the ringing of the telephone. As she reached for it, he strode to the door.

"Get some rest. I'll talk to you later."

With a wave, he grabbed his coat and left, clearly relieved to be going.

Ignoring the knot in her stomach, Callie answered the phone. The caller was Mick Earl, a casting director at one of the leading advertising agencies who had selected her for a couple of shoe ads her first fall in New York. She'd been extremely grateful to him for the work. There'd been so many other casting people since then that she couldn't honestly say she would have recalled all the rest, but she immediately remembered Mick. Like the dozens of people from the business who'd been calling this week, he hurriedly asked how she was before getting to the question that interested him: what had *really* happened?

At first Callie had been touched by the outpouring of concern from so many people in the industry. Her room was overflowing with flowers sent by the agency, Weston executives, total strangers. Then, once she'd been able to accept visitors, a constant stream of people came by, some of whom she barely knew. She had quickly discovered, however, that, like Mick Earl, they were blatantly curious to find out the inside dirt on her accident, and to learn if the famous Callie Stewart had really been as disfigured as the rumors said. It wasn't difficult to imagine the gossip going on about her throughout the industry.

Summoning all her resources, Callie skillfully deflected Mick's questions about the accident, then thanked him for calling. As she hung up, the door swung open and in stepped Fredericka Whiting, swathed in beige fur, holding two Henri Bendel shopping bags full of presents.

"My *darling*." She rushed over to Callie's bedside and dropped the bags, tossing her coat over the foot of the bed, then turning to clutch Callie's hand. She was dressed in a navy blue suit, her turban a navy and red paisley. "This is too terrible."

"Hello, Fredericka. It's nice of you to visit," Callie said, trying to smile.

"Don't be foolish, of course I would visit." She looked Callie up and down as if delighted with what she saw. "You're healing nicely. You have good doctors, I trust? You must have the best." She put up a finger warningly. "Be sure you have the best."

"They're very good. I trust them completely," Callie replied.

Fredericka pulled a chair closer to the bed and sat down. "Ve're so vorried about you at the agency. Everyone vorries about our girl. You are in much pain?"

"No; it gets a little better every day."

There was a brief silence. Callie saw Fredericka's eyes narrow slightly as she focused more carefully on Callie, taking the look she'd come for, assessing the damage, noting the patch, the stitches, the bruises. Of course the agency would be concerned about one of their biggest assets. Concerned enough for Fredericka to come in person.

"Thank you for worrying about me, but they tell me I'll be as good as new before long," Callie said, realizing as she spoke that it was futile to try to convince Fredericka that the permanent damage was minimal. Fredericka would make up her own mind about Callie's future, and that would be that. In fact, the decision had doubtless been made during the past few seconds. Callie wondered what it was.

"Sveetheart, you vill be *better* than new, I am sure." She crossed her legs. "But tell me about that eye."

"They took some glass out it. It's fine, really, I'm just cultivating a new pirate look."

Fredericka let out a loud, raucous laugh. "I like it. The look suits you." She stood, her mission completed.

"Please give my regards to everyone," Callie said.

The older woman was already halfway into her fur coat. "They all send their love, darling. Ve vant you to get vell right avay. Ve'll have a big party for you as soon as you get back, yes?"

Callie smiled. "How nice of you."

"Enjoy your presents, pet." Fredericka gestured to the shopping bags. "Ve love you."

You love me, Callie said to herself as Fredericka exited, *but will you help me when this is over, will you let me work again?* She hadn't told Fredericka the truth about her condition, the physical therapy and the surgery on her face and eye that lay ahead. No doubt Fredericka would make it her business to get the whole story anyway.

Tiredly, she pressed the control button to lower the head of the bed. First David, then Fredericka. If she let herself think about all of it, let herself feel anything, she would go crazy. Well, she thought bitterly, at least they'd distracted her from what she was usually thinking about. It was rare that she was able to escape her thoughts of Barbara Hutchinson and the little girl she'd left behind. Callie didn't know what she could do. She was sure the woman's husband wouldn't want to talk to her, probably couldn't stand to hear her name mentioned, so she didn't dare call. But hour after hour, she tormented herself with visions of the child weeping for her dead mother.

Alicia Stewart walked in.

"Everything okay, sweetheart?" she asked her daughter. "I saw Fredericka Whiting leaving."

"Everything's fine, Mom," Callie answered in a low voice. "But, please, nobody else today."

"Absolutely. You take a nap now." Alicia stroked Callie's cheek. "You have so many friends, honey, so many people stopping by. Isn't that nice?"

Callie closed her eyes, the skin beneath the bandage itching uncomfortably. *So many friends.* She envisioned little Julia Hutchinson lying in her bed at night, wanting her mommy.

Callie was restlessly picking at her dinner tray when David returned the next day. At the sight of him, she perked up and smiled. She was still wearing the eyepatch, but had put on a pair of sunglasses to hide it from the curious stares of her visitors that day. Now that he was here, she was glad she had them on, sparing him from having to look at the patch.

She smoothed her hair. During the night, as she had tossed in bed, unable to sleep, she realized that she couldn't go on without him, she just couldn't, and she wasn't going to let him slip away. Maybe he hadn't acted the way she wished he would, but he was no doubt having problems dealing with the accident. Of course, she'd thought, relieved. That was what this was really about. He had to fight off his own nightmares of that awful moment on the icy road, and she could only guess how terrible they must be. She'd find a way to make things right between them.

"Feeling better?" David asked, sinking down in a chair and going on without waiting for an answer. "I'm completely beat. We've been bogged down on the packaging for the Sunset colors. It's been a nightmare, Harvey, Aileen, and Craig fighting like cats and dogs. We're not getting anywhere."

He got up and crossed over to the window. Callie realized that, just like on his previous visit, he barely glanced in her direction. She pressed on.

"Want to tell me about it?" she asked helpfully.

"No, it's boring." He was gazing out at the street below. "Besides, I finally got away from it, even if it's just for a few minutes."

"You can only stay a few minutes?" Callie had been hoping they could talk about things, maybe get some of his feelings out into the open so she could deal with them.

He turned around, looking at her irritably. "You don't know what I had to juggle to get here now. Masterson is going to kill me for missing his meeting. I know you're sick, I know it's been tough on you, but I'm doing the best I can."

Hiding her hurt, Callie dropped her gaze down to her tray and slowly took a last spoonful of applesauce. It was obvious that David couldn't handle the fact that she was in this place. Nothing would change while she was still here.

That also meant there was no point in waiting to ask him about the other subject on her mind. *Might as well get it over with,* she decided.

"David," she said tentatively, "do you have any idea what Weston is going to do with me?"

"What do you mean?" He poured himself a glass of orange juice from a bottle sitting in an ice bucket on the windowsill.

"Will they wait for me to get better and let me come back to work?"

His answer was terse. "I haven't discussed it with any-body."

"What kind of protection does my contract give me if I'm hurt like this?"

David folded his arms across his chest. "Probably not much."

"Why?" Callie was alarmed.

"Come on," he snapped. "You were stupid enough to use a lawyer recommended by Whiting. What do you expect?"

Stunned, Callie stared at him. "What do you mean?"

David's tone was impatient. "Don't you understand the business by now, Callie? The agency has its own relation-ship with Weston. That relationship will go on long after you're gone from modeling. Sure, they wanted you to get a lot of money for the deal, but it wasn't in Whiting's best interest to antagonize Weston by fighting tooth and nail for you over every point. You could have gotten your own lawyer, but you asked Whiting, so they gave you theirs, of course. And he had *their* interests to consider as well as yours."

Callie's voice was a whisper. "Why didn't you tell me this before, when we started negotiating?"

He sighed. "Honey, it's obvious. I work for Weston. It would be a conflict of interest for me to tell you to go get a lawyer who'd get more money or concessions out of my company."

"A conflict of interest," Callie echoed in amazement. "You actually felt there was a choice to be made, whether to help your company or the woman you're marrying, the one you'll wake up with every day for the rest of your life, have children with, grow old and die with?" She shook her head. "And you chose to help the *company?*"

"That's a ridiculous way to put it," David retorted. "I have an obligation to Weston. Besides, that job is what supports me."

"I can't believe what I'm hearing." Callie leaned forward, but a sudden stabbing pain in her forehead made her fall back against the pillows immediately. "Don't I count for anything?" she went on quietly, pressing her hand to her head. "I make enough money to support us, anyway. What difference does the money make? You let me walk into something unprotected and did nothing about it."

"You had a lawyer. Don't act like I fed you to the wolves," he replied angrily. "It wasn't my place to get involved."

"Of course it was your place. If you loved me, it was your place." Callie's voice rose, her anger matching his. She ignored the throbbing in her head. "This is incredible."

"Stop making me out to be the bad guy," David yelled. "Nobody knew something like this would happen."

"A woman *died,* David," Callie exploded, her anger finally reaching the surface. "And I almost died myself. None of this seems to mean anything to you. All you're worried about are your office politics. You don't care about me, you don't care about anyone."

In a few long strides, he had crossed the room and retrieved his coat.

"I can't deal with this right now, Callie, I really can't. I have a lot of other things on my mind. Like I said, I know you're sick, but . . ."

Callie stared at him, too shocked to say anything more. She watched the door swing shut behind him.

So that's how it was. Now she knew there would be no wedding, no home to share, no children and growing old together. David didn't love her anymore. She wondered if he ever had. He hadn't helped her when it counted before and he wasn't there for her now when she desperately needed him. There was no use lying to herself, making excuses for his behavior. He was as cold as a stranger, uncaring and cut off from her completely. Her David.

The pain in her head intensified. Everything she had planned, everything she'd wanted. She'd had it, she'd *held* it in her hand. It was gone.

Over the next week, Callie lay in bed, the hurt of David's betrayal battling with the physical pain of her injuries. Her parents had left; they'd had to go back to their jobs. She was alone with her bad dreams, her tears over David, and her remorse and grief over Barbara Hutchinson.

The only people she still wanted to see were Kate and

April. But she noticed it was becoming less of a problem to keep people out. Fewer and fewer were coming to visit. The number of telephone calls dwindled as well. She supposed that interest in her and her misfortune was diminishing as the next scandal came along, the next hot piece of news traveled the circuit. She spoke to Grace on the telephone regularly, but despite the booker's genuine friendliness and concern, Callie could tell she was usually busy and feeling pressured to get back to her work. Thank goodness for April and Kate, she thought. They were always there to help.

It was Kate who was at her bedside the day Callie's doctor came to remove the bandages from her right eye and the side of her face.

"Good afternoon," Dr. Grant said cheerily, entering the room to find the two women deep in conversation. "Are you ready, Callie? We're going to take a peek at what's been happening under there."

Callie stiffened.

The doctor took her hand. "It's not going to be healed yet, please understand. Don't think this is the final result. But it's time to open things up."

Kate smiled. "Hey, with your luck, Cal, you'll look even better than before."

Callie nodded. "Okay, let's go ahead."

Kate pulled the curtain so Callie and doctor could have privacy, then stepped outside. There was silence in the room as the doctor cut away the gauze dressings, then carefully removed the eyepatch. He stood back and examined her face carefully, gently pressing on a few areas, asking if she was experiencing pain or any other sensation in various spots. When he was finished, he nodded.

"Do you want to see?"

She shook her head.

"It's not quite what we'd hoped, but we have every reason to be encouraged. Just remember it's going to take time."

"Thank you." Callie stopped listening as the doctor went on, encouraging her, giving her further instructions to help the healing process.

"Should I send your friend back in?" he asked as he was leaving.

"Yes, please."

Kate was back at her bedside almost instantly. She took a good look at Callie. "Well, okay, we're gettin' there," she said.

Callie bit her lip. "Give me a mirror. There's one in the drawer here."

Kate walked around to the nighttable, retrieved the mirror, and placed it in Callie's hand.

Callie took a deep breath. Then she looked.

Large black stitches ran from her eyebrow down along her upper eyelid, then continued from her lower eyelid partway down her cheek. Other stitches ran along her temple and up onto her forehead, disappearing beneath her hairline. The stitches were coarse-looking, and the skin around them was red and raw. Her right eye was swollen and puffy. The center of her eye was an eerie white, the original green of the iris only a hazy outline around the milky covering. Closing her other eye, Callie realized she could barely see out of the injured one.

She put the mirror down on the bed.

"It'll be okay, Cal, you know it will." Kate picked up the mirror, fiddling with it as she talked nervously. "Plastic surgery is incredible these days."

"It's all over, Kate," Callie said quietly. She was silent for a moment. "That poor woman died, and I lived." She took the mirror from her friend and gave herself one last look before putting it facedown on the table. "Of course, what punishment could be more fitting than this?"

17

The aroma of baking cookies filled the house. Callie inhaled deeply as her father carefully maneuvered her wheelchair through the front door.

"We're here," Frank called out.

"Frank? Callie?" Alicia's voice reached them just before she appeared in the kitchen doorway.

Breaking into a wide smile, Alicia rushed forward to kiss and hug her daughter, bending a bit awkwardly to put her arms around Callie in the wheelchair. Alicia had stayed behind while Frank went to get Callie out of the hospital in New York and bring her back to Bloomington to recuperate. Despite talking to Callie on the telephone every day, Alicia hadn't seen her in nearly two weeks.

"Sweetheart, how are you feeling? I hope the trip wasn't too much for you."

As she talked, Alicia quickly examined Callie's face, trying to make her glance appear casual. She did a good job of hiding her shock at what she saw, Callie thought, watching her mother's eyes grow wide as she took in the tracks from her stitches. But then Alicia caught her breath and brought her hand over her heart, and Callie knew she felt a stab there.

"It's great to be home, Mom," Callie said sincerely, wanting to comfort her mother. "I'm fine, really." She didn't want Alicia to know how exhausting the flight had been for her.

"Well, we're going to fix you right up here. Your room's ready, and you're to do nothing but concentrate on getting better."

"Maybe I'll go there now for a little while."

Callie looked at her father. "It was a long trip for you too, Dad. I'll bet we could both use a nap before dinner."

"Sure could."

As Frank wheeled the chair down the hall, Alicia called out, "Callie, I'll be there in a minute to see what you need, and I'll bring you some warm milk."

"Thanks, Mom," Callie answered gratefully.

Her father pushed open the door to her bedroom. She saw that her mother had put fresh flowers in a vase on the dresser, along with some magazines. The bed was already turned down, and Callie sighed with pleasurable anticipation at the prospect of slipping under the soft quilt, resting between the worn but freshly pressed pink sheets. Getting out of the chair was a slow process, her father awkwardly assisting her. Her broken ribs still ached with every movement, and her leg was difficult to manage in its long, heavy cast.

When she was finally settled, he pulled the quilt up over her and gave her a quick kiss. Her eyes were already closing.

"We love you, champ," he said. "Whatever we can do, you just name it."

She barely managed a thank-you before she was fast asleep.

"If the surgery works, I should be able to see again out of that eye. But everything is one step at a time." Callie took another bite of her mother's fresh banana bread and followed it with a sip of tea. She sounded detached, as if she were talking about someone else. "First, there'll be physical therapy for my leg when I get back to New York. Then they'll do the plastic surgery on my face."

Nodding, Frank sipped his tea. In the past week, he and his wife had been careful not to pressure Callie by questioning her about what could be done for her injuries and scars. The doctors had told them that nothing would be happening just yet, so there was no point in upsetting her unnecessarily. But for some reason, she had brought up the topic herself now.

"What do they say about your leg?" Frank asked. "How long will it take to heal?"

Callie shook her head. "Hard to say. It's pretty bashed up."

"Well, you're certainly looking much better," he said. The dark circles under Callie's eyes were almost gone, and she appeared more rested than when she'd come the week before. They'd gone for long walks every day, he pushing the wheelchair against the bracing January wind, the two of them saying little. He was pleased to see that the fresh air had brought back a bit of color to her cheeks. And she said that her ribs hurt her a little less each day, a great relief to him and Alicia.

But putting her battered physical self back together wasn't the only thing that mattered. All of Frank's best efforts at conversation and humor had produced only distracted replies and the smallest smiles from her. He often found her sitting in the wheelchair, staring out the window, tears running down her cheeks. But he couldn't get her to say anything other than that she was still upset about the accident. When he tried to pursue it, she politely but firmly ended the conversation and wheeled herself out of the room. And she absolutely refused to discuss why she'd broken off her engagement. However, her parents knew that she felt devastated, her silences and detachment a means of covering up the hurt.

The physical damage was something they could all live with. But if Callie's spirit was broken, Frank and Alicia didn't know what to do, how to restore it. When she was little, they had always known how to fix her hurts; now, they'd never felt so helpless.

"You've got to put in the effort for your leg, Cal. I'm sure you can get it back into shape," Frank said.

"I suppose." She spoke calmly, nothing in her voice betraying how she felt about the struggle ahead.

Frank felt another surge of rage at the injustice of what had happened to his little girl, rage he had been fighting back since the night of the accident. But he made sure his even tone matched hers. "There's no reason to say that. You've got to believe that you will."

They sat for a moment. Frank glanced at his watch.

"You keep checking the time," Callie observed. "Are you expecting something to happen?"

The front door opened.

"That's what I was expecting!" Frank smiled. "A little surprise for you."

Callie looked up to see Tommy coming into the house. She hadn't seen or spoken to her brother since the previous Christmas, when they'd parted on such bitter terms. The sight of him shocked her with the realization of how terribly she'd missed him. His blond hair tousled by the wind, he was tall and fit, his shoulders broad beneath his jacket. Seeing her there in the wheelchair, he stopped where he was. They regarded each other. He made no effort to hide his inspection of her, his eyes taking in the cast, the bruise marks on her arms, the injuries to the right side of her face.

"Hi, Tommy," she said almost shyly.

"Cal," he replied, shaking his head. "You look lousy."

There was silence in the room for a second, then Callie burst out laughing. Frank was surprised and delighted by the sound.

"I look almost as bad as you," she retorted to Tommy. "Are you here to be nursed back to health too?"

"No." He came closer, his expression gentle. "I'm here to spend some time with my big sister."

Callie stared at him. She'd been holding a petty little grudge, while he was there for her as soon as she needed him. She knew that Tommy had just begun his second semester at the University of Indiana. Her parents had told her only a few days before that he'd received some financial aid, taken out a large loan, and was working three different jobs to pay for his tuition. He'd done it all without a dime from her. She'd been horribly ashamed that her wounded ego had prevented her from even asking how he'd managed to get to college. He turned to his father.

"I came as soon as I could square things away for a little while. They won't miss me too much there."

"For once I'd have to say there's something more important going on than school," Frank replied.

Her brother looked back at her and smiled. He truly wasn't angry with her. Here he was, struggling to make a sum of money she could have covered in one check without giving it a second thought. She'd destroyed his pride, hadn't spoken to him since then, hadn't tried to get in touch with him for an entire year. But instead of being angry, he had gone to all this trouble to be with her. She wanted to cry at her selfishness.

"How about coming with your broken-down old sister into the living room," she said. "We can, as Granddad used to put it, sit a spell."

Tommy put his hands on the wheelchair's white leather grips, giving it an appraising look. "How fast do you suppose this thing would go down a hill?"

"We set up your furniture, but of course you'll want to do everything over so it's the way you want it." April fumbled in her bag for the key. She'd been talking nonstop on the way home from the airport. Callie knew her friend thought the chatter would cheer her up. It wasn't working, but she appreciated April's efforts.

"I'm sure it'll be fine," Callie said softly, shifting her weight slightly on her crutches. She waited patiently as April dug around in her red satchel. It suddenly seemed to Callie that she'd spent what seemed like half her life moving from one apartment to the next.

"Kate and I were so petrified, picking out a place for you.

We hope Seventy-fourth Street isn't farther uptown than you would have wanted. I mean, I thought I'd like it for myself, so . . ."

"This looks like a nice building. I'm sure I'll be happy here," Callie said reassuringly. "Besides, it was such a big favor, I can never thank you enough."

April dismissed that with a wave of her hand. "Don't be ridiculous. Naturally, you wouldn't go back to David's." She found what she'd been searching for, brandishing the key with a flourish. "Aha!" She inserted it into the lock, still talking. "How'd things go with your family?"

Callie smiled. The three weeks in Bloomington had been the best medicine she could possibly have had. Her parents had made her feel safe and protected, given her a place to nurse her wounds, both physical and otherwise, soothing her with love, but also knowing when she needed to be left alone. How ignorant she had been, thinking *they* were hicks. They were genuine, down-to-earth people who knew what was important in life. *She* was the one who had things twisted around.

They had helped her, even though she'd done her best to shut them out. At first she'd thought she'd never be able to stop thinking about David, to stop crying, to stop seeing his face at night while she lay there, praying for sleep to overtake her. She couldn't stop going over their time together, how they'd met, the wonderful months in the beginning, and his proposal. Then she saw the accident, the days in the hospital, that awful last conversation when she couldn't pretend anymore, when she had to face the truth about him. Where there was once a plan, a future for her, now there was nothing, just a frightening emptiness waiting for her back in New York. She was so afraid.

She'd cried alone in her room, not wanting her parents to see her misery, the racking sobs so painful to her bruised body. She thought she would die from her unhappiness. But slowly, very slowly, her grief had been replaced by other feelings. She was ashamed of herself for being so blind about him, for not seeing what kind of man he really was. And she was angry at him. He'd used her, he'd ruined her life, and he didn't give a damn. She was worn out by the power of her emotions, the sorrow and hate, the humiliation and fear. Her parents respected her demands for privacy, but their presence, the warmth of their comfort, was what got her from one day to the next.

If there was anything good to be said about the accident, it was what it had done for her relationship with her parents. She and Tommy had repaired things between them as well. As far as his college costs went, she had grappled with the question for days. She didn't want to diminish his accomplishment of getting the money for school himself. But she didn't want him to have to work so many hours when he could be studying or enjoying himself. In the end, she'd given her parents a check, asking them to tell Tommy his financial aid had been increased. She hoped that was the right decision.

"My family was terrific," she said to April. "I'm so glad I went there."

April threw open the door, handing Callie the key. "Now, tell me what you think."

They stepped inside.

"David left us a spare key to his place to let the movers in. But he wasn't around, so we didn't see him. I hope we took all the right things."

Callie saw that her friends had carefully set out the few pieces of furniture she'd instructed them to pack. There were dishes and pots and pans in the kitchen. All the walls were bare. Through an open doorway she saw a bed made up with the blue and white sheets she'd bought last summer. She loved those sheets, had enjoyed the crisp snap as she whipped them open and let them drift down slowly onto the bed. The thought flashed into her mind that David had made love to her on them.

The cold, unlived-in emptiness of the place was overpowering, but it was the sight of those sheets that nearly overwhelmed her. She swallowed, afraid she might break down.

"It's perfect," she said, managing a small smile. "And you did a great job setting it up. Thank you so much."

"Don't be silly." April went into the bedroom, unzipping Callie's suitcase and hurriedly removing its contents. "I've got to run to a booking, but Kate's coming by in about fifteen minutes. She said she was bringing Chinese food for the two of you and a good bottle of wine. Your telephone's installed, and the cable guy will be here tomorrow."

She came back into the living room, where Callie had flopped down on the sofa, her crutches propped beside her. "Can I get you anything before I go?"

Callie shook her head. "No, but I really appreciate—"

"Please, it's *nothing.*" April leaned down to give her a peck on the cheek. "Talk to you later."

The door shut. Callie was alone. She turned the key to the apartment over and over in her palm. A strange new place, all by herself again. David hadn't been interested enough even to ask April where Callie was going. And she hadn't expected the pain she felt at finding out that he had never bothered to check on the packing of her things. He hadn't cared if she took furniture she'd bought for them, anything with sentimental value from their time together, or even something that rightfully belonged to him. He didn't care if she erased every trace of her existence from his home. That hurt her in a way nothing else had.

The doorbell rang.

"It's open," Callie called out.

Kate stuck her head in. "What are you, nuts? You leave your door open and then you announce it to anybody who comes along?" She came in smiling, a brown bag with takeout food in one hand. "Hey, stranger. Glad you're back."

They talked as they unpacked the food, Callie leaning on her crutches, trying to help. Kate carried it all out to the dining room table in three trips.

"Dig in," she instructed, pouring them each a glass of wine. "The spare ribs from this place are delicious."

There was a time when Callie would have avoided all the food Kate had selected, opting for steamed vegetables to preserve her figure. She supposed it didn't matter anymore. But maybe she was wrong.

"Kate," she said, "what's the word on my Weston contract?"

Her friend reached for an egg roll and said noncommittally, "Boy, you don't waste any time. What makes you think I know anything about it?"

"Because you know everything that goes on," Callie replied patiently. "And I know you would have been on the watch for me because you're a good friend."

"You overestimate me." Looking down, Kate tore open a packet of duck sauce.

Callie smiled. "You're a bad liar."

Kate brought her eyes up to meet Callie's. "It's not important right now, Cal. You can deal with it later, when you're settled in."

"That bad, huh?" Callie took a breath. "I need to know."

"All right." Kate hesitated. "The word isn't good. It seems they're going to invoke some clause in your contract about your no longer maintaining the same physical appearance."

"They're dropping me completely? No second chance after my surgery?" Callie took a drink of wine, wishing her hand would stop shaking.

Kate nodded, her eyes showing how much she hurt for her friend. "I'm sorry, but it looks that way."

Callie ran her finger up and down the stem of her glass. "And David? What part did he play in this?"

"Oh, come on, you don't care about that," Kate said rapidly. "It's over between you, and you know how men can get. Besides, what do you expect?"

"Come on, Kate. And I want the truth," Callie said sternly.

"You're not being fair," Kate protested. "Don't put me in this position."

Callie stared at her, waiting.

Kate's voice was quiet. "He was one of the first to suggest dropping you."

Shutting her eyes, Callie let the pain wash over her. It was over for her then, really and truly. David had completely turned against her, making his betrayal of her public by suggesting Weston drop her. If Weston tossed her out, no one else would touch her, even if she could walk again, even if they could somehow repair her face. But of course there was no point in thinking like that anyway. She was deformed, scarred, her face and eye a hideous sight. Her modeling was finished forever.

The man she'd loved so much and her entire career, both gone in a flash. Why had she been given everything, only to have it snatched away? How long ago was it that she'd felt she was the luckiest girl in the world? She'd certainly had that wrong. Unlucky Callie, she thought miserably. Unlucky me.

18

There was Gloria Kendall up ahead. Alex Hutchinson reached for Julia's hand.

"Let's cross here, honey," he said, steering his daughter to the other side of the street and around the corner.

He continued holding her hand as they headed toward the Hudson River. There was just no way he could deal with Gloria today. She'd been a friend of Barbara's, from her exercise class or some such thing, and he knew the line of questions and sympathy he would be in for if he stopped to talk. He just couldn't do it anymore, couldn't keep it together to make polite conversation while trying to show how well he was holding up since his wife's death.

The truth was that he was holding up *lousy*. Nearly two months had passed, but he hadn't found any answers, any reason to feel that Barbara's death hadn't been a pointless waste. Numb at first, he had quickly lost the battle with grief, succumbing to the pain, fearful he would never find a way out of it. He didn't know how to cope with the emptiness of their apartment, the sudden blank slate of his days and nights where there had once been routines and schedules. At least he had his work. Teaching literature was absorbing enough to take his mind off everything else for the moment, although he would periodically find himself stopped midsentence during a lecture, completely at a loss as to what he'd just been saying. Most of his students knew about Barbara, and he was embarrassed to see the pity in their eyes.

His anchor, the reason he was able to hold himself together, was Julia. His daughter needed a parent she could rely on to be there for her. He sensed her clinging, her unspoken terror that he would leave her the way her mother had. Her need somehow made it a little easier for him to be strong, comforting her through all the tears she was crying for both of them.

Lately, though, he had found himself more angry than grieving. It had begun surfacing in small ways—his impatience when he tied his tie, cursing at himself when he dropped something or couldn't immediately find what he was looking for, an instant fury at other drivers on the road who cut him off. But it had grown steadily, a mounting sense of impotent rage, of wanting to hit something, to scream, to explode. *His wife was dead. Why?* He wanted answers.

Julia ran ahead of him, clutching a paper bag, the sun bright on her face. It was unusually warm, the kind of day that signaled spring wasn't too far away. Lovingly, Alex observed Julia's profile, the porcelain skin and fragile features, the long ponytail caught up in a plaid bow. She was so delicate, so precious. And he was so ill-equipped to raise her alone. He'd never realized all the things Barbara did for her, how much needed doing from morning until night.

"Daddy, I think I see a big fish out there." She pointed excitedly out over the Hudson River.

He came up alongside her. "Great. Where is it?"

She scanned the water. "I guess he's gone."

"Well, we'll keep looking for him." Alex stroked her hair lightly.

She shrugged, then opened the paper bag she was holding. Inside was a small bottle filled with pink liquid. Carefully opening the bottle, she retrieved the plastic wand inside and brought it out in front of her, waving it. Bubbles filled the air around them. Alex watched her rapt attention to her task. She had always adored bubbles. Since her mother had died there were few activities or games that still held her interest; Alex could only hope she would return to them in time. But blowing bubbles was, for reasons known only to her, an acceptable way to have fun in the midst of her sorrow. She was smiling now, holding her arm straight out and waving it back and forth as the delicate, rainbowed orbs filled the air around them.

"Aren't they pretty, Daddy?" she asked, spinning around in a circle as she produced more.

"They sure are, love." Thank goodness she was being distracted from thinking about Barbara for even these few minutes. Little girls weren't meant to lose their parents, he thought bitterly. They couldn't bear the monstrous weight of it.

A strong breeze carried a batch of her bubbles away.

"Look," she cried, "the bubbles are blowing out over the water. They're sailing away, just like little ships."

He smiled, but his mind abruptly went elsewhere, reminded by Julia's words of a conversation he'd had with Barbara several weeks before she died. He could envision his wife so clearly, sitting down to dinner with him that night, pouring another glass of her ever-present diet soda, her eyes bright. She'd been saying she was going to blow someone out of the water, and her mood was happy. What had they been talking about? Something about some guy at work whom she'd suspected was up to no good. It was coming back now, her elation at how she'd gotten the whole story on him and how she was going to ruin his career. He'd started to question her, asking why she was so happy about the whole thing, but something had interrupted them. Then the conversation had degenerated into an argument of some sort. He quickly pushed away the memory.

Alex took a deep breath, his anger returning. Was this what lay ahead of him, years of half-remembered conversations, snatches of words, images? The dimming memory of his wife haunting all his conversations and thoughts as he tried to forget? But he couldn't permit himself to forget: he would have to keep her alive for their daughter.

"Daddy, are you okay?" Julia was standing still, watching him with a frightened expression.

His anger must have shown on his face. Quickly, he knelt to reassure her, putting an arm around her shoulder. "Of course, honey. I was just thinking about something. What were you saying?"

By the time he had fed Julia dinner and put her to bed later that night, Alex was exhausted. But it was only his mind that was tired; his body refused to sit still. He went from room to room, unable to settle down, trying to read, attempting to go over some lecture notes, turning the television on, then immediately turning it off.

His mind went back to David Long. Maybe it was pointless, but Alex wanted to meet with him, to talk face to face with the man who'd been driving the car that night. He wanted some explanation, some apology, *something*. He supposed it shouldn't come as a surprise that this Long guy hadn't taken any of Alex's calls so far; he was probably afraid of what Alex might do.

Barbara had rarely confided in him about the people she worked with, so he didn't know what her relationship with David Long had been. She was usually too tired at night to discuss what went on at the office, or she claimed that the politics were too involved to get into. Maybe she *had* mentioned some of the people, and he hadn't paid attention properly. It was hard to tell now. But it was incredible to Alex that David Long had actually worked with Barbara and still wouldn't give her husband the time of day after being responsible for her death. Even though Barbara had died of a heart attack, if Alex had been the one in the driver's seat, he sure as hell would have felt responsible if someone else's wife had died that way.

His anger was rising again. There was also that Callie Stewart, the fancy model in the car with Long. He felt she was equally to blame. She'd actually had the audacity to send flowers to the funeral, no doubt figuring that that absolved her. They didn't care about Barbara or what they'd done. The model and her executive boyfriend. Disgusting.

He took a few deep breaths, trying to calm down. It wasn't helping, all this rage and no place to put it.

He went into the kitchen thinking he would grab something to eat. As he opened the refrigerator, he spotted the carton with Barbara's name on it, the carton of her things sent over by Weston after her death. He'd looked through the contents but hadn't known what to do with them, so he'd just shoved the box into the corner, planning to deal with it later. Now, as he gazed at it, he thought again of her remark about blowing some guy out of the water. What had she meant by that?

Shutting the refrigerator door, he dragged the carton out of the corner and lifted it onto the kitchen table. It was filled with papers and folders. There was a plastic bag bulging with Weston makeup samples along with a smaller one containing makeup that was obviously Barbara's, the jars and tubes open, half-used. Down at the bottom was her leather desk set, an assortment of pens, pencils, pads, and a jumble of all the other small items usually found in office desk drawers. He pulled out the folders and loose pages, scanning them for anything that might be connected to her comment. One of her colleagues had been doing something unethical, or maybe illegal. But what? This was just a batch of straightforward memos, reports, and charts, nothing out of the ordinary. If the answer was there, it was too subtle for him to see.

Ridiculous, he thought suddenly, feeling like a fool. He was sitting there pretending to be a spy, looking for who-knew-what, as if Barbara had left some secret behind. He stood up and tossed the papers back into the box, annoyed at himself. So what if one of the Weston people was ripping off the company? It wasn't his concern, certainly not anymore. Weston had stolen his wife from him, first when she was alive, then later when two of the people connected with the company killed her.

But he was going to have his talk; he was going to demand it. He had a right to know more than the official police version of that rainy night when his wife died. Somebody owed him an explanation. One way or another, he had to resolve this, had to hear that they'd *tried* to avoid hitting her but it was truly impossible, that they regretted what happened, that they even cared. Anything was better than sitting around feeling helpless. He needed to put the accident to bed in his mind somehow, to find a way to live with it. And a way to live with the fact that he'd gone home from the party that night and left his wife behind. With the fact that he was still alive.

Alex stood in front of the door trying to calm down. *I haven't even gotten into the woman's apartment and I'm already out of control*, he admonished himself. But he couldn't help it. He'd been angry before their phone conversation, angry on his way over here tonight. He could envision the evening ahead, the prima donna model sparing a few precious seconds to dole out a little phony sympathy, then patting him on the head and sending him away. He'd wondered if she might try to use her looks on him, play up to his male ego to appease him, shut him up; that probably worked pretty well for models. He imagined there would be a verbal battle, he demanding explanations, she acting self-righteous or attempting to dismiss him.

Wait a minute, he told himself, *let's get a grip here.* Actually, it was something of a surprise that he'd been able to contact her so easily. When he had decided to confront her, he had assumed she would behave just as her slimy boyfriend had, offhandedly avoiding him. Her telephone number was unlisted but he'd called Weston and been referred to her modeling agency. Once he had identified his connection to Callie, someone there had told him they couldn't give out her number but the message would definitely be passed on to her. Expecting that he would have to call many more times before reaching her, he was startled when the telephone rang later that same night and the caller softly identified herself as Callie Stewart. When he told her he wanted to have a talk with her, she had agreed at once and invited him to her home the following night.

He rang the bell and waited. He'd seen her photograph—was there anyone in America who hadn't?—but he'd never given her a thought until Barbara's death. All he remembered was that she was tall and blond, thin and beautiful, as one would expect any model to be. He envisioned a laughing, arrogant girl, with not a brain in her head, not a thought for anyone but herself.

The woman who answered the door that night was certainly tall and blond, but that was where her resemblance to his mental image stopped. He was taken aback to see her on crutches, one leg in a cast, large black sunglasses only partially obscuring scars on her face; he hadn't known she'd been so seriously injured in the accident. Now that he thought back, he'd never inquired what had happened to her. The police had told him she'd gone to the hospital, but he'd assumed it was minor, having heard that David Long suffered only a bruise or two. And he'd stayed away from reading the newspaper reports of the incident, keeping the papers out of the house where Julia might see them.

"Please come in," she said softly, taking his coat and balancing on her crutches as she slowly hung it in the hall closet. He noted how pale she was. Following her halting steps into the living room, he realized that every movement was painful for her.

The apartment was barely furnished, a tray of drinks and glasses set out for him, everything clean and neat, almost pristine. They sat facing each other, Callie choosing a chair, he positioning himself on the couch.

"What will you have?" she asked.

"Nothing," he said tightly.

She nodded and there was silence. Then she spoke again, her tone soft and apparently sincere.

"I hope you didn't have any trouble getting your message through to me. They're protective of us at the agency. You can understand why, I'm sure."

He nodded.

She looked pained. "I'm terribly sorry I didn't call you myself earlier. I should have, and I really regret it now."

Prepared for her to be cautious and defensive, Alex felt the wind being let out of his sails. He didn't know what to say.

"Do you live alone here?" He had no idea what made him ask that.

"Yes," Callie replied. "I've been here since the accident,

or rather, since I got back from my family's. They took care of me at first."

"Are they nearby?" *Why* was he asking her these questions?

"Indiana." She gave him a sad smile. "Too far away."

There was something so lonely about this girl. Suddenly Alex bristled, the reason he was there rushing back to him in full force. "But you have David Long, your boyfriend, of course," he said, the irony heavy in his tone.

Callie tilted her head, but he couldn't read her expression. "No, we're not together anymore."

Alex stood up in annoyance. This girl had to be acting, all sweetness and innocence.

"Look," he said, "you and Long killed my wife. I wasn't there. I never got to say goodbye to her. All I know is that I got a phone call telling me she was dead, and now my little girl has no mother."

Callie looked down at her lap, then back up at him. Her face was even paler than before.

Alex began to pace. "Yes, she had a heart condition, I know that, and technically it was the cause of death. But you knocked her down, your recklessness brought the heart attack on. I want to know what happened that night, what *really* happened, not the public version." His voice rose. "You owe me that much. Your boyfriend doesn't even take my calls. Does he think I won't show up in person if I want to, that he can just hide from me? What kind of a coward is he anyway?"

He saw Callie's jaw clench for a second.

"Well, for now, I'm here," he went on. "And you were in that car along with him. So you talk to me."

Her voice was so low he barely heard her. "What do you want to know?"

Sitting back down, he slammed his fist on the coffee table. The noise made Callie jump. "Why did my wife have to die?"

He waited for her to say the inevitable, that it was just an accident and couldn't have been prevented, that it wasn't her fault, she wasn't even driving. But all she said was, "I don't know. She shouldn't have."

Alex was thrown by her lack of resistance, her refusal to defend herself as he had expected she would. "What do you mean you don't know?" he shouted.

Callie flinched at his harsh tone, but her voice remained quiet. "We were driving out of the parking lot. I saw your wife in the road and we came very close to her, but David slammed on the brakes." She took a deep breath, remembering. "I thought everything would be all right. Then we hit some ice, I guess, and the car went into a skid. That's when your wife was knocked down."

"Did anyone help her?" Alex was frustrated, unable to grasp on to anything beyond the bare facts, but not even sure what he was trying to get at.

"I honestly can't tell you what happened to her after that." Callie paused. "The other car hit us and I went through the windshield. I didn't see anything else."

Her words silenced him.

Callie continued, "There's nothing I can say to make up for what happened to your wife. Please forgive me for not getting in touch with you, but I assumed you'd never want to talk to me or see me. And of course, there was the hospital for several weeks, and then Indiana." She looked away. "Things got a bit . . . overwhelming." Her gaze came back to meet his. "But that's no excuse."

He wondered what it had been like for her, weeks in a hospital with that leg and the lacerations on her face. Suddenly he realized that an injury to her face must be a model's worst fear. This girl's career was over. And he could only imagine what must have gone on with her boyfriend if they had split up after something like this. To his amazement, he found he was feeling sorry for her.

"I've thought a lot about you and your little girl," Callie was saying. "That may sound disingenuous, but it's true. I've never known how I could be of any help, though. All I can do is tell you I'm deeply sorry. I'd give anything to change what happened that night."

Alex ran his hand through his hair. He supposed this was what he had wanted to hear all along from her—that at least somebody was sorry for what happened. Now he realized that it accomplished nothing.

"Does your leg hurt you a lot?"

"At times," she replied. "The cast is coming off next week."

"Then it'll be healed?"

She shook her head. "Not right away. I'll be starting physical therapy."

His eyes met hers. "I'm sorry." They both knew he was apologizing for having come here, a chip on his shoulder, looking for someone to blame.

He stood up. "I shouldn't take any more of your time."

"There's something I want to ask you." Callie reached for her crutches and started easing herself up from the couch.

Alex put up a hand to stop her. "I'll let myself out."

She smiled gratefully. "Okay. But would you consider doing me a very big favor by bringing your daughter here one day? I'd like to meet her. If it's okay with you, of course."

Alex was surprised to hear himself agreeing to her request.

"Maybe Thursday afternoon after school," he offered. "My last class ends at three o'clock."

"Class?" Callie echoed.

"I teach English lit at Columbia."

"Yes, of course, I'd read that about you," Callie said. "I guess it's hard to connect a real person to the cold news reports."

Alex was surprised, not having considered that she might have cared enough to bother reading about him.

"Thursday's great. Thank you," she said warmly. "It means a lot to me."

He nodded. "Good night, Callie."

"Good night," she said. "I'm glad you came and gave me a chance to talk to you."

The strange thing was, Alex thought as he left, that she clearly meant it.

19

The waiter approached their table. "Something to drink, ladies?"

April smiled at him. "A glass of red wine, please."

Callie shook her head. "Nothing for me, thanks."

As the waiter left, April eyed her quizzically. "Given up drinking?"

"It makes me tired these days, and that's something I really can't afford." She patted the crutches propped next to her against the wall. "The cast may be off, but I still need my wits to maneuver on these."

April gave her a sympathetic look. "I understand."

"But, you know," Callie reflected, "I do feel better in general since I stopped. I didn't realize how much I'd been drinking before."

Her friend assumed a stern schoolmarm's voice. "Everything in moderation, missy."

Callie laughed, adjusting her sunglasses on her face. "Not a bad philosophy, at that."

"I suppose." April sighed. "I live a more moderate life since I got rid of Louie. It's better without the lows, but I admit to missing the highs."

Callie thought of David, of the elation she'd experienced the first time they'd made love, those weeks when she'd begun planning their wedding. All that paled in comparison to the feelings of betrayal she lived with now. Finding out how badly she'd misjudged him, how totally heartless he was—that was the worst. She'd invested all her dreams in him, only to discover that her wonderful fiancé was just a product of her imagination; David Long bore no resemblance to the man she'd wanted to believe he was.

She turned her attention back to April. "I know someone else will come along for you to love, someone who's perfect for you."

April brightened. "As a matter of fact, I met a guy on location in North Carolina. . . ."

Callie smiled. "See, it didn't take long."

The waiter brought April a glass of wine and took their lunch orders.

"How's Kate doing?" April asked. "I haven't spoken to her lately. Is she still dating Hal Arden? It's funny, the two of them finally getting together. She's been crazy for him for—how long? I remember her pursuing him that night of the movie premiere."

Callie suddenly realized that the night April was referring to was the same night she'd met David. "They're doing great," she said. "Kate's so happy, she's flying."

Kate had talked with Hal at the party after the screening, but it wasn't until she'd run into him again several months later that he had asked her out, for a ride on the Staten Island Ferry, of all places. Kate had loved that. Callie smiled, remembering how excited her friend had been. She hoped it would work out for them.

April took a sip of her wine. "And you—how are you doing?"

"Okay, I guess." Callie shrugged. "I'm getting there. Thanks again for picking me up from physical therapy today. I really appreciate it."

"Please, you've thanked me three times." April waved her

hand dismissively. "It's no big deal. Are you making progress?"

"I suppose so. They force me to move my leg, get things going. It's difficult, but the people who work there are wonderful, just amazing. They genuinely care about you. And they don't seem to know who I am, or at least they don't care, which is such a relief. I don't have to be Callie the model. I can look like a mess, and I can be mean and cranky, and they still have a joke to cheer me up."

"You, mean and cranky? I don't believe it," April said.

Callie smiled. "It's true. And the other people who go there for the therapy, they're so full of spirit. They have such terrible things wrong with them—they're much worse off than I am—yet they go on trying. It's kind of inspiring." Callie turned shy. "I know that sounds corny."

"Not at all," April responded. "I admire that you're finding something positive in all this."

Their food arrived and they started eating.

"You know what's strange?" Callie went on, spearing lettuce onto her fork. "The most positive thing that came out of all this is spending time with that little girl, Julia Hutchinson."

"You're still in touch with those people?" April asked, surprised.

"Not the father so much," Callie replied. "But he's let me see his daughter twice. We went to the zoo, which was sort of a fiasco with my leg, but it was fun anyway. And then I took her for tea at the Plaza. She seemed to enjoy it. A real grown-up thing, she said."

"I thought you said her father was angry and suspicious of you."

Callie nodded. "He was, and he was certainly entitled to be. But he brought Julia by one afternoon. I got ice cream cake, and we just sat around talking. It was nice. After that, I guess he either decided that the accident wasn't my fault, or he forgives me."

"So you like the little girl?"

"Very much. We don't talk about her mother—I wouldn't presume to do that."

April nodded.

"She's terrific." Callie smiled. "You know, the last time I saw her, she asked me to take off my sunglasses. I was afraid my bad eye would scare her since it's still white, but I did it. You know what she said? That it was neat, and I looked like an Alaskan husky with my two different-color eyes."

April chuckled. "I like that idea."

They finished their lunch, keeping the rest of the conversation light. Afterward, April dropped Callie off at her apartment, then headed downtown to a go-see. Callie stopped to get her mail, then went upstairs and flopped down on the couch. It had been nice to see April, but getting through lunch had exhausted her.

No, it wasn't just getting through lunch that had tired her, she thought. It was acting cheerful. Everything she'd told April was true—that the people at physical therapy were great to her, that she enjoyed seeing Julia Hutchinson. But she'd left out the fact that those were the *only* positive things she had to say. The actual work of rehabilitating her leg was demoralizing, her progress slow and painful. And every minute of the day was a struggle, dealing with the crutches, her body full of aches and pains, some of which might never go away. Her face was a horror she tried to avoid seeing whenever possible. It took forever in the morning to comb her hair so that it covered as much as possible of her scars yet still appeared reasonably natural.

Beyond that, there was always Julia to think about. Her mother was dead, and her father had no one to help him raise her. It was a tangle of pain and loss that Callie couldn't put aside for even a moment; if it wasn't in the forefront of her thoughts, it was an empty gnawing in her stomach, always with her. She felt responsible, yet she could do nothing to atone for it.

The depression that had become so familiar to Callie settled around her again. She sighed heavily, then reached for her crutches and slowly got up, making her way to the foyer to go through the mail, which she had dropped on a table.

Bills and junk mail. The new copy of *Vogue* was there, and

Callie studied the model on the cover. A pretty decent shot, she decided admiringly, good hair and makeup, the girl had some flair. She flipped open the cover and froze.

Inside was a richly colored two-page ad for Expectations, a new fragrance. A model in a red satin ballgown danced atop a table in an elegant restaurant, surrounded by admiring men in tuxedos, her eyes flashing, her devilish grin saying that she knew how to enjoy life to the fullest. It was Vida.

Callie was ashamed of the hot flash of envy that tore through her. Vida had the whole field open to her now, no Callie Stewart to compete with or get in her way anymore. She had years of modeling left, years to have a good time, spend her lavish paychecks, be admired and sought-after. Their little battle was over, and Vida had won.

Going into the bedroom, Callie opened the closet and pulled out her portfolio. She hadn't looked at it in a long time, since well before the accident; there hadn't been any reason to, once she was exclusive for Day and Night. She took off her sunglasses as she sat on the bed and placed the portfolio before her. Slowly, she flipped through the large plastic sheets. There she was on location in Barbados, a Panama hat in one hand, spinning so that the gaily colored skirt she wore fanned out around her; swathed in fur, her eyes closed dreamily as she stood beneath a streetlight in the heart of Rome; running down a street in San Francisco dressed in a tweed suit, a briefcase in one hand, two golden retrievers straining at the leash she held in the other; in an early Day and Night ad that was simply a full close-up of her face.

There were dozens more, and she was surprised that she could pretty much recall each shoot, the photographer, the atmosphere in the studio, the decision later to put the shot in her book. Watching the pages go by, she had the sense of how fleeting it had all been, how quickly her moment had come and gone. She'd given up college, all her long-term plans for the future, for this. And now what? She couldn't even play a game of her beloved tennis anymore. All that was left was her shattered face and body.

Tears of self-pity filled her eyes. Unlucky me, she thought bitterly once again.

The elevator doors opened and Kate poked her head out, spotting Callie and Julia waiting in a corner.

"Okay, come on." She waved to them.

Callie put an arm around Julia's shoulders and they hastened through the lobby to join Kate, Callie relying on a cane to help her walk.

"Has it started?" Callie asked Kate.

She nodded. "Don't worry. It's a mob scene, but they're all watching. No one will notice you slip in."

Callie smiled gratefully. It was Kate who'd had the idea that Julia might enjoy seeing a real fashion show, and in fact the little girl had squealed with delight when Callie invited her over the telephone. But Callie couldn't face all those fashion people just yet, so many of whom she knew. By having Kate sneak them in five minutes after the show began, she and Julia could remain in the back where they wouldn't be noticed, and leave immediately when the show ended, before anyone had a chance to realize that Callie was there. As an added precaution, along with wearing her oversized sunglasses, she'd hidden her hair in a turban. Regarding herself in the mirror that morning, she'd been amused to be reminded of Fredericka and her famous turbans. *Thanks for the fashion tip,* she'd told her old boss silently.

The pulsing rock music reached their ears well before the elevator stopped on the seventh floor. Grant Fola was one of Seventh Avenue's premier designers, and invitations to his shows were always scarce and sought-after. Many designers held their runway shows in larger venues, but Fola made it a point always to unveil his new clothing lines in his mirror-lined offices, building a special runway for the occasion and letting the store buyers and fashion photographers fight it out for a good view of the models.

Kate yanked open one of the heavy double doors with the large GF insignia etched into the glass. The place was packed, Callie saw. The most important guests—fashion editors and photographers from top magazines and newspapers, buyers from the larger or more prestigious stores—sat in the four long rows of chairs that had been set out; everyone else was standing, squeezed into every corner of the showroom.

"Follow me," Kate yelled over the music.

With difficulty, they made their way through the crowd along the perimeter of the room. Kate stopped at a wide ledge along one wall where a tall vase full of flowers was displayed. She set the vase down on the floor, then folded her hands together to make a step for Julia, signaling with her head for the little girl to hop up. Julia turned to Callie, questioning with her eyes if it was all right. Callie nodded.

Ensconced in her personal viewing area, Julia looked around, entranced. The models were coming down the runway in groups of two, three, or four, moving in time to the upbeat music, pausing, turning to display their clothes, then prancing back. They were a swirl of color, outrageous outfits, and attitude. The audience watched, many of them taking notes, some clapping when they saw a design they particularly liked.

Julia's eyes were wide as she took in the noise and sights. Finally, she leaned over to Callie.

"Why are they wearing such heavy clothes?" she yelled above the din. "It's almost summer. Aren't they hot?"

Callie moved in closer so Julia could hear her explanation. "These are for the fall season. The designers show the clothes really early, then they go to the stores where you buy them just before the weather gets cold. It's all done very far in advance."

Julia nodded gravely to show she understood. Callie smiled, then turned back to the action. Watching the models brought back so many memories, yet she was oddly detached. She could imagine them all backstage, the pandemonium that was typical of a runway show, each girl being assisted out of one outfit and into another within seconds. Frantically pulling at straps and zippers, changing accessories, they would be adjusting themselves until the second they stepped out into view, suddenly cool and collected, their expressions often appearing almost bored as they sashayed for the audience.

Runway was different from print work, the kind of modeling Callie was used to. She had observed that a successful runway model was more about personality and style than simply the right face. It was all in the way they moved, the way their fluid motions sold the clothes. If they had an air about them, the right *something* that was effective in showing clothes in a live setting, they could work for years, doing the shows in New York, Paris, and Milan season after season for years.

Callie was caught up in the spectacle, force of habit compelling her to scrutinize the models' hair and makeup as she took in the clothes, seeing who moved well and who looked uncomfortable. She scanned the audience, picking out editors she knew, faces in the crowd she recognized from business or her former social life. The show began to wind down, and at the end, Grant Fola was ushered out on the arm of a model wearing an outrageously lavish bridal gown of pearls and purple tulle. Callie hated to end Julia's fun, but she couldn't bear the thought of talking to anyone here.

"Come on, honey, it's over. We should go."

There was only a flash of disappointment in Julia's eyes before she obediently jumped down, Kate helping her to land safely. The three headed for the door.

"Thanks for getting us in, Kate," Callie said, ringing for the elevator. Callie could have arranged for her own invitation, but she didn't want anyone to know she'd be coming. She was grateful to Kate for making the whole thing so easy for her.

"Anytime." Her friend wasn't leaving yet, and she bent over to Julia, sticking out a hand, which Julia solemnly shook. "See ya, kid. It's been a gas."

Julia smiled. "Thank you, Miss—"

"That's Kate to you." She waved goodbye.

Back out on the sunny street, Julia was practically dancing with excitement as she walked beside Callie.

"Did you see all those clothes, so crazy-looking. The models were beautiful."

Callie grinned at her. "So you enjoyed it, I hope."

"Are you kidding?" Julia stared at her. "I loved it. Thanks for bringing me."

"Anytime."

Julia was looking ahead. She suddenly pointed. "There's Daddy."

Callie followed Julia's gaze. Julia had a piano lesson at five, and Alex had said he would meet them on the corner at four to pick her up. He was walking toward them, lost in thought, his navy trench coat billowing out behind him, his tie loosened. He looked slightly rumpled, but very handsome. Callie was startled by the thought.

"Hi, Daddy!" Julia ran to him.

Alex knelt, wrapping his arms around her. "Hello, angel. Did you have fun?"

"It was great. I want to tell you all about it."

"And I want to hear all about it," he replied, kissing her on the cheek. "We'll have time to talk, too. The school called—your piano teacher went home sick. No lesson today."

"No lesson?" the little girl repeated happily. "Then can we have some pizza before we go? Please, Daddy, please? It's right here." She pointed to a stand a few feet away.

He stood, giving Callie a smile and a shrug to indicate his helplessness at refusing his daughter. Callie noticed that he had a dimple in one cheek. "Want to come?"

She smiled back. "A little pizza is always a good idea in my book."

Alex passed out the three slices and sodas, and the two grown-ups ate contentedly while Julia gave her father a rapidfire account of the fashion show between bites. When she had finished and was engrossed in an ice cream cone, Alex turned to Callie. He seemed to be deciding whether he should speak.

"You look very different, your hair hidden that way," he finally said, smiling. "You have lovely hair, but it's interesting that way too."

Callie was taken aback by the compliment, since he had never before said anything to her about her appearance.

"I'm hiding, actually. Too many people at the show I didn't feel ready to see."

He nodded. "I've been avoiding a lot of people myself since . . . Well, it's not quite the same for me, but I know what you mean."

Callie twisted around to reach for a napkin, wincing at the pain in her leg as she changed positions.

"Are you okay?" Alex asked quickly.

"Yes, of course. It's nothing." Callie didn't want to complain to this man. She had only a painful leg and the damage to her face and eye to contend with; he had lost his wife.

Alex was watching her. "Everything back to normal with your leg?"

She hesitated. "We're getting there. It'll take a little while more."

Julia piped in to explain to her father, "Callie went for a lot of physical—" She paused, searching for the word.

"Therapy," Callie supplied.

"Yeah," the child went on. "But she's got to keep practicing using her leg. It hurts her a lot."

Callie stared at her. "Julia, how do you know it hurts me?"

"It's easy to tell," Julia said mildly. "You bite your lip and make a little face when it bothers you."

Callie's hand flew to her mouth. She hadn't realized that.

"You have to keep trying," Julia lectured her. "Don't be discouraged. You'll get better."

Callie smiled, touched. "You're right."

Alex was smiling as well. "I find she usually *is* right about things."

"What are we going to do now, Daddy?" Julia asked.

"Now that your appetite for dinner is ruined, you mean?" he asked teasingly. "I guess we won't be eating at our normal time, so we have a few hours. It's your choice."

She thought. "The park. Let's go to the park. But I want Callie to come too."

"You have to ask her if she wants to come, sweetheart."

"Will you please?" Julia turned beseeching eyes on Callie. She laughed. "For a little while."

Alex commented that they should pick a spot from which Callie could get home easily, so they took a taxi to Fifty-ninth Street and Fifth Avenue, where they entered Central Park. Julia played as Callie and Alex sat on a bench, idly talking about the sights in the park, the people passing, other spots in New York they both liked.

"How did you get into teaching?" Callie asked.

He laughed. "What else does a person who majors in English lit do in the real world?" His tone grew more serious. "Actually, I kind of fell into it, but then I discovered I really liked it."

"The students at Columbia must be very bright," Callie said. "I guess they'd be a good group to teach."

"Sure," Alex replied with a nod. "It's a cliché to say teaching is rewarding, but of course the thing about clichés is that they're usually true. Sometimes I think the students are bored or restless and don't seem to care at all. But at other times they're throwing out ideas and questions, so excited to have the material opening up to them—it's the greatest thrill."

Callie didn't want to tell him she hadn't gone to college, although if he thought about her age and how much time she'd spent working, he could have figured it out for himself. Still, even though she had no intention of bringing it up, there was something about him that made her think he wouldn't look down on her if she told him.

"You really like what you do," she said admiringly.

"Oh, yes." His tone imparted how much he loved his work. "The students challenge me, keep me on my toes. I suppose a lot of people think college professors are avoiding the real world, hiding in the ivory towers, but I don't care. It's sustained me and given me a lot of pleasure over the years."

They continued talking. Despite how much Callie was enjoying his company, when she felt herself tiring, she excused herself; she didn't want him to see the strain all this activity was causing her. He and Julia walked with her to Fifth Avenue and put her into a taxi. They stood on the curb while the cab pulled away, Alex's hand on Julia's shoulder as the little girl waved goodbye.

Callie leaned back against the car seat and closed her eyes with fatigue. As tired as she was, as much as her leg would hurt her later, it had been well worth it. This was the most pleasant day she'd spent in months. And Julia was right— she should keep strengthening her leg, keep at it. *In fact,* Callie thought, *I should stop complaining so much, to myself as well as to everybody else. It's time to stop feeling sorry for myself.*

I shouldn't feel unlucky, she thought with new resolve. *I should feel grateful for what I do have.*

She thought of Julia and Alex. They'd experienced something far more terrible than she had. Yet, they were managing to get on with things. And they were nice people. It felt good being with them. It felt real somehow. She liked that.

20

*C*allie filled a tall glass with ice cubes and water. Leaning against the sink, she drank it quickly. Then she poured more water into the glass and took it into the living room, sipping at it slowly. Wearily, she sat down.

Some days, she returned from her physical therapy feeling enthusiastic and full of resolve. On others, like today, she was depressed and discouraged, frustrated by her slow progress. Along with her broken bones, her therapist had explained to her, there had been soft-tissue damage, including her muscles and ligaments. The wrenching her back had taken kept it bothering her as well.

She'd put in so many hours doing the range-of-motion and strengthening exercises, plus gait training to eliminate her limp. Three times each week she showed up faithfully for the stretching and twisting, wiggling her toes, bending her knee, lifting and lowering her leg, sitting in the whirl-pool. She was inching along in her progress, using the weight machines, stationary bicycles, treadmills. Her therapist gave her exercises to do at home as well; sometimes she followed the regimen, but at other times she just couldn't face it.

She rubbed her eyes. In the beginning, her leg had been weak, like dead weight, and it *had* improved. But months had passed since the accident and she was barely comfortable walking without the support of crutches or a cane. Anything more strenuous, such as jogging or tennis, was still a goal for the future.

It was so frustrating. She'd put off dealing with her eye and the scars on her face until her leg was in better shape, but it was taking forever. She thought back to the days when she'd run onto a tennis court as if it were the place she most belonged, how easily she'd kept up a hard-driving game for hours, not a pain or a twinge anywhere in her young body. Now there were days when she felt eighty years old.

If Glen, her physical therapist, had been any less wonderful than he was, she didn't know how she would have gotten this far. But he was amazing—always upbeat, optimistic, quick to point out any advance she was making, no matter how small it was, and shrugging off any setbacks. She genuinely liked him and had great admiration for what he did.

Besides Glen, the other good part about her therapy was the time spent in the gym or whirlpool, where she had an opportunity to talk with the other patients. They traded notes, commiserated, shared stories. Callie had learned a lot from these people. They came to the center as a result of everything from sprained ankles and spinal cord injuries to strokes and cerebral palsy. Either they didn't know who she was or they didn't care, but it was a blessed relief not to have to talk about modeling or how she felt about the famous face, now ruined.

Callie also appreciated how much easier her lot was in comparison to those of the other men and women there. In fact, she had developed tremendous respect for her fellow patients. And she liked talking to them about their lives. It felt good to hear about their diverse backgrounds, to get lost in realities so different from her own. The modeling business had taught her a great deal about the world, yet there were things on a very different level to be learned from these people.

But she had her own life to piece back together at the same time, and so far she was doing a miserable job of it. Callie set her glass on the coffee table, so depressed she couldn't do anything but sit there staring out the window. She'd made no move to deal with her future. She just went from day to day, withdrawing from her friends a little more each week, finding she had nothing to say to anyone outside her family. She spoke to her parents nearly every day, and to Tommy twice a week. They all encouraged her, and even though she didn't respond all that enthusiastically to their pep talks on the telephone, she relied on those talks to get her through. But she couldn't come up with a good reason to go anywhere or see anyone. Kate and April, upset with the way she'd been retreating into a shell, were trying their best to cheer her up. But she just didn't want to go out at night, to have people stare at her in open fascination with her disfigurement.

She'd even stopped seeing little Julia Hutchinson. She recalled having a good time that afternoon of the fashion show, but her mood had taken a turn for the worse shortly after that, and she hadn't called the Hutchinsons since. They didn't need her hanging around anyway, interfering in the little girl's life. Julia should be with her family and friends, recovering from her mother's death, not hanging around with the woman responsible for killing her.

The ringing of the telephone made her jump.

"Callie?"

She was startled to hear Alex Hutchinson's voice.

"Hello," she said. "How are you and Julia?"

"We're okay, thanks," he said. "How are you feeling?"

"Fine, thank you." That sounded pretty stiff, she thought, but she was too depressed to care.

He paused for a moment, apparently hearing something in her voice, then went on. "You know, you're quite a favorite of Julia's. She's been asking for you."

"She's a sweet child." Callie's tone picked up slightly at the thought of the little girl. "I like her very much."

"Feel like a short visit with her next week? If it's convenient for you, of course." He sounded hopeful.

"Well . . ."

"Is something wrong, Callie? Are you all right?"

"Yes. Why do you ask?"

"You sound sort of, well, not like you did before."

She sighed. "I'm sorry, it's just that I haven't been myself, I guess."

He didn't say anything.

"It's . . . I don't know. I'll give her a call soon, though." Callie was uncomfortable with the conversation, but she was also confused, unsure what she wanted to say. She couldn't tell Alex that she was depressed, too weighed down with her problems to be good company for Julia. "It was nice of you to call me. I appreciate it."

"Sure."

"So, goodbye then."

"Goodbye."

As soon as she'd hung up, Callie felt even worse. Tears stung her eyes. Why were things getting her down this way?

She took a shower, then got into a comfortable pair of pants and a white T-shirt. Settling in on the couch, she picked up a book and started to read. She was sick of thinking about herself, of having lapsed back into feeling sorry for herself. Escaping into a good novel was exactly what she needed. Nearly two hours had passed when the doorbell rang.

Callie opened the door to find Alex and Julia standing there, he with a shopping bag in one hand and a pizza box balanced on the other arm.

"Hi, Callie," Julia said, beaming up at her.

Callie's heart melted at the sight of the girl. She'd forgotten how adorable Julia was.

"Hi, sweetie," she replied.

Her eyes rose to meet Alex's. Suddenly, she remembered that she wasn't wearing her sunglasses. This was the first time Alex would realize how ugly she was, see the scars on her eyelid, her white eye. She watched for his reaction, for even a flicker of distaste in his eyes. But he simply looked at her and smiled. There was that dimple again in his cheek, she noticed.

"We thought you might need a little company," he said.

He held up the pizza box, and his expression turned sheepish. "I'm not a great cook, so I hope this will do it for a dinner at home. At least I know you eat pizza from the last time we saw you."

Callie laughed. "Absolutely, I love it." She took a step back. "Come on in."

Julia bounded past her. "Daddy also brought a cake for dessert. One of his students made it for him."

"Your student?" Callie turned to him.

"She finished her thesis, and she said she made me this cake to celebrate all the free time she had now. Chocolate. Chaucer. Her thesis, I mean. Nearly killed her."

Callie laughed as they went into the kitchen and he put his packages down. "It's a mud pie. I admit I stuck my finger in it."

"I can't wait," Julia chimed in.

"You know," Callie addressed Julia in a serious tone, "I've read that you absolutely dare not eat mud pie unless you have an enormous glass of icy cold milk. It's considered a terrible breach of etiquette."

"Oh." Julia's face fell. "We didn't bring any milk."

"Fortunately, you've come to the right place. I have an entire half-gallon of frosty milk just waiting to be poured. We're going to eat mud pie till it's coming out of our ears."

As the pizza was being reheated in the oven, they all got busy setting the table and pouring drinks, Julia chattering about her role as a dove in her ballet-school recital. Callie was touched to observe the pride and love in Alex's eyes as he listened to his daughter. *But of course,* she thought, *if I had a child like this one, I'd burst with pride too.*

They sat down to eat. Callie tried not to wince at the shooting pain in her back as she pulled her chair in, but Alex must have noticed.

"Are you all right?" he asked, half-rising, leaning over to help her.

She waved a hand, indicating that he should stay seated. "It's nothing. The healing's going very well actually."

He picked up Julia's plate and deposited a slice of pizza on it. "No cast, no cane. That's great. Are you still going for the therapy?"

Callie nodded her thanks as he placed a slice of pizza on her plate as well. "It shouldn't be for too much longer. I hope."

"Is it difficult?" Alex served himself last.

"Sometimes. But at least in my case it's temporary, and I should be back to myself completely. Some of the people who go there can't say the same."

He took a bite of his pizza. "And once you're back to yourself, what will you do?"

Callie gave him a rueful smile. "Hard to say. Obviously, modeling's out."

"Oh." He said it so casually that she almost wondered if something was wrong with his eyesight, if he couldn't see what she looked like.

"So much has changed. I was going to be married, too, but that's not happening now, so it'll all be new."

"You and David Long." Alex took a long sip of soda.

Callie was horrified at herself. How could she have been talking this way, being so insensitive to him? He should have been married as well now, continuing the life he had already established with Barbara. It was because of her and David that he had to start all over again. For the moment, she'd forgotten the terrible reason he knew about David, the terrible reason he knew *her*.

"I'm sorry," she said very softly.

"Daddy, can I have more pizza?" Julia broke in.

"Of course, honey." He gave his daughter another slice, then turned back to Callie. "When did you two break off the engagement?"

"Right after the accident."

"*Right* after?" He echoed her words in puzzlement.

She wished she didn't have to talk about David, but she felt she owed Alex any explanation he wanted about David or anything else connected to his wife's death.

"After it happened, David was . . . unhappy with the way things turned out, I guess. Me. Us. I don't know." She faltered. She wasn't telling him the truth—that David had just walked out on her, no doubt because she was no longer the beautiful model he'd proposed to. She just couldn't bring herself to say it. "I didn't break it off, it just fell apart."

Alex was staring at her with an odd expression.

"Callie," Julia interrupted, bored with the adults talking to each other, "you didn't notice my new watch." She held up her wrist proudly. "See, it's got ballerinas on it. Daddy got it for me for my birthday. It's my first grown-up watch."

"I didn't know it was your birthday," Callie exclaimed.

Julia nodded proudly. "Last week. I'm seven."

"That calls for candles in our mud pie. And maybe a tiara for the birthday girl." She turned to Alex. "I have one inside I might be able to dig up, left over from a shoot." Standing up, she pointed a finger at Julia. "Promise you won't go anywhere."

Callie headed for the bedroom. Alex smiled after her.

Music filled the air, as all around them the other concert-goers enjoyed the warm summer evening, sitting on lawn chairs and blankets, picnicking, drinking wine, or just watching the dusky sky. The strains of *Aida* floated to the outer edges of the vast space, now inhabited by thousands of New Yorkers.

Callie, Alex, and Julia sat on a large yellow blanket, finishing the remains of the picnic Callie had packed. Alex picked up a bunch of green grapes and stretched out as he ate them, leaning on one elbow. His daughter moved over to snuggle up against him, and he stroked her hair easily as the three of them talked.

"I've been in New York for so long, I can't believe I've never come to one of these," Callie said, biting into a chocolate chip cookie. She looked around once more at the elaborate dinners set out, the candelabras, buckets with champagne. "It's obviously about more than just listening to the music."

"Absolutely. Opera in the park is just as much about the food and company," Alex replied.

Julia pointed to a distant spot. "They have about a hundred balloons over there."

They all looked. Clusters of balloons were tied to three picnic hampers, where a group of about twenty people gathered in their own party.

Alex smiled. "Next time, we'll bring balloons too."

"Can we, Daddy?" Julia asked excitedly.

Callie lay back and closed her eyes, listening, slightly adjusting the tan patch she wore over her eye. What a pleasant surprise, having Alex invite her to come with them tonight, relaxing here in the balmy night air, a perfect evening to enjoy Central Park and the music.

She'd seen Alex and Julia twice since that night he'd brought the pizza to her apartment, and each time she'd found them easy to be with. They were both very aware of any little pain or difficulty she might be having, but instead of making a big deal about it, they apparently realized it was better to treat her as if it were nothing. She appreciated that. At the same time, though, they encouraged her to keep up with her therapy exercises, to keep trying. She had to admit she'd derived strength from their support. Except for a slight limp, her leg was pretty much healed now. The next step was plastic surgery for her face. But that was too scary to contemplate just yet.

She rolled over onto her stomach. Julia had lain down next to her father and her eyes were growing heavy with sleep. Alex and Callie exchanged smiles at the sweet sight of a little girl drifting off to sleep.

"More wine," he asked Callie softly, not wanting to disturb his daughter.

She shook her head. "No, thanks, I'm fine."

They sat in comfortable silence. Julia's breathing became deep and regular.

"She's such a happy girl, even in spite of things," Callie said finally. "It's so nice just to be around her."

"Yes," Alex replied. "It's taken a while, but it seems to be coming back. I'm amazed at how well she's dealt with losing her mother. There are times, of course—the nights are the worst. And sometimes I see her just sitting, doing nothing, and I can see she's feeling so lost. But she pulls herself together and goes on." He shook his head. "Incredible, the courage in this child. She adored Barbara."

Callie turned to gaze at him. "You've never talked to me about her."

Alex spoke gently. "What good would it do?"

Callie looked down at her hands. "I can keep saying I'm

sorry, but I guess you know that I am. Besides, it doesn't help anything."

"No, but thank you for saying it."

She rolled over to face him more fully. "Alex, I'd do anything to change what happened."

"Callie," he said gently, "it's all right. I know how you feel. It wasn't your fault, and I don't blame you."

"If only . . ."

"Look, we all can say 'if only,' but it doesn't do any good. You're entitled to go on, to have your own life." He poured wine into his glass. "I see how you're consumed with the accident, with your injury, but you should put it behind you. Look ahead to your future."

"I can't see any future," Callie said so quietly he could barely hear her.

"Don't you want to go back to work at something?"

"Yes, I do want to work." As she spoke, Callie reflected how miserable she would be sitting home doing nothing on a permanent basis; she was already getting stir crazy now that her leg was better. Of course she wanted to work. "The problem is that I don't know what to do with myself. What am I skilled at besides modeling?"

"Do you have some other interests that lend themselves to a job?"

"There's nothing I can do with my tennis on a professional basis anymore," Callie said ruefully.

"Think about it. There must be things you like that you could translate into a new career." He leaned forward. "Seriously. Tell me whatever comes into your mind, no matter how silly it might sound at first."

She thought for a bit. "You know, this may sound strange, but the thing that's been the most interesting to me over the past few months has been talking to the other people at my physical therapy."

She reached for a plum and bit into it. "It felt good to get outside myself. Modeling demands that you focus so much attention on yourself, on how you look, on the way you behave with everyone. There, I could just talk to people and learn. I liked hearing about their lives, finding out what made them happy or sad, how they accomplished different things. It was an unusual circumstance, so people shared unusual things with each other."

"I can understand that," Alex said.

Callie reflected as she finished the piece of fruit. "It was learning about them that I liked. I wish I could find something that would allow me to do that professionally somehow. Just go around and learn about people." She looked at Alex, feeling foolish. "That sounds childish and ridiculous."

"Not at all," he answered. "I like to see people learn, so I teach. You want to talk to people. There are lots of professions where you could incorporate that, I'm sure."

Callie lay back and closed her eyes again. There was a long, peaceful silence. She imagined that Alex was relaxing too, just listening to the magnificent music floating through the night air. Then she sensed his presence, that he was coming closer to her. With a start, she felt his lips lightly brush against her cheek. Her eyes flew open.

He was pulling away, looking almost as surprised as she was.

"I apologize. I shouldn't have done that," he mumbled.

Callie didn't know if she was more shocked that he had kissed her or at how embarrassed he appeared now. She touched her cheek. It had been such a nice, soft kiss. She smiled.

"No need to apologize."

He averted his glance. "You looked so beautiful, just lying there."

She sat up. The last man who kissed her—other than her father and brother, of course—was David. It had been a very long time. She realized that since the accident, she had somehow assumed no man would ever want to kiss her again, would ever want to come that close to her scarred face.

"Thank you for that," she murmured.

They were both quiet. Julia stirred and sighed lightly in her sleep.

21

A group of eight-year-old girls, all clutching violin cases, pushed by Alex, laughing and talking in raised tones to one another. He pressed against the wall, trying to make room for them. Noisily, they disappeared around a corner. Several other children came along, each holding a different musical instrument, on their way to class.

Alex was early to pick up Julia from her piano lesson; she wouldn't be finished for another fifteen minutes. He spotted a bench at the far end of the hall and went to sit down. This was a good time to review his notes for the new lecture he was incorporating into his American literature class. But he set his briefcase down, making no motion to retrieve anything from it. He was thinking about Callie.

He couldn't imagine what had made him kiss her the previous week when they were at the opera in Central Park. She had just been irresistible, lying there looking like a princess, like Sleeping Beauty. He smiled briefly at the image, thinking he was spending an awful lot of time reading Julia's books aloud to her; the characters were starting to become as real to him as they were to his daughter. But he knew Callie was self-conscious about her eye—usually hidden behind a patch—and the scars on her face, and he wished he could find a way to reassure her that they were unimportant. The truth was, he barely saw them anymore when he looked at her. Still, he understood that she believed they were the *only* thing anyone saw.

His smile turned into a frown. Callie had paid a high price for that night in the injuries to her body and the end of her career. But she shouldn't have paid *any* price at all. It was that David Long who was the villain in all this, the only one who'd walked away unhurt, and apparently untouched emotionally as well. Alex couldn't understand how Long could have broken off his engagement to Callie. He'd killed a woman, even if it *was* an accident, and put Callie in the hospital, nearly killing her too. Then he left her there, her life in shreds. What kind of man would do such a thing? Even if he didn't love her anymore, any decent human being would have waited until she was recovered and strong enough to deal with it before he called off their marriage. His mind went back to Barbara's words about someone cheating Weston and how she was going to expose him. Could she have been talking about David Long?

Alex sat up with a start. Maybe Long had hit Barbara deliberately. Was that possible? No, it was too crazy an idea even to consider. He shook his head. *I'm really losing my mind,* he admonished himself.

But what about Callie? There wasn't much point pretending to himself that he wanted to keep in touch with her just for Julia's sake. His daughter had definitely taken to her once she'd agreed to the first meeting. Alex had simply told Julia he was bringing her to meet a woman who'd been hurt in the same accident Mommy had been in; he'd purposely neglected to mention that Callie had been in the car that hit Barbara. And now Julia had become attached to Callie. As had he.

It was all a bit hard to fathom. He was finding Callie Stewart—the woman he had recently blamed for his wife's death—to be the one person whose company he enjoyed. With Callie, it was easy and comfortable. Other than his daughter, there wasn't anyone else he wanted to be with, no one he had anything to say to. After the first time they'd met, they hadn't discussed the accident, and they didn't have to. Somehow he felt good with her, and those were the only times he could say that since Barbara had died.

He twisted around in his seat. The guilt about Barbara again. It had been with him for months, always near the surface. He didn't know how he dared to have the kind of feelings he was having toward Callie when his wife was dead just over eight months. But he couldn't pretend he wasn't attracted to Callie, to her kindness, her vulnerability, her magnificent smile that filled the room with sunlight when he was fortunate enough to elicit it. There was something that felt right about being with her.

It was odd, too, since she came from such a different world. Imagining the circles she had traveled in to be so glamorous, he wondered how his boring life must appear to her. Yet, the other night she'd seemed almost afraid to confess that she hadn't gone to college, as if he would think less of her. She was sharp and clever, certainly just as bright as any of his students; what she needed to learn from books could be taken care of easily. Her innate intelligence, the warmth in her voice when she talked to him or Julia, her obviously genuine interest in what they were thinking— these were the things that mattered.

Looking up, he observed that a number of other parents had gathered in the corridor in the past few minutes, waiting for their children. He watched two women talking familiarly as they passed the time. A little boy came running out of one of the rooms, straight over to one of the women. Kneeling down, she adjusted his shirt collar and took his music case from him. She waved goodbye to the other mother as they left.

If she were still alive, Barbara wouldn't be among these mothers coming to fetch their children in the late afternoon. She'd always worked until seven or so at night, but she'd made arrangements to have Julia picked up from wherever she went after school. Alex wondered now why he'd never picked Julia up from her piano lesson before. She'd started taking lessons the preceding year, and his last class on Thursdays hadn't run past three o'clock; he would have been available to do it. But Barbara had never asked, and he'd never offered.

She'd arranged so many things in their lives, and everything had operated so smoothly, so efficiently. Oddly, it was one of the things he'd disliked about her. Of course it made things easier, having someone to organize every detail of their lives. Still, he would have gladly traded that for a little spontaneous fun with her. He didn't know what she was like at the office, but at home she was rigid, completely inflexible, quick to make decisions, and always anxious to get her schedule in place. And she would never do anything that wasn't thoroughly researched in advance.

Just last year, he'd suggested that the three of them go to Europe for the month of July, rent a car, and drive around, going wherever the mood struck them. Barbara had stared disdainfully at him. First of all, she'd informed him in annoyance, she could never take that time from her job. When he reminded her she had three weeks vacation and could ask for a fourth week unpaid, she'd laughed, telling him that a four-week absence would knock her right out of the loop at work. He hated when she used expressions like that, that hard-edged business lingo that proved she was as tough as the next guy. She was always talking about playing hardball, bottom-lining it, running with the ball. He'd tuned all that out, telling himself he doubtless did a million things that drove *her* crazy. But it was symptomatic of all the other changes she'd gone through since they'd gotten married.

No doubt about it, she wasn't the same person once she graduated from business school. She was consumed with her job, with advancing her career. In the early years of their marriage, she would have jumped at the chance to travel through Europe. They couldn't have afforded it then, but when they could, she didn't think it worth leaving Weston. Even if they were to go to Europe, she'd continued, the idea of roaming around with no set itinerary and no reservations was utterly unappealing; they'd wind up sleeping in the car, unable to get a hotel room because of the throngs of summer tourists. Alex hadn't mentioned the idea again, seeing in her face that she'd dismissed it with finality.

A man and woman hurried past him, their voices raised in anger.

"You won't give an inch," the woman was saying. "You're selfish and you always have been."

"*I'm* selfish?" her husband retorted. "You haven't thought about another living soul since the day you were born."

Alex winced at the familiarity of their words. When Barbara *had* made time for him, that was usually the way it ended up, the two of them fighting. Typically, it was about something inconsequential, their anger over important things misdirected into petty arguments. They'd had some knockdown, drag-out fights as well, but those had died out in their last few years together. They'd even lost the passion to fight on a grand scale, he reflected.

He stood up, shaken. He'd forgotten it all, blocked out all the bad things. Since her death, he'd remembered only what was good about Barbara, the qualities that had made him fall in love with her. There was nothing wrong with that, but he was denying the truth. They'd been heading for a divorce. It had been on his mind for about six or seven months before she died, but he'd found himself unable to broach the subject with her. She'd made a few cracks that made him realize she'd been thinking along the same lines. So whom was he kidding? His marriage hadn't been good for a long time. They had Julia in common, which kept them together longer than they would have otherwise. But there was little love or communication, or even trust, between them.

I'm sorry, Barbara, he addressed her silently. *It was over and we both knew it.* He walked to the water fountain, shaken by his thoughts and confused by the sense of relief flooding him now that he had admitted the truth.

He'd been mourning his wife with an overpowering sense of guilt that he hadn't begun to understand until now. He shouldn't feel guilty that he'd been left alive while his wife had died. Maybe he had wanted to divorce her, but he hadn't wished her to die. And he hadn't caused her death by contemplating the divorce. It happened the way it had, and there was nothing that could alter that.

She had been his wife and the mother of his child, and he would always love her in a special way for that. But he was allowed to go on. And it was okay for him to have feelings for another woman. Certainly, he should proceed with caution where Callie was concerned, both for his own sake as a man and for his daughter's sake—she was an emotionally vulnerable child with a growing attachment to this woman. But he shouldn't be holding himself back because he felt guilty about wanting to leave Barbara. He would keep Barbara's memory alive for Julia, and he would paint her in the most glowing terms, both because that's what the child needed and because Barbara had truly been a good mother, and she deserved that. But he should say his goodbyes to her, let her go. And go on himself.

A heavy set of double doors was thrown open, and a dozen children came spilling out, talking, laughing, jostling one another. Several minutes passed before he saw Julia emerge, eyes downcast, looking over the sheet music she held in her hands. He recognized the determined set of her mouth as she studied the piece. It was Barbara's. *Good for you,* he told Julia silently. *Your goals will be your own, but you'll have the drive to go after them. We should thank your mother for that.*

Smiling, he called out his daughter's name.

Callie bent over to pick a flower, then straightened up, twisting it in her hand as she spoke. She and Alex had been walking along the country road for the past half-hour, talking about their families, getting lost in the warm sun and fragrant air of the late September day.

"Now it's all okay, but I still feel terrible about what I did to him," she said.

Alex regarded her. "But your brother seems to have forgiven you. Why can't you forgive yourself?"

Callie smiled at him. "Don't you think you'd feel bad if you made your brother scramble that way, when you had more money than you knew what to do with?"

"You never know," Alex said. "It may have made him feel pretty good about himself to earn that money. You said before that he would have hated having you pay his way through school."

Callie shrugged. "Looking back, I can see that I was pretty wrapped up in myself most of the time. What I did to him was typical, treating people like they were at my disposal, being annoyed if things didn't go just as I wanted them to."

She stopped to face him. "Even after the accident, everything was always about *me*. My leg, my eye, my career."

"That's not true," Alex protested. "You cared about Julia, you were always interested in her. Besides, the accident *was* a lot to deal with."

Callie paused, unsure if she should say what was on her mind. She plunged ahead.

"I don't know what I would have done if it hadn't been for you and Julia. You've been my greatest supporters, my cheerleaders. I can never thank you enough."

Alex took her hand and they resumed walking, neither one saying anything. When he had invited Callie to come to Vermont with him for the weekend, she had been nervous but not surprised. They'd seen more and more of each other as the summer had progressed. He'd become an important part of her life, and she hoped she was the same to him.

She remembered the night she realized how much he and Julia really meant to her, the night Julia had broken down in her arms, sobbing for her mother. Callie had volunteered to tuck Julia into bed while Alex was in the kitchen washing their dinner dishes. She'd thought her heart would break as she sat on the edge of Julia's bed, rocking the little girl, murmuring soothing sounds, helplessly wondering what to do. At that moment, she knew her warm affection for Julia had blossomed into love, that she would do anything to spare the child from further hurt. She didn't want to be without Julia again. She didn't want to be without Alex. And she thought she'd seen the same feelings she was developing for him in the way he looked at her, touched her hand, gently kissed her good-night. She prayed she was right.

The week before, Alex told her that Julia was going to stay

with some cousins in Boston for the weekend, and he wondered if she would like to take a trip to an inn he'd heard about. Having deposited their bags in the two rooms he'd booked for them, they'd immediately gone outside, stopping at a small restaurant for a delicious lunch of homemade soup and fluffy omelets, then coming here to walk. Callie wondered what would happen later when they went back to the inn. She was scared but at the same time ready for whatever happened. Her leg was nearly back to normal, her limp only slightly noticeable when she hurried or got tired. Other than the damage to her face, her body had recovered.

The question was, would he want her that way, would he be able to get past her disfigurement? He'd convinced her to take her eyepatch off this weekend. It wasn't the first time he'd seen her without it, but she'd never gone this long with her bad eye exposed. Maybe seeing her that way for so many hours had disgusted him. Perhaps the idea that he thought of her in romantic terms was just a case of wishful thinking on her part.

They decided to drive for a while, stopping to walk down a street of small shops, buying some coffee beans and freshly made jams to take home, lazily passing the afternoon. The sun was setting as they headed back to the inn and went off to their separate rooms to shower before dinner.

Nervously, Callie selected her outfit for the evening. She wanted to look her best. Strangely, though, she realized that she now had a different idea of what her best *was*. In the old days, as she'd come to regard the time before the accident, she would get so dressed up at night, all glittering and sexy, the star of the show wherever she went. Now she wanted to seem softer, more approachable. She shook her head with amusement at herself as she picked through the clothes she'd hung in the closet. In some ways, it occurred to her, she was returning to the girl she'd been before she'd come to New York to model.

Dressed in a pale blue sweater over beige pants, Callie was putting a thin necklace of liquid gold around her neck when Alex knocked on her door. Letting him in, she felt a flutter in her stomach. He was so attractive in a simple white shirt and tan chinos. They smiled at each other, glad to be together again after the brief separation. Leaving the inn, they each instinctively reached for the other's hand.

Alex had chosen a French restaurant, where they shared tastes of everything they ordered, enjoying a bottle of wine, relaxing in the intimate, candlelit atmosphere. For dessert there was a Grand Marnier soufflé for Callie and chocolate mousse for Alex. It was nearly eleven when they finished.

"I'm completely stuffed," she said as they returned to the inn. "But what a great dinner." Her tone grew formal. "An excellent selection, monsieur."

He bowed and said, his tone matching hers, "For you, mademoiselle, it was not nearly good enough."

They went up the carpeted stairs to the rooms. Callie paused outside her door, hesitant. Alex took a step closer to her. Gently, he brought his palm up to her face and lay it on her cheek. She gazed up at him, her heart beating frantically. His hand moved to stroke her hair. Then, slowly, so slowly, he leaned over and kissed her.

Callie's eyes closed with the pleasure of his nearness. His kiss was so warm and sweet. Without thinking, she slid her hands up his arms and around his neck, feeling herself drawn into him as if that were the only place to be. She felt his arms go around her and their kiss grew more intense. When Alex pulled back from her, she let out a soft breath, not wanting it to stop.

"Do you want to go inside?" he asked, his voice ragged.

She nodded. They quickly opened the door. As soon as they were in the room, they came together again, but this time the restraint was gone. Hungrily, Callie drank him in, drawing her hands along his back, his face, through his hair. He pulled her to him, the strength of his hands on her communicating the depth of his desire. They stayed that way for a long time, their mouths searching, tasting the kiss that had been so long in coming. Their breathing was faster as they moved to the bed and lay down together, not wanting to be apart for even a second.

Clothing fell away. Callie felt a moment of self-consciousness, remembering that she was no longer the famous face of beauty but a scarred, disfigured face. Then she felt Alex's finger gently tracing the lines of her scars as he kissed her tenderly, silently telling her it was all right, he knew what she was thinking and he didn't care at all about that.

She opened her eyes, smiling up at him, stunned by the combination of passion and tenderness in his expression. Jean had been good to her in bed, but she hadn't known the depth of feeling she had for Alex. David had been a whirlwind of sex, a heady thrill. Yet she had never felt the caring from him that she sensed in every movement of Alex's hands, the way he drew his lips along her face, her neck, her shoulders. Alex didn't care if she was the Day and Night girl, he didn't care if she was even pretty. He wanted her the way she was, and the power of his desire was overwhelming as she gave herself over to him, happily slipping into the sweet haze of their lovemaking.

When it was over, they lay silently, catching their breath, neither one wanting to break the spell by speaking. Finally, Alex rolled up onto one elbow, running his hand through her hair as he looked down at her.

"I care for you, Callie," he said softly. "I have for a long time."

"I care for you, too," she answered, hoping he wouldn't see the tear of joy sliding down her cheek. "I want to make you happy."

"You do." He kissed her lingeringly. "Let me make *you* happy as well."

She sighed with pleasure at his words and slipped her arms around him.

The rest of the weekend passed by in what seemed like seconds. On Sunday morning they had brunch at a restaurant overlooking a lake, then returned to the inn to spend the rest of the day in bed, both of them relishing the gentle caring as much as their passion.

When they got back to New York, they were together every minute they could find. It was Alex and Julia who were with Callie when she went to the hospital for the plastic surgery on her face, Alex consulting anxiously with the surgeon beforehand as Julia presented a frightened Callie with the colorful cards she had drawn for her in school. When it was over, Alex sat with her every minute that he didn't have to be in class. Back at her apartment, he tended to her well past the time she insisted that she was perfectly fine and he could stop worrying.

The operation had minimized the scarring along her forehead and her eyelid, and the doctor told her he was exceptionally pleased with how it had turned out. It was a full three weeks after the procedure before Callie permitted herself to take a good, close look in the mirror. She was startled to discover her old face reemerging. Her whitish eye was another matter, and she could still see only light and shadow out of it. But it seemed her face would pretty much return to normal.

In a strange way, Callie thought, all those marks had taught her a few things about herself and the rest of the world. She followed the faint lines with her finger. She certainly wouldn't miss them. But she wouldn't try to forget about them either.

22

Callie raised her voice to make herself heard, leaning in slightly to Alex as he glided her smoothly around the dance floor to the band's Latin beat.

"Where did a college professor learn to rumba like that?" she asked playfully. "I'm having a hard time keeping up."

He laughed, spinning her out and away from him, then sharply pulling her back in. "We're not all moth-eaten old fogies, you know. Some of us do get out once in a while."

The song ended. Callie and Alex made their way back to their table. They were sitting with April and her new boyfriend, Tyler, an architect she'd met when she decided to do some renovations on her apartment.

"You two make a nice picture out there," April said to them.

Callie didn't respond. In the back of her mind, she'd been wondering if her gait was totally back to normal, if she appeared to be off-balance in any way. She didn't have the nerve to appear in public without her sunglasses on, and it had initially taken an act of willpower just to get up and dance.

As if reading Callie's mind, April leaned over and squeezed her hand. "It's as if it never happened," she whispered.

"Thanks for the compliment," Alex said, responding to April's earlier comment. "But it's just that Callie makes me look good."

Callie smiled lovingly at him. He always knew what to say.

A friend of April's stopped by the table. Peggy was a producer for one of the local television news shows. Callie had met her once before, and they'd liked each other, but the opportunity to get together again had never presented itself. She was with a pleasant-looking, slightly older man, who she introduced as Lucas James, the executive producer of *A Time & Place,* a national feature news show. Greetings were exchanged all around. As April and Peggy talked, Lucas turned to Callie.

"It's nice to see you again," he said with a smile.

She tried to hide her embarrassment; she had no recollection of ever having met the man.

He saw that she was at a loss. "It was a party at Zack Roman's place. But I'm not surprised you don't remember. You were the center of attention, everyone wanting a few seconds to bask in your reflected glory as you glided through the room, bestowing waves and kisses."

"In other words, I was making a spectacle of myself," Callie said with a smile. "How awful that sounds."

He laughed. "Not at all. You were a thing of beauty and a joy to behold. Women as beautiful as you aren't held to the same standards as everyone else."

"I'm not sure that's such a good thing," she remarked.

Lucas tilted his head. "I heard about what happened to you, as everyone did, I suppose. You look absolutely wonderful. It can't have been easy, going through all that."

Callie was reluctant to discuss it. "Thank you, but it could have been far worse. I'm fine now."

He was watching her, an appraising look in his eyes. "We take beautiful women so for granted," he said. "We stare at them, we're drawn to them, but in a way, we don't really see them. I was struck by it that night at the party, too. I talked to you briefly, and you were so charming, so bright. Yet everyone seemed to just want to look at you, to be near you, be part of your—" he searched for the word, "your aura."

"Some people enjoy that," Callie replied. "I always found it a very strange aspect of being a well-known face."

He pulled out his wallet, extracting a business card. "Please give me a call sometime, won't you? I'd like to talk to you about some business."

Callie took the card. "What do you mean?"

"Hey," Tyler broke in at that moment, "here they come."

All the heads in the room were turning in the same direction. Peggy and Lucas moved back to their own table.

Kate and Hal had slipped off to change out of their wedding clothes and were ready to leave now for their honeymoon in Bali. Both of them had had grave doubts about having such a traditional wedding, but in the end they'd decided to go the whole way with it. Originally dressed in a beige, antique lace wedding gown, Kate now wore an acid-green suit with tights and suede pumps of the same color. Clearly relieved to be out of his tuxedo, Hal was back in his usual outfit of black jeans and a white T-shirt with a black jacket.

"They sure do go together, don't they?" Tyler said, smiling. Callie knew that he and April had often double-dated with Kate and Hal over the past few months; they'd become a close foursome. It was nice for them, she thought. She was surprised that she didn't feel left out, but the truth was that she and Alex were perfectly content to be alone or with Julia. They'd rarely sought out other couples.

"They're sensational," Callie said truthfully.

"It's so great for Kate," April gushed. "She's absolutely glowing."

Tyler stood up, raising his glass of champagne. "Long life and lots of happiness," he called out affectionately. "Maybe even some kids, too."

There was rousing applause and cheering in the room. Kate and Hal looked embarrassed but pleased. They waved, their parents coming to hug them, friends crowding around, everyone shouting goodbye. Once they'd made their exit, the guests began gathering their belongings.

Callie and Alex retrieved their coats and stepped outside onto the dark Manhattan street. Alex held his hand up for a taxi.

"It was a nice wedding, wasn't it?" Callie mused, burrowing into her coat collar for warmth; the November night had turned cold. "I'm so glad for Kate."

"She's a fun girl. A good friend to you, too, I've seen," Alex said, putting an arm around her as he searched for an available cab.

"Absolutely." Callie was pleased that he'd noticed. David would never had said such a thing about one of her friends; they'd been interchangeable to him, practically invisible. She observed Alex's profile, his strong chin and clear eyes.

"I hope the ceremony didn't make you sad, thinking about the past," she said tentatively. It had been on her mind the whole evening, that attending Kate's wedding with her might bring back memories for him. Alex had hinted lately that his marriage to Barbara had been in some trouble at the end, but that didn't mean he wouldn't have memories that could still sadden him.

"Sure, it reminded me. I imagine weddings remind practically everyone of their own. But you don't have to worry, it didn't upset me," he said. He was quiet for a moment, thinking back. "Ours was just a tiny affair, maybe twenty people, dinner at a restaurant."

"Kate couldn't have managed anything smaller than a hundred fifty people, I'm sure." Callie laughed. "She's knows a million people in New York. There must be plenty of ruffled feathers out there anyway."

An empty taxi finally appeared. Alex hailed it and opened the door for Callie to slide in. Getting in beside her, he gave the driver his address.

"You know," he said to her, as the cab pulled away from the curb, "it wasn't my wedding I was thinking about in there. It brought back memories of Barbara, but there was something she said—I kept turning it over and over in my mind."

"What do you mean?"

"She told me somebody at Weston was selling out the company. She knew who it was and was going to expose him. I've been pushing it away since she died, but it was back tonight."

Callie was confused. "Pushing what away?"

He turned to look directly at her. "I'm wondering if it was David."

"David?" Callie said uncomprehendingly.

"Yes. I wonder if she had the goods on whatever David was up to, and he hit her that night intentionally."

Callie's stomach lurched. "Alex, that's crazy. Do you know what you're saying?"

But even as she spoke, she was recalling how it had seemed to her that the car sped up just before they hit Barbara, how she'd tried to tell David to slow down.

"Why is it crazy?" Alex asked. "If she was going to ruin him, maybe get him thrown in jail, who knows what he might have done."

"You're accusing him of something so terrible . . ." Callie trailed off, growing visibly upset. "He would never have done that."

"What makes you so sure?" Alex's tone was sharp. "Look at what he did to you. Do you really know what he was capable of?"

His words were like a slap in the face. She hated to be reminded how she'd misjudged David. It was humiliating enough to think she was about to marry a man who could abandon her in the hospital without a backward glance. But this—this was far worse.

"Please," Callie protested. "It couldn't be true."

"It *could* be true," Alex insisted. "Callie, for once, admit what a rotten guy he was. Admit that he used you."

Defensively, she lashed out. "You don't even know him. You're letting your imagination run wild. And you don't know what was between us, so don't pass judgment on me."

"Oh, come on," Alex said in exasperation.

Callie's anger rose. It wasn't that she wanted to protect David, but she hated having Alex see her weakness for having been with him.

Alex went on. "I don't know how you could have chosen that lowlife to begin with."

Her tone turned sarcastic. "I'm sorry you don't approve of my choice in men."

"You're right, I guess I don't," he said curtly.

Callie's mouth was set. "Maybe I'm still making bad choices."

"What's that supposed to mean?" he snapped.

She leaned forward. "Driver, please pull over. I'm getting out."

Alex put a hand on her sleeve. "Callie, stop it, this is ridiculous."

"That's too bad." She snatched her arm away. "I'm going home. Good night."

The cab pulled over and she got out as quickly as she could, ignoring Alex's protests. Slamming the door behind her, she began walking. She was infuriated even further when she heard the cab pulling away; Alex hadn't gotten out to come after her.

It was nearly thirty blocks to her apartment but she wanted the fresh air, so she ignored the passing empty cabs and walked. With every block, her anger subsided. But in its place grew a terrible fear. She'd always tried so hard to avoid confrontations; how had she lost her temper that way to Alex? He would never want to see her again.

All he'd done was tell her what he was thinking. Yes, it was a shocking idea, but that didn't mean she had to jump on him that way. It was just that she didn't want to admit that David could be capable of such a thing, that she could have loved a cold-blooded killer. She'd struck out at Alex for voicing her shame and fear. Now she had angered him, and he would leave her. She'd ruined the best thing that had ever happened to her. A lump formed in her throat. She'd never learn.

As she turned the corner to her building, the sight of Alex standing in the dim light beneath the canopy made Callie's heart leap. He spotted her coming down the block and hurried to meet her halfway.

"Callie," he said quietly, "please forgive me. I upset you. I never want to do that again."

He was apologizing. It hadn't even occurred to Callie that he would do such a thing.

"No, it was my fault. I don't know why I made such a scene." She reached out to touch his hand, and he pulled her toward him.

"There's no reason for us to fight. Not about this or anything, ever, I hope." He pressed his lips to her hair. "I love you."

Callie put her arms around him and held on tight. He hadn't left her. They'd argued, but the world hadn't come to an end. He still wanted her. She closed her eyes. He even said he loved her. He'd never said that to her before.

"I love you, too," she whispered. "You'll never know how much."

". . . so Fredericka thinks this redhead is the next big thing. She's been taking her all over New York, introducing her to the right people." Grace's voice over the telephone was amused. "But the girl has this horrible, squeaky voice. It doesn't matter for print work, of course, but everybody's snickering."

Callie felt a rush of sympathy for the girl. "She must know they're making fun of her. That has to hurt."

Grace laughed. "Don't worry about her. The rumor is she's about to sign a million-dollar contract with Getabout Jeans. She was in yesterday telling us she would laugh all the way to the bank. 'As high-pitched a laugh as I want,' was how she put it. She knows the score."

"Oh." The fast-flying gossip of the business seemed far away to Callie now.

Grace's voice grew more serious. "There's another rumor around. About Weston."

Callie didn't say anything. Normally, she tried not to think about Weston or anything else connected with David or the accident.

"They say the company is in some trouble. Apparently, several of its new product ideas and marketing angles have been scooped by competitive lines. It's quite the scandal."

Callie's stomach turned over. That night in the cab a few weeks back, when they'd had the fight—was that what Alex had been talking about when he'd said someone had sold out Weston?

"There's my other line ringing, I gotta go," Grace said. "Great talking to you, sweetie. Please come visit when you can."

"Thanks for calling," Callie said sincerely. She appreciated that Grace still kept in touch.

"Oh, wait!" Grace exclaimed. "Hang on." She put Callie on hold and was back in a few seconds. "I forgot to tell you—Vida's moving to Australia! She met this guy, a record producer from there, and wants to marry him. But he said she could either go home to Australia with him or end it. And the guy's insisting that she give up working, just stay at home after they're married. She's going. Austin's cutting her loose from Whiting."

"Vida's giving up modeling?" Callie was nonplussed.

"Can you believe it? And she says she's happy for the first time in her life. Well, goodbye for real." Grace hung up.

Callie stood there, reflecting. Vida was leaving, and if Callie had still been modeling, she would have emerged the victor in their little war. No more competition, no more anxiety about losing jobs to her. Callie thought about Vida living in Australia. Even if Vida was madly in love, she would still keep up with the business, still follow what everyone was doing, who was on top, who was falling. From her own experience, Callie knew there would come a day when Vida felt left out, forgotten; she might even be bitter about having walked away from it when she was so successful. Callie supposed she could derive some nasty pleasure from that. But she was surprised to find that she didn't get any satisfaction from the thought. It seemed so ridiculous to enjoy Vida's leaving the business. Callie was simply glad for her, glad that she'd found somebody who made her so happy. He must be really special. Maybe as special as Alex.

Callie realized she had to get moving; she was due to meet Alex in front of the Metropolitan Museum of Art in fifteen minutes. Her mind went back to Weston's problems as she hurried toward Fifth Avenue. She forced herself to think about David in the months before the accident—his mood swings, his edginess, the changes that had come over him.

But to think that he could have seen Barbara Hutchinson crossing the street and coldly, calculatingly, stepped on the gas . . . She shuddered with horror.

Alex was standing next to the fountain in front of the museum, a large gray envelope tucked under his arm. As soon as she saw him, she sensed something was wrong. His face was grim as she approached and he leaned over to give her a quick kiss on the cheek.

"What is it?" she asked anxiously. "It's not Julia, is it?"

"No, she's fine," he hastened to reassure her. "But I have something to tell you that may upset you."

She felt herself tense up, then let out a breath. "Okay. I'm ready for anything."

"Let's walk." He took her hand. "I was in midtown yesterday on an errand, right near Weston," he began. "I decided to go up and say hello to Annie, Barbara's old secretary. They'd been together for about five years. I knew her, and I liked her very much."

"You once mentioned that she gave Barbara the silver picture frame in your living room," Callie reminded him.

"Right. Well, she told me she still had a box of Barbara's things—she was very embarrassed that it had never been returned. Apparently it was way in back on the top shelf of Barbara's closet there, and Annie found it herself just the other day when she was cleaning the place out for yet another executive to move into—it seems three different people have already occupied that office."

He paused, taking the envelope out from under his arm. "The box was full of papers Barbara obviously didn't want anyone to see. Research and notes on ideas she was working on. She was very secretive about stuff like that, I know. She believed people would steal her ideas if they could."

He sighed, remembering Barbara's suspiciousness.

"Anyway, this was in it as well." He handed the envelope to Callie. "Someone at the Miracle Corporation must have really disliked a guy named Lawrence Richards. They went into his private files to get these and handed them over to Barbara."

They sat down on a bench. Callie opened the clasp and pulled out a sheaf of papers as Alex continued talking.

"Confidential memos outlining Weston's future plans for different products, plans that no outsider could know about. Canceled checks made out to David Long, drawn on a bank in Maryland and deposited into another account down there for Long. Plus several other documents, all of which make it patently obvious: David was selling Weston's secrets to Miracle, via this Richards guy."

Callie scanned the top page in her hand, a memo on Miracle's letterhead outlining Weston's launch plans for a new fragrance. Lifting up the paper, she saw a copy of a check made out to David Long for ten thousand dollars. She was afraid she might be sick to her stomach.

"It's true, then," she said quietly. "David had a reason to want Barbara dead."

Alex nodded. "I'm sorry, Callie."

She looked at him. "What are you going to do?"

"That's what we need to talk about." He took her hand. "What are *we* going to do?"

Callie pretended not to notice the faces staring at her, the whispers up and down the corridors of the Weston offices. With Alex beside her, she looked straight ahead as they walked toward Joseph Mann's office. She was glad no one could see the panic in her eyes behind her sunglasses, that no one could tell how hard it was to expose herself here. The secretaries' whispers continued.

"It's her, Callie Stewart . . . I hear she's blind, so that guy must be leading her . . . killed Barbara Hutchinson."

Callie noticed Alex's clenched jaw; he too heard what was being said. The carpeted corridor seemed to stretch on for miles. Finally, they reached the end and turned the corner. Mann's office was straight ahead.

"Good morning, Miss Stewart." His secretary leaped up, her voice a shade too loud as her eyes hurriedly searched Callie's face, judging the damage. "So lovely to see you again."

Callie was grateful when Alex spoke for them both.

"We have an appointment with Mr. Mann. Is he ready for us?"

The secretary was openly staring at Callie, obviously

wondering what was behind the sunglasses. "Oh, yes, yes." She forced herself to turn away, opening the door to her boss's office.

Joseph Mann got up from behind his desk and came around to greet her.

"Callie." He spoke just the one word as he shook her hand.

"Hello again, Joseph," she answered. "I'd like you to meet Alex Hutchinson."

Mann turned to Alex. "There are no words to ease the loss of a wife, but I'm truly sorry about Barbara. We thought very highly of her around here, in every way."

"Thank you." Alex was gracious, although Callie knew he resented the way Weston had stolen his wife's time and attention for years. He felt little warmth toward the company or anyone in it.

The older man directed them to the sofa. "Now, what did you want to talk to me about?"

Callie and Alex looked at each other. She indicated with a nod that he should be the one to speak.

"We believe that Barbara's death wasn't an accident. That David Long deliberately tried to run her over. Or maybe he planned to come close enough to make her *think* he was going to run her over. I doubt he could have known about her heart condition, so he wouldn't have realized a scare like that could actually kill her."

Mann stared at him. "David Long is a very respected part of Weston's team."

"Nonetheless," Alex said, "it's true."

The other man turned to Callie. "You believe this?"

"Unfortunately, yes."

Mann sat there for a moment, trying to take it all in. "If you suspect David of this, why haven't you gone to the police? Why come to me?"

"Because David's motive for killing Barbara was that she was about to expose him for selling Weston's secrets to Miracle. He was the reason your competitor kept getting the jump on you."

Mann turned ashen. "We suspected somebody of selling information. But David—never."

Alex reached into his briefcase, extracted the gray envelope, and handed it to Mann. There was silence in the room as he read the contents. When he was finished, he stood up.

"Callie," he said, "to tell you I appreciate what you're doing doesn't come close. You're quite a lady to help us this way after everything that's happened."

She smiled sadly. "I only wish none of it were true. But the modeling and all the rest is unimportant compared to what Alex and his daughter have suffered."

Mann nodded. "Would you two mind waiting outside for a minute?"

Alex put a hand on Callie's lower back and escorted her out. "Are you okay, honey?" he asked her worriedly.

"Thanks, I'm fine." She squeezed his other hand gratefully.

In another moment, Mann emerged from his office. "Please come in again."

When they were reassembled in his office, he went on. "Now that we have a motive for David to kill Barbara, this is a very different matter than it was before. It's small comfort now, but we'll try to find some justice for you. For her."

The intercom buzzed, and his secretary said, "Mr. Long is here."

Callie instinctively took a step back, frightened; she hadn't expected to encounter David in person. The door opened at once to reveal him standing there.

He was still as handsome as she remembered, dressed in an impeccably tailored charcoal gray suit, his hair neatly combed. But now she saw something around his mouth she'd never noticed before, a cruel hardness. At the sight of her, his eyes briefly narrowed with displeasure, but he quickly regained his impassive expression.

"Callie." He nodded to her, his voice pleasant and even. "You're looking well."

She didn't say anything. How could he talk to her like that, as if they were two friendly acquaintances? She shuddered. He was a monster.

"David, this is Alex Hutchinson, Barbara's husband," Joseph Mann said.

After a split second's hesitation, David extended a hand

311

to Alex. "I'm so sorry about Barbara. It was such a rotten break, and I liked her so much. We were great friends."

Alex remained still, his hands motionless at his sides. "I'll pass on the handshake," he said evenly.

David lowered his hand. "I understand," he said gently, crossing over to Mann's desk. His tone became businesslike. "Your secretary said you wanted to see me immediately."

Mann regarded him steadily. "How long have you been selling information to Miracle?"

"What?" David appeared confused.

"You heard me."

"Joseph, you can't be serious. I'd never do that, and you know it." He turned to Callie, anger on his face. "Do you have something to do with this?"

Mann said sharply, "I'm the one asking the questions here. You talk to *me.*"

David looked back at him. "Your information is wrong. If there's a leak, I swear to you I'm not the one."

Callie was amazed at how sincere he sounded. If she didn't know better, she would have bet her life he was telling the truth.

"You *swear* to me?" Mann crossed his arms over his chest. "I see. Would you also swear that you had nothing to do with Barbara Hutchinson's death, that you didn't deliberately try to hit her?"

David looked as if he'd been slapped in the face. "How could you even suggest such a thing?"

"Because I know that, somehow, Barbara figured out that you were the one talking to Miracle. You had to be worried she would blow the whistle."

"I don't believe this!" David was shocked, indignant. Then his tone turned angry, and he pointed to Callie. "She told you all this, didn't she?" He shook his head. "Come on, Joseph, you know better than to believe a jilted girlfriend. She wants to get back at me. Her face got cut up, she lost the deal with us—it's revenge." He lowered his voice and practically hissed, "But she's *lying.*" Nodding as if in sudden realization, he looked at Alex again. "The two of you are in this together. You have a little romance going?"

Mann looked at Callie. "You want to show him?"

She picked up the papers on Mann's desk and extended them in front of David. "The bank account in Maryland, the canceled checks—everything was here in Barbara's papers."

Her eyes met David's, and she was shocked to see the hatred for her in his gaze. The atmosphere was thick with ugly silence.

"Mr. Mann, they're here," the secretary's voice over the intercom interrupted them.

He pressed an intercom button and replied, "Send them in."

The door opened to two policemen. David's eyes grew wide.

"This is the one." Mann pointed at David and the policemen walked over to him.

"You'll have to come with us, sir," one of them said.

"Oh, stop it, this is crazy!" David yelled. "Joseph, you can't do this, you *can't!*"

Callie couldn't watch any longer. She left the room, Alex right behind her. Back in the hall, she took a deep breath and exhaled slowly. It was over, finally and truly over. She was relieved and sad at the same time, and, suddenly, overwhelmingly tired.

23

Wearing only his boxer shorts, Alex returned to the bedroom carrying a tray that held two mugs of herbal tea and a plate of oversized chocolate chip cookies. He set it down on the bedside table, handing Callie one of the mugs before climbing back into bed beside her. It was nearly ten-thirty. They'd finished making love half an hour before and had been lying there talking until Alex suggested a snack.

Callie, naked under the down comforter, put her tea on the small table on her side of the bed, then leaned over, reaching across his chest for a cookie.

"Did you check on Julia?" she asked.

Alex nodded, stroking the soft, bare skin of her shoulder. "Still sound asleep."

"This cookie is absolutely delicious," she said, chewing with great enjoyment as she lay back. "There was a time when I wouldn't have dared eat these, especially late at

WITH A LITTLE LUCK

night. Way too fattening. It's just going to sit in my stomach like a rock, right?"

"Right," Alex agreed, smiling. He turned and swooped down upon her, gathering her in his arms. "Fat or thin, you're mine, all mine. If you're fat, there's just more of you to love."

Callie kissed the tip of his nose. "A gallant sentiment."

Alex lay back on his side of the bed and reached out toward the clock radio. "Besides, I know you're not supposed to eat after midnight, and I don't want you to be too hungry in the morning. What time do you want me to set the alarm for?"

Callie stiffened slightly. "I'm supposed to be at the hospital at nine-thirty."

"Sweetheart," Alex reached for her hand, "it'll be all right, I promise you."

She bit her lip. "The operation on my face was bad enough. But my eye—it's too scary."

"You want to see out of it again, don't you?" Alex asked soothingly. "This is the only way. It'll be over in no time."

She sighed. "There's no point being a baby about it. I know I have to do it. But I can't help being afraid. It's just . . ."

"Anyone would feel the same." Alex put his arm around her. "But you have a great doctor. I'll be there every minute. It'll be fine. Please, try not to worry."

"Thanks, Alex." Callie snuggled in closer to him. "You've been incredible through all of this."

He paused, then seemed to make up his mind to go on. "I could be incredible for you through more things, if you wanted. Things in the future."

She looked at him, confused. "What do you mean?"

"If we got married."

She pulled back onto one elbow. "What?"

"Callie." Alex put down his tea and sat up straight. "I love you. Julia loves you. We hope you love us back."

She smiled. "You know I do."

He spoke softly. "Then will you marry me?"

Callie fell back against the pillow. "Oh, Alex, I'm . . . I don't know what."

315

He frowned. "You could try *happy.*"

"Of course I'm happy," she hastened to reassure him. "But the last time I agreed to get married, it was for all the wrong reasons."

Alex bristled. "You're comparing marriage to me with marriage to David Long?"

"No, not at all. I'm comparing myself to the way I was then. So much has happened." She hesitated, thinking. "I haven't taken charge of getting my life back together, not completely. And I need to do that myself, *take care* of myself. I wanted David to take care of me, and that wasn't right."

"You were different then," Alex argued.

"In a lot of ways," Callie agreed. "But I want to stand on my own two feet, not depend on you to be responsible for me. Then I can come to a marriage with a clear conscience, knowing I'm doing it for the right reasons."

"You don't love me enough." Alex looked away.

Callie put her hand on his arm. "That's not it at all. I love you more than anyone in the world. Try to understand." She searched for the right words. "Models live in a world where everyone tells them what to do. Where to go, how to dress, how to stand or tilt their head—*everything*. I don't know, maybe you have to be a certain kind of person to be a model, because you follow all those instructions willingly."

"Do I tell you what to do?" Alex asked. "Is that it?"

"Of course not," Callie replied quickly. "But, as a person, I need to get out and decide for myself what to do now. It's as if I'm starting a new life. This time, I have to be in control, make my own choices, take my own risks. I don't even know yet if my eye will be better."

Alex looked at her dejectedly. "So the answer is no."

"I love you," she said softly. "Please ask me again—when the time is right."

He didn't respond, just reached over and turned out the light. In the dark, they came together, their arms going around each other. Callie kissed his cheek. The tension was thick, but as they lay there silently, the familiar feel of each other's body acted as a soothing balm. Slowly, they relaxed. Their breathing became regular, and they drifted into sleep.

In the morning, no mention was made of their conversation. Alex had taken two days off so he could be with Callie while she went through the surgery. On the way to the hospital, he appeared calm and cheerful, although Callie didn't express any further concern; she was keeping her fears to herself.

As she was escorted away to be prepared for surgery, Alex finally permitted his nervousness to surface. Her doctor had explained that she would be having a triple procedure. Not only would he be removing the cataract that had developed as a result of the accident, and then implanting a lens; he would also be doing a cornea transplant, because her cornea had been so scarred from the pieces of glass that had been embedded in it. The doctor was confident, but Alex found the whole thing frightening. If it didn't work, she might not regain her sight in that eye. Alex had deliberately minimized it the night before, but the truth was that he admired Callie's courage, the way she'd voiced just a few misgivings and then faced it without any further complaint.

The operation took two hours. Callie spent another two hours in the recovery room before she was wheeled out to her room. She was wearing a bandage and a hard shield over her right eye to protect it. Alex sat with her until visiting hours ended and the nurse on the floor demanded that he leave.

The doctor came to Callie's room early the next morning and removed the coverings over her eye. Whereas the day before she could see only light and shadows out of it, today she could discern fuzzy shapes and colors. Her vision would continue to improve, the doctor assured her; the operation had gone extremely well. Alex appeared in the doorway to her room just in time to see Callie break down in tears, the tension of the whole event finally being released in a rush of joy and relief.

"Don't cry," he said, putting his arms around her. "You'll get your bandage all soggy."

He was rewarded by the sound of her happy laughter.

"I love you too, Mom," Callie said into the phone. "See you then."

She hung up, pleased. It was all set. Alex, Julia, and she would go to Indiana for Christmas. Funny, she thought, she'd never considered taking David home to meet her family. But it seemed important to her that they get to know Alex, get to care for him as much as she did. Of course, they would fall madly in love with Julia right away, just as she had, Callie was certain.

Forcing herself to return to what she'd been doing when the telephone rang, she picked up the newspaper and, with a sigh, went back to perusing the want ads. When she'd awakened that morning she'd decided to get moving on the future. It was so easy to keep drifting along, enjoying her time with Alex and Julia, letting the days slide by. But that wasn't bringing her to anything productive, to deciding or discovering what she wanted to do with herself. There were no more excuses to fall back on. Her body was almost completely healed. The scars on her face had been nearly resolved by the earlier surgery, and what was still visible was fading or hidden by her hair. Her vision was improving every day, the only traces of the operation a few dark stitches apparent just upon close scrutiny; they too would eventually be gone.

She tossed the paper down on the kitchen table in disgust. *How ridiculous,* she told herself, *as if I'm suddenly going to find a new career this way.*

The ringing telephone rescued her once again.

"Hello." The masculine voice was pleasant but brisk. "Callie? Joseph Mann here. How are you?"

"Joseph, what a surprise." Callie couldn't imagine why the head of Weston would be calling her, much less calling her at home.

"Let me get right to the point," he said. "I understand you've been undergoing all sorts of rehabilitation and surgery. They tell me you're pretty much recovered. On a personal note, let me say again that I'm so sorry for what you've been through, I truly am."

"Thank you." Callie couldn't figure out what he was getting at. At the same time, she wondered how he knew what she'd been up to, and who *they* were, the ones who'd told him she was recovered.

"Anyway, I wanted to know if you'd be interested in coming back to work for us. It wouldn't be as the exclusive Day and Night girl, of course. But there's no reason you shouldn't do some modeling for us. If you have any scars or marks, we can work around it, I'm sure."

Callie was speechless. This was the last thing she'd expected, being asked to model again. Was it an act of pity on Mann's part? Maybe he felt responsible in some way; Callie's job, David, the Weston party where the accident occurred—they were all connected to his company.

As if reading her mind, Joseph said, "This isn't charity or guilt speaking. You were always the look we wanted, and that hasn't changed. Your face and body are back. So we want *you* back." His tone was sincere. "Please say yes."

Callie's mind raced. To be back at work, back in the industry. She'd been gone and forgotten, but this could be a sensational comeback. Everyone would be talking about it. And she would be working again. Modeling was what she knew, what she was good at.

Still, she knew she shouldn't jump in with both feet just yet. "I'll have to think about it," she said to Joseph. "But thank you for asking."

"Not at all," he replied. "There are certain things that happened here which I feel rather bad about."

Callie knew he was referring to the way she'd been so unceremoniously dumped from her contract.

"I can't make that up to you, and as I said, this isn't about the past anyway," he went on. "But you're ready to work again, and we're ready to have you come back. It's good business. Call me when you've thought it over."

With a click, he was gone.

Callie inhaled deeply. What a shock, Joseph Mann personally asking her to come back. Should she do it?

She couldn't think. Grabbing her coat, she decided a walk might clear her head. It was a warm afternoon, mild for early December, and she headed toward Central Park.

Everybody would talk about it—that's what she had just told herself, and it was true. Callie Stewart's comeback. She could imagine the way people in the business would scrutinize her photographs, looking for the scars, speculating about what the makeup was hiding, how much airbrushing had been done to the pictures. Anyone who'd been on the set with her would be grilled for the inside scoop on Callie's face. There would be speculation about Weston's motives: if Callie herself thought they were offering her work out of pity, the word around town would say the same or worse. She'd be an object of curiosity, the latest gossip, a has-been who didn't know when to walk away, desperate to stay in the game.

She pushed all thoughts on the subject out of her mind, walking briskly through the park and coming out on the West Side at Eighty-fifth Street. Without having any particular destination, she went over to Broadway and headed uptown.

It was time to move on. She shouldn't be making decisions by considering what other people would say or think. That was her old insecurity talking. She couldn't permit herself to fall into that trap again.

She walked along, feeling as if a weight were being lifted from her shoulders. *I'm free to do what I want,* she thought. *It's not a burden, deciding what new path to follow. It's a luxury, a new chance to become practically anything.* By telling her she *could* come back, Joseph Mann had shown her that she didn't have to.

She suddenly noticed where she was. One Hundred Sixteenth Street, the entrance to Columbia University. Smiling, she turned and entered the campus. So she *had* had a destination after all, she realized.

Stopping to ask one of the students for directions, she made her way to the admissions office. Inside, a young woman sat behind a desk. Callie walked up to her.

"Excuse me," she said. "I'd like some information, please."

Epilogue

Callie stopped by her secretary's desk.

"Anything earth-shaking happen while I was at lunch, Helene?" she asked, slipping out of her coat.

Helene smiled, proffering three pink message slips. "Just three phone calls, Ms. Stewart."

"Thank you."

Callie glanced through the messages as she went into her office. One was from the head researcher at the lab where Callie was doing a story on sleep deprivation; the second was from one of the staff producers wanting a meeting at three o'clock; the last was from the real estate agent in Connecticut saying that she'd located a house that met nearly all of Callie's requirements.

Hanging her coat on a hook behind the door, Callie slid into her chair and put down the messages. She had to get into the editing room and get going on this week's piece. It was a story about physical therapy. Working on it had been a true labor of love, and she'd gotten permission to tape at the therapy center where she'd done her own rehabilitation, interviewing Glen, her own therapist, and for the first time talking publicly about her experience in putting her body back together. Yanking open a desk drawer, she pulled out her notes for the edit session. She wanted the piece to be really special when it aired on Thursday. Having lunch with Kate and April today had been a treat, but now she needed to clear her mind of everything else.

Helene buzzed her on the intercom as she was about to leave. Callie glanced at her watch. She *had* to get going.

"Yes?"

"Lucas James on line one."

Callie sat back down and reached for the telephone. "Put him through."

She would always have time for Lucas. They'd had just that brief, casual conversation back at Kate's wedding, yet he hadn't forgotten that he'd asked Callie to get in touch with him. During her second year as a student at Columbia, she'd summoned up all her nerve and contacted him, asking if there was something at the network he thought she might be able to do part-time while she was in college. He'd gotten her a job as a researcher on *A Time & Place,* and she'd happily dashed back and forth between the show's offices and her classes for nearly a year, working, learning, soaking it all up.

From there she'd gone on to newswriter, then associate producer, and finally producer. By then she'd graduated from Columbia and was on staff full-time. It was in March of that first year out of school that Lucas informed her they'd decided she was ready and they were putting her on the air. She'd done soft-news features for a while before settling into her current niche of science and health stories.

"Callie?" Lucas's voice was affectionate. In the years since she'd joined the show, the two of them had become good friends. "How're you feeling?"

"Great, thanks. Couldn't be better." Callie smiled. "Thanks for asking."

"All right, then. We're in my office looking at applicants'

WITH A LITTLE LUCK

tapes—you know, someone to do the new fashion and beauty segments. We're down to five. As I recall," he said exaggeratedly, "you had a bit to do with that field once. Want to come by to give us your input on some test stories we might have them do?"

Callie was flattered. "I'd be delighted, but I think I'll be editing until about six o'clock. Is that okay?"

"See you then."

Fashion and beauty. It was all still a part of her and always would be. Strange, she thought, that it was the accident, the worst thing that had ever happened to her, that had unleashed her desire to get to this point. Her removal from the world she'd known during those months of recovery, her time in physical therapy, the realization that she was lucky to be alive—it had all made her more aware of other people. The curiosity that that had unlocked in her had led to this job, to wanting to spend her time talking with different people about their lives and interests.

But it was modeling that had enabled her to actually get here. In some ways, she had moved on from it, grown past the concerns that used to trouble her so. She didn't worry so much about her looks, her weight, what everyone thought of her, and whether she dared disagree with them. That was all over; she was more comfortable with herself now. Still, modeling had given her so much, even beyond the fame and money. It had taught her discipline, how to behave, how to stay focused. And it had opened the doors for her. It had brought Lucas to her in the first place and smoothed the way when she was out doing stories, people recognizing her even before she was associated with the show, still interested to meet the ex-supermodel Callie Stewart.

She glanced up at the wall near her office door. Alongside several photographs of her with various luminaries, doing pieces for *A Time & Place,* hung her diploma from Columbia and a few cover shots of her on *Vogue* and *Bazaar,* as well as a fashion shot of her taken in Paris on her first modeling trip there, a younger, more innocent-looking girl in bicycle pants, resting in the sun. She was equally proud of all of them, all the pieces of her life, all the people she was.

Callie dialed another number. The phone rang repeatedly before someone answered.

"English Department," a young woman's voice said.

"Is Professor Hutchinson there, please?" Callie asked. "It's his wife."

"Just a second, I'll see."

Callie was put on hold.

"Hi, sweetheart." Alex got on the line. "What's up?"

"I know you're busy and I've got to run too, so I'll be quick. Lucas wants to see me at six. That means I'll be late getting home. Can we manage?"

"We'll miss your smiling face, but Julia told me she's planning on trying out a new recipe tonight, so the two of us can eat, and you take your time. We'll keep something hot for you."

"You're a saint. Have I told you that lately?" Callie smiled into the phone.

"You have, but I'd like to hear it several times a day," Alex answered with a laugh.

"Julia's deciding to be a world-famous chef is the best thing that could happen to our dinnertime. I feel guilty. She's practicing, and we're reaping the benefits of her hard work."

"Remember, last month she wanted to be an architect, and the month before that a pilot. This will pass shortly."

"I guess you're right," Callie agreed. "It's nice that she sees so many choices ahead of her. She's growing up so fast."

"Don't remind me." Alex sighed. "Now, on to you. How're you feeling?"

Callie rubbed her rounded stomach gently, smiling. At that moment, she felt the baby inside her give a kick.

"Great. And getting bigger every minute."

"Don't work too hard, honey," Alex said, concern in his voice.

"I won't," Callie promised. "See you later."

Their conversation over, she gathered her notes and grabbed a pen. She would spend the afternoon doing something she enjoyed totally, something she found completely fulfilling in different ways every day of the week.

Then she would go home to Alex and Julia, the two people she loved most in the world. And in a few more months, there would be a new family member to love.

Not bad, all of that coming from what was supposed to be just a summer job in New York City.

"Lucky Callie," she whispered gratefully. "Lucky me."

About the Authors

KIM ALEXIS, whose face has graced the covers of over four hundred magazines and who has been featured in five *Sports Illustrated* swimsuit issues, is one of America's leading supermodels. She was Fashion Editor on ABC's "Good Morning America" for three years and currently hosts "Healthy Kids" on the Family Channel and "Ticket to Adventure with Kim Alexis" on the Travel Channel and has her own radio show called "Bet You Didn't Know That." Kim has completed seven marathons and now endorses a fitness product for Fitness Quest. Kim and her husband are happily married with five young children.

CYNTHIA KATZ has coauthored five books, including her most recent novel, *Relative Sins*, published under the name Cynthia Victor. She lives in Connecticut.

"WIN A DAY IN NYC WITH SUPERMODEL KIM ALEXIS"

(Official Entry Form)

Name _____

Address _____

City/State_____**Zip**_____

Daytime phone _____

Date of birth _____

Send entries to:
Pocket Books
"Win A Day in NYC With Supermodel
Kim Alexis" Contest
Marketing Dept.--13th floor
1230 Avenue of the Americas
New York, NY 10020

See next page for full contest details
and official rules

1023A

Official Rules

1. No purchase necessary. To enter, submit the completed Official Entry Form (no copies allowed) or send your name, address, daytime phone number and date of birth on a 3" x 5" card to the Pocket Books "Win a Day in New York City With Supermodel Kim Alexis" Contest, Marketing Dept., 13th floor, 1230 Ave. of the Americas, New York, NY 10020, along with a 50 word or less answer to the question, "One Perfect Highlight in the Day of a Supermodel—Your Personal Diary Entry." All entries must be original and the sole property of the entrant. Essays must not have been previously published or won any awards. All entries must be received by November 15, 1994. Pocket Books is not responsible for lost, late or misdirected mail. Winner will be selected on basis of their answer.

2. Essays will be judged on the basis of originality(45%), creativity(45%), and grammer(10%). Decisions of the judge(s) are final.

3. One entry per person. Entrants must be residents of the U.S. and be between the ages of 13-18 years of age (as of November 15, 1994). Void in AZ, FL, MD, VT, CAN, P.R.
and wherever else prohibited by law. Employees of Pocket Books, Simon & Schuster, its suppliers, affiliates, agencies, participating retailers, and their families are not eligible.

4. Prize: Two days and one night in New York City for winner and his/her parent or legal guardian. Includes, round-trip coach airfare from major airport nearest winner, airport transportation to and from New York City airport to hotel, one night accommodations (double occupancy), meals during stay, a makeover and haircut for the winner at a New York salon, lunch with Kim Alexis, opportunity to accompany Kim Alexis on certain of her scheduled job engagements, and to visit other New York City attractions. Approximate retail value: $3000. Trip dates to be determined by Kim Alexis, Pocket Books and the winner, and must be within 6 months of notification. No substitution or transfer of prize is allowed.

5. All federal, state and local taxes are the responsibility of the winner. Winner will be notified my mail and will be required to execute and return an Affidavit of Eligibility and release within 15 days of notification or an alternate winner will be selected.

6. Winner grants Pocket Books the right to use his/her name, likeness and entry for any advertising, promotion and publicity purposes without further compensation to or permission from the entrants.

7. For the name of the winner, available after November 15, 1994, send a stamped self-addressed envelope to Prize Winner, Pocket Books "Win A Day in NYC With Supermodel Kim Alexis", Marketing Dept., 13th floor, 1230 Ave. of the Americas, New York, NY 10020. For a copy of the Official Rules, send a stamped self-addressed envelope to Official Rules, Pocket Books "Win A Day in NYC With Supermodel Kim Alexis", Marketing Dept., 13th floor, 1230 Ave. of the Americas, New York, NY 10020.

1023B